BLACK LIES, RED BLOOD

Also by Kjell Eriksson

The Hand That Trembles

The Demon of Dakar

The Cruel Stars of the Night

The Princess of Burundi

BLACK LIES, RED BLOOD

Kjell Eriksson

Translated from the Swedish by Paul Norlen

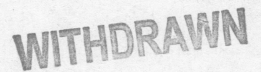

MINOTAUR BOOKS

A THOMAS DUNNE BOOK 〰 NEW YORK

A THOMAS DUNNE BOOK FOR MINOTAUR BOOKS.
An imprint of St. Martin's Publishing Group.

BLACK LIES, RED BLOOD. Copyright © 2008 by Kjell Eriksson. Translation © 2014 by Paul Norlen. All rights reserved. Printed in the United States of America. For information, address St. Martin's Press, 175 Fifth Avenue, New York, N.Y. 10010.

www.thomasdunnebooks.com
www.minotaurbooks.com

The Library of Congress has cataloged the hardcover edition as follows:

Eriksson, Kjell, 1953—
    [Svarta lögner, rött blod. English]
    Black lies, red blood / Kjell Eriksson ; translated from the Swedish by Paul Norlen.—First U.S. edition.
        p. cm.
    ISBN 978-0-312-60504-9 (hardcover)
    ISBN 978-1-4668-4067-6 (e-book)
    1. Policewomen—Fiction.   2. Missing persons—Fiction.   3. Murder—Investigation—Fiction.   I. Norlen, Paul R. translator.   II. Title.
    PT9876.15.R5155S8313 2014
    839.73'8—dc23

                                                        2013032881

ISBN 978-1-250-04263-7 (trade paperback)

Minotaur books may be purchased for educational, business, or promotional use. For information on bulk purchases, please contact the Macmillan Corporate and Premium Sales Department at 1-800-221-7945, extension 5442, or write to specialmarkets@macmillan.com.

First published in Sweden under the title *Svarta lögner, rött blod* by Ordfronts Verlag.

First Minotaur Books Paperback Edition: May 2015

10 9 8 7 6 5 4 3 2 1

BLACK LIES, RED BLOOD

One

"You're different," said Ann Lindell.

A tired phrase, a worn-out expression, but there was no other way to put it.

"Is that a good thing?"

Anders Brant was lying with his eyes closed, one hand on his belly, the other behind his neck. She observed him: the dark, sweaty hair by his temples, the trembling eyelids, given a violet-red hue by the first morning light, and the beard stubble—"my scourge," he said, as he always had to shave—which had scratched her.

He was not a powerful man, not much taller than she was, with a boyish body that made him look younger than almost forty-four. From his navel down to his pubic hair a dark, curly strand ran that resembled an exclamation point.

His face was thin and lacked strong lines, although when he smiled it came to life. Maybe it was his casual manner that first aroused her interest. Later, when she got to know him better, the picture got more complicated. He was just different in that way, often carefree and a little roguish, but with an inner fervor that was sometimes seen in his eyes and his gesturing hands. Then he was anything but carefree. As she observed his relaxed facial features, it occurred to her that his attitude reminded her of Sammy Nilsson, the one colleague she could confide in and discuss things other than the trivialities of work.

"I don't know," she said, in a tone more ominous than she intended, now feeling even more banal.

But perhaps he understood: She was in love. Until now neither of them had hinted at anything like that.

And was that good? He was different in every conceivable way from the men she'd been with. There weren't many really, two somewhat longer relationships—Rolf and Edvard—and a few short-lived ones, but the few weeks with Anders Brant had really shaken her up.

For the first time in a very long while she felt desired. He made no secret of his longing for her. He might call her at work and whisper things on the phone that left her speechless, and then when they met he drew her to him; despite his slender body his hands felt powerful. Sometimes she warded him off, afraid that Erik would surprise them, and also afraid of the rush she felt in her body, as if they were doing something forbidden.

"Hugging won't hurt you," he would say. "Relax."

He courted her, and he talked; never had Ann's apartment been filled with so many words. Talk, but never about before and later, always about the present. Unwilling to offer details about his past, not a word about his plans or dreams.

Ann knew absolutely nothing about his family, other than that he was the oldest of four children, and that his mother lived somewhere in south Sweden. His father had left early on; it was unclear whether he was alive. When she asked he simply mumbled something about "the old man was too damn gloomy."

Few things surprised him. He noted her own biographical details without showing any great interest, and did not connect her experiences to scenes from his own life.

He showed the greatest interest and engagement when they were watching the evening news together. Then he sometimes got agitated, or cynically scornful. Journalist colleagues that he thought were not doing their job gave rise to derisive, in some cases spiteful, comments.

Despite this singular apathy with regards to the private sphere, he was present; she never felt bored or overlooked. He glided into her life without a lot of fuss. She liked that. She thought the contrast to her life, so heavily scheduled for so long, would have been too great if he broke out in impassioned declarations of love and constructed romantic castles in the air.

It was as if he took it for granted that they would be together.

Sometimes she noticed a certain restlessness in him. He would fall silent, lose focus, and almost be dismissive, even if he did not verbalize his irritation. On a few occasions he left her on the couch or at the kitchen table and went out on the balcony. Those were the only times she saw him smoke, slender cigarillos that he enjoyed with eyes closed, leaning back in the wicker chair she once got as a present from Edvard. Then he wanted to be alone, she realized that.

After smoking his cigarillo he always brushed his teeth, which she also appreciated.

"I have to leave," he said, abruptly interrupting her thoughts. "I may be gone a week or two."

He got up from the bed, hurriedly dressed, and left.

✦

Two

The place was just as miserable as the dead man's life must have been. An unnecessary place—cold, windy, and hard—without beauty or the slightest finesse. The plants that had worked their way up out of the coarse gravel radiated chlorophyll-deficient impoverishment and misery. It was a place of exile, a Guantánamo for plants.

Ola Haver even thought that the workers who laid the foundations—reinforced, poured, and graveled—forgot they had ever been there. There was no pride over the surroundings.

His father had once expressed such a thought, as they drove past a viaduct and an intersection along a highway. His father put on the brakes for no reason and stopped by the side of the road.

"What a shitty place," he exclaimed, while he inspected the slopes of crushed gravel with a look of disdain.

He explained that many years before he had been involved in building the viaduct, but then totally forgot this non-place. It was the first time Ola Haver heard him say anything negative about a work site. Otherwise he had the habit of proudly pointing out all the buildings and installations he had worked on.

A non-place where the woeful, soiled figure at Haver's feet had been killed. He was lying on his stomach with a cracked skull and arms outstretched, as if he had been thrown out of an airplane into the sea of air and immediately, brutally struck the ground. A failed parachute jumper.

That was what Ola Haver saw and thought. Why here? When and how? He read the dead man: the grip of his hands on the gravel; the battered knuckles; the greasy hair, carelessly trimmed at the neck; the heavy boots, sloppily tied with colorful laces; the stained pants; and, not least, the desperation written on the half of his face that was turned upward in a peculiar way. Haver got the idea that the unnatural angle was because at the moment of death the man tried to twist his head to look toward the sky one last time. Was he a believer? That was the policeman's completely irrational thought, and even if it seemed unlikely, he wished that had been the case. He got to see the sky. Because even if the dead man had been an incorrigible sinner, God would show mercy on a man who died in such an ignominious way, Haver was sure of that.

How old was he? About forty-five, at a guess. They had not found a wallet in the man's pockets or any document that might reveal his age or identity.

And why here? Because his life had looked just like this. Perhaps the man lived in the vicinity? A hundred meters away there was a derelict job-site trailer, perhaps that was his home.

When? He suspected it had been a while since the murder occurred, perhaps a full day. In due course there would be papers about that.

Like a dark shadow his father's apparition hovered over the scene. Often, far too often in his opinion, thoughts of his dad and his unexpected death came up. He seldom if ever talked about it, but the realization that he had now lived longer than his father tormented him.

In the background he heard the technicians talking. Morgansson was the one doing all the talking. Johannesson was taciturn as usual. Haver was standing too far away to hear what they were saying.

Allan Fredriksson was poking around in his seemingly aimless way. I guess he's looking for unusual plants, thought Haver, not without bitterness. His colleague's passion for nature showed no limits. Even at the scene of a murder he was assessing, registering, and systematizing, coming out with eccentric comments for the context about plant and animal life. Indoors, in furnished rooms or in public spaces, he looked lost. Fredriksson was in his element outdoors, even if it was at a place condemned by humans. It made no difference for plants and insects. For them there was always something to feed on, and the same was true for the Boy Scout Fredriksson too.

More and more Ola Haver had come to loathe Fredriksson's capacity to brush aside the deeply inhumane aspects of the violent crimes they were there to investigate in favor of quiet observations of nature. It was undignified. Death to Ola Haver was such an awful event that nothing was allowed to disturb his focus. Every time he stood before a lifeless body he thought about his father. Fredriksson on the other hand talked about sprouting life, woodpeckers, strange insects, or whatever caught his eye. Haver was struck by thoughts of meaninglessness, while if anything, Fredriksson became exhilarated.

Maybe I'm just envious, thought Haver, as he observed Fredriksson's forward-leaning figure. His colleague's thin coat was unbuttoned and fluttered around his skinny body when the wind picked up between the concrete pillars.

Was it perhaps a hopeful sign that Fredriksson could perceive life and a future in the most miserable environments? Haver felt a sting of bad conscience. Who am I to have interpretative preference? Fredriksson is neither a worse nor a better policeman than any one of us, so why judge his enthusiasm for nature? Maybe it's his way of processing reality, making it comprehensible and bearable.

In the corner of his eye he noticed Johannesson approaching. The technician, who had only been on the unit for six months, walked slowly, as if he was hesitating. Ola Haver trembled unconsciously, made a vehement motion with his shoulders as if he was shaking off something unpleasant.

"How's it going?" Johannesson asked.

Haver chose to overlook the question.

"What have you found?"

The technician made a vague gesture.

"I think this is the murder scene," he said. "Two blows and that's it. The old guy fell down immediately after the first blow and then took one more on the back of the head. But I guess the doctor will have more to say about that."

The old guy, thought Haver; the murdered man might be younger than him.

"A slip of paper in his back pocket," said Johannesson.

"A slip of paper?"

"That's all we found."

Out with it, thought Haver. In the background Fredriksson coughed. He had complained that morning about feeling lousy.

"A telephone number," said Johannesson at last.

Haver stared at the cars on the road below the place where they had found the murder victim. The traffic was heavier. They don't know a thing, he thought. All these people going to work now, happily unaware of how close death is.

"A telephone number?"

The technician held up a plastic bag with a slip of paper in it.

"I think it's a phone number anyway. Do you want to write it down?"

Haver nodded and produced paper and pen. Six digits, three of which were fours. Always something, he thought, three fours, that beats two pairs. Who called you? Who were you going to call?

Fredriksson approached. Johannesson smiled at him unexpectedly.

"I'm going up to the trailer," said Haver and pointed.

From the road the bellowing honk of a truck was heard. Johannesson twisted his head and studied the intense stream of vehicles, and if he intended to say anything, he quickly changed his mind and went back to the dead man with an expressionless face.

Haver set off before Fredriksson reached him.

You died in a place with a view, thought Haver, looking out over the scene of a crime that in the tabloids would surely be described as the "homeless murder" or something like that.

The trailer had flat tires, but was otherwise in reasonable shape. The hitch looked new. It was a yellow, smaller-model Valla trailer, with sitting room for four, Haver guessed. It was squeezed in between a pair of sizeable spruce trees, representatives of what not that long ago could be characterized as countryside, or perhaps the borderland between city and country. Now the expanding city had eaten its way in, chewed up and spit out the former forest and replaced it with roads and interchanges.

The door was closed. Haver pulled on a thin glove and pushed down the handle with one finger; the door opened easily on its own. To the left was what had once been a changing room but all the lockers were now removed. Against the one wall stood a camp bed without sheets, with a gray blanket in a pile at the foot. On the opposite side were several large plastic crates with covers and an enormous toolbox. A helmet was hanging on a nail. He could have used that, thought Haver.

He pulled on his shoe protectors and stepped just inside the door to get an overview. This was soon done, with a floor surface of perhaps ten square meters.

The trailer had probably been the dead man's home. If not, there was a connection here. It was a homeless person's temporary refuge.

In the space to the right was a table attached to the floor and four chairs. The tabletop was covered with various pieces of trash, a roll of steel wire, a packet of hard tack, a pile of used paper plates, but no bottles or beer cans, Haver noted with some surprise.

He left the trailer and went back to the technicians.

"You can look at the trailer too."

Morgansson nodded.

Fredriksson was still strolling around, but when he saw that Haver had come back, he came closer.

Haver looked at the dead man one last time, turned on his heels, and went toward his car. He was seething with bitterness. No one, especially not Fredriksson, was allowed to say anything! Then he might get furious and blurt out things that he would always regret. It was bad enough that he left his colleague in the lurch.

Before him his father, the burly construction laborer, dropped down without a word, his hand fumbling over his throat, choking to death from a wasp sting.

By leaving he was protecting his father, who was murdered by an insect. He was protecting himself, clenched one hand around his heart, to prevent an inner explosion.

Once at the car he changed his mind, but turned the key in the ignition anyway, put it in gear, and drove off. Fredriksson could do what he wanted, he can ride back with the technicians, he thought shamelessly.

✦

Three

She suddenly remembered the sting. Did he spank her? Shamelessly she had thrust up her buttocks. It was as if his hands were still resting heavily around her hips.

She drew in air, deeply, and breathed out, lowered her gaze and let it rest, carefully turned her head, and sniffed. He had licked her armpit. To start with it felt strange, bordering on unpleasant, but suddenly well-being took over. That was how it started, with his tongue.

"... two blows to the head ... the injuries ..."

Allan Fredriksson's voice in the background broke through her hazy thoughts for a moment and she raised her head and observed her colleague on the other side of the table. He met her eyes and the flow of words ceased for a moment before he continued.

"... the place where the discovery was made is probably identical with the scene of the murder."

Ottosson sniffled and took out a gigantic handkerchief. The violent nose-blowing made Fredriksson look up from his notes.

"Try echinacea," he said.

Ottosson shook his head while he carefully folded up the handkerchief.

"*Rövballar.*" Why had he used that dialect word? Was he from Skåne? Probably not. She seemed to recall him saying disparaging things about people from Skåne, that they were provincial and lethargic, which no one could accuse Anders Brant of.

Anders was smart. She realized that right away, and he quickly understood connections. But now it was his penis she was thinking about. Smart or not, he was the most all-around best lover she had encountered. He made her feel beautiful and desirable. He saw lines in her body like no one before. I'm over forty, she protested, but he just smiled, and caressed her across her back and down over the rounding of her rear. "Dead man's curve," he said, letting his hand continue toward her womb and she had lightheartedly parted her legs, but his hand made its way across her thigh toward the hollow of her knee.

He was slow but sometimes heated as well, and he sometimes talked about Tantric sex, which she'd never heard of. Always attentive to her mood and desires, he was, in short, a "keeper" as Görel would put it.

For three weeks they had been seeing each other, but only at her place. It was the most practical, he thought, saying that his place was cramped and that he didn't like to clean. She thought it was a good arrangement, as she avoided having to get a babysitter. Erik had not taken any great notice of the man who came and went. Anders was always gone before Erik woke up in the morning, and Ann was not sure whether he knew that Anders slept over. One evening they played computer games together, and the next morning Erik asked where the "old man" had gone.

They had made love three times in the past twelve hours—that was more than she had done the last two years before meeting Anders. She glanced at the clock; it was only an hour since he had slipped out of her.

She felt her belly contract. He had licked her like no one else, along her spine down toward the tailbone, and further, parted her cheeks and let his warm tongue run. Carefully he had drawn patterns with the tip of his tongue.

". . . that's what I think."

Fredriksson fell silent.

Lindell reached for the pen that was on the table in front of her.

"Do you have a fever too?" asked Fredriksson.

"No," Lindell assured him.

"You look a little warm."

She laughed. She heard how wrong it sounded, girlish and nervous. Her colleagues around the table observed her: Haver with a look of admiration, Beatrice mildly indulgent, and Ottosson with that unbelievable furrow between his eyes. Fredriksson looked completely uncomprehending while Sammy Nilsson smiled and made the V sign.

"I'm just a little—"

"A little what?" said Ola Haver.

He knows, thought Lindell. Their eyes met before she looked away. With a mental exertion of will she tried to gather her freely floating limbs and thoughts, and return them to her body.

It only struck her now that she had declined an invitation from Ola Haver and his wife Rebecka the evening before. Every summer they organized a barbecue. She had been there the past few years but this year she stayed away. No doubt they had discussed her absence.

Ann Lindell looked at Fredriksson.

"What do we know about his circle of acquaintances?"

"Have you had a stroke, Ann? Allan was just telling us that we don't have an identity."

Sammy Nilsson's words made her look down at the table top.

"I was somewhere else for a while," she said quietly.

"Where were you?" asked Beatrice Andersson.

He licked my armpit, she thought, and smiled and raised her eyes.

"I was in a place you've never been, Beatrice," she answered after a few seconds, still smiling. "If you'll excuse me, I have to make an urgent call."

She got up and grabbed the notebook and pen. It shows, she thought as she left the room, well aware of their looks.

"Urgent," she mumbled quietly to herself outside the door, and grinned.

After her panicky flight from the morning meeting, Ann Lindell barricaded herself in her office, unplugged the phone, and sat down, not at her desk, but in the visitor's chair that was pushed up against the wall between a pair of gigantic file cabinets. The office was so small that the chair was always in the way when it was in front of the desk. If anyone were to crack open the door and look in, they would think she was out. She also felt like she needed to be somewhere else.

Little by little the satisfaction of the early morning had turned into a feeling of vague worry.

She was sore, but above all confused. She had to stick to what had happened. It had been a long time since she needed to handle emotions like passion and hope. Regret and longing she had been able to parry with pretty good success. But this? Should she make a comparison to Rolf or Edvard, two past lives? Can you start from zero, she asked herself, and immediately knew the answer.

They had met a couple of months ago at Görel's and sure, she had been interested even then, and she sensed it had also been Görel's intention to bring them together. She had tried earlier without any results and jokingly complained about Ann's lack of involvement.

He had an open face and she liked that, got the idea that it corresponded to what was inside him. She needed a man like that, a man who talked about what he liked and thought, without reservation. She longed for painful honesty. No obstacles, no unspoken reservations, no point-taking.

Then she had not heard a word from him, even though he had said something about calling, but as the days and weeks passed she had resigned herself.

A month later he called. They decided to have dinner, the most civilized act two people can do together, as he put it. He suggested an Italian restaurant far up on S:t Olofsgatan and she said yes. She arranged for Erik to sleep over with a playmate from preschool. Anders Brant would pick her up and arrived half an hour early. She was still in her underwear, peeked through the peephole in the door, wrapped a stained bathrobe around herself, and opened the door.

They never made it to the restaurant. Ten minutes after he had stepped into her apartment they were in her bed.

This had been going on for three weeks. Violent fucking, there was no other word for it. He was loving. Unaccustomed to all this attention, these hands and this tongue, this cock, made her confused to start with, and sometimes she thought it was too good, too much of a good thing.

This morning he got out of bed, drew his hand over his sex, which in all likelihood was sore too, and said that he had to go away for a week, maybe two. She asked where he was going but did not get a reasonable answer. That's how much of an investigator she was! I got caught with my pants down, she thought gloomily, still intoxicated and tired.

A shiver of fear passed through her. Would he come back? She tried to calm herself by thinking: Why *wouldn't* he come back? He seemed happy with her. He came of his own free will, seemingly gladly and often to her home and bed.

After an hour there was a careful knock on the door. She knew it was Ottosson. The door was opened slowly by the unit chief who peeked in, and discovered Lindell between the massive cabinets.

"How are you? You look a bit tired out," he began unusually directly, without commenting on her placement in the office.

She could tell that Ottosson was exerting himself to sound relaxed, despite the furrow between his eyebrows.

Lindell pulled the chair out into the office, patted him on the arm, and sat down behind the desk. Ottosson took a seat in the visitor's chair.

"Warmed up," he said, and it took a second before Lindell understood that he meant the chair.

"I've been thinking about something," she said. "Ask around at 'The Grotto,' they might have some idea who he is."

"Ola and Beatrice are on their way there," he said with a smile.

"The Grotto" was the fixed point in existence for many of the homeless. The operation was run as a non-profit by a few activists and got some municipal backing and private sponsorship. There the mournful existences that no one really wanted to take responsibility for or even know about, could get a meal, some clothes, and consideration.

Lindell nodded and smiled back. Ottosson's wrinkle smoothed out somewhat.

"How was the barbecue last night?" she asked.

"Ola postponed it, so you'll get another chance."

She realized he was wondering what she'd been doing the night before, what was so important that she chose it over the traditional barbecue. Perhaps he thought it was a demonstration on her part, a way of communicating that she was not in sync with the others at the unit.

"That's nice," she said without any great enthusiasm.

Ottosson was drumming his fingers on the armrest.

"So, what do you think?" she asked.

Ottosson leaned back in the chair. His fingers became quiet.

"The usual," he said. "A wino has too much to drink and kills another wino."

"But there was no alcohol in his body, was there?"

Lindell's face suddenly turned red. What if I misunderstood that too?

"No, but maybe the murderer had a little under his belt."

"And the phone number on the scrap of paper?"

"No one answers. Berglund is checking on that."

"Whose account is it?"

"His name is Anders Brant, some kind of journalist."

Ann Lindell stared at Ottosson. Her mouth opened, but not a word came across her lips. Unconsciously she raised one hand as if to say: *Hold up, repeat that!*

"You know him?"

In the midst of her confusion she marveled at how easily her boss read her.

"Tell me," Ottosson continued. "Has he interviewed you?"

Lindell shook her head.

"No, we've just met casually," she said.

"What's he like?"

"I don't really know," she said.

Ottosson observed her.

"What connection do you think there is between the murdered man and Brant?"

"Not a clue," said Lindell.

"But if you know him."

"I don't know him."

"But something—"

"Don't you hear what I'm saying? I don't know him!"

She braced her feet in the chair as if to get up but sank back with a sigh.

Ottosson put his hands up in a defensive gesture. This had happened before, these moments of collapse in their otherwise familiar relationship. No powerful collisions, and their quarrels never dragged on and seriously poisoned their collaboration. It would not happen this time either, Lindell was clear about that.

Ottosson smiled at her. The wrinkle of worry was gone. It was as if he strove to lure her over a boundary, to get her to expose herself, say something that might explain. He knew her so well. Ottosson was conflict averse but also wise enough to understand that out of anger something might come loose from his otherwise reserved colleague. The iceberg Lindell might calve a piece out into the sea, a frozen clump that would drift away leisurely and slowly melt. She knew his tactics and her own weakness with respect to him.

This time you won't get any confidences, she thought gloomily, but she braced herself and let out a short laugh, a gesture and a grimace that might indicate resignation, not due to Ottosson, but rather a kind of excuse, evidence of self-insight: Yes, this is me, Otto, and you'll have to put up with it.

"I do have my cold case," she said, and he took her hint.

"Okay," said Ottosson. "You don't know him, but soon enough we will. Sammy's going to check up on this Brant. And how's it going with the girl?"

"I can't make heads or tails of it."

In April a sixteen-year-old girl had disappeared from her home in Berthåga. Lindell had expended considerable effort trying to figure out what happened, but had not found anything, or anyone, who could explain why Klara Lovisa Bolinder was as if swallowed up by the earth.

Every year a number of Swedes disappeared from their homes; the majority ran away of their own free will from their everyday lives, their jobs, and their families. For understandable reasons, the investigating police occasionally thought.

Klara Lovisa's disappearance on the other hand was a mystery. Lindell had stared at photographs of the young girl, the best one taken only a week or so before she disappeared. It depicted a blonde, laughing girl, with long, straight hair parted in the middle, blue eyes, and a classical nose that hinted at Roman blood in her veins. She was smiling into the camera. Her eyes were confident, she trusted the photographer.

It was a girl you noticed. Lindell sensed that from the first moment, which was also confirmed by her family and friends. Even more peculiar was that absolutely no one had noticed Klara Lovisa after she left home on April 28, 2007, to go into the city and shop for a spring jacket.

"I want to find her," said Lindell quietly.

Ottosson nodded. He leaned forward and placed his hand on Lindell's. They both knew that in principle the odds of finding Klara Lovisa alive were equal to zero.

✦

Four

The visit to "The Grotto" had produced an identity, an ex-wife, and a handful of names that might be characterized as Bo Gränsberg's friends, or at least acquaintances.

The manager of the refuge for the homeless, Camilla Olofsson, looked at the photograph of the dead man for a long time.

"Bosse was a considerate man," she said at last, but neither Ola Haver or Beatrice Andersson took her words at face value. It was a common reaction; very few people wanted to say anything bad about a dead person. Instead their positive qualities would usually be emphasized.

"He was considerate," the manager repeated. "He helped out. He was handy too. Nothing was left undone. I remember when we were going to . . . it doesn't matter."

Ola Haver stepped aside. Beatrice took a step closer.

"No one deserves to die like that," she said.

Camilla Olofsson nodded resolutely.

"Can you help us? We need a list of names, persons who maybe can tell us about Bosse, what he did, who he associated with, what plans he had."

"Plans," the manager said flatly, fixing her gaze somewhere far away. "He was happier recently," she said at last. "It seemed more positive, life, I mean. He came here a couple years ago, when he was really bad off. Then it went up and down."

"But now he was happier," Beatrice observed. "Did he say anything that explained—"

"No, nothing. Bosse didn't talk much. He kept most of it inside. He was trying, you could see that, but it was a struggle. He never recovered after the divorce. And then the injury, of course."

"What injury?"

"I don't really know how it happened, but he fell on the job, he was a construction worker. He broke his one arm and shoulder. Sometimes I could see that he was in pain."

"Do you know the name of his ex?"

"Gunilla Lange. I think she lives in Svartbäcken. I have a brother who lives up there and I've seen Gunilla around there a few times. She's been here a few times, dropped off clothes and that sort of thing. I liked her. I think she cared about Bosse too. She asked how he was doing. Maybe he was too proud to take any help from her, so she donated clothes here instead. Maybe they were his old clothes, what do I know?"

"He never talked about a job or apartment, or anything like that?"

Camilla Olofsson looked at the police officer.

"Job and apartment," she sniffed. "You don't know what life is like for these men and women."

"No, I don't," said Beatrice. "But you do. That's why I'm talking with you."

"Why the hell does he have to die for all of you to get interested?" said Camilla.

Besides Gunilla Lange's name, they also got a list of a few names—five men and a woman. According to Camilla Olofsson it was likely that the men on the list would show up at "The Grotto" later in the day.

Beatrice Andersson phoned Berglund, who promised to spend a few hours of the afternoon at "The Grotto," to possibly make contact with a few people who could provide information about Bosse's recent doings.

Am I grieving for him? She had repeated the question silently to herself since the police left her. They must have talked at least a couple of hours, then shook hands and said good-bye. The female police officer was sweet, complimented her on the curtains, asked whether she had sewn them herself. Not everyone noticed such things. The other one's gaze had wandered, as if he was ashamed or afraid of her.

Yes, I'm grieving, she decided. I am grieving the life we could have had. For sixteen years they had been married, for two periods, like a soccer match. A long first half, which lasted twelve years, was good. Then came the accident.

They had no children. She mourned for that. Maybe him too. Of course that's how it was. He loved kids. During all those years they had barely talked about it. They were both responsible for their childlessness, so why should they gab about it? She knew, purely rationally, that it was idiotic, but after the abortion, when she was nineteen, an intervention that he had supported, she saw childlessness as a punishment. She—they—had a chance, and they blew it.

Would things have been different with a child? Doubtful. Children were love, but not life, she had heard a girlfriend say once, and that phrase had etched itself into her awareness.

Their lives, mainly Bosse's, had developed along a path that no one could have foreseen. He had always been a proud man, and that would become his great torment. Pride was easy to bear as long as he had something to be proud of, but then what?

She told the police about his work, about the years when he came home sober, full of life, and just proud. He worked hard and made good money. And then: a single nerve in his body that was torn apart and made him useless as a scaffolder. Unable to raise his arm. The pain. Being useless, looking up at the facades and knowing.

"How did it happen?" the male police officer asked, the first time he had shown any deeper interest in Bosse's fate.

She told about the accident and how it had upset Bosse's life forever, and along with it their life together. He could not blame anyone, it was his own mistake, his eagerness to get it done quickly, that doomed him to idleness. He cursed his own clumsiness, called himself an "amateur."

Like so many others he chose liquor. He said "booze," never alcohol or more specifically vodka, gin, or whiskey. Booze it would be. She thought it sounded crude, but that was probably the point. There was nothing sophisticated, nothing enjoyable in Bosse's drinking habits. Booze was oblivion. Booze was hate. Booze was separation from life.

She got up, went over to the window, and looked out over the yard. In the background was a glimpse of the newly constructed police building.

They didn't have far to go to convey their message. How could anyone work as a police officer? A high-rise full of crime, hate, lies, guilt, and sorrow. She should have asked how they put up with it, but suspected there was no good answer.

The clock in the living room struck one. Soon Bernt would come, he was taking off early to visit the construction industry health office later in the afternoon. They would have scalloped potatoes and fried pork loin. She would tell about Bosse's death. Bernt would not ask many questions. She understood that deep inside he would be relieved, perhaps even happy. He was jealous that someone else had been so significant in her life, before she and Bernt met, a kind of retroactive jealousy that she never understood. Bernt had also been married before and talked freely and easily about his former wife.

He would not want to see her tears or listen to her stories. And she would try to please him. Cry now, not later, she thought. And she cried, cried over a wasted life. Bosse's. And perhaps her own, she wasn't sure. Her demands on existence had never been all that great, but she sensed that there was another way to live.

From the oven came the aroma of the casserole. She took out the pork and started cutting it up into slices. He liked them thin and only lightly fried. Suddenly her movements stopped. The police wanted her to come to the morgue and identify her former husband.

"You are the next of kin, from what we understand," the female police officer had said.

So it was, she thought, I was and am his next of kin. The police would pick her up at three o'clock.

How many slices will he want? The sight of the pork nauseated her. She set the knife aside. How did he die? It had not occurred to her to ask about that. What if they'd made a mistake and the dead man was someone else?

After the visit with Gunilla Lange, Ola Haver and Beatrice Andersson decided to look up the other woman on the list, for the simple reason that she was the only one with a permanent address, on Sköldungagatan in Tunabackar.

Ingegerd Melander was drunk, not conspicuously, but enough to make Haver feel uncomfortable. It was still only the middle of the day. He was immediately seized with antipathy, studied the woman's slightly worn features, the wrinkles that ran like half-moons on her cheeks, and which deepened when she screwed up her face to conceal her intoxication. This had the opposite effect.

Her hair was pulled up in a ponytail, which still made her look a bit girlish. Behind the ravaged face Haver could sense a woman who had once been really attractive.

"I'm going to the store," she said for no reason when they introduced themselves.

"We're here for Bosse Gränsberg," said Ola Haver.

Beatrice glanced furtively at him.

"May we come in and talk a little?"

Ingegerd Melander shook her head lightly and her noticeable confusion increased, but she stepped to one side to let them in.

They sat down at the kitchen table. Beatrice did not say anything about curtains, because there weren't any. The kitchen was otherwise strangely clinically clean. Not a gadget to be seen on the kitchen counter, the table, or other surfaces; no potted plants adorned the windowsill. The only thing that suggested any human activity was a wall calendar from Kjell Pettersson's Body Shop. Ola Haver noted that yesterday's date was circled in red.

"I have some bad news," Beatrice Andersson began.

"It always is where Bosse is concerned," said the woman.

"But you haven't had a visit from us before on his account, have you?"

The woman shook her head.

"What's he done?"

"Nothing, as far as we know," said Ola Haver. "He's dead."

At that moment he loathed himself and his work. The impulse to get up and rush out of the apartment was almost too much for him.

The woman's body contracted as if she had been given an electric shock, and she collapsed across the kitchen table, as if she were an inflatable doll someone had stuck a pin in. Just then the outside door opened, and they heard someone calling, "Hello in there!"

Beatrice leaned over the kitchen table and placed her hand on the woman's trembling shoulder. Ola Haver stood up. A man came into the kitchen whom Ola Haver immediately thought he recognized.

"What the hell are you doing here?" said the man.

In his eyes there was a mixture of surprise, suspicion, and fury.

"My name is Ola Haver and I'm a police officer."

"I can see that!"

"We have some bad news."

"You always do," said the man.

He glanced over Haver's shoulder.

"What have you done to Ingegerd?"

"Bosse Gränsberg is dead," said Haver.

"Huh?"

The man swallowed.

"Dead?"

Haver nodded.

"What the hell! Why's that? Did he kill himself?"

"No, someone else killed him."

Ola Haver saw the scene before him: Bo Gränsberg lying in the gravel.

Ingegerd Melander suddenly sat up, raised herself halfway, one hand resting heavily on the kitchen table while the other pointed at the man. Her hand was shaking. Her whole body was shaking.

A string of saliva ran from the corner of her mouth. Her face was beet red and her cheeks wet with tears. Hate, thought Ola Haver. That's what hate looks like. She wanted to scream something but there was only sound somewhere far down in her throat, and she lowered her hand.

"That was why," she mumbled.

"What do you mean why?"

"I turned forty."

Ola Haver glanced at the calendar. She sank down on the chair. Haver signaled with his hand that the man should follow him into the living room.

"What the hell is this?"

"Murder," said Ola Haver. "Bosse was murdered."

"I don't understand a thing," said the man.

"What's your name?"

"Johnny Andersson. Why?"

What a nutcase, thought Haver. He recognized the name from the list they got from Camilla Olofsson at "The Grotto."

"So you knew Bosse too," he said. "What do you think happened?"

"Me? How should I know?"

"When did you last see him?"

Johnny Andersson suddenly looked scared.

"You don't think . . ."

"Answer the question," said Haver, not able to hold back his fatigue and irritation. From the kitchen loud sobbing was heard.

"A couple days ago," said Johnny sullenly. "You can't just storm in here like the fucking Gestapo—"

"Where and when?"

"We met in town. It was last Sunday, maybe."

"What time?"

"In the morning."

"What were you doing?"

"We just ran into each other. You know, down at S:t Per."

Haver nodded. The little square in the middle of downtown where he and Rebecka used to meet when they were going to do something together. "See you by the fountain," she always said.

"How was he?"

"Well, same as usual. We talked a little. He was like he usually was . . . what should I say? A little bent."

"Bent?"

"It's like he curled himself up, made himself smaller than he was."

"He was a hundred eighty-six centimeters," said Haver for no reason.

"Right, that tall."

The man seemed to ponder the fact that there was at least ten centimeters difference between the dead man and himself.

"He didn't seem worried, agitated, or depressed, or anything?"

"Where that's concerned, was concerned, Bosse made you guess."

"One thing," said Haver, lowering his voice. "Did Bosse and"—he made a movement with his head toward the kitchen—"did they have a relationship?"

Johnny Andersson looked to the side. Now he's going to lie, thought Haver.

"Yes, before."

"When was before?"

"A month or two ago, maybe."

"They broke up then?"

Johnny nodded. Haver was not equally convinced that he had been served a lie, perhaps mostly because that lie would crack easily. He sensed that Johnny was interested in the woman in the kitchen. There was something in his attitude, but maybe mostly the tone he used in the cheerful call when, so free and easy, without ringing the doorbell, he stepped into the apartment.

"Who ended that relationship?"

"Ingegerd."

"In other words, Bosse was unhappy. Was there a rival?"

Johnny shook his head.

"Not as far as I know," he said.

There was the lie, thought Haver.

When the two police officers left Sköldungagatan they felt dejected. The mood did not lighten until they came to the crossing with Luthagsleden.

"Sometimes it's better when there are two of us," said Beatrice Andersson at last.

Haver nodded. Beatrice turned right.

"Bosse and Ingegerd had a relationship previously," said Haver.

"Yes, she told me that. She thought that he would congratulate her on her birthday anyway."

"Why did she break up with him?"

"Too much partying, she maintained. The strange thing, or Ingegerd thought it was strange, was that Bosse had stayed sober since the day she broke off the relationship. Stone sober."

"He wanted to become a better person and make everything all right," said Haver, catching himself using a careless, almost belittling tone.

Beatrice squinted at him.

"How are things at home?" she asked mercilessly.

"What do you mean?"

"Do you want to become a better person and make everything all right too?"

Haver looked at her and the fury made him clench his fists.

"Admit it," said Beatrice. "I have eyes and ears. You're feeling terrible. You're not doing well."

"What does that have to do with you?"

"It affects your job."

When the light turned green at Sysslomansgatan she gunned the engine and took off long before the other motorists.

"And mine," she added.

"Up yours," said Ola Haver.

Beatrice made a quick left turn onto Rackarbergsgatan and slammed on the brakes so that Haver was thrown forward and caught by the safety belt.

"Listen," she said, turning toward her colleague. "You need to cool down! We work together. We depend on each other. I can take a lot, but when I see that it's affecting people we meet in our work, then it's gone too far. Right now you are not a good policeman, do you see that?"

Haver stared straight ahead. More than anything he wanted to get out of the car.

"We know each other well, we've worked together for many years, so I can be frank. You're not a trainee, you're an experienced, capable detective. So act like one."

Shut up, he thought, but said nothing. Beatrice did not let herself be silenced by his stone face.

"Take sick leave if you're feeling shitty. Go somewhere. Do something you think is fun. In the worst case, get a divorce!"

She pushed forward the gear shift and the car rolled off up the hill. They had intended to check on an address in Stenhagen, where a former coworker of Bosse Gränsberg lived. A man whom Gunilla Lange knew was on long-term disability and whom Bosse often talked about. According to his ex-wife, they had seen each other several times during the last month.

But as if by unspoken agreement they returned, in icy silence, to the police building.

◆

Five

As soon as Ottosson left, Lindell took out the phone book and looked up Anders Brant's number.

With increasing agitation she punched in the numbers. She wished he would pick up the phone and explain how it all fit together, but after a half-dozen rings an answering machine came on: "Hi, you've reached Anders Brant. I can't come to the phone right now. Please leave a message." Anders Brant, the man who made her feel pleasure like never before, the man who made her feel hopeful. When she heard his voice the thrill from the morning returned, the satisfaction and excitement. He didn't say he wasn't at home, just that he couldn't come to the phone.

She had never called him before. She did not even have his cell phone number. He was always the one who made contact, and until now she had not found that strange. Now it felt all the more peculiar.

Now he did not pick up the phone and what was worse, he was involved in a murder investigation. He had suddenly gone away. She called again, with the same result. For a moment she considered leaving a message, but decided not to.

Someone other than Anders Brant might listen to the message.

Who was he? A journalist, he said, freelancing now after resigning from a magazine she had never heard of, much less read. A cultural magazine, he explained, which in his taste had become a little too stuck-up. He mentioned something about a "battle-ax" in the editorial office he didn't get along with.

What did he write about? She didn't know. Cultural articles was the most likely candidate. Here Ann felt that she was in foreign territory and no doubt that was also the reason she had not shown any great curiosity. She did not want to admit how ignorant she was in that area.

They had not talked that much really, mostly cuddled and made love, and Ann had not protested, starved as she was for skin and touch.

And now he had gone somewhere. She did not know where and she did not know how she could quickly and easily find that out. A week, maybe two, he had said. She guessed it had to do with work. Was he in Sweden or abroad? Perhaps Görel knew something? Ann had no idea where and when they had met. Görel was not someone you immediately associated with cultural magazines.

She went to the Eniro website and searched his cell phone number. The phone was turned off and an automated message said something about a voice mailbox.

All in all, Anders Brant was one big question mark. She guessed that the reason the murdered man had a slip of paper with a journalist's phone number on it was purely professional. But what could Bo Gränsberg have to say to a cultural journalist? Perhaps they were acquaintances from before, perhaps even related?

There were too many questions. She decided to talk with Sammy Nilsson and then Görel, but that would have to wait until this evening. Reaching her at work was difficult and not greatly appreciated.

It struck her that her girlfriend had not called during the time Brant was tumbling around in Ann's bed. Didn't she know that they had met? She must be curious, but if Brant hadn't said anything to her, then Görel must have guessed that her attempt at procurement had not succeeded. She usually called now and then, but the past few weeks there had been complete silence, and Ann had not thought about contacting her. I've had my hands full, she thought, and could not help smiling to herself, on some level very satisfied with the experiences of the past few weeks. And she did not want to believe that it was over. It couldn't be over. But why this aching, unpleasant feeling, which also expressed itself physically, that the whole thing was over, that for a few weeks she had been able to look out over landscapes that were not her true domains. A temporary visit.

Ann Lindell got up with a heavy sigh. Never, she thought, it can never be really good, never uncomplicated.

Sammy Nilsson did not answer either. In Lindell's experience, that could be due to two things; either he was talking with a "customer," as he insisted on saying, or he was exercising. Considering the circumstances she believed in the first alternative. She left a message and asked him to call her as soon as possible.

Then she sat down at the computer to do some research. She typed "Anders Brant" in the search field and after a moment or two the screen was filled with information. There was a total of 2,522 hits, even if many of course came from the same source.

The first entry was a short article published in the Swedish Society for Nature Conservation magazine, about biofuel, followed by some longer articles about Putin and Russia printed in a magazine she was not familiar with, followed by an opinion piece on the same subject published in *Dagens Nyheter*.

Lindell skimmed through the text. A different Anders Brant emerged than the one she knew. His tone was polemical, but quiet nonetheless. He formulated himself well, she thought, and felt a touch of pride in his ability. We were fucking that same day, she thought. *Dagens Nyheter* inserted his article on the editorial page and Anders inserted a different article in me, she thought, smiling in the midst of her confusion.

The phone rang and she saw that it was Sammy Nilsson.

"Good," she said. "I'm wondering about that Brant."

"I am too," said Sammy. "I'm actually at his residence."

Lindell's face turned red.

"Where does he live?"

"In Svartbäcken. No one's home. I've talked with some of his neighbors and one of them saw him leave the house with a suitcase yesterday morning. He came home at eight in the morning in a taxi. It's good to have old ladies around who keep an eye on things. But this time it was a guy, Mr. Nilsson, like Pippi Longstocking's monkey."

"Suitcase," she said stupidly and could not hold back her disappointment, even though he said he was going away.

For a brief moment she considered telling about her relationship with Brant. Sammy was someone who could take it without getting upset or criticizing her. On the contrary, he would think it was exciting. He would congratulate her and say that there was nothing to worry about. Lie low, he would encourage her, you're not working on the case. We'll find Brant, question him, and remove him from the investigation.

Just as the words were on the tip of her tongue, ready to be spit out, because that was how she felt now, she had to spit Brant out, get rid of the bitter taste in her mouth, Sammy continued.

"Well, sure, that messes everything up. He was only carrying a small suitcase, which the neighbor believed was a computer case."

"He's a journalist," said Lindell.

Sammy laughed.

"We know that," he said. "How's it going?"

"Super!" said Lindell.

It struck Lindell that Brant must have called for a taxi when he left her apartment. Now he was Brant and not Anders.

"Then he took off in another taxi half an hour later," Sammy continued.

"Have you checked the fare?"

"Will do. He took Uppsala Taxi. The monkey noticed that."

Lindell took a deep breath, trying to think of something intelligent to say.

"I see," she managed to say.

"Why do you ask? Do you have anything new concerning our writer friend?"

"No, no, I was just curious, I knew you would be checking up on him. Ottosson mentioned something about it."

Sammy Nilsson did not say anything. Perhaps he was waiting for more? But why did he say "monkey"? Sammy's last name was Nilsson too.

"We'll be in touch," said Lindell at last, when the silence became too tangible.

"We'll do that! Bye!"

After the call Lindell sat for a long time, brooding about whether she should go to see Ottosson and tell him what she had been unable to say to Sammy. But she decided to lie low. On the screen his name was shining and she shut down the computer.

"Jerk," she said.

Listlessly she opened a folder that contained the latest about Klara Lovisa. At the top was the photograph and as usual Lindell studied it carefully before she browsed further and produced the hastily jotted down notes from yesterday.

A man in Skärfälten, just ten kilometers west of the city, had seen a young girl in the company of a man. The description tallied, and the witness had even specified the right color of her jacket and pants. They were walking together at a slow pace on the road toward Uppsala-Näs.

A day after the disappearance, when the media had reported on the case, the man, Yngve Sandman, called the police tip line, but since then no one had shown any interest in questioning him further.

Yesterday he had called, somewhat bitter but mostly surprised at the lack of action, and was forwarded to Lindell.

"I have a daughter myself," he said.

Lindell could not explain why no one from the police had been in touch. Carelessness, she thought to herself, but obviously could not say that. Always with disappearances, especially when young women were concerned, there was an abundance of tips and observations. Mostly they led nowhere. The man's call had no doubt drowned in the flood of calls.

Ann Lindell got his information again and promised to be in touch within a day or two. Now it had been exactly twenty-four hours and she made the call. They agreed that she would drive out to see him right away.

"It was here," said Yngve Sandman, pointing. "I was on my moped and they were walking there, on the other side of the road."

Lindell looked at him.

"So they were walking on the wrong side," Lindell observed, as if that were significant. "You were on a moped?"

"Yes, I collect mopeds and was out test-driving an old Puch. It's older than me. It doesn't go fast and I was able to get a good look at them."

"Tell me how they were walking, what they looked like and that."

"She was walking closest to the road. They weren't walking particularly fast, didn't look stressed. But they didn't seem to be talking with each other, not right when I encountered them anyway."

"How did the girl seem?"

Yngve Sandman shrugged his shoulders.

"Well, what should I say? I thought she was pretty, if you know what I mean."

Lindell nodded.

"Did you get the impression that they knew each other? She didn't look scared or anything?"

"Well, two friends out walking, that's what it looked like. But actually you can be afraid of a friend too."

"How were they dressed?"

"I've told you that, first in April and then yesterday to you."

"Tell me again."

"She had dark-green pants, almost looked military with a couple of pockets in front on the hip, and a light-blue jacket. Pretty short, I thought, it was cold that day. I didn't think about her shoes, if I had to guess they were black, some kind of boots."

Mr. Sandman guesses right, thought Lindell. Klara Lovisa had on a pair of short, black boots the day she disappeared.

"And him?"

"Blue jeans and a jacket with a hood, which he had pulled up. It was dark, maybe blue. Workout clothes, I think."

"What did he look like?"

Suddenly the sky darkened and they looked up. A dark cloud passed quickly and the sun was hidden for a few moments.

"Around twenty-five, maybe younger," said Sandman, as the sun returned. "Light hair, but the hood concealed most of his head."

"Glasses?"

The man shook his head. He looked away along the road.

"I got the sense that he was walking a little funny, but that may be because he was walking halfway in the ditch, if you know what I mean?"

"Was he limping?"

"No, not exactly, but in some way . . ."

They stood quietly a moment.

"I have a daughter myself," he said. "If she disappeared, I mean."

"Yes," said Lindell. "It's too awful."

"Does she have any siblings?"

"No."

He shook his head and stood quietly a moment.

"Looks like rain," he said, as another threatening black cloud drew past.

"Did you drive back the same way?"

"Yes, I turned up at Route 72. Although I stopped there awhile and adjusted the moped. It was running a little shaky and I had to tighten a brake wire."

"How long did it take before you came past here again?"

"Ten minutes, maybe fifteen."

"And then the two of them were gone?"

"Yes, not a soul on the road."

"What time of day did you see them?"

"Around eleven thirty."

Klara Lovisa had left home on Saturday the twenty-eighth of April one hour earlier. Lindell looked around. Fields, a few houses, a narrow country road that made its way down toward the valley. She had driven this way perhaps a dozen times. What was Klara Lovisa doing here? What was the likelihood that she was the one Yngve Sandman had seen? And who was the young man?

Klara Lovisa did not have a boyfriend, not officially anyway. Her girlfriends had spoken about an Andreas, whom she had dated since seventh grade, but he had been removed from the investigation long ago. The day of her disappearance he had been in Gävle with his mother.

Could the young man by her side be an unknown admirer, someone she was acquainted with, or in any event recognized? It seemed as if she had been walking on the road voluntarily. If this was even Klara Lovisa.

Sandman was her last straw. He seemed lucid and not someone who was only trying to get attention. She cursed the unknown associate who had neglected the early information. Then the observation was close to fresh, now almost two months had passed.

Ann Lindell decided to use the folder she had already put in order during the first week of the investigation.

"I want you to look at some photographs of young girls."

"I see," he said, not seeming particularly engaged.

Lindell browsed a little back and forth, held out the first photo. He shook his head. There was a similar reaction to photos number two, three, and four. At the fifth photo he lingered a little before shaking his head. He firmly rejected girls six, seven, and eight, and all the others that followed.

"Then we have the nineteenth and final picture," said Lindell.

"It looks like a parade of Lucia candidates," he said. "But I didn't see any of them here."

"Certain?"

Sandman nodded immediately. Lindell took out the twentieth picture, which she had left sitting in the folder.

"That's her," he said immediately.

He did not need to say anything because as he was looking at Klara Lovisa he took a deep breath and made a gesture with his hand as if to illustrate that it was here on the road he had seen her.

"It's her," he repeated. "Poor girl."

Lindell was not convinced. Sandman may very well have recognized the picture from the newspaper, but it reinforced her impression that he was not a crackpot. All too often the "customer" was so eager to please that he, for some reason less often she, would do everything at a confrontation to "recognize" someone, perhaps not point out anyone definitively but still show some hesitation, as if it were impolite to consistently be a naysayer. He had denied any recognition, including the one he believed was the last picture.

"Thanks," she said. "You've been a very big help."

Yngve Sandman looked almost helpless.

They walked back toward the parked cars. There they remained standing awhile in silence. The sun once again broke through the clouds. It was like a staged alternation between shadow and sun, which in turns let the landscape, the stony meadowland up toward the forest, and the fields with the spiky corn on the other side of the road, bathe in light, and then be swept into a slightly mysterious darkness.

"The human factor," he said at last.

"What do you mean?"

"It's not allowed to happen in my work. I mean, when I called you the first time someone dropped the ball, it's obvious, isn't it?"

Lindell could not help but nod.

"Then perhaps she was still alive?"

"Yes, that's how it is," Lindell admitted. "Then we would have been in a better situation."

"And her parents too, even if . . ."

Yngve Sandman looked down at the roadside. By his feet a dandelion was growing. He kicked at it so that the yellow flower was separated from the stalk.

"I live up there on the rise," he said without prompting, and pointed. "You don't see the house but it's behind there. It's a nice house, paid for. I live almost for free. The children have moved out. I get by. I tinker with my mopeds. The woods are full of berries and mushrooms."

Lindell looked in the direction he was pointing. An area as good as any, she thought. She had a vague memory that once she had picked mushrooms in the vicinity, but maybe it was on the other side of Route 72.

"Stina left a few years ago."

He said it without bitterness, just a statement. And he smiled.

"How many kids do you have?"

"Two. And you?"

"A boy," said Lindell. "He'll start school in the fall."

"I was early," he said. "I have a windmill on the lot," he said with unexpected eagerness. "It's really ugly but it was my dad who built it. I mean, if you were to come by, you'll see the windmill."

"What kind of work do you do?"

"Air traffic controller."

"You're used to details," said Lindell, and smiled back. "You can't miss anything."

"That's how it is. For me the human factor doesn't exist."

"It was nice to meet you," said Lindell, extending her hand. "Although the circumstances could have been better."

"It doesn't feel good, I mean this," he said, taking her hand in a slightly awkward motion and throwing out his other arm.

After a period of silence Ynvge Sandman tried to smile again, but it was more like a grimace.

Lindell sensed that he was a man without great pretensions, a man who did not let himself be surprised, whose equanimity would not be disturbed too easily. She sensed the equanimity was acquired, perhaps even forced. For behind his tinkering and berry picking she sensed a very lonely person.

And now that balance had been disturbed. A girl's disappearance worried him, that was clear, but what exactly was going on in the man's mind she obviously did not know.

They separated, walking to their cars. Lindell raised her hand as she drove away. He remained standing outside his car, peering along the road, and did not appear to see her greeting.

Stone dead for centuries, thought Lindell, and then comes a whole swarm of men. He had hit on her, it was quite clear: single, children moved out, a hint of solid finances, and an honorable job. And then a comment about the windmill that showed a romantic side. Yngve Sandman was no tough guy; he maintained a hideous windmill for sentimental reasons.

But he was right, if their procedures functioned then perhaps the disappearance would have been solved. If it really was Klara Lovisa he had seen. And Ann Lindell was becoming more and more convinced of that as she drove at a slow pace back toward the city.

In line with Berthåga she got an impulse to turn and drive to the home of Klara Lovisa's parents. Her mother was probably home. She had been on sick leave from her job at the Swedish Medicines Agency since the disappearance.

But she continued toward the city. Before she visited them again she should refresh her memory, go through some of the many interviews that were filed in binders piled in her office.

Over 150 interviews had been conducted during April and May to try to chart the girl's life, contact points, and movements during the time before she disappeared.

Perhaps in the binders there would be a single sheet of paper that might tell about a blond, young man wearing jeans and a dark-blue jacket with a hood. A man who made Klara Lovisa abandon the thought of buying a spring jacket and instead lured her out of town.

✦

Six

Beatrice Andersson had never seen a T-shirt that stained. It had once been white but was now covered with spots. She could not keep from staring. A dark whirl of hair stuck out at the chest. When he took hold of the T-shirt and pulled it away from his substantial stomach to study the variety of colors for himself, she observed that the man also had hair on the back of his hand and fingers.

Göran Bergman laughed.

"Yeah, I know," he said. "If you're selling laundry detergent you've come to the right place. Solvent would be even better."

There was a pungent odor coming from the apartment, mixed with the smell of coffee.

She introduced herself and asked if he had time for a brief conversation.

"Sure," he said. "It's time for a coffee break anyway."

He stepped to the side and let her into the apartment. On the floor below the coat rack, which held only two garments, was a wastebasket, a bucket of kitchen scraps, three pairs of shoes, all heavy work shoes, and a pair of sandals.

He pushed the wastebasket to the side.

"I'm in the middle of painting," he said with his back to her, disappearing into the kitchen just to the right. "You don't need to take off your shoes!"

Beatrice Andersson followed. The kitchen was small and dominated by an easel. The half-finished painting depicted a forest glade.

"Okay, and what does the police department want with someone like me?" he said, taking out two mugs and pouring coffee without ceremony.

"Fresh brewed," he said. "Sit yourself down! Is this about the car? Has someone burned up my car?"

"You haven't read the newspaper?"

Göran Bergman shook his head.

"It got too expensive, and there's just a lot of crap in it anyway."

She took a sip of coffee and waited until he sat down across from her.

"I don't have good news. Your friend Bo Gränsberg was found dead yesterday. I'm sorry."

Bergman slowly lowered the mug and stared at her.

"I see, he couldn't take it anymore," said Bergman.

"He didn't die by his own hand," said Beatrice.

"Someone killed him?"

"Yes, it's that bad."

Beatrice told how and where Bo Gränsberg was found.

"How did you find me?"

"His ex-wife said that you and Bo got together."

Göran Bergman nodded. He fixed his eyes on the painting.

"He liked that, although it's ugly as sin. I thought about giving it to him."

"Where would he hang it up?" Beatrice asked.

Bergman gave her a look of surprise.

"You worked together?"

"Yes, for many years. He was the best. We were the best, that's how it was! Damn it, we were the fastest and the safest scaffolders in town."

"But then he injured himself?"

"Yes, so fucking stupid. And here I sit with damaged legs. Did you ever hear the like, I'm forty-eight and my knees are shot."

"What were the two of you up to?"

"I see, Gunilla gossiped," said Bergman with a crooked smile, and started to tell her.

The idea was that the two old workmates would start a company, scaffolding construction, of course, but other things too. What the "other things" might include was not clear from Bergman's exposition. He thought they had the know-how and the contacts, plus a solid reputation, even though Bosse's was somewhat tarnished, but no one could take from him the almost twenty years he had worked in construction and on building facades.

They could no longer perform the purely physical aspect, erecting the scaffolding, but Bergman thought—and Beatrice had no reason to doubt him—they could organize the work like nobody else. They knew all the tricks, they had a good sense of people and a realistic picture of what the job involved.

How much of a problem do I have with construction workers, wondered Beatrice. When she dropped off Haver at the police building and said she was thinking about visiting Bergman alone, he asked how much she knew about construction workers. As if he was an expert, simply because his father had been in the industry. She was well aware of his father's reputation and above all his early, unpleasant death, and for that reason she did not say anything. Everyone on the squad knew that this was a sensitive chapter in their associate's life, something he was still wrestling with after all these years. There was no reason to add to his burden, but she felt a certain sense of triumph in having gotten Bergman to talk so freely.

Because Bergman was talking away. It seemed as if he had repressed the thought of his friend's death, and everything sounded to Beatrice very intelligent and thought out. They had done what many others who were going to start a new business did not have the sense to do, that is, market research. Bergman had called around and personally visited thirty or so "actors on the market," as he put it, the majority of them, if not acquaintances, known from before anyway.

"Capital," Beatrice interrupted the torrent of words.

Bergman abruptly fell silent, but recovered fairly quickly.

"Exactly," he said with emphasis. "Cash is required, not enormous amounts, but still."

Beatrice suspected that Bo Gränsberg did not have any concealed assets.

"A direct question: Do you have that kind of money?"

"Not exactly, but quite a bit."

"And Bosse?"

"He was going to arrange it," said Bergman, looking unhappy, because he was smart enough to realize that Bosse's violent death might have concerned money.

"He was going to put in a smaller portion," he explained. "Not fifty percent, that is."

"How much?"

"Around a hundred and fifty grand."

"That's a lot of money for an unemployed, homeless person."

Bergman nodded. He turned his eyes away. Suddenly he realized that there was a coffee mug in front of him and he took a gulp.

"Lukewarm," he said.

"What do you think?" Beatrice asked.

"What do you mean?"

"How was he going to get hold of a hundred and fifty thousand kronor?"

Göran Bergman took another gulp.

"It's a bit sensitive," he said at last. "I don't know if I should talk about it, but you've met Gunilla, Bosse's ex, she's a really good lady, you know. She has always—"

"Can she come up with that amount?"

Beatrice had the impression that Gunilla Lange lived quite frugally, but on the other hand, perhaps that was why she could invest so much money on a homeless, alcoholic former husband.

"A hundred anyway," said Bergman.

"That's a fair amount," said Beatrice, and Bergman nodded in agreement.

"Why? Bosse was perhaps not the safest investment you could imagine."

"No, but the fact was that he was sober for a couple of months. He really believed in this project, and I did too. I know we would have made it work. And I think Gunilla saw that too, she had seen him in his prime. He made decent money back in the good old days."

"But then he was sober, uninjured, and had a well-ordered life," Beatrice objected.

"That's true, but he really wanted to. Adamantly. 'This is my chance,' he said."

"Was there anything between Bosse and Gunilla?"

"No, no, but I think they still liked each other a lot. He often said that."

"But he had another woman, from what I understand?"

"That one," said Bergman. "She's just after money. Do you know that old hag is a gambling addict? She can sit in front of those machines for hours on end. And sometimes she goes to Åland and gambles away tons of money on roulette."

"She never wins?"

"Ingegerd is a loser," Bergman maintained.

"And then she broke up with him?"

"She did," said Bergman bitterly. "And Bosse had a relapse and got stinking drunk for two days. Deep down he knew that Ingegerd wasn't good for him, but he was still depressed, because you need someone to hug now and then."

Beatrice nodded.

"Do you have someone to hug?"

"Oh, sure," he said. He smiled that crooked smile again. "Ursula is her name. The best thing that's happened, they always say, but for me it's true. A good lady like that is like a gift from above. She's the one who gets me to paint too. She took a few paintings to a gallery in town and this fall I'm going to have a show. Can you imagine that?"

He shook his head and observed the painting on the easel again.

"Not that one maybe," he said, laughing nervously, but soon became serious again. "But Bosse got back on his feet! He sat here and sweated and shook for a whole day. And I made coffee and painted and we talked and talked. He crashed over on the couch and came out like a human being. The next day he went and picked up a few things he had with that bitch. Bosse was strong sometimes. I know we would have managed it! Östen, the guy from the gallery, was here and took a look. He wanted to see more paintings. He called me a naivist and damn it, I probably am naive sometimes, but Bosse and I would have made the company work."

"I think so too," said Beatrice.

Bergman gave her a quick look. His eyes were misty.

"In a way I expected this," he said. "Bosse was a very sad man."

✦

Seven

Over the two days after Bo Gränsberg was found the image emerged of a man who had just gotten back on his feet. It was Beatrice who used Göran Bergman's words at the morning gathering.

At the time of his death Bosse Gränsberg was forty-four years old, born in Domkyrko parish. His parents, Gerhard and Greta Pettersson, both worked at a clothing company, his mother as a seamstress and his father as a kind of factotum watchman and chauffeur. When Bo was five years old they changed their surname to Gränsberg, after the place in inland Västerbotten where Gerhard was born.

He had no siblings and his parents had been dead for many years. According to Gunilla Lange, he had pleasant memories of his upbringing and she had never heard him say a bad word about his parents.

What Beatrice produced about his adolescence barely deviated from the pattern for a working-class boy: no brilliant performance in school, with his best grades in math and PE; after completion of elementary school, training as a construction worker at the Boland School, and then a job right away as a carpenter at BPA. There he stayed for five years before he took a job as a scaffolder. Göran Bergman was one of his co-workers.

Bergman was the primary source of information, and his opinion was that then, at age twenty-five, was the best time of Bosse's life. He had been with Gunilla for several years, they rented a two-room apartment in downtown Petterslund, he was hardworking and earned good money, his involvement in sports gave him friends and strengthened his self-esteem.

Then came the accident. A faulty anchor in a facade, his own mistake; in one stroke, a single bolt changed his life. At first he was hopeful, even though the doctor at the construction industry health office was pessimistic about his chances of returning to his old job, and encouraged him to get retraining. Bosse on the other hand was convinced that the injury would heal; a construction worker has to take a few knocks, he reasoned. But as the months passed and the pain did not subside, his mood became more and more bitter and contrary. He turned to the bottle for consolation. Until then, according to Gunilla, he had a relaxed attitude toward alcohol, drank no more than most, and despised those who couldn't handle liquor.

After repeated promises of sobriety, and just as many relapses, Gunilla left him, even though she was still in love with him. She left him to protect herself, aware that wives of alcoholics could never control their own lives, but always became victims, whether or not they drank themselves.

Bosse moved to a studio apartment in Eriksberg, intensified his drinking, was sent to a treatment center but soon quit the program, and then his decline accelerated. After a year he was evicted from the apartment. Bo Gränsberg became one of a growing army of homeless people.

The change came during the late winter of 2007. Göran Bergman and Gränsberg had kept in touch the whole time, even if during the most difficult periods it was sporadic, when the idea of a joint investment in a scaffolding and service business for construction companies came up.

Bergman was convinced that they would succeed, and as he was presenting his case Beatrice let herself be convinced with him. When it came to scaffolding, the naivist amateur painter was a realistic pro. She had also made inquiries among others in the industry, and all had testified to his capability and enterprise.

Gränsberg got similar ratings, even if they were darkened by his drinking in recent years. But the majority were prepared to agree with Bergman: Their business concept was not crazy at all. The chance that they would succeed was fairly good.

"It's cruel," said Beatrice after her presentation. "After so much misery, just when he starts getting back on his feet again, he gets clubbed to death. He was on his way back up again, but got knocked down for good."

"Thanks, Beatrice," said Ottosson, coughing and looking slightly helpless.

The squad chief was known for his soft heart when faced with human shortcomings, but also of man's capacity, out of degradation, perhaps impotence and hate, to shake it off, stagger on, and simply get back up. That kind of thing always made him teary-eyed.

Berglund's afternoon session at "The Grotto," where he spoke with a dozen of Gränsberg's "brothers in misfortune," as he put it, resulted in a similar picture.

"He was a good guy, that's how you can summarize the whole thing," said Berglund.

"Hallelujah," said Riis. "Are we at a Salvation Army meeting? Aren't there any stains? The guy drank and was a tramp. How did he get money? No thefts or minor assaults, not even shoplifting? He was no angel, was he?"

"Tell about the trailer," Ottosson encouraged Morgansson. Ottosson was ashamed of Riis, mainly perhaps because Fritzén, the prosecutor, was present.

Morgansson explained that they had found three fingerprints in the job site trailer, besides Gränsberg's. Two had been identified. Johnny Andersson and Manfred Kvist, two homeless men, had left their prints in a number of places. Both had also admitted that they visited Gränsberg, but could not say when, other than that it was during the past month. Kvist had slept over on one occasion on the floor in the trailer. That was at the end of May.

They had not found anything of great interest, no alcohol or narcotics, and nothing that looked like stolen goods.

Morgansson's report was brief and concise as usual. Lindell observed him during the presentation and found that he had been getting better and better.

"The third print?" she asked.

"Well," said the technician with a quick glance at Lindell. "We found it on the cover of a notebook, the ordinary kind with a shiny black cover and lined pages. It looks brand new, the price tag is still on the back, and nothing was written in it."

"Can it be the sales clerk's print?"

"Probably not," Morgansson drawled. "Unless we're talking door-to-door sale of notebooks, because we found the same print on one of the windowpanes, the one by the table. Or pane, it's actually plastic. My theory is that the unknown individual was sitting at the table, pushed up the window to get a little fresh air, and then locked it with an adjusting screw. Or maybe simply opened it and threw something out the window, but that doesn't change the picture. The print is there."

Morgansson stopped talking and they realized by his expression that he was done.

"Perhaps the man in the car," said Sammy Nilsson.

Everyone turned toward him.

"I got a tip today. I was rummaging around at the murder scene and ran into two guys doing cable work. As you've seen, a cutting runs along the road past the murder scene. This morning there were people there. They were doing some excavation work, cable laying or something. I realized that they must have been there awhile and stopped. To summarize, they had seen a car parked fifty meters from the discovery site, approximately where we parked ours. That was Monday, they were dead sure of it. Tuesday and Wednesday they were at a different job. We found Gränsberg on Tuesday, when he'd been lying there a full day, according to the medical science."

"What kind of car was it?" Ottosson asked.

"The guys in the cutting said a white one, a little run-down, make unknown."

"When?"

"After their coffee break at eleven it was just there. Then it disappeared without them noticing it. They were down in the cutting of course and had limited visibility."

"Anders Brant has a white Corolla," Sammy Nilsson continued. "Eight years old. It's in his parking space."

Ann Lindell looked down at the table. Damn jerk, she mumbled inaudibly, over and over again.

"And he's still missing?" asked Fritzén, the prosecutor.

"Yep," said Sammy. "He packed up and left Tuesday morning."

"We'll have to go into his apartment," said Fritzén. "There's no other alternative. We'll bring in the car too."

"Doesn't he have a cell phone?" asked Fredriksson, who had so far been silent.

"Not turned on," said Sammy. "I've checked the flights on Tuesday. He left home about eight and we know he went to Arlanda, terminal 5, international departures, that is. There are countless conceivable destinations."

"Check them all," said Fritzén. "He must be on a passenger list."

"Madrid," said Ola Haver. "He went with Spanair to Madrid. The ticket was purchased on the Internet on Friday of last week."

Ottosson smiled broadly and gave Fritzén a look. For once Sammy Nilsson looked disappointed, not to mention taken by surprise. Beatrice also grinned and made a thumbs up in the direction of Haver, who however did not abandon the poker face he had put on the past week.

"I'll be damned if it wasn't that hack who was there and smudged his prints in the shed," Riis commented.

To him all journalists were rabble.

"You said that Brant came to his residence early Tuesday morning by taxi. Where did he take it from?"

Lindell stared at her colleague and then turned her gaze toward Sammy Nilsson, who seemed to have recovered after Haver's unexpected initiative as far as Madrid was concerned.

"Vaksala Square," he said. "According to the taxi driver he was walking along Vaksalagatan and hailed the car."

Lindell exhaled audibly. Brant had evidently walked some distance from her home, but she realized that her concealment could be discovered at any time. Maybe her phone number was jotted down in an address book in his apartment? Her secret—that she and Brant had been lovers, or whatever other people would call it—would crack the day they checked Brant's calls from his home phone. Almost certainly he had called her from there. What would she say? That he had called for an interview? That he was an acquaintance of a friend that she got together with now and then? Or should she go see Ottosson and tell him what was going on?

With every minute it was getting harder to be honest, with every second that passed she looked more and more like a liar, and even more important in the eyes of her colleagues, one who was obstructing a murder investigation.

Maybe he'd only called her from his cell phone? She seized that straw, even if it was fragile, and decided to wait and see. If only she could make contact with him first!

On Tuesday evening she phoned Görel, who had no idea where Brant might conceivably be, nor how he could be reached. She had no e-mail address for Brant. When Lindell asked, it turned out that they had met at a salsa class. He was not much of a dancer, Görel thought. Lindell mumbled something and thanked her, and quickly ended the call by blaming Erik.

Is this how they feel, it struck Lindell, the ones who are questioned by us and stick with half-truths and evasions as long as possible? They don't need to be guilty of anything, but shame or misdirected loyalty makes them stand out as tortuous liars.

The prosecutor decided on a house search, "on weak grounds," as he himself admitted, but they did not have much to go on. The hope was that they would be able to establish that it was Brant's prints in the trailer. And the car would be brought in for technical investigation, even if the chance of directly linking it to the crime scene was not that great. For one thing several days had passed, for another the installation workers had not seen the parked car at close range. Besides, the road up to the area where the trailer stood was coarse, crushed gravel. So no one was counting on any certain tire prints, even more so as several police vehicles had used that same access road.

The group discussed further, reinforced by the prosecutor's decision, how the investigation should otherwise be run. Berglund was eager to continue talking with the homeless at "The Grotto." Beatrice Andersson's task was to have yet another conversation with Gunilla Lange and her new husband, Bernt Friberg. Based on that she might possibly question Göran Bergman again. Ola Haver would devote himself to the Madrid lead, and seemed content with that when he got up and left the room. Beatrice looked after him, but when he turned in the doorway it was Lindell's gaze he sought.

"So how are things going for you?" asked Ottosson, turning toward Lindell, when the discussion on Gränsberg was taken care of and the prosecutor had hurried off.

To hell, she thought about answering.

"With the disappeared girl, I mean."

"I realize that," said Lindell in a curt, slightly fatigued tone. "Well, I've found a witness," she continued, telling about Yngve Sandman's observations, and that she judged it to be a hot, credible tip.

"Found" did sound good. She did not mention that the tip had been neglected the day after the disappearance.

She had renewed contact with the parents and some of Klara Lovisa's friends, to try to ferret out whether there was possibly anyone in her circle of acquaintances who might match the young man by the road-side, but had not produced anything new.

"I'll keep rooting. Maybe there's an unknown young man around here now with a life on his conscience."

"You think she's dead?"

Lindell nodded and Ottosson got that furrow between his eyebrows.

"Klara Lovisa was not a girl who disappears of her own free will," said Lindell.

Lindell was aware that such a judgment was risky, because what can you know about another person's thoughts? They had experienced this before, how an apparently well-functioning youth ran away, to resurface again after a while, in another city, in another country. It might take a day or two, but even six months or more. She herself had a case with a young girl who after two years was found in Copenhagen. Maybe that was why Lindell had been assigned Klara Lovisa? If it could happen once, then . . . perhaps Ottosson had superstitiously reasoned.

After the meeting Lindell returned to her office. She sensed that her colleagues were starting to notice her self-imposed isolation more and more. She withdrew, she no longer took part in coffee breaks, in-stead she hid out by herself.

From hope to despair; the contrast was almost too much for Ann Lindell. For a few weeks she had lived in a rush, overwhelmed to start with and in a state of surprise at experiencing something like that, so courted and desired, perhaps even loved. Anders Brant had taken her on a journey she had never been on before, or thought she would ever experience.

The love story with Edvard was one thing, it had been amazing in many ways. She had truly loved that man, more than she realized when they were caught up in the relationship.

Then came the night with a strange man she met at the bar, and from having too much to drink, but also to satisfy a vague need for intimacy and mutually explicit lust, they staggered home to her bed. He was a man she would never see again, married besides. She had been his fling, and afterward it just felt wrong and messy. Improbably enough she got pregnant, but kept the father uninformed, and the relationship with Edvard fell apart.

Edvard had been good, but he was too melancholy, sometimes hard to reach and convince that life did not only have to mean hard work. She liked his seriousness but with the years had realized that it was best for both of them to go their separate ways.

With Anders Brant it was different, he was more easygoing. He was relaxed, didn't make things more complicated than they were. When it came to sex he was exceptional, she had to admit. Never before had she experienced such rapture. He was alternately tender and intense. Perhaps it was a game, but it was a lovely game.

What surprised her was that she knew so little about him. He had mentioned a few things about his work; he preferred to write about social movements, he said, whatever that meant. Perhaps he noticed her uncertainty and for that reason had not expounded on that topic. She understood enough to know that he was not a sensationalist who took his job lightly. He sometimes showed indignation, which made him verbose. Then he talked about justice. A bit vaguely, she thought, and when she jokingly said something to the effect that she too worked in the service of justice he fell silent for a moment. Judging by his expression he was prepared to make an objection, but at the next moment said something in the same easy tone as hers about "the best justice money can buy." She had heard that phrase before and was not particularly impressed.

"You mean that I just work for the wealthy?"

"No, not at all," he answered. "It's just an expression."

Exactly, she thought, it's just an expression, but what does it express? But she didn't say anything.

It was one of the few times they talked about her work. He showed surprisingly little interest. Normally people she came in contact with asked her to talk about it, wanted to hear a few cases described, wondered whether it was a nasty chore to be a police officer, and if she was afraid. More than a few would offer drastic examples of their own and others' encounters with crime.

On another occasion he asked her what the penalty for blackmail was. I guess it depends on the circumstances, she answered a little vaguely, uncertain what the penalty scale looked like. The fact was that she had never worked with any cases like that. When she asked why he was asking, the answer was that he was just curious in general and then said that he had read a book about the Italian mafia. Then he dropped that subject.

But she was sold. And she started to hope. She started dreaming and looked at Erik and wondered to herself whether he would want a stepfather. Brant had no children of his own and for her it was too late to think about another.

The train had not left for her. "You're on the track," as Görel preached to the point of nagging when she tried to get Ann to become more active and involved.

Now she was active and involved, and with a man who had disappeared and left lots of question marks behind him, both professionally and personally.

She must get hold of him, that was the dominant thought in her mind. It was meaningless to try the cell phone again. He had it turned off during the trip, she was sure of that; perhaps he turned it on when he wanted to make a call.

E-mail remained, and she was sure that Brant delivered his articles electronically. She called information, got the number to the Swedish Society for Nature Conservation and asked to be connected.

She asked the switchboard for the editor of their magazine and immediately got to speak with a man with the bizarre name Gunnar Göök, or did he say Höök? She explained who she was and that in an investigation she had to make contact with one of the magazine's contributors, who was traveling and could only be reached by e-mail.

Göök was hesitant, gave roundabout answers, asked who this concerned, expressed doubt about the correctness of giving out an e-mail address to just anyone, started talking about protecting sources.

"I'm not just anyone, and you are definitely not disclosing any sources," said Lindell. "I suggest that we hang up and you call the Uppsala police switchboard and ask to speak with Ann Lindell, so you know I'm a police officer."

"As if that would change anything," said Göök.

"This is a murder investigation," Lindell explained. "Does that possibly change the situation? Brant is in no way suspected of a crime but may be in possession of very essential information. Hang up now and call!"

To her surprise Göök obeyed and a few minutes later the phone rang and she got what she wanted without further discussion. She thanked him for the help and hung up.

She stared at the hastily scribbled Telia address. He probably checks his e-mail on the Internet, she thought. If he really is in Spain then that's no problem.

Her message was brief. *Call me immediately! Important! Repeat: Call me immediately! Ann.* Then she sent an SMS with a similar message, but with even more exclamation points.

No cooing, no questions about how he was doing or where he was. There was no room for that, and she was doubtful whether she could formulate anything personal without feeling even more mendacious than she already did where Brant was concerned.

Even if she was taking a risk, because others might read her e-mail and SMS, she now felt better. She had done something anyway and not just sat there like a fool, waiting for the roof to crash down on her.

✦

Eight

The building manager let the two police officers in without apparent excitement.

"What'd he do?" he asked again.

"Nothing," said Sammy Nilsson flatly, for the third time.

"But something?"

"Yes, something for sure, but nothing we know about!" Morgansson responded. "Now you can go. We'll shut the door behind us when we leave."

Anders Brant's apartment consisted of two rooms, a kitchen, and a minimal bathroom. Sammy Nilsson and Morgansson remained standing a moment in the hall, apparently indecisive, before they pulled on their protective clothing and gloves.

"I guess I'll try to secure a print to start with," said Morgansson, entering the kitchen with his bag.

Sammy Nilsson started in the combination bedroom/office. There was a bed in the middle of the room, made with the spread neatly on top. The walls were covered with books from floor to ceiling, except the one long wall, in front of the window facing the courtyard, where a board was mounted on a pair of sawhorses.

There was not much on the makeshift desk: an old-fashioned file holder next to some piles of books, a jar with various pens, a notepad, and a mug with remnants of dried coffee. No computer, but a router with blinking green lights.

There were two file cabinets under the desk. Sammy pulled out a drawer full of papers and plastic folders in various colors with a sticker in the right corner. The one on top was labeled *Agrofuel*.

He pulled out drawer after drawer. Mostly computer printouts and newspaper clippings, but the bottom drawer to the right was full of office supplies—a hole punch, a stapler, a box of paper clips, and other things you would expect to find in a home office.

Sammy Nilsson did not feel inclined to go through all the papers, even if he realized he would have to do a quick browse. But he left the desk for the time being and took a look at the bookshelves. Quite a lot of fiction, Sammy noticed some titles he had too. *The National Encyclopedia* and various other reference works and dictionaries took up an entire section. There was also what Sammy assessed as "political literature," a lot about environmental issues and globalization, strikingly many in English.

A thinker, Sammy decided, and left the room. The living room was easy to survey. A lounge suite consisting of a 1960s-era leather couch and two armchairs that were certainly trendy but looked needlessly uncomfortable, a teak coffee table decorated with some tea lights on a ceramic plate, a TV and DVD player on an IKEA shelf, a tall floor lamp with a brass base and three lampshades—Sammy's parents had one like it—a storage unit that housed a BW brand stereo system, and a collection of CDs, mostly blues and classical music. A pair of speakers were mounted on the wall.

That was all. Borderline impersonal, Sammy thought. Easily taken care of was his next thought, and that granted him some consolation, considering all the papers in the other room.

"Find anything?" he yelled toward the kitchen.

"Just one print so far, and I assume it's Brant's," Morgansson answered.

Sammy Nilsson sat down in an armchair and had his prejudices confirmed.

If Brant really had visited Bosse Gränsberg's trailer on Monday, the same day Gränsberg was killed, he was in a bad way. But what motive could there be?

Sammy's thought process was interrupted by the technician, who was standing in the doorway. In his hand he was holding the new prints.

"It's him," he said curtly.

"Are you dead sure?"

Morgansson did not answer, but looked at Sammy with a blank face and turned on his heels. A new Ryde, thought Sammy. Eskil Ryde was the former head of the tech squad, now retired. He had always been dead sure.

Sammy got up with effort from the clearly defectively designed arm-chair and returned to the bedroom, positioned himself to stare at the bed, and carefully raised the spread. He folded back the blanket just as carefully and viewed the sheets below.

On the nightstand, with a small drawer that he only noticed now, was a book by Samir Amin. God, what a serious guy, thought Sammy Nils-son, pulling out the drawer. Inside was a half-empty package of a for-eign brand of chewing gum—Sammy had an impulse to sample it—and an open package of condoms.

Originally it had contained twenty condoms; four remained. Other-wise in the drawer there was a subway ticket—Sammy Nilsson guessed New York—some pens and a small pocket calendar for 2006, which he quickly browsed through. It was jotted full of tiny but completely legible text, about meetings and conferences, dental appointments, and other trivia that fills a person's everyday life. Exactly to the day one year ago Anders Brant had made a call to a woman. In any event there was a re-minder there with three exclamation points: *Call Rose!!!* Sammy looked around for a phone and found it stuffed into the bookshelf.

He peeked at the sheets again; the sight made an almost too intimate impression. It bothered him that now they were violating a person's in-tegrity. Then he turned his attention to the desk. He shuddered at the thought of the piles of papers, but started with what seemed most cur-rent, the files on the desk.

Everything was neatly labeled, apparently research material, perhaps the basis for articles. A mixture of computer printouts, handwritten notes, and newspaper clippings.

The first folder contained a number of texts in Russian and was marked *Putin* the second file simply *MST,* it too filled with texts in a foreign lan-guage, probably Spanish. Under it was a file with an abbreviation equally unknown to Sammy, and whose contents were surprisingly like the others. Once again in the same language.

Morgansson came into the room.

"Anything exciting?"

Sammy turned and held up a plastic folder.

"Working materials, presumably," he said, holding out the thick bundle.

The technician browsed a little.

"Most of it's in Portuguese," he said, handing back the file.

Are you sure, Sammy was about to say, but caught himself and nodded. "The kitchen?"

"Nothing remarkable. Reasonably clean and tidy, everything washed, the refrigerator emptied as if he were just leaving on a trip, no waste bag. I've found two different prints, his own and one other, left on a vase and on the front of the stove."

"Where the hell is the guy?" said Sammy Nilsson. "I don't like this."

Morgansson sneered.

"I mean, we barge in on a completely unknown person. Think about it. Do we really have reason to trespass?"

"We'll have to see," said the technician, showing no great enthusiasm to pick up the thread.

"I mean—"

"I know what you mean," said Morgansson. "Now I'll do the bed."

Sammy Nilsson nodded. From the courtyard outside the sound of a heavy truck was heard. He went over to the window. It was the tow truck that would bring in Brant's car. Alongside him stood the building manager, who was saying something to Nyman. The trainee stretched, made a gesture as if to move Nilsson aside, waved with his other hand to the driver of the tow truck, as if he needed any assistance to back into a wide open area, thought Sammy Nilsson. The only thing that might get in the way was probably Nyman himself.

Sammy Nilsson turned away. He could not shake his aversion. They were treating Brant as a possible suspect and on very flimsy grounds at that. It was now clear that he had visited Gränsberg's trailer, and there was much that suggested he had done so the day the murder was committed. The fact that he travels abroad the following morning may be flight but just as easily a planned trip. That he booked it as long as a few days before departure meant nothing.

A journalist, thought Sammy Nilsson, a politically oriented freelancer, would he kill a homeless former scaffolder? Well, unexpected things happen, he reasoned further, but the probability, how great was it?

"Listen, do you think Brant is our guy?"

Morgansson stopped, still leaning over, turned his head, and observed his colleague.

"No," he said, somewhat unexpectedly for Nilsson, but did not develop his viewpoint.

"I'll be in the living room," said Sammy.

Morgansson nodded and continued his work.

Nilsson sat down in the other armchair with a vague hope that it might be somewhat more comfortable, and continued thinking. He could hear the tow truck leaving the parking area.

Morgansson came into the living room a few minutes later and sat down in the other chair.

"He hasn't changed the sheets for a while," the technician observed. "I've secured two different types of hair, one light and one very dark. There are stains besides, probably semen, on one of the pillows."

"My God," said Sammy Nilsson.

"Maybe she had a pillow under her ass," said Morgansson.

Then a few minutes of unforced silence followed. That was one good thing about the guy from northern Sweden, thought Nilsson, he knew the art of keeping quiet without making it feel strange. But it was Morgansson who broke the silence.

"So, what do you think about Haver?"

Sammy looked up with surprise.

"What should I think about him?"

"I'm sure you've noticed how difficult he's been, mostly goes around sulking and snaps at everyone. I think Beatrice is really sick and tired of it."

"I guess he's tired and worn out," said Nilsson, feeling some discomfort.

"We all are more or less," said the technician. "This is different."

"He'll probably get out of his slump," said Nilsson.

"I think it's on the home front," Morgansson continued, who obviously did not want to let go of the topic.

"With Rebecka, you mean?"

Morgansson nodded.

"We know nothing about that," said Nilsson, and now his tone was plainly unsympathetic.

"Maybe it's something with Lindell?"

"What?"

"She hasn't been herself either recently."

"You mean that Ola and Ann might be together?"

"Depends on what you mean by together, I don't know," Morgansson retreated.

"Well, you know her better than most," said Nilsson.

Morgansson's cheeks immediately turned red. He's jealous, that bastard, thought Nilsson. Lindell and the technician had had a brief affair, shortly after Morgansson moved there from Umeå.

"She seems to be off her game," said Morgansson. "Completely absent for long periods."

"It's Klara Lovisa that's haunting her."

Morgansson shook his head.

"It's love," he said.

"And the reason is Haver, you think? That those two would . . . and that Haver is thinking about divorce, is that what you're thinking?"

"Something like that," said Morgansson.

Sammy Nilsson shook his head.

"Never," he decided, getting up from the chair.

Morgansson laughed awkwardly.

"Nice chairs," he said, patting the armrest.

✦

Nine

Andreas Davidsson had a distinctive hair style; his head was shaved on the sides with a short Mohawk on top. In one earlobe he had an earring. He had adopted this style in an attempt to look tough, Lindell believed, but he only radiated fear.

"You finished ninth grade last spring," she noted.

He nodded.

"What will you be doing this fall?"

"Graphic design at GUC," he answered.

"Is that good?"

"Mm."

Is this what Erik will turn into, thought Lindell, taciturn and a little sullen, unwilling to look you in the eyes?

"First I want to say that we do not suspect you of anything. You were in Gävle when she disappeared. We know that you and Klara Lovisa were seeing each other last year, wasn't that the case?"

Another nod, and now the boy appeared on the verge of tears.

"Then she broke up with me right after New Year's," he said. "On New Year's Day."

Lindell nodded. She knew all this from when they questioned him back in April.

"Do you have a new girlfriend?"

Andreas shook his head. Lindell sensed that he still thought a lot about Klara Lovisa. Not only because she disappeared in a dramatic way, but because he was still in love with her.

"Was any other boy interested in her? I mean, did she hint anything?"

His jaws tensed, and he gave her a quick look.

"She didn't say anything, that she had met someone else, or something?"

"No, she just left."

"But perhaps you suspected—"

"No, I said that!"

"Okay," Lindell backed up immediately. "I believe you, but as you understand this can get a little tedious. I want to know what happened, just like you. Did she say anything at all about other boys? I mean, she is pretty."

"There was someone stalking her last fall," Andreas said suddenly.

"What do you mean by 'stalking'?"

"Well, he was after her."

"Who was it?"

"I don't know. She didn't want to say anything, just said something about some retard who was trying. He was going to invite her to Stockholm."

"I see, why did she tell you that, do you think?"

He responded with a sigh.

"To make you jealous, perhaps?"

A bird, Lindell thought it was a blackbird, came hopping across the lawn in front of the terrace where they were sitting. She observed the bird and thought about how she should keep coaxing.

"What were they going to do in Stockholm?"

"Shop and go to Gröna Lund, or something, I don't know."

"But there was no trip to Stockholm?"

"Not as far as I know."

He smiled a joyless smile.

"Do you think it was someone from school?"

"No, it was someone older."

"How much older?"

He shrugged.

"He had a driver's license, anyway. She said that."

"When exactly was this? Fall, you said."

"Maybe some time in September."

"And then she didn't say anything about this unknown admirer?"

"No, nothing."

Lindell felt sorry for the boy in front of her, for his way of nervously and unconsciously taking hold of his left wrist with his right hand and twisting it around, back and forth, as if he was trying to slip off a bracelet, and inhaling through his nose as if to steel himself to not start crying. It was torture to make him go through this again.

It was summer break, he should be doing fun things, celebrate that nine years of school were over, lie on a beach or whatever, instead of meeting a police officer and recalling the girlfriend he still dreamed about. There was nothing exciting about that, only regret. The memory of Klara Lovisa would fade, but Lindell was convinced that for his whole life he would remember her shoulder-length hair, lovely profile, and tender young breasts, which perhaps he had caressed. Perhaps they had slept with each other, perhaps it was the first time for both of them.

"What happened last fall with Klara Lovisa? Were things going well in school for her, did she do anything special, did anything happen that you can recall?"

"No. Everything always went well for her."

"Nothing out of the ordinary, something that made her worried, something that maybe passed quickly, but that she was sad or angry about for a while?"

"No, not that I remember."

"Did you sleep with each other?"

Andreas's cheeks turned beet red, and then his ears. His earlobes appeared to be red-hot. He shook his head.

"She didn't want to," he said quietly.

"But you wanted to?"

He nodded.

"She wanted to wait."

"Until when?"

He shrugged his shoulders. She observed his hands, very powerful for belonging to a young boy, but still unproven, both at work and perhaps at caressing. His nails were well-cared for.

"Thanks, Andreas," said Lindell, extending her hand. "I'm sorry that I stirred everything up again."

He awkwardly took her hand.

"I think about it every day," he sniffed, and now the tears burst forth. "I think about her all the time."

She continued holding his hand in hers, squeezed it.

"She was so fine, and now she's gone! She's dead, isn't she?"

"We don't know," said Lindell, squeezing his hand even harder. She realized that there was nothing consoling to say.

"We liked each other. A lot."

"I understand that. You're a good guy."

She refrained from saying that he would surely meet another girl to fall in love with. That was not what he wanted to hear right now.

Lindell turned out of the driveway at Andreas Davidsson's home, after speaking a little with his mother, a woman with a limited vocabulary, who followed her out with a tormented expression.

What a shitty job, she thought, and she immediately thought of Anders Brant. Now was when she needed someone to call, someone to make plans with for the evening, and then the jerk goes and gets dragged into a murder! And puts her in a pinch besides. If he had just said where he was going, she thought, realizing that would not have changed the situation appreciably.

She forced herself to think about Klara Lovisa and the unknown admirer who wanted to invite her to Stockholm. A handsome guy who knew how to hit on a younger girl, but in her case had evidently lost out. Older, Andreas had said. Where, in what context, does a teenage girl meet an older guy? Was it the son of someone in the neighborhood?

She knew she was on the right track. Or at least convinced herself of that, because for lack of anything else this was the only thing that had any substance.

September 2006, she thought. Klara Lovisa is courted by a guy with a driver's license, but turns him down. How does he react? Does he give up or keep trying? Klara Lovisa did not say anything else about it to Andreas, but that didn't need to mean squat. Maybe she had let herself be influenced by continued courtship, and then broke up with Andreas after New Year's?

Lindell put on the brakes and checked in the rearview mirror before she made a U-turn and took the same way back.

The woman of limited vocabulary was at a total loss for words when Lindell turned onto the driveway to the Davidsson house again and got out of the car. She just stared at the police officer.

"I forgot to ask Andreas one thing," said Lindell. "Is he still at home?"

His mother opened her mouth but said nothing. Lindell was seized by a strong distaste when passivity was so obviously given a face.

"Is it okay to go inside again?" she asked.

The woman did not answer but managed to point toward the door and nod. Lindell opened the door and called the boy's name. His head almost immediately stuck out from the second floor. He looked perplexed, and a little worried.

"Just one thing," said Lindell.

The boy took a few steps down the stairs.

"What did you do on New Year's Eve?"

"Me?"

"Yes, you."

"I was with some friends."

"Not with Klara Lovisa?"

"No, she was at a different party."

"With who?"

"Her soccer friends."

"She played soccer?"

"Well, not then. She quit, but she was at their party."

Lindell stood silently a moment.

"When did she quit?"

"The team, you mean? Last fall. They had a few matches left. She said that some of them were mad at her because she quit right then."

"What's the name of her team?"

"The Best."

"The team is called 'The Best'?"

"Yeah, like, they wanted to be the best."

"Were they?"

Andreas shook his head.

"Thanks," said Lindell, pushing open the outside door with her elbow.

The woman was still in the same spot. She had a planting trowel in her hand.

"Nice kid you have," said Lindell.

"He hasn't done anything," said the woman. "So why are you coming here all the time? We were in Gävle! He has nothing to do with the case! He wasted all his time on her, and not just time either!"

Lindell stopped in pure surprise that Andreas's mother could express more than five words in sequence.

Magdalena Davidsson took a couple steps closer to Lindell. She raised the planting trowel threateningly.

"If you only knew!"

"Knew what?"

"He had to run around with those advertising flyers, selling socks and God knows what, just for her."

"You mean Klara Lovisa?"

The woman stopped a moment and stared at Lindell.

"Why don't you say her name? Her name is Klara Lovisa."

"I know that perfectly well! He fell behind in school. She wanted things and Andreas couldn't say no. He's too nice, way too nice, I told him that. And now you're persecuting him. He has nothing to do with this!"

"No, no one has alleged that either, but he knew Klara Lovisa well."

"He doesn't need this pressure. He has to put this behind him. This fall he's going to study, start high school. It's going to be a lot of work for him."

GUC, thought Lindell, he won't have to work too hard there, not if you were to believe half of what Sammy Nilsson had to say anyway. He had a nephew who took his qualifying exams there last spring.

"I'm sure it will work out," said Lindell politely.

Klara Lovisa had been in dance class at the Vaksala School and would have continued with dance at a school in Stockholm this fall.

✦

Ten

The police work puzzles, Sammy Nilsson thought as he observed his associates in front of the whiteboard. Maybe he picked up that phrase from some book or comic he read in his youth, he didn't know.

On the whiteboard were a dozen names, two of which were women, Gunilla Lange and Ingegerd Melander.

The strange thing was that all of them, with the exception of Anders Brant who had moved there with his family as a ten year old, were born and grew up in the city, a fact that Berglund pointed out. Uppsala was a city people moved to; many came to study or teach at the two universities or got jobs in industry or healthcare. A service city, which at one time had been just as much an industrial city. Berglund mentioned once how few students there had been well into the sixties, before the education explosion started. How then there were brick factories, shoe and coat factories, Uppsala Ekeby with its ceramics, a wire-mesh mill that then transitioned to making synthetic wires for the paper industry, a silk-weaving mill, as well as soap factory, breweries, chocolate factory, and bicycle manufacturing.

The university had expanded and now there were tens of thousands of students, while the industrial epoch was only a memory. Replacement in the form of a pharmaceutical industry and high-tech laboratories could not compare with the time when the streets and residential neighborhoods of Uppsala were filled with regular folks, as Berglund put it.

Typical for the new era was that the two areas that were most talked about, where the jobs of the future were concerned, were production of antiwrinkle compounds and development of computer games.

But everyone on the whiteboard, except Brant, was a native and stemmed from the other, for the most part vanished, Uppsala.

They were all acquainted with the murdered man. One of the two women, Gunilla, had been married to him, and the other, Ingegerd, had a relationship with him until quite recently.

One of them, Göran Bergman, had worked with Gränsberg. The others had been drinking with him, except for Bernt Friberg, who lived with Gunilla Lange. None of those questioned had any idea what connection Brant had with Gränsberg, but his work as a journalist was the only reasonable explanation.

There were ten names in all. One of them perhaps was the murderer. Purely instinctively they ruled out Göran Bergman, whose grief seemed to be genuine. Nine remained.

Which of them could conceivably have a motive? All of them, the three investigators decided.

Berglund thought it was a drinking thing.

"There was a spat in Gränsberg's trailer that went downhill," he thought. "It started as an argument about something trivial, then out came an iron pipe and suddenly one of the combatants was lying there."

Beatrice believed it might be Bernt Friberg and the motive would be jealousy.

"He was opposed to Gunilla's loan of a hundred thousand to her ex-husband," Beatrice asserted. "She told me she hadn't talked about her plans, but that Friberg found out by accident and then went completely nuts."

"Did it come to fisticuffs?" Berglund asked, and Sammy Nilsson smiled at his word choice.

"Not that I know, but Friberg seems to be a hot-tempered type, who easily boils over," said Beatrice. "When I questioned him he sat with his fists clenched the whole time, his face was bright red and when I brought up the subject of Gränsberg and his good relationship with Gunilla,

Friberg spit out his words. He was really furious, even though he ought to be a little calmer with Gränsberg out of the game."

"He didn't even try to keep a straight face?" Sammy Nilsson asked. "Now he could sit there and pretend to grieve and talk nicely."

Beatrice shook her head.

"I believe in Brant," said Sammy Nilsson, "and that is for a single reason: He was demonstrably there."

"It's not established," Beatrice objected.

"The gravel that was in the tire on his Toyota comes from the road up to the trailer, I'm dead sure of that. We have his prints there, and then he leaves."

"The trip was planned before the murder," said Berglund. "It was booked a few days before."

"Perhaps the murder was planned," said Sammy Nilsson.

"Why?"

"That's our job to figure out," said Sammy Nilsson and smiled.

"The brothers in misfortune, then, as you call them," said Beatrice, turning to Berglund. "Do you have any favorites?"

Berglund shook his head. Beatrice had hoped he would come out with a name, because they all had great respect for the older officer's intuition. He had hit it right many times, above all in the cases where the victim's and murderer's background was like his, that is, what he always summarized as "east of the Fyris River."

"Brant and Gränsberg are the same age," Sammy Nilsson said suddenly. "Can that be something?"

Berglund understood immediately what he meant.

"You mean they were in school together?"

"I'll check on that," said Sammy Nilsson.

Beatrice continued the brainstorming. "If we don't believe it's a drinking thing or jealousy, what motive is there? What can Gränsberg know or have that is so valuable that it motivates violence? He was not a rich man, owned no property, and actually had nothing anyone else could conceivably be after."

"An old grudge, perhaps?" Sammy Nilsson tossed out. "Something that happened many years ago. Maybe Gränsberg cheated the murderer out of money, didn't pay back a loan, or whatever."

"And now the rumor got out that Gränsberg was going to invest a lot of dough to start up a company with Bergman," said Berglund, picking up the thread. "Then the murderer saw his chance to collect the old debt. Gränsberg obviously refused and the result was a few blows to the head."

"We'll have to question Bergman and Gunilla Lange again," said Beatrice. "Maybe they have some idea."

"What about the alibis for his buddies?" Beatrice asked.

"Tolerable," said Berglund, consulting his notes, which was a change from before.

Since Berglund's operation, when a tumor was removed from his brain, his memory had gotten worse, that was apparent to everyone at Homicide. Before, he could reel off names and connections like running water. On the other hand this might be a completely normal sign of age. Berglund only had a few months left until retirement.

"Manfred Kvist we can probably count out completely," said Berglund. "In the morning he actually had a foot care appointment, he showed me his feet, and if there's someone who needs foot care it's dear Manfred. From there he went straight to the Mill and met some buddies. They had a little aquavit, Manfred was going to arrange something to go with it and went into Torgkassen. When he came up to the register he didn't have enough money and there was a little kerfuffle. That's confirmed by two employees. Then he and his buddies went out on the square to have lunch, that is, a seventy-centiliter bottle of aquavit and a lukewarm hot dog. A guy who sells flowers at the square thought they were yelling too much and told them so. He knows Manfred from before and was quite certain he was part of that merry troupe. Mustafa, or whoever it was, had been to buy flowers that morning and was quite sure it was on Monday."

Berglund read from his notes and started up again.

"In the afternoon he was at 'The Grotto,' that's quite clear and then—"

"We can probably remove him, in other words," said Sammy Nilsson. "The others?"

"Two of them, Johnny Andersson and one Molle Franzén, you surely recognize them," said Berglund, looking up, but both Beatrice and Sammy shook their heads. "They're a little unclear about what they were doing on Tuesday. Both had been drinking pretty heavily the whole weekend and probably on Monday as well and don't remember too much.

"Johnny maintains in any event that he visited his aged mother at a home for the elderly in Svartbäcken, he does that every Monday afternoon, but when I spoke with her she remembers even less than her son. She's obviously senile. A woman on the staff claims to maybe remember Johnny, but she also said that she may have been mistaken about the day, it might have been Tuesday."

"I saw Johnny Andersson at Ingegerd Melander's, it seems like he's taken her over after Gränsberg," Beatrice interjected.

"We actually do have one thing on him," said Berglund. "A break-in and assault three years ago. He got one year, tried to escape, and got an extended sentence."

"What was that about?" Sammy Nilsson asked.

"The usual, he and a buddy broke into a car repair shop, took a little money and some tools. Then they didn't agree on how they should divide the spoils and Johnny knocked his buddy down."

"Cozy," said Sammy Nilsson.

"And then Molle Franzén," Berglund resumed. "He says he was at 'The Grotto' although no one there remembers him. But most of these guys have a tendency to get the days mixed up. And why shouldn't they?"

"Camilla, the manager," asked Beatrice. "Doesn't she remember?"

"Same thing for her, the guys come and go. If it's not something special, it's impossible for her to keep track of who is there on a particular day."

"Are there more?" asked Sammy.

"Victor Skam, who is known as Victor the Looker, because he's so monstrously ugly, barely remembers that he's ugly, much less what he did last Monday. He seems weak, to say the least, it's a question of whether he would have the strength to kill anyone."

"Is his name really Skam?"

"Yes, I think it's a Norwegian name."

"Thought so," said Sammy.

"Olle Olsson," said Berglund. "A little crazy and brooding, always carries a Bible with him. A plague according to many, when he gets going with his verses. Once he was a locomotive engineer and cracked up when he ran over a teenage girl at the crossing in Bergsbrunna. If you ask me we can rule him out, even if he can't say what he was doing on Monday."

Berglund took a breath.

"Nice work," said Sammy.

"There are a few more," said Berglund. "There are quite a few in town, I mean in those circles where Gränsberg was found. Some are full-time homeless, others come and go, maybe get a temporary nest for a while and then are out on the street again, or they crash with a friend for a month or two, then the buddy gets tired of it."

"But these are the ones he hung out with?"

"The chief mourners," Berglund confirmed.

"An odd little group, I mean Gränsberg seemed to be one with ambitions," said Beatrice. "Why would he associate with these particular guys?"

"An odd group," Berglund agreed, "and they all have ambitions, but the level changes."

"Like at Homicide," said Sammy, and was rewarded with a grin from Beatrice.

"It might very well be someone outside of this quartet. There are so many sketchy characters," said Beatrice, unconsciously giving her interjection that lecturing tone that had irritated so many in the building over the years.

Berglund observed her in silence.

"He's out there, that much we know," he said, closing his folder. "Sit down for a day at 'The Grotto' and look at the old guys, those 'sketchy characters.' Among others you'll meet a cousin of mine, a genuine Berglund. It might be him. Sure. It might be Sundin, once upon a time Uppsala's most skillful carpet layer, or Foot-Nils, an incorrigible wife-beater who got run over by the Route 6 bus ten years ago, or in any case his right foot did, it might be him. Roger Gustavsson, raised on amphetamines since his first drop of breast milk, is crazy enough to kill half the city. It might even be a woman, Bella, who was raped as a seventeen year old and got epilepsy to boot, and over the years became a worthy heir to Knife-Emmy, who wreaked havoc in the city in the sixties. Do you want more names? Bertil Wall, known as the 'Finance King,' worked at a bank at one time. Now he collects cans. Kurt Johansson, who I played soccer with three decades ago, whose old lady ran off with the mailman of all people, went straight to the dogs. An incredibly nice guy, he was sentimental even as a teenager, but it's obvious, one day maybe he'll club someone down. We don't know."

This time Berglund didn't need the support of notes. Sammy and Beatrice were convinced that he could continue his recital for a very long time. There was an unusual sharpness in his voice, but Beatrice was wise enough not to take all the blame for the verbal attack, but also wise enough to realize that she was the one who triggered it.

"Excuse me," she said, "I didn't mean to be impudent."

"But you were," said Berglund calmly, but unexpectedly.

He got up slowly.

"I'm tired," he said.

Sammy gave Beatrice a quick look.

"Go home," he said. "You've been slaving away with those old guys."

He sensed that Berglund had run into his cousin at "The Grotto."

"You're only working part-time," he added.

Berglund thoughtfully gathered up his papers. Sammy and Beatrice waited for some words of wisdom from the veteran who knew Uppsala inside and out, but the old man remained reserved, as if the long lecture on "brothers in misfortune" was his description of the situation in the investigation and perhaps not only that.

"See you," he said, giving Beatrice a nod and Sammy a look, before leaving the room without further ado.

As Sammy Nilsson went past Lindell's office the door was open, which was unusual enough that he noticed it. She was talking on the phone, but signaled with her hand that he should wait.

He leaned against the doorpost. He was still feeling the gloom that Berglund's words, and above all attitude, summoned. The old man is starting to get up in years and they aren't hatching that kind of cop anymore, he thought.

Lindell was talking away. She unconsciously stroked her hand over her hair where a few strands of gray were showing, but that in particular was not a good lead-in to a conversation with her, Sammy Nilsson assumed.

She was talking somewhat surprisingly about soccer and when she hung up, that was exactly what she wanted to talk about with him.

"Listen, Sammy, you coach young boys and that sort of thing, do you know a team called 'The Best'?"

"Yes, maybe. Wasn't that the team that allowed over a hundred goals last season? I think it was in the paper. A girl's team. They've renamed the team 'The Worst,' I heard."

"Klara Lovisa played with them until some time last fall," said Lindell.

"Was that why she disappeared?"

"Stop your joking now. A dumb question: Is it common for guys to coach girls soccer?"

"Yes, it happens. Pretty often actually, maybe in the majority of clubs. There's a shortage of female coaches. Do you have something going?"

Sammy Nilsson sensed what Lindell was looking for.

"Maybe," she said. "Now I've talked with three of her teammates. They had a party on New Year's Eve. A group of girls decided to celebrate the arrival of the new year—and then she just leaves, at eleven thirty after receiving an SMS. Strange, huh?"

"Well," said Sammy, "not so strange perhaps."

"On New Year's Day she breaks up with her boyfriend, who she's been with since seventh grade, a really sweet, nice guy."

"And?"

"Lay off, you get it! She got an SMS from a guy and left. The thing is that none of her friends understands why she broke up with Andreas and no new guy showed up during the winter or spring. 'She just got secretive,' as one of her friends said."

"You think she was dating someone in secret?"

Sammy Nilsson suddenly saw Lindell and Haver in his mind and could not keep from smiling.

"What are you laughing at? What is it that's so incredibly entertaining?"

Nilsson's smile got even broader when he heard how irritated she was and saw her cheeks turn red.

"Sneaking around," he said. "That's exciting."

"Lay off!"

Nilsson put his hands up in a defensive gesture, but so high that it looked like he was protecting himself against a blow. Lindell observed him and shook her head before continuing.

"I also think that this is an older guy with a driver's license. And I think that on April twenty-eighth he took Klara Lovisa on a trip to the country and that was the last thing she experienced in life."

"I'll be damned," said Sammy Nilsson.

"And where does a fifteen-year-old girl meet an older guy? Not at school, but—"

"In so-called club activities," Sammy Nilsson filled in. "You think it's that young man who was seen in Skärfälten?"

"Yes, pretty much dead certain in fact," said Lindell. "Now it's just a matter of finding him."

"And the ex-boyfriend?"

She shook her head.

"He was in Gävle visiting his grandmother at a home."

"Who says so?"

"His mother."

"Have you checked with the old lady at the home?"

"Yes, one of our colleagues up there visited her. The fact is that the grandfather was a superintendent on the detective squad. He's dead now but the colleague had met the woman previously, at a party."

"A confused police widow," said Sammy Nilsson. "They're reliable."

"Who said she's confused?"

"She can't be that old, but lives in a home."

"Around seventy, if I remember right."

"You see."

"You mean that—"

"The mom wants to protect her son, Andreas is keeping a straight face, and the old lady is confused and confirms what her daughter tells her to confirm. She is questioned by a colleague who is sympathetically inclined, because he happened to work with her husband. Just like that the boy has an alibi."

Lindell sat quietly a while.

"You really stir things up," she said at last.

"That's my job," said Sammy Nilsson.

It can't be wrong, was a sentence that came back in her head again and again, after Sammy had left her.

Now there was quite a lot that was wrong. Klara Lovisa was missing and probably dead. That was just so very wrong. Her own theory, about a young man with a driver's license, rested on shifting sand and would easily collapse. How wrong can you be! If Sammy Nilsson was right after all, that Andreas's alibi was constructed within the family, then that was wrong too. Sinking her teeth in the poor boy again simply felt rotten.

And Anders Brant was wrong! She checked her e-mail repeatedly; not a word from him. Just a lot of drivel that didn't mean a thing, either personally or professionally. Within the corps there seemed to be a whole cadre of salaried bullshitters who did nothing other than produce completely meaningless messages.

The latest however was from her mother, who with the help of the neighbor lady Olofsson's computer and willing assistance for a while now had been sending e-mails almost every day.

This time it was about her father and his "depression." He was asking about her! Lindell did not believe that for a moment. Vacation was approaching and Mom wanted Ann to come to Ödeshög. "Dad wants you to." So wrong! Feeling that way about your parents created a bad conscience, that was a given, but Lindell had learned to live with it. Nowadays she accepted that she found no joy in returning to her childhood Ödeshög. Am I a worse person for that, she would ask herself. On one level she obviously liked her parents, they had given birth to her and raised her, gave her a secure upbringing, she had never wanted for anything, the ties to the person she had been and had become were with them.

Gratitude, that was how she might summarize the feeling she had, but there was no affection any longer. When they met there was a brief period of the joy of recognition, exchange of the mandatory gossip, but then only silence and embarrassment. Having arrived at that stage her mother became sharp and impudent, made comments and demands that Ann perceived as pinpricks and intrusions on her own life, a life far from Ödeshög and the stuffiness of her girl's room.

Her father looked at her with an expression of doubt and admiration, as if he was asking himself: Is this Ann, my daughter? Then indifference took over and he showed no real interest in her life and doings, and the two slowly glided into a kind of anonymity with each other, a mood that suited her better than her mother's meddling.

For many years she had tried to mobilize some form of enthusiasm, convince herself that love for your parents is something you feel automatically, anything else is unnatural and a sign of baseness. But Ödeshög and even the briefest coexistence with her parents seemed like pure exile, a feeling that was reinforced leading up to this summer.

In her mind she had planned to spend the major part of her vacation with Brant. Then he and Erik could also start getting to know each other. How that would turn out no one could predict.

But Ödeshög, sitting with a cup of coffee on the increasingly neglected terrace, staring at the hedge of bridal wreath and plastic flowerpots planted with dispirited marigolds and bright violet petunias and listening to her mother's increasingly macabre rigmarole about the neighbors' lives and supposed ill will—never!

Sports Club The Best's coach for the women's team was named Håkan Malmberg, Lindell figured out after speaking with one of Klara Lovisa's soccer buddies, Elina Strindberg. He was single, but had "a really cute son," according to Elina. She thought the coach was on vacation. He often rode his motorcycle through Sweden and sometimes down on the continent. So too this summer. Elina Strindberg could also tell that for a short period Malmberg had an assistant coach, "Freddy something," who was "like, twenty-two" years old.

Lindell had cautiously inquired about Freddy under the pretext that perhaps he knew where Malmberg was to be found on his motorcycle odyssey.

Elina did not think so at all; the reason that Freddy's sojourn on the team was only a couple of months was that Malmberg did not like the "snob," as he called his coaching assistant.

Lindell asked Elina to think about whether she could ferret out Freddy's surname, perhaps she could look in some old papers or call around to her friends, and then possibly also check whether anyone had Malmberg's cell phone number. Of course she could. Lindell sensed a certain excitement in the girl's voice; it was not every day you were asked to help out in a police investigation, and Lindell poured it on by saying something to the effect that the general public was the police department's best friend, a cliché she hoped did not sound like one in Elina's ears. Lindell gave the girl her cell phone number and encouraged her to call whenever she wanted, even in the evening.

Elina called after only half an hour. Freddy's last name was Johansson and coach Malmberg was quite rightly on a motorcycle vacation. Lindell got cell numbers for both of them.

"Think if everyone worked that efficiently," said Lindell, and praised Elina for her quickness.

The girl sounded charmed when she explained that she was happy to help find Klara Lovisa, but then asked carefully whether Freddy and Håkan were "suspects."

"No, not at all," Lindell reassured her. "We're just trying to map out everything and everyone around Klara Lovisa."

Elina, who to that point sounded eager, seemed to hesitate a moment.

"Freddy's a little untethered," she said.

"What do you mean by that?"

"Well, a little strange, like that."

"That he's a snob, you mean?"

Lindell understood that that was not what made Elina want to talk about the assistant coach, but wanted to get her started. No doubt she and her friends had aired Freddy's "strangeness."

"He doesn't say much," Elina said at last.

"Maybe he's shy?"

"No," said Elina hesitantly. "Well, maybe," she quickly changed her mind, "but he looked so strangely at . . . he seemed . . ."

"He looked strangely at the girls on the team?"

"Uh-huh."

"At you?"

"Yes. He is cute and that, and—"

"So in the beginning you were a little interested?"

"Not exactly. Maybe."

"Was he interested in more than one? Klara Lovisa or another?"

"Klovisa thought he was really super."

"You call her Klovisa?"

"Yeah, didn't you know that?"

"No," said Lindell, writing down the nickname on the pad in front of her.

She thought it was strange she hadn't heard that nickname before, but there was a lot that was strange with this investigation. That some dumbass had lost track of Yngve Sandman's call was unforgivable, and that Klara Lovisa played soccer had escaped them. She had missed that!

"Was that why he had to quit as coach? I mean that he was taking liberties."

"No, no, he never did anything. It was just Håkan who got mad at him, a few times."

"Did he have different ideas about coaching?"

"No, it was something else, I think. Håkan just didn't like him."

"But the girls liked him?"

"Some," said Elina, and now her voice had lost all its previous certainty and eagerness.

"Thanks, Elina, you have been super nice for letting me take up your time."

"It's just cool," said the girl.

So cool it is, Lindell thought, when they ended the call.

In between checking her e-mail, if Brant were to decide to respond, she called the two numbers she got from Elina, with meager result. Håkan Malmberg had voicemail anyway and Lindell left a message.

Where Freddy Johansson was concerned, the answer signal sounded like that number was no longer current or that Elina had given her a wrong number.

She also searched on their names and did not find a single notation. Pure as snow.

Suddenly the cell phone beeped. She grabbed it and stared at the display: Message received. It was Charles Morgansson reporting that fingerprints from the murdered Bo Gränsberg had been found in Anders Brant's Toyota.

Lindell knew she had to do something. And Klara Lovisa's disappearance was something. Otherwise she would only obsess about Brant.

She left the police station, got in the car, and drove north on Svartbäcksgatan. An hour later she was there.

✦

Eleven

It started like a play with comic elements and ended as a tragedy.

By late afternoon the exchange of words had already escalated. Powerful explosions, outbursts of fireworks, interleaved the quarrel, which played out over several hours, coming in waves, temporarily subsiding, then suddenly picking up again with renewed energy and intensity.

The curtain that was gradually lowered by the setting sun made no difference. The men seemed inexhaustible. What was the quarrel about? Impossible to say. Anders Brant could only sporadically make out what was being said, and perhaps it was long-term accumulated enmity about a number of unrelated things that now exploded; when one conflict was thrashed out, the next one began.

Alcohol was surely fueling the flames. At one point Anders Brant saw one of the men disappear down the street and return a short time later with a bottle of Mulata Boa. He recognized the label at a distance: a seductive mulatto in a bikini strutting and holding up a bottle.

The bottle was passed around. In that respect no distinction was made between the different parties; everyone got their allotted share of the devastatingly strong liquor.

It was like a staged play, with actors who were only periodically visible on the stage. A stage which once had been a floor and now nothing more than a concrete surface, exposed to sun and heavy downpours, covered with miscellaneous junk: some rusty tin cans with plants, a stack of iron pipe, broken lounge chairs, a parasol without canvas, a cracked toilet seat, and much more which in other countries would have gone to the dump.

He had been drawn to the window by the furious shouting, went back to the computer, but then returned to his lookout point. There was something engaging about the whole thing, as if it wasn't serious, as if they were just performing a stage play, and only for him. It would not look good if the only available audience left.

During the entire performance three younger men acted, going in and out of the part of the building that was still somewhat intact. An older man sat in a discarded beach chair placed against a wall. He did not take part in the exchange of words, but followed it attentively, twisting his head as if he was watching a tennis match. And then the woman, the one who was now screaming in agony. During the quarrel she had tried to mediate at first, but was finally drawn into the dispute. It was hard for him to determine which party she favored. Perhaps her loyalty shifted?

When the fireworks were at their most intense the parties took a break. One of the men, perhaps the one now stretched out in the alley, laughed at one point and said something to the old man in the beach chair, who joined in the laughter and did a thumbs up, a gesture that could mean anything in this country—a greeting, general approval, or a positive response to a direct question.

Now he was no longer laughing. His neck was broken, you didn't need to be medically trained to realize that. The old man got up from the beach chair and stared uncomprehendingly at the spot where the young man had stood before.

It was murder. Anders Brant had seen the hand. Or was no one there?

"He was pushed!" he called out in Swedish, without thinking about it. The old man heard the scream and raised his eyes.

Or what had he seen? He glanced at the sky as if to check whether this might involve some kind of weather phenomenon. There was a full moon and perhaps some clouds had quickly moved past and placed a temporary curtain over the moon, and in doing so created this shadow-like, reptilian movement. But no, the sky was clear and innocent, the moon a secure cheese-yellow.

True, the light from the street was faint and only cast a pale glow over the remains of the building, but from his outlook, a window perhaps six meters right above the alley and a few meters above the level from which the man fell down, he had the best imaginable view. It was not a mirage!

Perhaps it was not a premeditated act, with an intent to kill, but the hand had pushed mercilessly. It must have made contact somewhere between the shoulder blades. So if not homicide, then it was manslaughter.

No muscular strength was required, as the man who gyrated down and broke his neck against the stone of the alley had been leaning over the low wall with his center of gravity past the top, which perhaps reached his thigh. A little tap, then it was done.

The perpetrator had been hidden behind a higher section of wall, what had once held up a roof, and not all that long ago.

So easy to kill, it struck him, as he observed the commotion in the alley. It was an old truth, a blow that goes wrong, an antagonist who takes a bad fall, then it's over.

He was strangely calm, even though a human being had just died before his eyes. He registered it all with ice-cold precision: the old woman who came running; the excited children—where did they come from, so many, so quickly?—loudly babbling and gesticulating; the crowd at the bus stop at the corner where the alley came out at the main street, curious, their necks craned, but not wanting to miss the bus; the woman who stood leaning over the wall and screamed uncontrollably; and then the man, the one who stepped out of the darkness, placed his hand on the woman's shoulder and said something. Was it him? Was that the hand, which now consoled, but which half a minute ago was an instrument of death?

Out of the dead man's mouth and ears blood was running over the uneven cobblestones, blood mixed with the white paint that had spilled the night before and stained the pavement.

Anders Brant happened to think of peppermint sticks. Then he raised his eyes and looked at the man again. He was still standing quite passively, with his hand on the woman's shoulder. The question was whether he had looked over the edge of the wall at all. Suddenly he removed his hand from the woman's shoulder and made a gesture that could mean anything at all. He threw out his arms and lowered his head as in prayer; he looked almost dejected.

Then he raised his head and met the gringo's eyes for a few moments, before he unexpectedly smiled, turned on his heels and in a shuffling gait disappeared into the ruins, as if he was completely exhausted.

He was part of the multitude of homeless, one of many in this country. Was he a killer? Who was the man in the alley? Were they related to each other?

Anders Brant forced himself to look down at the corpse once again, which someone had now turned on his back. Brant could see the whites of his eyes shining. His hands were resting against the surface, with the palms open and fingers extended. Perhaps they were brothers; there was a certain resemblance.

Someone pulled out a cardboard box from the pile by the wall. Perhaps the man had picked it up himself. The family that was staying in the half-razed building collected junk. Brant understood that from the carts in the alley.

Now a cardboard box that had once contained a Consul brand freezer became his shroud.

The sound of sirens came closer and closer, and soon a police car drove into the alley. The blue light on top was pulsing. Two men got out and stood quietly for a few moments observing the scene, before they went up to the body. The one pushed the box aside with his foot.

Should I go down, he wondered.

The other policeman peered up toward the facade, looked indifferently at the woman who was draped over the wall, in utter despair, no longer capable of screaming out her desperation. Anders Brant saw her upper body contract as if in convulsions.

"Is this your husband?" the policeman shouted, but got no answer.

A man from the crowd took a few steps toward the policeman and said something, pointed at the lifeless body and then toward the building.

I am actually a witness, perhaps the only one, Anders Brant continued reasoning to himself. Should I tell about the argument and the hand I thought I saw?

Suddenly the old man, the one Anders Brant had seen sitting in the beach chair earlier, stepped forward. A woman sobbed and tried to hold him back, but he freed himself and with stiff joints fell laboriously down on his knees beside the dead man. He extended his hand and closed the wide-open eyes.

The crowd was quiet. The one policeman crossed himself and that served as a signal for the others, who all crossed themselves.

Even the traffic stopped before the calm that spread out over the alley.

The old man placed his hand on the dead man's chest, held it there several seconds before he pulled himself up in a standing position, with the assistance of helping hands.

"The gringo is crying," shouted one of the boys in the crowd and pointed.

Anders Brant closed the window, backed into the room, and sank down in front of the computer, just as it was going into sleep mode.

The voices on the street had become louder, the death had become a concern for the whole neighborhood, the minimal favela that was interspersed among the more regular construction.

He had stayed at the simple but well-run *pousada* on many occasions over the years and could study how the surroundings had changed. The first few years he was often afraid about coming home too late, always took a taxi up to the entry. He never carried large amounts of cash, and definitely no rings or gold chains around his neck.

The horror stories of robbery and assault marked his initial time in the city. Now after several trips in the country he was experienced, knew how to behave, and security had also gradually improved.

The death in the alley of course did not fundamentally change conditions in the area, but he was still brought back to the aching uncertainty of earlier years. He had experienced a murder, he no longer doubted that he had been a witness to a violent crime. The hand had been there, the shove likewise.

What frightened him, and made him increasingly agitated, was the man's indifference. Even the hand on the woman's shoulder seemed like a mechanical action without any deeper meaning, scornful.

Then the smile, when he left the woman alone by the wall. He had looked down across the gap of the alley, observed the gringo in the window, and then smiled. What was the meaning of that? Perhaps it was a grimace, of disgust or sudden pain, perhaps of regret?

The man's serene calm was the most frightening. The message was clear: *I know you saw what happened, but that doesn't matter. No one will believe you, and more important: You will never dare say anything.* It was a concealed threat, that was becoming increasingly obvious to Brant.

He moved nervously in the creaking chair, considered peeking out, but did not want to expose himself more. The boy's shout that he was crying, moved as he had been by the old man's clumsy but also very dignified manner, created an unwelcome interest in his presence.

Perhaps the police would pay a visit? What should he say? That he was drawn to the window by the noise that the crowd was making and had not seen any of the preliminaries?

The incident would of course affect his remaining time in the city and definitely his writing. He was known for writing sharp, but somewhat dry and factual prose. He did not try to fan the flames, but instead let facts speak for themselves. Would he be able to describe the situation of the homeless in this country in his quiet way, an assignment for the Swedish newspaper *Dagens Nyheter* that would surely produce enough surplus material for several more articles?

Could he simply take the incident in the alley—now in his mind it was an "incident," not a murder—as the starting point for the article? Could he do that without mentioning his own passive but still central role in the drama?

He got up from the chair, forced himself not to look out, and went to the kitchen to make a cup of coffee. The usual, secure puttering with the coffeemaker, the characteristic aroma of the scouring powder the landlady had used all these years to clean the floor, and the liberating feeling that the kitchen window faced in toward the courtyard, all together meant that he relaxed somewhat.

But the worry came back: When thoughts of the "incident" were pushed aside by everyday impressions, he returned in his mind to why he originally sat down at the computer. It was not often he turned on his cell phone, and this time among all the expected reminders and inquiries there was Ann's brief message, distinguished both by the slightly desperate tone and the affectionless address. She had not even added an "XOX."

What could get her, a woman he had gotten to know as a very level-headed person without a lot of fuss, to send such a message? Only one thing. And he felt very tired, perhaps even scared, even if he did everything to stow that feeling away in a distant, inner corner.

He had meant to send an e-mail and try to explain his headlong flight from home, in any event present some kind of half-truth. She certainly perceived it as running away, what else could be expected?

Could he explain how it all fit together, and do that without having her push him away? A single mistake and he would be punished. Because there was a punishment waiting. He feared that he had definitively lost Ann, a woman who in a rare, unexpected way had taken hold in him.

When had she figured out the truth? And how? Did she know the whole truth? He didn't know. If she had only given him a little more information in her message, it would have felt better. And how successful would it be to offer a half-truth if the whole picture was now clear to her? He would be exposed immediately as a notorious liar.

"Isn't that what I am?" he asked himself.

The water started boiling and he made his coffee; sat down at the kitchen table, listened out toward the alley, where it was still noisy.

I'll wait, he decided, and immediately felt better.

✦

Twelve

The coffee shop outside Laxå was just as rundown as the exterior promised. Håkan Malmberg had hoped for a surprise, that the cracked canary-yellow paneling, the rusty sheet metal roof, and the misspelled sign along the side of the road was a front.

But the interior was even more decrepit, with broken chairs and tables, worn textiles, and incredibly dusty plastic flowers. The coffee was lukewarm and the cheese sandwich dry as dust, the only thing he dared buy because of the obvious risk of food poisoning where the other sandwiches were concerned, sweating behind a smudged plastic cover:

meatballs with red beet salad and shrimp sandwiches swimming in mayonnaise.

He was alone in the place. He understood why.

Despite the meager snack, he felt satisfied and did not let himself be discouraged by the fact that he would probably need to stop for food once more before Uppsala.

It had been a fine trip, a mini-vacation of over a week. He went to Koster for the first time in his life and visited an old acquaintance who had moved there permanently, spent a few days in Gothenburg, and unexpectedly ran into a childhood friend he had not seen for at least fifteen years. The last two days he camped at Kinnekulle, swam in ice-cold Lake Vänern, and finished the red wine he had bought in Gothenburg.

Now he turned on his cell phone for the first time since Koster. Five voicemails and eight missed calls.

He listened to the messages. The first few were not sensational, two from motorcycle buddies, who like him were out and about and wondered where in the world he was, two from his sister, who wanted help moving. The fifth message was all the more worrisome.

A woman from the police, Ann Lindell, was looking for him in "an urgent matter." It was about Klara Lovisa.

Håkan Malmberg pushed aside the plate with the remains of the roll, got up immediately, and left the place.

"Bye now and welcome back," a voice was heard, but he did not turn around and did not answer the greeting. There was nothing to say thank you for here either, he thought bitterly, suddenly enraged at the whole place. How the hell can you work in such a dive! Not even keep it clean. He resisted the impulse to go back in and scold the woman behind the counter.

"All these bitches can go to hell!"

It was more than a two-hour drive home. Just as he was kick-starting the motorcycle, he got the idea to turn west instead on E18 and go to Oslo. There he had bike buddies and could disappear for a week or two. Then maybe it would blow over. He had nothing waiting in Uppsala.

"She can move herself," he muttered.

It was the third time in as many years that his sister was moving, always in the summer, and she always expected him to help out.

He pulled out on E20 and placed himself aggressively close to the centerline and the cars he would pull up alongside of and, one after another, put behind him on his ride.

✦

Thirteen

Bernt Friberg's and Gunilla Lange's relationship could be summarized in a single word: skin.

They crept together like two animals in darkness. Gunilla breathed against his shoulder and he hid himself behind her ear.

He's a fine person, Gunilla would think, when she heard his heavy breathing. She knew what he did during the day, felt the weight of his body, the twitching muscles.

I love you, Bernt might mumble, before he passed out.

The hours of skin counterbalanced much of what felt incomplete.

She stared into the darkness. They were lying close together, he with one leg over her thigh, she with her arm resting on his shoulder. It looked like any late evening, they always lay close together, wordlessly storing up skin from the other.

"What is it?" he said, twisting his head. She felt his words against her throat, and she heard that he was worried. Not angry, just worried, a feeling he often expressed in darkness.

"I'm thinking about Bosse," she said without fear.

What else could she say? Betray Bosse by saying: "Nothing?"

"Don't think like that," he mumbled.

What do you mean by "like that," she wondered.

"He's gone," he said. "Now you have me."

"I know," she answered.

She waited awhile for him to continue. Normally he would rattle off a long litany, but he remained silent.

"He wanted so much to get away from this life," she said instead, encouraged by his silence.

"I doubt anyone really believed in that company, other than Bergman, but he was wounded too."

"What do you mean?"

"He sits at home dabbing at canvases and daydreaming," said Bernt.

"I believed in their company," said Gunilla. "I know what he could do, what they could do."

"That was then," said Bernt, with sharpness, but still consoling in tone.

"He deserved a better fate."

"You have me," Bernt repeated.

They were still lying close together, but none of the customary calm was present. Suddenly he placed his hand on her breast, caressed it carefully, took hold of the nipple between his thumb and index finger and mumbled something she could not interpret.

She did not want his hand on her breast but against her will the nipple stiffened. She freed herself carefully from his hold by turning over. She felt how he stiffened and how he pressed himself against her back and buttocks. His breathing became heavier. Without wanting to she became damp, and she thought about Bosse as he forced himself inside her.

When in the middle of the night she woke up he was no longer in the bed. He usually got up once during the night, but there was no sound of flushing from the toilet.

She pulled aside the cover, swung her legs over the side of the bed, and sat that way for a few minutes before she got up, pulled on her bathrobe, went up to the closed bedroom door, and listened. The apartment was quiet.

The door creaked a little as she opened it. She heard a faint sound from the kitchen and happened to think of a puppy she had as a child. A puppy that never was more than a puppy as he was run over at only three months old, who at night would whine at the foot of her bed, unable to jump up onto it.

He was sitting at the kitchen table, naked, with his shoulders tensed, his head resting in one hand. In front of him were two bottles of beer. One was empty, the other half empty. Bernt, who would not have a drop for weeks, not even a beer.

"What's going on?"

He started and turned quickly around. In his eyes there was fear. His hairy chest heaved in a deep breath.

"I woke up," he said as he exhaled.

"Were you dreaming?"

He shook his head. She knew that it would be as good as impossible to get him to talk, but she made an attempt anyway.

"I liked what you did," she said, realizing how crazy that sounded. "I mean, it was nice for me too."

She guessed it was something like that he wanted to hear.

He said nothing, raised the bottle, and took a gulp.

"Won't you come and lie down?"

Another shake of the head.

"I might as well stay up. I'll be leaving soon."

She looked at the clock on the stove. 4:13.

"You can sleep another hour," she said.

At a quarter to six he had to be at Heidenstam Square. He and four workmates met there every morning to carpool down to Jakobsberg. They had done that since March. In the fall there would be a few weeks in town before the commute to Stockholm started up again.

In that respect they were alike, Bernt and Bosse. It felt good in the morning, like a continuation of her life with Bosse. Bernt was also in construction and always left home early. Bosse had never been exactly talkative in the morning, and Bernt wasn't either.

"Why do you have to work on a Saturday?" she said.

"You know how it is," he replied.

She knew. How many weekends hadn't Bosse worked?

"Shall I make you a cup?"

He did not answer and she took that as a yes.

They drank coffee together. She glanced at him.

"Aren't you cold?"

"Yeah," he said.

She went for the cover in the bedroom and draped it around him. He looked surprised, but smiled, took a sip of coffee.

"That was good," he said. "I needed to warm up."

"What are you thinking about?"

It was as if Bosse's death made it possible to ask such a question at four thirty in the morning. She did not understand how, but that's how it was.

"About us," he said. "You are so dear to me."

She reached her hand across the table and took hold of his. I will never forget this moment, she thought.

He looked tired. His beard stubble was shiny black.

"I didn't mean you any harm," he said.

"What do you mean?"

"With all this," he said after a long time.

She still did not understand, but waited for a continuation.

"Jerker's not doing well," he said suddenly.

"Does he have a cold?"

"No, it's his lungs. He has a hard time breathing."

Jerker Widén had been Bernt's workmate for many years.

"Angina, maybe."

"They don't know. But he's worried, of course."

"What are you worried about?"

He looked quickly at her.

"Losing you," he said.

Gunilla started crying. She withdrew her hand and hid her face. Bernt started talking with a fervor that at last made him fall silent, embarrassed by his own words.

"Don't say that," she said. "You don't need to explain everything. I know."

"I'm thinking about Bosse too. I didn't want it to go that way, just that he would disappear from your life. I knew you still cared about him. And then that money."

"He needed it," she said hotly.

He nodded.

"I'll be on my way now," he said. "I can stop by the storeroom."

He got up and left the kitchen. She understood that nothing more would be said, and she was grateful for that.

As he went past Gunilla he stroked her across the back, and in the doorway he turned around.

"We need that money too," he said.

She nodded, did not want to discuss it.

"Jerker wants to sell his boat," he said.

She stared at him.

"Should we buy a boat?"

"We need to get out a little," he said, unusually defensive.

"A boat?" she repeated, looking like he had suggested they should sail around the world.

"It's in Skarholmen," he said, nodded and disappeared. The lock clicked as he carefully closed the outside door behind him.

Gunilla shook her head. He had never mentioned being interested in the sea or boats. Was it Jerker who put that idea in his head? They were like clay and straw. Of course they had discussed her loan to Bosse, and now that it was no longer relevant, the money could be plowed into a boat project.

"We need to get out a little," he said, and in principle she agreed, but she would never literally throw her money into the sea.

She had heard Jerker talk about his boat, but did not even know if it was a motorboat or a sailboat. It didn't matter. A boat was just not going to happen!

✦

Fourteen

"Why did you lie?"

Andreas Davidsson had not once looked Ann Lindell in the eyes, but instead continued stubbornly staring down between his feet. Sometimes he made a movement with one foot; Lindell did not see it, but heard the scraping sound of the sole against the pavestones.

They were sitting, like before, on the terrace. Lindell invited his mother to sit with them, but Andreas refused. Then he would not say a word, he explained. His mother did not put up a fight, on the contrary she sneaked off immediately. Did she have any idea that she too would be questioned? Lindell suspected more and more that she suffered from some defect, which made her incapable of fully understanding the consequences of their family lie.

Lindell had explained to both of them that she would tape the conversation. Andreas was over the age of fifteen and therefore liable for a criminal offense.

"I don't know," he forced out.

"If you can speak louder, that would be nice," said Lindell, moving the tape recorder a little closer to the boy. "Okay, this is how it looks: Klara Lovisa disappeared on her sixteenth birthday. You and your mother have maintained the whole time that on that Saturday you were in Gävle visiting your grandmother. Your grandmother supported that version. Until yesterday, when I visited her. Then she was clearly having a pretty good day. You know she's often confused, that's not news to anyone in your family, is it?"

"Naw."

"She was angry at you, do you know that? Because you didn't come that Saturday. It was not only Klara Lovisa's birthday, but also your grandfather's. She was angry because you stayed home."

"She's so screwy," said Andreas.

"Yes, sometimes she's a little confused, we know that, but the problem for you is that your aunt, who I didn't even know about until yesterday, confirmed your grandmother's latest version, the true version. She was also there at the cemetery and at dinner. She is definitely not confused. I talked with her too. She remembers the dinner very well and that your grandmother quarreled with your mother because you weren't there. You were still in Uppsala, weren't you?"

He did not answer.

"Can you stop scraping your feet and answer the question instead!"

He shook his head.

"What does that headshaking mean?"

"I was at home."

"Good, now we don't have to argue about that," said Lindell. "It's nice when you say what really happened."

The next question was a given, but she chose to wait in silence. After a while, no more than half a minute, Andreas looked at her for the first time, a momentary glance. Lindell nodded and tried to look encouraging.

"What did you do on Saturday the twenty-eighth of April?"

"I was at home, like I said."

"The whole day?"

"Yes."

"A Saturday? It was a beautiful spring day. You didn't go outside even once?"

"No."

"Did you have any visitors?"

"No."

"Did anyone call?"

"I don't remember."

"Were you waiting for someone to call?"

The answer was delayed, and came in the form of another shake of the head.

"Perhaps you thought that Klara Lovisa would be in touch?"

"Lay off! Haven't you understood that it was over?"

"It was her birthday."

"I know that!"

"Did you send an SMS to wish her happy birthday, perhaps?"

Suddenly Lindell felt sorry for the boy. He was suffering all the torments of hell before her eyes. She understood now why he stayed at home. He had been waiting for a response from her. He must have sent her a text message, maybe said something about wanting to see her.

"You didn't go to her house, did you?"

"No."

"When did you find out that she had disappeared, did you see it in the newspaper?"

"I knew it before. Klovisa's mom called here."

"On Saturday evening?"

"Yes, she wondered if I'd seen her."

"And then your mom decided that you should lie, that you had been in Gävle?"

"We didn't know anything."

"So the lie came about when you read in the paper that she had disappeared," Lindell observed. "But you had no reason to pretend. You were home the whole day and had no contact with her, so why this song and dance?"

"I don't know."

"You did have contact with her, didn't you? Think now, before you tell another lie. They often crack. I know that, I'm a police officer, I've questioned hundreds like you. The truth almost always creeps out."

"I texted her," he said at last.

"When was that?"

Andreas pulled out his cell phone. Lindell understood that he had saved his message and she felt a stab in her heart.

"Nine twenty-two," he said.

"What did you write?"

"'Happy sixteenth birthday. Can we meet?'" he read from the display.

"You got no answer."

"No."

She could imagine his anguish, first before he sent it, then afterward, while he waited for a possible reply from Klara Lovisa.

They sat in silence. Lindell peeked at her watch. In an hour she should pick up Erik, who was at a birthday party on Botvidsgatan. A playmate at preschool was turning seven.

She guessed that the boy spoke the truth where the SMS was concerned, and sensed that he had not seen her that Saturday. In April they had already asked all the neighbors around the Davidsson house if they might have seen Klara Lovisa, but no one had seen or heard anything.

"Where you did usually meet?"

"Here or at her house," said Andreas.

"But when you wanted to be by yourselves?"

"By the crematorium, behind there kind of. There's a place where they pile up old gravestones, so they can use them again. Recycling, kind of."

Lindell could not keep from smiling at his word choice, but it didn't seem to be the most romantic place for a date. At that moment she remembered that the first time she saw an erect penis was at a cemetery in Ödeshög.

"May I borrow your cell phone?"

"Why? That's what it says."

"I just want to check," said Lindell, reaching out her hand.

After a slight hesitation he handed over the phone. She read the message. He had left out an "XOX" at the end. She went back a step and checked incoming texts. If he had gotten a reply from her, she guessed he would have saved that too. But there was no SMS from Klara Lovisa.

She handed back the phone.

"Thanks," she said. "It's good that this came out, isn't it?"

He nodded.

"Will I be punished?" he asked.

"No," said Lindell, and turned off the recorder.

The one who should be punished is his mother, she thought.

Andreas sat with the phone in his hand. Wonder how many times he's read his message, wondered Lindell, more gloomy than content at having cracked his alibi.

"One thing, and now the tape recorder is no longer running," she emphasized. "When I asked you whether you had slept with each other, you said that Klara Lovisa wanted to wait. Wait until when?"

"Until she turned sixteen," said Andreas.

Back in the car she wondered about the significance of Andreas's final statement. Certainly he had hoped that he would be the first. An SMS could create contact, that was his obvious thought.

Lindell did not believe that Andreas had any part in her disappearance, but obviously that could not be ruled out. She looked at her watch again. Erik would not like her arriving late, and she saw that she still had time to take a look at the area around the crematorium and cemetery.

She headed in that direction, and when an elderly woman came walking along Berthågavägen she braked to ask about the place where the church stored old gravestones. The woman looked perplexed at first, and then nodded encouragingly, as if she thought Lindell was going to choose a gravestone, and pointed out the way.

Lindell got out of the car. The woman's face made her think about her parents, that one day, perhaps in the not too distant future, she would have to choose a stone.

The area was an open yard where stones in all forms were laid out like on parade. She read some of the stones. Some of the inscriptions were almost worn away by the teeth of time.

She strolled around, turning in behind a wooden fence and surveying the ground. Weeds were growing luxuriantly between piles of gravel and chunks of concrete. Had Klara Lovisa and Andreas, despite everything, seen each other here on her birthday? Perhaps Klara Lovisa was happy that he remembered her birthday, even if she rejected his overture to resume the relationship. Could Klara Lovisa be buried here?

Andreas seemed to be a careful guy, but Lindell knew the problems that raging hormones in combination with disappointment could create.

She left the place with a sense of oppression, as if she had trespassed. The same feeling as when you are witness to a stranger's sorrow.

She understood that it was this place, so lacking in finesse, that she would associate with Klara Lovisa. This would be her resting place, until they found her.

✦

Fifteen

Itaberaba–Portal da Chapada, it said on the wall of the bus station. Gateway to the inferno might be more like it, thought Anders Brant.

For an hour he had fought with flies, stared blankly at the blaring TV, had a cup of overly sweet coffee, and turned down several taxi drivers.

He should have taken the first offer, but indecisively lingered at the station. The trip had taken four and a half hours, and once at his destination he felt mostly like getting on the first available bus back.

He was sweaty and strangely irritated at the people around him. He found himself looking for faults: one was too fat, another had ridiculously ugly clothes, and the third was talking nonsense. This behavior was quite unlike him.

He was usually not easily annoyed. If anything he was tolerant of people's ideas and ingenuity, but now he felt as if the whole city, the bus station anyway, was one big taunt.

He had been in Chapada before, stayed at a hippie-influenced guest house in Lençóis and from there went out on various adventures, hiked in the mountains, rode a spavined horse during a three-day tour with a guide who talked about sex most of the time, and rafted down a river together with three Dutch women, all of it pleasurable and exciting. He liked Chapada, but not this time.

Now there were no outdoor arrangements waiting. The anguish made him sweat even more. He had a second cup of coffee. The man behind the counter asked what bus he was waiting for.

Anders Brant only shook his head and pretended not to understand, but realized that as a gringo he stood out, all the more so as he did not seem to be on his way anywhere, but hung around like a homeless person trying to pass the time.

He went up to the wastebasket, threw away his plastic mug, and decided it could not wait. Going back with unfinished business would be both silly and irresponsible.

He had prepared what he would say. In his money belt was an envelope with cash. When he left the bus station it was with a feeling of fateful distress, as if he could not have done this any other way, at least that's what he told himself. There had really been no choice, everything had worked toward this ignominious end.

Obviously there had been a choice at one time, he could have left the place, even after they established contact and started exchanging small talk in that way Brazilian women are so good at, demure and flirtatious at the same time. But he wanted to hear the music group that would appear an hour or so later and decided to wait. In the interim he could just as well pass the time with a little company. She introduced herself as Vanessa. He ordered a beer, which they shared, and then another.

If he had left the concert and instead taken the last ferry back to the island, then he would not need to go back to Itaberaba like a scoundrel, with words and money ready, but without honor. You got horny, it was that simple, admit it, you idiot, he thought, heading for the first available taxi. I should have gone home, given myself a hand job and woken up at sunrise, sober and free.

The taxi ride was short, maybe fifteen blocks or so. It cost 8 reais. Brant gave him ten, got out of the car with sweat running down his forehead, and headed for the blue-painted house with the light red wall she had described.

A few children were playing on the street. A gas peddler pulled his cart as he called out that he was in the neighborhood. Anders Brant looked around in hope of finding something, a sign that would give him a chance to leave the field. Maybe Vanessa might come walking with a guy at her side? Then he could sneak away behind the ice cream seller's hut, observe them, let him give her a passionate kiss, which could not be misunderstood, before he continued up the street. He would wave at the man and then disappear through the gate to the blue house.

Fantasies! But could he simply, untruthfully make up a man? A rival. Go back to Salvador and then from Sweden write a letter, filled with anguish and injured fury.

Give up! Vanessa is a good woman and you're a childish prick. Go up to the gate now and ring the bell, don't tell her everything, but enough. Offer her support, money, whatever, to make things easier and smooth. Give her everything except your faithfulness and love. Give her betrayal. Then flee. Fight back the disgust and bad conscience, keep building on the myth of Anders Brant, the unreliable Swede, who for twenty years never paid for sex or even started a relationship on all his travels in Third World countries. On the contrary, he had maintained, with a type of moral superiority, that it would be cruel and unjust.

The men, Scandinavians, Germans, Americans, or wherever they came from, who with the power of the dollar bought sex and temporary intimacy, for a day, a week, a vacation, to feel like kings, with their cocks as a scepter, left devastated women and a sick system behind them, a prostitution economy.

Vanessa was no whore, and he was no traditional john. They had not met with a business transaction as starting point, there had been genuine attraction and sincere joy, perhaps love. He did not know whether he was in love or if he was only a victim of the Western middle-aged man's need to feel potent and desirable.

He could not see a life together with Vanessa, it was that simple. She had many good qualities, she was beautiful as a dream and easy to be around, in short, an amazing woman, but still there was no future for the two of them. She could see a future, but he could not.

Of course he had asked himself why, but could not formulate an explanation that was entirely convincing. So how could he convince her?

It was more a feeling of inequality. He would always be the stronger one, the one with money, and above all the one who had a possibility to leave. Then, when he did leave, and he would sooner or later, he would leave a Vanessa with considerably worse opportunities than she had today. She was twenty-nine, talked about children, inconceivable for him. He was fifteen years older and could not imagine becoming a father at that age. Besides, it was doubtful whether he had the purely physical prerequisites. During the last two years of a five-year relationship with a woman they had tried to have a child, but failed. Two years later she was pregnant by another man and now had four children, no fertility problems there.

Were those only excuses to be able to flee with honor intact, albeit somewhat tarnished? No, he answered himself.

He did not want to give up his independence and he did not want to tie Vanessa down in a relationship, it was that simple. There was nothing chauvinistic about this, he maintained, on the contrary it was an expression of concern for her.

He still felt like a traitor.

The bell rang. If only she weren't at home, he thought before the door opened. First surprise on her face, which quickly changed into a broad smile. He tried to smile.

She ran up to the gate. He adjusted the money belt.

✦

Sixteen

Lindell met Fredrik Johansson in town. When she got hold of him—once again it was Elina who helped locate a current cell phone number—he was on his way to a workout session at the old Centralbadet, and they agreed to meet first at the Cathedral Bridge.

"I have to get going," he said. "I'm going to meet some buddies and work out, I told you that."

"Okay," said Lindell. "Let's meet here in an hour, then we'll go up to the police station."

He turned on his heels and disappeared without a word. Lindell started to follow him but stopped at the square and sat down on a bench. She watched as he slipped into the health club.

Her stomach was growling but she could not bring herself to go to the Kurdish hot dog vendor on the pedestrian street, much less fight the crowds for a nondescript daily lunch special at a restaurant.

She decided to wait on the bench. There was a lot to think about with the investigation of Klara Lovisa's fate, but she immediately started speculating about Anders Brant—who he really was, what he had to do with Bosse Gränsberg, and where and why he had gone away. Somewhere warm, she decided. He was strikingly tan all over his body, obviously he had sunbathed naked. "I go away sometimes," he said casually when she asked whether he'd been on vacation, but did not explain where, or whether it was for pleasure or business.

What hurt was just his casual attitude. For him perhaps it was just a short-term love affair, one of many. There was no doubt that he appreciated her company and their sex together, he had both said and shown that openly. But there was something, and it was only now that she could put it in words, something tacitly apathetic in his attitude, as if he did not really take their developing relationship seriously.

Then, and that was only a few days ago, she had not thought about it that much, fully occupied as she was with simply experiencing this rebirth in the area of love. The intoxication of passion made her inattentive. Now she had a serious hangover, with the demon of loneliness perched on her shoulder. He jeered at the futile castles in the air. He would remain sitting there a long time, she realized that.

Treachery, she thought. It is treachery if he leaves me now. It is treachery if he is mixed up in something illegal. I am never going to forgive him! Or myself either!

Those were her thoughts on the bench. It was summer, people were strolling slowly along, enjoying the heat. A few tourists photographed the milldam. A young couple lifted up their children so they could peek over the railing of the Cathedral Bridge and look down at the current. Lindell could sense their delight and the parents' quiet joy, which even at a distance could be seen on their youthful, innocent faces. There was a playfulness in the woman's manner when she set her kid down on the sidewalk again. The man said something and she smiled at him. That's what being a couple looks like, thought Lindell, bitterly envious.

The onset of her period did not make things any better, the plague that had started hitting her again with full force and made her body slack and her mood low. It was as if nothing mattered when the periodic torment approached.

And she had dreamed of a vacation together! A vacation full of laughter and intimacy, Ann, Erik, and Anders on an expedition somewhere, it didn't matter where and how, just the idea of a joint project made her laugh to herself and move with a different lightness.

Was it over? Unconsciously she was becoming convinced that this was the case. She would be sad, but not let herself be totally crushed. She would put up walls inside, hate her way out of the pain, convince herself that it was good for her and Erik when Brant definitively disappeared from their life.

Beside her on the bench an older man was sitting straddle-legged, with his hands resting on a cane. He was dressed in heavy shoes, gabardine pants and a worn jacket, with a soiled hat on his head. His face was weather-beaten. Wind and sun had hollowed out furrows in his cheeks and made his skin leathery. Lindell imagined that he was a Greek shepherd, sitting on a mountain slope watching his herd.

Tell me something, she wanted to encourage the old man, tell me about your life.

Suddenly he turned his head very slowly, as if the movement required the greatest effort, and observed her. The whites of his eyes were streaked with red.

"A beautiful day," he said.

Lindell nodded and smiled.

"I usually sit here, or there," he said, pointing toward a bench on the opposite side of the square. "It depends on the sun."

His accent reinforced her impression that he came from the Mediterranean. Why not Greece, she thought?

"Are you from Greece?"

He nodded, but showed no surprise at her correct guess.

"People come and go, I watch them. In the summer it's mainly the women I'm interested in. I like fluttering skirts."

He laughed, a boyish, giggling laugh.

"Unfortunately I don't have a skirt on," said Lindell.

"You don't look like you're in a skirt-wearing mood."

" 'Skirt-wearing mood'?"

"Yes, I think about laughter when I see a beautiful woman in a beautiful skirt. But today a skirt would not suit you so well."

Lindell looked down at her black jeans. They didn't look too happy either.

"He's coming back," said the Greek.

"Who?"

"And when he does, you should put on a skirt with beautiful, happy colors."

Lindell stared at him, both moved and agitated by his words. He raised one hand from his cane and placed it on her knee. It felt as if his hand weighed a ton.

"Now Grandpa's going home," he said.

He removed his hand, got up laboriously, and took a deep breath.

"Are you a shepherd?"

"No, land surveyor, but now I don't have any land to survey. Trust me," he continued after a short pause, without looking at her, and went his way. A few seconds later he had disappeared.

What did he mean? Lindell stared at the building where the man had gone around the corner. Had he seen her and Freddy on the bridge, how he left her and how she followed him a little indecisively but then sank down on the bench? That he improbably enough thought they were a couple? She could be Freddy's mother!

Or was her quandary about the disappeared journalist so clearly legible on her face? Perhaps the old land surveyor was psychic?

And this talk about skirts! She could not see him however as a peeper who sat drooling over skirts blowing up and exposing women's legs. His whole way of expressing himself was too singular and his eyes too wise for that.

She smiled to herself and decided to consider him a bearer of a favorable message that everything would work out. Brant would come back, everything would have a natural explanation, and she would wear a skirt in happy colors. Did she even have such a skirt?

Freddy Johansson approached on foot exactly one hour after they had gone their separate ways. Lindell gave him a smile from a distance that she hoped would express her appreciation that he was so punctual. They walked in silence to Lindell's car and drove to the police station.

In contrast to Andreas Davidsson, Freddy Johansson looked her in the eyes when he spoke. He also adopted a considerably tougher attitude.

"You sent a text message to Klara Lovisa last New Year's Eve," Lindell stated, taking a chance.

"I don't remember that," he answered. "Maybe I did."

"Where did you send the text from?"

"I was in town."

"With friends?"

"The party broke up right before twelve o'clock. There was a little trouble. Then I went home."

Lindell asked for the names of his friends and Freddy listed off a handful of names and some cell phone numbers, which she wrote down.

"You went home alone?"

"I already said that."

Lindell squinted at her notepad, browsed back a few pages, pretended to read something, and then fixed her eyes on the young man before her. She understood why he irritated some people. His full lips were drawn up, making him look like he was sneering superciliously all the time.

"Okay, then," she sighed. "What did you write?"

"I didn't say I sent her a message. You know how it is, you text here and there."

"You liked Klara Lovisa, I've understood."

"She was cute," said Freddy.

"Did you have a relationship?"

Freddy laughed. The superior sneer disappeared, and he suddenly looked more human, with a boyish, almost cute expression.

"She was jailbait, sort of, you know, a little flirty."

"And you're a grown man?"

He did not comment on that.

"She was fifteen. You know she turned sixteen the day she disappeared?"

"It was in the newspaper."

"Did you text her and wish her happy birthday?"

"No," said Freddy, shaking his head.

He drew his hand through his mop of hair.

"What do you really want? Am I suspected in some way?"

"We're just checking up on a few things," said Lindell curtly. "Do you have a driver's license?"

"Yes, what about it?"

"A car too perhaps?"

"No."

"Do you ever borrow a car? From your parents perhaps?"

She suddenly got the feeling that she was completely on the wrong track. Why should this twenty-two year old have anything to do with Klara Lovisa's disappearance?

"It has happened. Damn, you're really inquisitive!"

Lindell waved her hand to interrupt him.

"We would like a photo of you."

He immediately took out his wallet and removed a minimal photo, no larger than a passport picture, and handed it over.

"That's nice," she said. "But we want a proper photo."

"Why? Fan picture, or what?"

Now it was Lindell's turn to shake her head.

"Come along with me now, and we'll get this taken care of right away. Then you can go home."

✦

Seventeen

She hugged him hard and long, and when she released her hold she nudged the money belt, laughed, and said something jokingly about the rich gringo with the artificial stomach.

He freed himself from her embrace.

"Shall we go in?"

She stepped to one side and as he passed through the doorway she caught him again, pressed herself against him, put her head against his shoulder. Her hair smelled of lemon.

She was wearing a white dress, with several clasps depicting birds tucked into her hair.

"I'm so happy," she whispered. "I've been longing for you."

He nodded and looked into her amazing eyes.

"We have an hour before Mama comes home. She's nervous, you should know."

He nodded again.

"But she won't be home for an hour."

She caressed his cheek.

"You're warm," she said, pulling on his T-shirt and fanning a little air in toward his upper body.

"Take a shower," she suggested, leading him into the house, toward the bathroom.

He sensed what that hour might involve. Vanessa was extremely physical, as she herself put it. She loved bodily contact, was often ready for touch, took the initiative. The modesty she had shown at first had completely disappeared and was replaced by an openness that was a match for his.

"I think I'll shower later," he said, and his voice sounded considerably rougher than he intended.

"Are you tired? Do you want to rest before Mama gets here?"

He noticed a moment of disappointment in her eyes. He shook his head.

"Just a little thirsty."

"I'll get a beer, then we'll sit in the shade behind the house."

She went toward the kitchen. He watched her. I want her, he thought, suddenly aroused.

They sat down on the patio. A bird, whose call Anders Brant recognized very well, called out its encouraging song: *come-on-along, come-on-along, come-on-along.*

She poured the beer, carefully as usual, and set a glass in front of him.

"*Skål,*" she said.

The first word in Swedish that she learned.

"*Skål,*" he said, and reciprocated her smile.

His dehydrated, exhausted body greedily soaked up the cold beer. He immediately felt the effect of the alcohol. Maybe it will make this easier, he thought, and emptied the glass.

She observed him, but her smile had faded somewhat. She poured more beer. Her eyes rested steadily on his face.

He leaned his head forward, wiping his sweaty forehead. The belt pressed against his stomach.

"What's that bird called?"

"I don't know," she answered immediately, as if she didn't care to listen, as if birds were the last thing that interested her right now.

"I hear it a lot," he said.

She nodded.

"It's a pair that lives here. They're building a new nest," she said, pointing toward a scrubby tree in one corner of the yard.

He looked at the tree, took a gulp of beer, then let his eyes wander around the garden.

"It's nice here," he said.

"That's Mama's doing. I don't do a thing."

He knew that she was looking at him and he smiled, but avoided her eyes, pretending to be interested in the plants growing by the wall.

"Bougainvillea," he said, pointing to the one plant that he could identify.

"What is it, Anders?"

Now! Now or never. He gave her a quick glance.

"I guess I'm a little tired," he said, and was seized by the desperate thought of staying in this sweaty, dusty city, moving into the house, living with Vanessa and her mother.

He looked at her. Their eyes met. What more can I want? He continued his train of thought, what more can a man, and a human being, demand from life? She loves me, this is an amazing country where I feel at home, and maybe I would be happy here.

She looked searchingly at him.

"What is it?" she repeated.

"I'm thinking about us," he answered at last.

It felt like he was about to start crying.

"About us, about everything, about life."

She nodded with seriousness like a trembling in her face, as if now she was beginning to understand the extent of his ambivalence and lack of enthusiasm. That the simplest question in the world to answer for him was the cause of great anguish.

"It feels a little strange," he said. "With us and everything, I mean."

Make it easy for me, he thought, put me up against the wall, get furious, throw things at me, kick me out onto the street!

But none of that happened. Instead she got up and disappeared into the house. He listened to the sound of her steps moving across the tiles and then up the stairs to the second floor. Then there was silence, only the *come-on-along* of the bird sounded like a stubborn admonition.

Anders Brant wiped the sweat from his brow, reached for the bottle, but it was empty. He went to the kitchen to get another one. The refrigerator was well filled: there was salami, cheese, natural yogurt, which she knew he liked, vegetables, chicken sausage, a package with a kilo of "beef Paris," and on the topmost shelf, in a transparent plastic container, a cake.

He stared at the abundance, and realized that Vanessa and her mother had stocked up before his visit. With the refrigerator door still open he looked around the kitchen, and the impression of an approaching party was reinforced: plates of mango, graviola, pineapple, passion fruit, and bananas. A beautiful glass bowl was heaped with *umbu*, the fruit that was a specialty in the dry inland and which Vanessa liked so much. They had *umbu* the morning she stayed over at his *pousada* for the first time. She had stood looking out over the harbor area and the bay and ate, apparently relaxed, fruit after fruit. He was still lying in bed and observed her back and shoulders, her bottom and thighs. She had a way of resting more on one leg. He thought she was the most beautiful woman he had ever seen, an impression that was reinforced when she turned her head and gave him a smile. On her chin a few drops of fruit juice glistened.

He took a bottle of Brahma, carefully shut the refrigerator door, and returned to the patio. Vanessa had not come back.

He poured the beer, took a drink and waited, increasingly intoxicated. The bird couple flew back and forth to the tree. In their beaks they were transporting building materials. Occasionally their *come-on-along, come-on-along* sounded.

Twenty minutes passed. He got up, wandered indecisively across the patio, but sat down again. Beer bottle number two was empty. He wanted more, even though he was really feeling the effects of the alcohol, and a minute or two later he was on his feet again, stumbled, went toward the kitchen, but changed his mind, stopped, and looked toward the stairway. Not a sound was heard in the house. Soon her mother would come home.

Maybe he could make use of the drama from the day before, in order to retreat in a dignified way. He had not said a word about what he had witnessed. What if he now hinted that he was shocked and depressed, that he could not make any decisions in that state of mind? Then perhaps he could return to Salvador with a few vague words about meeting later, postpone the whole thing, prepare her for the inevitable.

He thought about the most recent e-mail he had sent to Vanessa. In it he had written that they had to meet to discuss things, and let her know that he would go to Brazil, partly to visit her in Itaberaba, partly to collect material for a couple of articles.

He thought she would understand, that his e-mail was a signal that perhaps it would be best to end the relationship. The deliberately vaguely worded message would give her a warning. He could never live with Vanessa. He realized that after he met Ann.

It was obvious that Vanessa had drawn quite different conclusions. She had seen it as a confirmation of their relationship, that he was coming to discuss their common future, so she filled the refrigerator with delicacies and awaited his arrival.

"Vanessa!" he called toward the upper floor, but got no response.

He went up the stairs, looking around. To the right was a small room with a TV and a few armchairs, to the left a corridor with four doors, one of which was ajar; that was the bathroom. He listened outside the other rooms but heard nothing.

She was sitting at a desk in her bedroom. Hanging on the wall was the poster they bought in Salvador. On the nightstand was a pile of books. The one on top was a Portuguese–Swedish dictionary.

She was sitting very quietly, with her back to him. She must have heard him but did not turn around.

"Vanessa, what is it?"

She turned her head and observed him. He had expected a tear-filled face, but her expression was calm, resolute.

"Are you still here?"

He was shamelessly happy, but at the same time somewhat upset at her coolness.

"Do you want me to leave?"

He wished that she would tell him to go away, but she only shook her head with a joyless smile at his childishness.

"I have a hard time talking about . . ." he began, but got no further.

"*You* have a hard time finding words? You, who are constantly orating?"

"I don't want to leave you."

"Who's forcing you?"

He owed her a reply.

"I wrote a letter."

"I don't want your letters," she said in a cutting tone.

In the money belt was the letter, written the day before with great effort, before the murder of the homeless man. In the envelope there was money too. In the letter he explained that it was enough to pay for her education to become a web designer, something she had dreamed of doing for several years, that the money should be seen as a gift, nothing else.

Now he could not bring himself to bring out the letter, and above all not the money. To her it would look like he was trying to buy himself free. The rich man with the money belt, who amused himself for a while, then tossed her a tip and went his way.

"Okay, you don't want anything," he said, throwing out his arms in a gesture of resignation, but his face remained beet red, recalling her unfeigned delight at the gate and the well-stocked refrigerator.

She looked at him with contempt and he left the room—the room where they should have made love, talked, and dreamed—and stumbled down the stairs and out of the house. On the paved path—he noticed how artfully the small black-and-white stones were set in a sensuous pattern—he almost ran into a woman. He noticed her terrified expression before he hurried on.

"Excuse me," he mumbled, and ran out through the gate, calmed down somewhat so as not to attract too much attention, but continued hurriedly down the street. He felt how the sweat immediately forced its way out of every pore in his body. The sweat of shame. The headache, reinforced by the beer, and now the unmerciful sun, sat like a clamp around his forehead.

He walked toward the sun, toward the south, hoping that the bus station was in that direction, aware that he had carried out the most reprehensible of all actions: treachery against a person who loved him and trusted him. He had never before hated himself the way he did at that moment.

After a few blocks a feeling of relief came over him. It was done! He tapped his hand over the money belt. The letter he would tear to pieces.

Suddenly he stopped. A feeling of ambivalence came over him. He looked around, peered along the street. Perhaps she was standing there, hoping that he would change his mind, that she might call him back, that her love had overcome the icy cold and the unconcealed contempt of a humiliated person she had shown.

He spotted a few children at the ice cream seller's canopied wagon, but no white dress, no Vanessa. He sensed that she and her mother were now united in a hateful, perhaps tearful, verbal thrashing of the faithless gringo.

Tears welled up in his eyes, seized as he was by the tragic element, by his own sentimentality, but also struck by a dash of self-pity for the deeply unjust judgments that were now being pronounced and which would mark their recollection of him for all time. He had tried! He was not malicious. His intentions had been good. He thought he loved her, that they would be together.

And how strong really was her own conviction? Hadn't she also played a game, where hindsight had caught up with spontaneous passion? That alternative could not be overlooked. Her ice-cold contempt and immediate reaction—aloofness, no attempt to convince, no pleas, no tears—what was that a sign of?

For a few seconds he stood there irresolutely, took a few steps, stopped again, turned around, looked, took a few steps, a ridiculous dance of self-betrayal, when deep inside he knew that there was no way back.

Brant put up his hand and hailed a motorcycle taxi. He got a helmet from the driver and experienced a liberating sense of anonymity as he put it on. He straddled the motorcycle and was seized by the impulse to lean his head against the driver's back, which was decorated with the name Kaka and the number eight.

The conveyance took off over the cobbled streets. It moved quickly. Brant fumbled with his hand behind his back and took hold of a bracket.

In ten minutes they were at the bus station and when he saw the ugly building just as a bus turned around the corner, he knew he had done the only right thing.

On my way, he thought. Never again Itaberaba. Never again Vanessa. He paid the motorcycle driver and gave him twice what he asked for the ride. Now I can be generous, he thought bitterly.

Although he was convinced he had made the right decision, anxiety pricked him like angry mosquitoes. Another bus came roaring, black smoke welled out of the tailpipe and the chassis rattled. He stood there in the sun. It was over 30 degrees Celsius in the shade.

"Who am I really?" he mumbled.

A car passed with music booming out of the open trunk. He saw women and men, playing children; he saw vendors of *caju* and ice cream, he heard shouts and laughter; he saw Brazil, and the ambivalence tormented his body, increasingly exhausted by the sun and the alcohol.

"I am a piece of shit," he continued his monologue.

Angry and friendly honking marked buses that arrived and departed in a steady stream, stinking and rattling highway ships that careened around the building, and gear boxes clattered and scraped their bearings as they took off.

He realized now that he was a scared gringo. A gringo who would never be anything else either. He was scared, scared of losing something, perhaps a comfortable existence, the freedom of the vagabond, perhaps also the myth of Anders Brant, world traveler, the world's conscience, the fighter for good.

The insight came suddenly, like an unforeseen smack to his solar plexus, and he was forced to support himself against the wall and take a deep breath.

He leaned forward, supported his hands against his knees and vomited. A cascade of beer splattered against the stone pavement on a small square under the scorching sun of Bahia.

✦

Eighteen

Finally, thought Urban Fredlund, the last building!

Soon he would be lying on the couch, with a cup of tea on the coffee table and a double toasted ham, cheese, and pepper sauce sandwich, his specialty every Sunday morning for the past twelve years.

Urban Fredlund did not have many pleasures in life, even less so since the woman he was living with left him ten years ago and Mirjam died a short time later. He was not sure which of the two losses he took the hardest. He had gotten Mirjam from an animal-lover and butcher, a Swede-Finn who spent his days butchering animals on a conveyor belt, and then went home to a menagerie.

That cat was special, just like his Sunday morning specialty.

In the C entry, the last one, he realized that this particular Sunday his specialty would have to wait.

5:45 A.M. A lifeless body in a stairwell in Tunabackar, female, middle-aged. Probably stone dead. Wounds on the face and back of the head. Found by a newspaper carrier. Ambulance and patrol car were on their way.

That was what Sammy Nilsson found out when he got the call. The clock on the night stand showed 5:49. Angelika was turning restlessly by his side. Perhaps she had noticed the phone ringing, but Sammy Nilsson was sure that in a few minutes she would be sound asleep again.

He would have to drag himself out of bed and take off. Along with Beatrice, he was on call over the weekend, which to this point had been surprisingly quiet. Now the calm was over.

Of course he could not know who the woman was, but he could guess. He remembered the address from the board where they had written down Bosse Gränsberg's acquaintances. But it could also be a neighbor lady or acquaintance of Ingegerd Melander or a visitor to someone else in the building. No point in speculating, he thought, while he took a quick shower. In fifteen minutes he would find out. The dead woman was not going anywhere.

A patrol officer was standing by the entry. He held his nose demonstratively while Sammy Nilsson parked next to an ambulance and got out of the car, but the gesture was not directed at Nilsson or detectives in general.

"The paper carrier puked," said the uniformed colleague, whose name Sammy recalled just at that moment.

"Hey, Bruno!"

His colleague nodded good-naturedly, noticeably pleased at being addressed by his first name.

Sammy did not hurry, but instead looked around. The building was a typical 1950s construction, yellow plastered, with three entries, four floors, a gravel yard with a number of abused trees and bushes shaped into balls, overflowing bike racks, a misplaced trash room that had been added in later years, and a grilling area where a grouping of chairs had been set out.

Could they have planned it to be any less inviting, wondered Sammy Nilsson.

"She's stone dead, and clearly has been awhile," said Bruno.

"Has the doctor arrived?"

That was a pious hope at six o'clock on a Sunday morning.

"We were first on the scene, besides them," said Bruno, nodding toward the ambulance.

"I guess I'll go take a look," Sammy said. "Are you the one who propped open the door?"

"It smelled really awful."

"And the paper carrier?"

"Sitting with an old lady on the second floor. Says 'Melkersson' on the door."

"Is he shook up?"

"Yeah, you know," Bruno replied.

Sammy Nilsson knew.

"And your partner?"

"Ortman is guarding the lady."

Sammy turned his head and studied the directory on the wall in the stairwell. *I. Melander* lived on the top floor.

At that Beatrice Andersson walked in. Nilsson was expecting his colleague.

"Now maybe we can get a quick identification," he said to Bruno. "Bea was here a few days ago."

"Oh, shit."

"The homeless guy who was killed, you know, he had a connection here."

Beatrice nodded at Bruno. Sammy stepped to one side and let her in.

"Is it her, do you think?"

They went up the stairs together. The stench of vomit became stronger and stronger.

"The newspaper carrier," Sammy explained.

"What the hell had he been eating?"

They stepped over the vomit on the third floor.

"An apple and strawberry yogurt," he said.

"You're too much!" Beatrice exclaimed.

The woman was on the landing between the third and fourth floors. Someone had placed a kitchen towel over her head. Sammy noted the neatly embroidered monogram. Her right hand tightly clutched a trash bag. At her feet was a newspaper. Sammy read the headline on the front page: *Henhouse Burned Down in Alunda.*

Ortman was standing halfway up the stairs. The pale, expressionless face testified that he had had more enjoyable assignments.

"Okay?"

Ortman nodded.

Bea leaned over, lifted the blood-stained hand towel, put it back immediately, and straightened up.

"It's her."

"That sucks," said Sammy.

"Any curiosity seekers?"

Ortman shook his head. Can he talk, Sammy wondered, and tested him with a question that reasonably required a somewhat more advanced reply.

"The newspaper carrier? Where is he?"

Ortman managed it by making a motion with his head and pointing one floor down.

Sammy started to laugh.

"This job really sucks!"

Beatrice stared at him. Sammy fell silent, but burst into laughter again when he saw Ortman's dismayed expression and bewilderment.

"You can go ahead and switch with Bruno for a while, so you get a little fresh air," Sammy said to Ortman. The patrol officer disappeared down the stairs.

"And you! Do you know if Forensics is on their way?" Sammy called after him.

"Think so," was the answer.

"He can talk," said Sammy.

"Shape up," said Beatrice. "I'll go up, you take the paper carrier," she decided on the division of work. "We'll save time that way."

Urban Fredlund had apparently recovered somewhat. In front of him on the table was an empty glass.

"Would you like some too?" Maja Melkersson asked. "There's nothing like a glass of cold milk in the morning," she continued, taking Sammy Nilsson's reply as a given, as she immediately set out a glass, got a jug from the refrigerator, and poured in milk.

"Yes, that was good," said the carrier.

"It's the least I can do," said the woman. "You run here every morning and make sure I find out who's died."

Sammy Nilsson guessed that she was referring to the obituaries in the local newspaper, but this particular morning her comment sounded macabre, to say the least.

"Can you tell me a little," said Sammy Nilsson, as he sipped the milk and nodded appreciatively at Maja Melkersson, who was observing him.

"I noticed the smell first," Urban Fredlund began.

"What smell? Was there already vomit when you arrived?"

"No, that's my fault," he said, giving Sammy Nilsson a quick look. "I'm sorry about making a mess."

Sammy Nilsson made a deprecating gesture.

"It smelled like garbage," the carrier continued. "Old cheese, mainly. Then when I came up to the third floor I saw . . . I saw the legs first."

"You went up and looked?"

"Of course, I had to check whether or not she was injured."

"But you knew right away that she was dead."

Urban nodded.

"Then I ran halfway down the stairs. I thought I would make it outside, but I didn't."

"That's nothing to be ashamed of," said Sammy Nilsson. "Did you recognize her?"

"No, but there aren't too many you recognize on your route. Most of them are still asleep when I'm working."

"You didn't see anything strange, anything that was different, in the yard or in the neighborhood?"

"No, it was a typical Sunday morning. Quiet and peaceful. Until now."

Sammy Nilsson wrote down his name and contact information.

"One thing," said Urban Fredlund. "Could you deliver the last newspaper to Wilson, at the very top? It's probably on the stairway."

Sammy Nilsson nodded, said thanks for the milk, and left them.

In the meantime the forensics technicians had arrived, the inexhaustible Morgansson and the considerably less energetic Johannesson.

"We don't really have time," said Morgansson. "We were just getting in the car to drive up to Dalarna."

"Dalarna?"

"Yeah, a young kid in Hedemora was cut down with an ice pick last night," said Johannesson. "Half of Dalarna is down with the flu, our associates in Falun anyway, so we have to intervene."

"But there must be more than the two of you in Forensics?"

Morgansson smiled apologetically.

"They've got it too. Haven't you noticed that half the building is coughing and sniffling? Jakobsson is the only one who's healthy, but typically he's on vacation. That's the situation."

"How's it look?" Johannesson asked. "Can the apartment wait until tomorrow? I mean, it looks like an accident."

"Okay," said Sammy. "But wrap up the trash bag, then I'll take it along and put it in your fridge."

Sammy continued up the stairs and stuffed the newspaper into Wilson's mail slot. The door to Ingegerd Melander's apartment was open, but only slightly. He took hold high up on the door frame and pushed it open.

Beatrice was in the kitchen. She had put on protective socks and gloves. There was a smell of smoke and old, dried-up beer.

"He's lying on the couch sleeping, evidently dead drunk," she said. "I thought I would look around a little before we wake him, if that's even possible."

"Who is he?"

"Johnny Andersson, her new boyfriend. Ola and I met him here the last time."

"No one else?"

"No."

"Is this a crime scene?"

"Doubtful," said Beatrice. "It looks like she started tidying up, went to take out the garbage, and fell down."

"Anything exciting?"

"Not so far. There's been a party, that much is clear."

The kitchen counters, which on her first visit had been almost clinically clean, were now overflowing with plates, glasses, and food scraps. Sammy counted three whole bottles of liquor, all empty, plus a fair number of beer cans.

"There were several of them," he determined.

He counted six large serving plates and just as many table settings. On the stove was an ovenproof dish that presumably contained potato casserole. Three jars of different kinds of herring were on the kitchen counter, all empty.

He lifted the lid of a saucepan, in which there were three new potatoes left. In a frying pan was half a sausage, which someone had bitten off in the middle, perhaps a final nighttime bite.

Sammy sighed and put the lid back on. It reminded him that he had not had any breakfast.

"Shall we wake up Mr. Andersson?"

"I'd like to look around a little in peace and quiet first," said Beatrice.

"You've had breakfast, I'm guessing."

Beatrice ignored his comment.

"Let's take the bedroom first, that's where women hide their secrets," she said.

"Shouldn't we let Morgansson—"

"There's nothing that indicates a crime," said Beatrice.

"But if she was going out with the garbage, why just take one trash bag? It's full of shit here, enough to fill a container."

"She took the worst of it, what smelled bad," said Beatrice.

"I think we should wake up Johnny anyway to get his version," Sammy insisted.

His feeling of discomfort had increased. He didn't like Beatrice's somewhat lecturing tone either.

"If I wake up our snoozing friend, you can look around a little. Then we'll save a little time too."

Beatrice shrugged and went into the bedroom.

The only thing Johnny Andersson had on was a pair of fairly clean underwear. He was lying with one leg stretched out on the couch and the other foot resting on the floor. His hands were clasped on his hairy chest. He was snoring lightly.

Sammy Nilsson observed him a few seconds before he took him by the shoulder and shook.

"Time to wake up!"

Johnny moved restlessly, hiccoughed, but did not wake up.

"Johnny!"

Another shake. No reaction. Sammy bent down over the sleeping man, whose breath defied all description.

"What did you eat yesterday?" Sammy mumbled, and shook the lifeless body again, this time considerably more brusquely.

Johnny Andersson opened his eyes and looked confusedly at the policeman.

"What the hell!"

"Sammy Nilsson, police."

"Huh?"

"You heard me. Sit up, we have to talk a little."

It took several minutes to get a more or less clear picture of what had happened the night before. Johnny was hungover but still capable of giving an account of what had gone on. About a dozen "acquaintances" had celebrated. Ingegerd had won a little money on the lottery, Johnny explained. At midnight most of them disappeared. He himself passed out.

"What the hell are you doing here?" he asked suddenly.

"There's been an accident," said Sammy. "Ingegerd fell on the stairs."

"What do you mean, stairs?"

"She went out with the garbage."

"Typical," said Johnny. "Everything has to be so fucking tidy."

"She fell badly."

"Was it the neighbor lady who complained?"

"Listen up now! Ingegerd fell and struck her head. It was really bad, she's dead."

Johnny stared at the policeman, shook his head, and fumbled for a bottle on the table, but knocked it over.

"Dead?"

Sammy Nilsson nodded.

Johnny stared at the vodka running over the edge of the table and dripping down onto the carpet. He took a glass and captured a few drops, which he knocked back at once. He was ready to repeat the maneuver, but Sammy Nilsson took the glass out of his hand.

"This is not the time to drink," he said gently. "We have to talk a little."

"What the hell, she's dead? Are you sure? What the hell is this?"

He got up suddenly, took a few steps, and stopped in the middle of the room.

"But what do you mean, she's in the bedroom!"

"No, that's my associate Beatrice, whom you met the other day."

"Where's Ingegerd?"

"Sit down, Johnny. There's nothing we can do now. You have to tell me who was here last night and what happened."

"Happened? Nothing happened! I said we were partying. Is that illegal, maybe?"

"Sit down."

Johnny obeyed unexpectedly and sank down in an armchair. He reached out and righted the bottle.

"So where should I go now? Tell me that."

Beatrice came into the living room and observed Johnny Andersson, who raised the empty glass and brought it to his lips, set it down with a surprised expression, as if the very thought that there was no more vodka was incredible.

"Okay, I think it's best if you come along with us, then you can tell us what happened yesterday and who was there. You can't stay here anyway."

"What do you mean, I said we were partying."

"But we have to get that down on paper, as a formality," said Sammy.

"So where will I crash?"

"We have comfortable single rooms," said Beatrice before she disappeared out into the stairwell.

"We'll leave in a few minutes," said Sammy.

✦

Nineteen

Anders Brant was the key, Sammy Nilsson was sure of that. Bosse Gränsberg's violent death was not strange per se. That a homeless person with substance abuse problems was beaten to death was, in the eyes of many, not surprising. Many of the victims, and the perpetrators as well, were in that category.

The only thing that deviated from the pattern was the journalist. They had demonstrably had contact: Brant's fingerprints had been secured in the trailer, and the scrap of paper with the telephone number they found in the murdered man's pocket proved this was not a coincidence.

Sammy Nilsson stood in his office in front of the desk with his hands at his sides, his thinking pose. There was something he had said to Lindell, something that might have significance for his investigation, but he could not remember what it was.

He went over the most recent meetings with Lindell. Recently these had been brief; she seemed to be more than allowably absent at the moment. Was there perhaps something to what Morgansson had hinted, well, maintained actually, that Lindell and Haver were having an affair?

Sammy laughed. That would be something for Ottosson to brood about, a love story at Homicide, with all that would entail.

They had talked about Brant. Lindell asked about the journalist, where he lived, they had very briefly discussed her investigation of Klara Lovisa, but Sammy Nilsson could not find any entry there to his own pondering about the duo Brant–Gränsberg.

He decided to return to Brant's apartment. Maybe the answer was there, something he and Morgansson had overlooked. The papers they found in his apartment and only looked at in passing seemed harmless in this context. From what Sammy Nilsson could understand this was background material and drafts of articles. He feared the day when Brant came back and discovered their trespassing. Journalists were a sensitive breed.

Morgansson had found a handful of fingerprints, but not Bosse

Gränsberg's. None of the others were on file. Nothing they had seen in the small two-room apartment seemed suspicious or could link Brant more closely to the murdered man.

While he was searching for building manager Nilsson's phone number he thought about whether it was necessary to contact the prosecutor, but decided to wait. Knowing Fritzén, he would question whether another visit was appropriate.

Mr. Nilsson was not hard to convince to provide the master key once again, and they agreed to meet outside Brant's apartment half an hour later.

His curiosity was even greater this time. Sammy Nilsson explained the visit by saying that he had probably forgotten his glasses, it was nothing more dramatic than that. The building manager looked skeptical and offered to help with the search, but Sammy declined the offer.

The apartment gave an impression of abandonment, much more tangibly than the other day. Maybe he's left for good, thought Sammy Nilsson, while he made an initial round of the kitchen, bedroom, and living room.

If you were going to leave, what would you definitely not leave behind? He did not see any valuables, the pictures seemed mediocre, a few graphic prints and a couple of posters were what adorned the walls. He let his gaze wander across the apartment, pulled out the drawers in a small dresser in the hall, but like the time before found nothing exciting. He returned to the bedroom, as if driven by a haunted spirit.

Something ought to speak to him! He scanned the spines of the books. Should he leaf through every book? That seemed both dusty and superfluous. Brant was not suspected of any crime. His eyes fell on a framed photo on the bookshelf. He had noted the picture during the previous visit without finding it remarkable, seeing it instead as a memory from the past left out as a reminder.

It depicted a bandy team, fifteen or so young men in club uniform, a couple of coaches, a type of picture Sammy Nilsson had seen often. He himself had a number of such photographs, stored away in some drawer. Maybe that was why he hadn't paid attention to it the last time.

He should have known better. In the everyday objects that fill a person's home is where the story is found.

He took down the photo, studied the faces more closely. He was as good as certain that the third man from the left in the back row was Bo Gränsberg. Diagonally below him, crouching on one knee, must be Anders Brant. It was taken perhaps twenty or twenty-five years ago. The team members radiated a kind of moving innocence, their open, exhilarated faces testified to success, perhaps unexpected. Sammy had both experienced that and seen the rush when the improbable happened on the field, the feeling that did not really take hold, but simply burst forth in an exhilaration reminiscent of the unfathomable euphoria of love.

The two coaches looked guardedly happy, more aware that they were part of a picture that would show up on the sports pages of the local newspaper and decorate the clubhouse and many homes.

Sammy Nilsson knew what happened after the photo session. The players would hug each other, and once again go over the decisive moments in the match just ended. Temporary misses that created irritation and anger would be transformed into jokes and friendly banter. Everyone was a winner today.

He studied the one he believed was Bosse Gränsberg a little more carefully. He had pulled off the mouth guard from one bracket and a scar on his chin shone white.

He picked up the cell phone, dialed information, and asked to be connected to Gunilla Lange.

She answered cautiously, saying her surname. Sammy Nilsson introduced himself.

Yes, Bosse had played bandy for Sirius in his youth, Gunilla recalled, and he got the scar on his chin as a junior. An ice-skate blade that hit his chin.

Who could he talk with, did she recall any coaches or players? Gunilla Lange suggested that he contact Lasse Svensson, the restaurateur, who had been a player and was still active in the club. Gunilla Lange thought maybe he could give him the information he needed. She remembered that Bosse and Lasse said hi when they ran into each other. A few times she and Bosse had also visited one of Svensson's restaurants and exchanged a few words with him there.

Before they ended the call she asked why he was interested in Bosse's bandy friends.

"We're just trying to chart out Bosse's life," Sammy Nilsson answered, thinking that sounded a little peculiar even to him.

"But it's almost twenty years since he stopped playing sports. That can't have anything to do with the murder, can it?"

"Probably not," said Sammy.

He stuck the photo inside the waistband of his pants, pulled his T-shirt over it, and left the apartment. The building manager was standing in the yard, outside the entry.

"Unfortunately, the glasses weren't there," said Sammy. "But they were the cheap kind. I lose a bunch of them every year."

The manager did not look convinced.

"Does this have anything to do with that donna?" he asked. "I mean, that you're running around here all the time."

"What donna?"

The superintendent smiled, judging by appearances very satisfied in having caught the policeman's interest.

"I don't like to pry into people's personal lives," he continued.

Of course you do, thought Sammy, that's why you're a building manager.

"Well, there's no donna involved," he said in an indifferent tone, making an effort to leave. "We just want to exchange a few words with Brant."

The building manager took a step to the side as if to block Sammy's way.

"Is she one of those concealed refugees?"

"I'm in a bit of a hurry," said Sammy.

"She stayed here," said the manager quietly, and now he put on a conspiratorial expression. "A nice-looking lady, there's no doubt about it, curvy and dark, but extremely mysterious."

"I see, and when was this?"

"A month ago. The association would really like to know who—"

"Mysterious, you said."

"Yes, she hardly ever went out."

Sammy sensed that the package of condoms and the pubic hair in Brant's bed now had an explanation.

"I guess they had other things to do," he said.

"Yes, I believe that," said the manager, now noticeably amused by the direction the conversation had taken. "Now I call him the journal-*lust*."

"You have no idea what her name is, this dark beauty?"

"Not the faintest."

"When did she disappear?"

"May seventeenth was the last time I saw her. That's Norway's national day. They went off in Brant's car, and when he came back a few hours later he was alone. Since then I haven't seen a trace of the gal."

The old man is unbelievable, damn it, thought Sammy Nilsson, but with mixed emotions. Mr. Nilsson was certainly a real plague in the condominium association through his uninhibited curiosity, but also a reliable source of information.

"Thanks for now," he said, going around the manager and heading toward the car.

"She was really black and curly haired!" Nilsson shouted after him.

Sammy stopped short and turned around. The manager had an expectant, almost greedy expression on his narrow mouth. Sammy went back and stood quite close to him.

"And that bothers you quite a bit, huh? That she was dark and curly haired? Are only Aryans allowed in your little Nazi association?"

It was like always on sunny days, full of people at the Åkanten Restaurant, which had one of Uppsala's best locations, in the middle of town, right by the Fyris River and the milldam. In the background rose the spires of the cathedral and the roof of Skytteanum could be seen on the other side of St. Erik's square.

Sammy recognized several of the lunch customers, and he stopped to exchange a few words here and there.

"Here on business, or is it hunger that drives you out into town?" asked an old friend from the indoor bandy gang.

"Nah, I'm just going to have a little talk with Lasse Svensson. Have you seen him around?"

"Yeah, he glided by just a minute ago, in a turquoise shirt and silver vest."

"Nice outfit," said Sammy.

Just then he caught sight of the old bandy player, who had been a Swedish champion in the sixties, and now owned a number of restaurants in town. He stood leaning against the iron railing toward the river and was having a discussion with a man Sammy vaguely recognized, a trumpet-playing municipal official whose name he could not recall. Sammy immediately went up to the two, aware as he was that Svensson was considerably more mobile than he ever was on the ice.

"What do you know, hey there, out patrolling?" said Svensson, extending his hand. "Yes, you must know Boris," he continued. "He talks even more than I do."

Sammy Nilsson smiled and nodded at Boris.

"That's not possible," he said. "Excuse me for disturbing—"

"No problem," said Svensson. "Are you here to eat?"

Sammy shook his head.

"There's something I think you can help me with," he said. "Maybe we can step aside a moment, if you have time?"

Svensson led him one flight up, where Hyllan and Guldkanten were, and they sat down on a couple of armchairs.

Sammy took out the picture of the bandy team.

"Sirius," he said, and Svensson immediately reached out and took the photo from his hand.

"I'll be damned," he exclaimed. "A relic from the past. Where did you find it?"

"Do you recognize anyone?"

"What a question! I've played with most of them, even if they're a few years younger. This is the B team, but several of them made the jump up to the A team. Some continued in Oldboys."

Sammy Nilsson guessed that there must be more than ten years between Bosse Gränsberg and Lasse Svensson.

He took out a notepad and pen.

"If we start in the upper right," he said, "that's Ville Lagerström."

Then followed the whole team, with the exception of a couple of players Svensson recognized, but whose names he could not recall.

It was confirmed for Sammy that Bo Gränsberg and Anders Brant played bandy together in the 1980s.

"It's the murder, right? I read about it in the paper, horrible."

Sammy Nilsson found no reason to deny that it was Bosse Gränsberg who was the reason for his curiosity.

"But what does this gang have to do with the murder?"

"Probably nothing," Sammy Nilsson answered. "But we're checking up on everything. Can you tell me a little about the guys in the picture?"

Sammy got biographical information about all of them, some brief, others more exhaustive. Most of them still lived in town.

"Rolle lives in Edsbyn, where he played a few seasons, he met a lady up there. Svenne I don't know, I seem to recall he actually became a cop somewhere in south Sweden. And Patrik, he was a little special, became something in finance in Norway of all places."

"Is there anyone you think might have associated with Bosse later on?"

"Doubtful," said Svensson, after studying the picture awhile. "Bosse went into the construction industry and got married. I've met his wife too, a real looker back in the day. I get the idea that he mostly worked, no time left over for bandy. He was a workhorse even on the court. Never gave up, even if we were way behind."

"This guy," said Sammy and pointed. "Oskarsson?"

"Well, not a buddy of Bosse directly, not off the court, I mean. Oskarsson works at PEAB, some kind of quality guy."

"And Brant?"

Svensson shook his head.

"No, definitely not, he's a journalist, an investigative one. But he was quick, reminded me a little of Alfberg in his skating style, small build too. I actually read something Brant wrote, about Brazil. Do you know I've been there twenty-six times? An amazing country."

"Not too much bandy."

"But soccer."

"Jakobsson then? He looks like a real joker."

"He was too, and still is. He has a gas station, or had, it went broke.

But I don't think he and Bosse had anything to do with each other. Perra has always had a little trouble holding on to his money, but somehow he always lands feet first."

"In contrast to Gränsberg," said Sammy. "Jeremias Kumlin?"

"Became a stock guy, or something, accountant maybe. He eats here sometimes. Works with something in Russia, I think he said. Not Bosse's type. I think Boris knows him, but on the other hand he knows half the city."

They went through the list name by name. Sammy Nilsson took notes. He looked at the list.

"Work," said Svensson, who sensed what Sammy was thinking. "It's like the restaurant, one thing leads to another. You can never relax."

"That's not your thing," said Sammy politely. "Relaxing, I mean. But it's going well, isn't it?"

"Sure," said the restaurateur. "Guldkanten ended up high on White's list."

"What's that?"

"A ranking of restaurants all over the country."

"Congratulations, that must feel good," said Sammy Nilsson. "And thanks for the information. I wish everyone could keep track of things like that. If you can squeeze out the names of those last two, I would be grateful."

He left Åkanten hungry, even though Svensson offered him lunch. He wanted to get back to the police station and his computer. Thirteen names. Among them, Anders Brant.

✦

Twenty

Sammy Nilsson had just logged onto the computer when the phone rang. He picked up the receiver with a sigh. It was Ottosson.

"My office," he said, and hung up.

Sammy Nilsson stared at the receiver in amazement. He had never been summoned to his chief's office in such a brusque manner. Ottosson usually poked his head in and tactfully asked whether you had any time to spare.

Sammy Nilsson suspected what this was about. In pure protest he lingered in front of the computer a few minutes and then slowly took the fifteen steps to Ottosson's lair, actually the smallest office on the unit.

He entered without knocking.

"Well, the staff sergeant is calling."

"Sit down," said Ottosson.

Sammy Nilsson sat down, more curious than worried.

"We've received a complaint," Ottosson began.

He saw himself as a servant of the general public, a somewhat antiquated attitude in the opinion of many of his colleagues, and if there was anything that worried him it was complaints.

"Your namesake, Nilsson, first name Konrad, phoned. According to him you conducted yourself shabbily this morning. He feels offended. And I know how you can be. If a building manager is nice and helps out, you have to adapt. And what were you doing there anyway? Going into the apartment once was borderline official misconduct, that could only be justified if we had indications that Brant was in danger, or something like that. But running there every five minutes doesn't hold up."

Shabbily, thought Sammy, he makes it sound like I defiled the stairway.

Ottosson observed him gloomily, but Sammy could not take him seriously. He understood that he was now expected to give his version of the incident, but a sudden sense of fatigue came over him. He decided to bypass Konrad Nilsson and overlook Ottosson's exaggeration.

"I've found a connection between Brant and Gränsberg," he said.

"I see," said Ottosson. "But you should have spoken with me first, or Fritzén."

"Sure, but I didn't have time. Or rather, I had no desire."

"Desire or not, we should . . ." Ottosson began, but did not complete the sentence.

Nilsson told about the photograph, the connection between Brant and Gränsberg, and his idea of digging further to perhaps find a thread worth tugging on.

Ottosson listened but looked moderately impressed.

"You called him a Nazi."

"He is one," said Sammy.

"He has filed a formal report."

"He can stick it up his ass."

"We may have problems, even more so when Brant comes back. He's a journalist, and if the building manager gets it into his head to rile up the reporter it can get really unpleasant."

"We'll deal with it then, Otto," said Sammy tiredly. "Right now I want to work."

He got up from the chair. Ottosson seemed to want to say something more about the collision of the two Nilssons but in the end only let out a sigh.

"Have you seen Lindell?" he asked.

"No, she's probably at the Savoy."

The Café Savoy was Ann Lindell's retreat when she needed to collect her thoughts. For many of her colleagues it was a completely inconceivable environment for thinking, with families with screaming kids, retirees eagerly conversing, and the rattle of cups and plates.

Freddy Johansson now looked considerably more docile. He smelled of sweat and his gaze wandered between Lindell and her notepad, which she was browsing in a little absentmindedly.

"Let's go over this again," she said. "A witness saw you together with Klara Lovisa walking on the highway at Skärfälten about twelve o'clock on April twenty-eight. You deny it, but will not submit to a lineup. What are you scared of, if it wasn't really you?"

"There's so much bullshit," Freddy mumbled.

"Yes, on your part."

"I wasn't there," he repeated for the fifth time.

Ann Lindell sat quietly a moment. The ceiling light in the interview room flickered and Freddy looked up in fright. His attorney, Gusten Eriksson, coughed.

"I don't think we'll get any further," he said.

Lindell ignored his interjection. She had encountered Eriksson before, and he was not known for being the sharpest.

"I'll give you one more chance," she said. "You can tell me in your own words why the two of you were in Skärfälten. Perhaps there's a very natural explanation, what do I know?"

"My client has—"

"Otherwise I'll hold you on probable cause suspected of kidnapping. And as you understand, the charges can quickly get a lot more serious."

"Now you're pushing it to the breaking point," said the attorney, raising his voice. "You have nothing that connects Fredrik to Skärfälten. Besides, it has not been established that the poor girl really was there."

"Freddy, tell me!"

"I don't know anything," he said.

"Okay," said Lindell. "Then I'll tell you: Your parents own a Volvo, metallic blue, last year's model, right? You borrow it sometimes, you've admitted that. On Saturday the twenty-eighth of April it was towed from Skärfälten, from a bus stop approximately two hundred meters this side of the side road down to Uppsala-Näs. I have the documents from the towing company here," said Lindell, holding up a red plastic folder. "It was towed to Uppland Motors. The problem was electrical, a copy of the garage bill is here too. It was picked up on May second by your dad. Who drove the car to Skärfälten, if not you?"

Fredrik Johansson had been staring down at the floor the whole time. When Lindell fell silent, he gave his lawyer a quick glance before he looked at her.

"I was there," he said hoarsely. "Klovisa and I went for a ride, then there was car trouble. She took off."

"Wait a minute now," Lindell interrupted. "She took off, what do you mean by that? Did she start walking back to town, or what?"

"I don't know, she got tired of waiting."

"She didn't say anything?"

"'I'm splitting,' she said."

"In what direction?"

"I don't remember."

"And you stayed by the car?"

"Yes."

"You were seen on the road toward Uppsala-Näs. How do you explain that?"

"It must have been someone else."

Lindell snorted.

"Pull yourself together, Freddy. You are linked to the scene, we have a credible witness who picked you out among photos of forty different young men. The witness has even described the clothes you had on. Clothes that in all likelihood we are going to find at your house."

"I didn't do anything," Freddy sobbed.

"Perhaps we should break for a while?" Gusten Eriksson interjected, now considerably tamer.

"I don't think so," said Lindell, forging ahead. "You knew it was her birthday. You had, or did have, a relationship, but had not slept with each other. You knew she wanted to wait, and just until her sixteenth birthday. You called her up and suggested a little drive. You wanted to screw Klara Lovisa, or what? Perhaps she said something previously, like 'you'll have to wait.' On Saturday the twenty-eighth of April you didn't want to wait any longer."

Fredrik Johansson was crying.

"Now we'll take a short break in the questioning of Fredrik Johansson," said Lindell. She turned off the tape recorder, got up, and left the room.

Outside the interview room she took a deep breath.

"Klara Lovisa," she mumbled, leaned against the wall, and closed her eyes.

She knew that she could, and would, crack Fredrik Johansson. She would let them wait fifteen minutes and then take apart the last of his lies. Gusten Eriksson would not offer any resistance, now when he understood that his client could be linked to Skärfälten on the day in question. Perhaps he would try to convince Fredrik to present the whole thing as an accident, that they "bickered" as he was always saying, and that he shoved Klara Lovisa and she fell. Something along those lines. Noncriminal homicide, or in the worst case manslaughter, would most likely be the attorney's line.

Lindell's line was homicide. She called Allan Fredriksson, whom she had caught a glimpse of in the corridor, and the new trainee, who might as well be there to listen and learn.

Oskar Nyman came running almost right away, Fredriksson took a few minutes. In the meantime she told the trainee what this was about. He smiled greedily, which she did not like, but she excused him, he was probably tense.

"I see," said Fredriksson, when he came sauntering in.

"Wipe off the grin," said Lindell. "It's not over yet."

"You're such a joker, Ann," said Fredriksson.

"Nice work," said Nyman, imitating one of Sammy Nilsson's favorite expressions. Lindell looked at him with surprise, and then started laughing, presumably for the first time since Brant left her bed.

I'll give him an hour, thought Lindell, when the questioning resumed at 1:22 P.M. Nyman sat down on a wobbly chair by the door. Fredriksson took a seat alongside Lindell. On the other side sat Fredrik Johansson, twenty-two years old and the much older Gusten Eriksson.

Fredrik had been crying and sweating; it smelled musty in the small room. The ceiling fixture flickered again. Lindell took that as a starting signal.

An hour passed without Fredrik Johansson providing a single new piece of information.

"Straighten up now!" said Nyman. "Show us what the hell you're all about!"

This was a totally unexpected intrusion and completely violated what Lindell had advised the trainee: Sit in, but don't say anything.

"Now that's just about enough," said the attorney.

"Sit down, Nyman," said Lindell in a sharp tone, but Nyman did not let himself be stopped.

"Sit here and lie to our faces, what's that like? Monkeyshit, I'd say. It's shameful, damn it!"

Fucking amateur, Lindell was thinking, when Fredrik burst out in a tearful, stammering harangue.

"I don't know why she didn't come back! We were in the hut, we had fun for a while, but she didn't want to, we bickered a little, then I split. I don't know what happened! Do you get that? I liked her."

He fell silent suddenly and stared straight ahead.

Nyman nodded, Lindell could see a hint of a satisfied sneer in his usually rather expressionless face, before he returned to his seat by the door.

Lindell waited until the sobbing subsided before she continued.

"What hut?"

"The old hunting hut, or whatever it is. I don't know."

"Where is it?"

"In Skärfälten."

"Then that was you and Klara Lovisa walking on the road," Fredriksson observed.

Fredrik raised his head and nodded.

"Speak into the microphone," said Nyman.

"Yes," said Fredrik. "It was us."

He looked at Nyman and then at Lindell.

"Was it that old guy on the moped who saw us?"

Lindell nodded.

"Speak into the microphone," said Nyman.

Allan Fredriksson could not keep from smiling a little.

✦

Twenty-one

The door-to-door questioning in the apartment building where Ingegerd Melander broke her neck produced a unison response: On Sunday evening there had been noisy partying and quarreling in Melander's apartment. Several neighbors could testify to loud music, people coming and going, someone had urinated in the bushes in the yard.

"We've complained so many times, you just don't have the energy anymore," said the closest neighbor, Anja Wilson, a woman in her thirties. "Nothing happens."

At eleven thirty things calmed down considerably. Several of the partiers noisily left the apartment. But the music continued until midnight. Soon after that a violent tumult arose.

"It sounded like they were smashing apart the furniture," said the neighbor directly below Melander's apartment.

The police had found a battered chair in Ingegerd's bedroom, that was all. But a chair in the hands of the wrong person can produce a lot of noise, as Beatrice put it.

Then it was quiet.

"Johnny Andersson fell asleep," Sammy Nilsson speculated.

No one heard when Ingegerd fell down the stairs.

"She died immediately in any event."

Beatrice looked at him. They were sitting in the police station cafeteria, discussing Melander's case.

"She didn't have that much alcohol in her body," said Bea.

"Enough for a stumble."

Sammy Nilsson did not want to think about the unfortunate woman. While they waited for the medical examiner's report and the autopsy, Beatrice organized the door-knocking and compiled biographical facts about Ingegerd Melander. There was a sister in Norrköping who had now been informed. She questioned Johnny Andersson again, and in the meantime Sammy had devoted several hours to the thirteen names from the bandy team. During the afternoon the list had expanded to fifteen, when the restaurateur Svensson called and added the remaining two players on the photo.

So far Sammy had not found any sensational information. Five of the bandy players were in the crime registry for minor offences, just as many in the enforcement office's files, one of them was in hospice, dying of cancer, and two had been living abroad for a long time. They had the same address at a resort in the Philippines. Sammy immediately drew the conclusion that they were pedophiles.

The list had been reduced to twelve names. Sammy had managed to contact seven of them. All of them knew that their old teammate had met a violent death. None of them had been in contact with Gränsberg in recent years, in principle since he put his ice skates on the shelf. Sammy fished cautiously about Anders Brant, but had not produced anything substantial.

Now he did not want to sit and speculate about an alcoholic woman's unlucky fall and death, but instead get hold of the remaining five individuals.

"It's typical," Beatrice continued. "The woman dies while she's cleaning house and the man is sleeping off his bender."

Sammy Nilsson sighed.

"What did Johnny say?"

Beatrice reported that he confirmed that they had quarreled, nothing serious according to him, as he had been too drunk. Drunk talk, he called their exchange of words, no physical violence had occurred. The broken chair he explained by saying that Ingegerd barricaded herself in the bedroom and placed the chair against the door to keep Johnny from coming in. "I wanted to cuddle a little," he explained. When he tried to force the door the chair fell into the room and when he entered he stumbled on it, took hold of it in fury and threw it against the wall. There was also a mark on the bedroom wall, approximately at chest height.

"Breaking apart a chair is physical violence, wouldn't you say?" Sammy objected.

He could picture the scene in his mind.

"Yes, but he didn't hit her, just the wall."

"She had a really nasty bruise on her arm and shoulder," said Sammy.

"From the fall on the stairs, Amrén thought."

Jonas Amrén was the medical examiner, whom Sammy had christened "Loose Lips" because he was so uncommunicative.

"It will probably turn out that we put Melander in the files," said Sammy.

"We can't prove a crime was committed," said Beatrice, with a bitter tinge to her voice.

Sammy Nilsson sensed that she suspected that Johnny Andersson assaulted Melander and perhaps flat out pushed her down the stairs, but both knew that at the present time there was nothing that supported such a scenario. There was nothing to run to the prosecutor with.

"When we released Johnny this morning he only talked about Ingegerd Melander's apartment, whether he had a chance to take it over."

"It's a municipal rental unit, isn't it?"

"Of course, Uppsalahem has its own waiting list, but he was carrying on about buying it under the table somehow. Not a word that he was sorry she'd broken her neck."

"He wants to move on with his life," Sammy said casually and got up. "And I have to attend to the teammates."

✦

Twenty-two

Tuesday morning was promising. The sun shone in between the windowsill and blind. Ann Lindell was already awake by five o'clock. I've got to make a longer curtain, she thought, something she'd had in mind since spring.

Perhaps she was wakened by the sunlight, or possibly by the dream, traces of which now lingered in her mind. It had been a real mishmash. Fredrik Johansson, Klara Lovisa, and Anders Brant had been there, as were Sammy Nilsson and Ottosson. It was not a good dream. Eroticism, work, and a desperate sense of loss, of getting too late a start in everything she did, made her wake up sweaty and worried.

"I miss you," she mumbled, pushing off the overly warm covers.

Anders Brant had not been in touch, either by e-mail or SMS. Maybe he was in some kind of trouble and could simply not communicate, but she pushed that unpleasant thought aside.

If it had not been for everything that was hard to explain about Anders's disappearance, it would have been a thoroughly good morning. She was well on her way to cracking the mystery of Klara Lovisa's disappearance. Today would be decisive. She had decided to take Fredrik Johansson to the scene in Skärfälten; he was going to show them the hut. A dog handler would go along. She was certain of finding Klara Lovisa somewhere in the surroundings.

A good day, except for Fredrik who would be arrested for homicide, alternatively manslaughter; she was equally sure of that.

Klara Lovisa's mother had called the day before, just as Lindell was about to leave work to hurry to the preschool. They had not spoken for a while, but Lindell was certain that the rumor that Fredrik Johansson was being questioned had spread among Klara Lovisa's friends and on to her mother as well.

Lindell had not told her everything and definitely not the truth.

Fredrik was being questioned simply because he might have information that was interesting; that was her white lie.

Now when he had been held in jail overnight the rumors would intensify.

Her body wanted to stay in bed. She was far from rested; the turbulence of the past few days had left its mark. A week before she had been unreservedly happy, satisfied, and slightly optimistic. Now the picture was more divided.

But there was also a more prosaic reason that she was dawdling. The dream had made her wet; in the vacillation between dream and waking up she could feel his hands on her body. There was a tingling in her abdomen as she thought back to the Brant of the dream and how he had recently been in her bed.

She drew her hand across her belly, but it felt wrong to touch herself, that would be admitting that Brant was gone for good. Self-stimulation would only mean a return to her former life's meager substitute for real love, so she let her hand rest.

Instead she got out of bed, pulled on the blind so it flew up with a bang, opened the window, and observed the blossoming mock orange bush in the yard. She hoped that a breeze would carry a trace of its aroma to her.

Even though she had not yet showered she pulled on a recently washed T-shirt, just to take in the citrus-scented fabric softener. In the building opposite there were many retired eyes up early, who would enjoy getting a look at a bare-breasted police officer. Here everyone knew who she was. It had attracted some attention when the very first week she was driven home in a marked police car.

The birds were also experiencing a lovely morning. They were going full tilt, broods of baby birds had to be fed. The building manager had set up lots of birdhouses in the lindens on the grounds and on the little back building. Lindell could sometimes see him studying the sparrows and titmice, and whatever else there might be. She thought the caretaker preferred the feathered tenants in the little houses to those in the bigger building.

She was filled with a great sense of calm from standing by the window and observing the rising sun just peeking over the roof of the neighboring building, the persistent yet leisurely and lazy flight of the small birds back and forth, the abundant blossoms and sweet aroma of the mock orange, which reminded her of something from the past, everything combined to help the unpleasantness of the dream subside.

The move had done her good. She was feeling more and more at home in the area. Admittedly the buildings had a somewhat lower standard, but they were more comfortable, the contact between tenants was better, the little yard with two groupings of chairs and a grill invited neighborly interaction.

Erik had grumbled at first but soon adapted and found two new friends at a comfortable distance, one in the adjacent entryway. In the fall he would start school, and Ann had decided to move well in advance of that.

It was not until she was moved in that she realized how ingrown the old apartment had been, ingrown with old thoughts, too many late evenings with too much wine and, not least, memories of Edvard. The new apartment, besides being roomier, felt like a fresh start, and in that connection Anders Brant fit in very well.

A deep sigh and one last sniff to soak up the mock orange, before she went to shower. In fifteen minutes Erik should get up, and he was not a kid who could leap out of bed, quickly wolf down breakfast, and then run off to preschool. He needed plenty of time, first slowly getting dressed, perhaps some quiet play before it was time for a drawn-out breakfast, which he exploited to satisfy his curiosity in the most wide-ranging areas. Many mornings Ann was completely worn out from fending off all his questions. She had never met such an inquisitive person, either adult or child.

The preschool staff testified to the same thing and joked that Erik would be an excellent policeman. Then I'm a bad police officer, Ann thought, because she was not particularly curious and over the years had become less and less interested in her surroundings. Many times she was completely indifferent to her friends' talk about this and that, even about issues that concerned current politics and the world situation. She had become aware of that during the weeks with Brant. She had never seen so many news stories in such a short time as the evenings when Brant visited her.

She showered off the dream sweat with a feeling of confidence. She convinced herself that everything would work out, including the mystery of Klara Lovisa's disappearance, a vacation destination, Erik's starting school, and, not least, her relationship with Anders Brant.

At exactly nine o'clock in the morning four cars rolled onto a small yard, or more precisely a minimally arranged turning area.

Out of the first car stepped Ann Lindell, Allan Fredriksson, and from the backseat a stout uniformed officer named Jarmo Kuusinen, who was keeping track of Fredrik Johansson. In car number two were the technicians Morgansson and Kraag, who had recovered from his illness, with two patrol officers in the backseat. Then came the dog handler Vidar Arleman with his companion Zero. Completing the motorcade was the prosecutor, Sixten Molin, who was leading the preliminary investigation.

It was seven weeks since Klara Lovisa disappeared. Zero let out an unexpected bark and perhaps that expressed everyone's emotions. As with most visits to the scene of a crime, there was tension in the air. During the drive Allan Fredriksson had not said a word about the surroundings. Kuusinen confirmed the myth of their neighbors to the east as a taciturn, rugged breed. No one doubted that Fredrik, who had given Lindell directions in a few words, was nervous. His previous somewhat arrogant attitude had been replaced by a pale slump. He was already sweating and the weather outlook was for 26 to 30 degrees Celsius in eastern Svealand.

Sixten Molin was as usual somewhat slow, both in movement and in speech. He smiled often, a bit too ingratiating, Lindell thought, but for the most part he was a competent professional.

Vidar Arleman also had reason to feel worried. Zero was not his dog. His had died unexpectedly only a week before, and Zero's regular handler was in bed with a fever.

One of the two patrol officers immediately started taking spades out of the trunk, but was stopped by his colleague, and now they were waiting around in the shade of a tree.

Morgansson and Kraag were the only ones who looked somewhat relaxed, taking out their bags at a leisurely pace and surveying the terrain.

Kraag pointed out something that had drawn his attention, Morgansson looked up and laughed. Lindell looked in the direction in which Kraag had pointed but could see nothing other than some birch trees and stacks of wood.

Between the birches a path led in toward an area with lichen-covered flat rocks and marshy depressions in between. Perhaps that's where she's lying, thought Lindell and inspected Fredrik Johansson. He was standing stock-still, with Kuusinen beside him, staring at the hut.

Lindell had a hard time believing this was a hunting cabin. In that case why would it be here? Fredriksson thought it was more likely an old shed for forest workers.

"It's reminiscent of Gränsberg's last residence," he said. "Shall we get going?"

Lindell had deliberately held back so that the young man could calm down a little and get used to the sight of the place, but now she nodded and went up to Fredrik.

"How does it feel?"

"Not good," said Fredrik, and his entire physiognomy underscored his discomfort.

"So this is where the two of you went? You've been here before?"

"With Sis and Mom to pick mushrooms. We parked here and when I got tired of mushrooms I went back to the car. Then I discovered that the hut was unlocked."

"So you thought it would be suitable for a romantic encounter with Klara Lovisa?"

Fredrik nodded.

"No one would see us. Klovisa was . . . she didn't want anyone to find out."

"I understand," said Lindell. "So you came here, it was the end of April, admittedly sunny, but wasn't it a bit chilly in the hut?"

"No, I didn't think so anyway. Although Klovisa thought it was a little disgusting in there."

"Was she happy otherwise? I mean, it was her birthday and all."

"Yes, I think she was happy."

Fredrik sobbed and Kuusinen watched with contempt as he hid his face in his hands.

"You went in," said Lindell, starting to walk at the same time. She nodded toward Kuusinen, who took hold of Fredrik's arm and shoved him forward. In the corner of her eye Lindell saw the prosecutor and Fredriksson trudging along.

They came up to the hut. Lindell took out a plastic glove and carefully opened the door with two fingers. A musty smell struck her.

She stepped up on the flat rock that served as a step, peeked in, and turned toward Fredrik.

"Not exactly a love nest," she said.

Fredrik stared at her blankly.

"You went into the hut and then what happened?"

"We were there and then . . ."

"You started making out, in other words," Kuusinen unexpectedly interrupted in his melodic Finland Swedish.

"And then Klara Lovisa didn't want to anymore, was that it? You said she changed her mind."

Fredrik nodded.

"You also said yesterday that you started to quarrel, what does that mean?"

"She said she wanted to, but then it turned out so wrong. She just wanted to go home."

"But you wanted to?"

He did not answer.

"Did you quarrel? Did you take hold of her, shake her?"

"No, I tried to hug her, but then she hit me."

"You didn't hit back, as a reflex, I mean?"

"I got totally sick of it and just left."

"How long were the two of you here?"

"Maybe fifteen minutes, no more. Then I left. I knew that Klovisa wouldn't change her mind. She's always been super stubborn. I promise, that's what happened!"

"And she stayed here?"

"I don't know."

"You didn't feel lousy?"

"Yes, afterward, but then it was too late."

"Okay," said Lindell, looking at the prosecutor, who shook his head.

"Now you can ride back to the police station, and we're going to do an investigation of the hut. But I think it's good that we've gotten this far. You've been helpful."

Kuusinen made a face that clearly showed what he thought of Fredrik Johansson, took him by the shoulder, and more or less turned him on the spot.

Lindell watched how Kuusinen, Fredrik, and Fredriksson got into the car. Fredriksson made some elaborate maneuvers to wriggle the car out of the yard and it then jolted me out of sight.

Lindell had made an agreement with Sixten Molin to ride with him back to Uppsala.

"What do you think?" she asked.

"It doesn't look promising for our dear Fredrik," said Molin.

"Now we'll let the dogs loose," said Lindell.

"The dogs?"

"Zero, Morgansson, and Kraag," said Lindell.

Vidar Arleman did not need to worry. Zero, who was first allowed to sniff a few of the garments the police had obtained from Klara Lovisa's parents, immediately marked by the door to the hut, even if the dog handler did not believe that Klara Lovisa's scent was still lingering after two months. Zero was not allowed to go into the hut. The technicians wanted to do their work first.

Arleman then led the dog in wider and wider circles around the shed, searched the ground, and then the edge of the forest that surrounded it. In the gap between the birches, where the path disappeared, Zero whimpered and marked toward the path. Arleman knew then that it would go that way. He released the dog, who eagerly bounded away with his nose a centimeter or two over the ground.

Arleman walked slowly after, while the others waited at the start of the path. Thirty meters into the forest Zero stopped suddenly. There the vegetation opened into a glade.

Lindell, who got a flashback to another forest and glade in Rasbo a few years earlier, followed after Arleman. Halfway she turned her head and saw the prosecutor nodding and smiling.

We smile when we find bodies, thought Lindell, because she was sure now that they would find Klara Lovisa.

Zero disappeared behind a thicket, and then the confirmation came with a few short, sharp barks.

At 12:20 P.M. on a numbingly beautiful day in June, Klara Lovisa Bolinder's body was dug up. It was covered by a meter-thick layer of dirt, branches, and moss.

She had been buried lying on her back with her arms along her side. The body was half decomposed. Lindell could not avoid seeing the worms crawling.

But there was no doubt that it was Klara Lovisa, enough of the face was preserved to make identification possible. In addition the clothes tallied with what she had been wearing.

"She was going to buy a spring jacket," said Lindell, who could not hold back the tears.

Arleman had returned with Zero to the car as soon as they started digging, while the others stood gathered around the pit, as if they were at a funeral.

The prosecutor Molin was obviously moved, Kuusinen swore softly, long strings of words that further reinforced his image, while his two colleagues rested with both hands on the spades looking distressed, as if they regretted having contributed to the whole thing. Morgansson slipped up behind Lindell and for a few seconds placed his arm around her shoulders.

Kraag was the only one who was working. With video camera and still camera he documented what had come to be Klara Lovisa's resting place for a few months.

Lindell already realized that something did not add up but was unable to really think about it. Her thoughts were occupied by the gruesome task of telling Klara Lovisa's parents that their daughter had been murdered on her sixteenth birthday and buried in the forest, perhaps after being raped.

She took a final look at the remains of Klara Lovisa, the blonde hair, now soiled by dirt, the thin hands and tongue that poked out and had rotted in many places, giving her face a clown-like expression, as if in death she was sticking her tongue out at them. She had never before experienced anything worse than this. She had an impulse to climb down into the opened grave, pull away the clump of moss that disfigured Klara Lovisa's forehead, arrange, straighten, and wake her to life.

Hatred against the person, or persons, who had done this made her sob, before she collected herself and raised her head. Kuusinen stood on the other side of the pit, framed by multiple stems of a sallow bush. Their eyes met. He had stopped swearing and now looked almost lost.

From the deep forest birdsong was heard. The wind was filtered between the tree trunks, made the branches of the sallow bounce, pleasantly turned a few leaves, brought with it aromas of summer.

I promise you, Klara Lovisa, thought Ann Lindell, that I will . . . Then the words stuck, she became uncertain what she should promise, what she could promise, and what such a promise was worth.

She turned around, aimed for the path, and tried to move intentionally forward toward the car, without sidelong glances and thoughts. She heard the prosecutor following in her tracks.

From her back pocket a peep was heard from her cell phone. Lindell took it out and checked the display, *New message received*. It read: *Little shook up right now. Witness to a murder. May be problems. I'll be in touch. Hugs. Anders.*

Lindell stared at the display.

"Yes, it feels too awful," said Sixten Molin, the prosecutor, who misunderstood her surprise.

"This is so fucking unbelievable!" Lindell exclaimed.

She struck the roof of the car with her hand, had an impulse to toss the cell phone to the ground, stamp on it, eradicate Brant, but instinctively turned around so that Molin would not pick up on the extent of her consternation, which she realized was written all over her face.

The prosecutor was ready to get into the car, but stopped in midmotion and looked at her with surprise.

"How are you? Is something else going on?"

Lindell shook her head with her eyes directed into the forest.

✦

Twenty-three

When the call was over he stood for a long time with the receiver in his hand before it occurred to him to hang up. Through the window he stared unseeing at the back side of the lot, before it slowly took shape: the worn-out swing set that only the neighborhood children used now and then; the apple tree which during the spring, despite the onslaught of canker, blossomed like never before; a pale-green, moss-infested lawn hidden under piles of brush, a pile that was now growing before his eyes, turning into an image of how he understood life.

The day before he had done what Henrietta had been nagging about for several weeks, pruned the hawthorn hedge down to an acceptable level. Now the brush had to be removed. He had no desire, he had no time. He loathed hawthorn, with thorns that poked so infernally and straggly branches that were impossible to load onto the trailer efficiently. He would have to make several trips. Besides, his own trailer was uninspected and he would have to go out and rent one.

We should have planted something besides a hedge, he thought. There were lots of things they should have done differently. We should live somewhere else, not in this shitty country, he sometimes thought.

These thoughts had come and gone recently, but he always pushed them aside as unrealistic. There were so many other things that occupied his time. The morrow would always have to wait, that's how it had felt for several years now. The dreams would have to wait.

There had been too much work, but he couldn't complain, that was what he had foreseen and planned for, understood already when the Wall fell. Then he had been at the SE Bank main office, one of the successful ones, a pup who had now grown into a, well, what? A fighting dog? A clever poodle? Or a tired Saint Bernard?

No, he decided, I'm an experienced hunting dog with a sharp nose, a foxhound.

And things had gone well. The company he started in 1993 established itself as one of the most successful on the Eastern European market. It gave him great satisfaction that he had been right. That he had done the right things in the right order and in the right place, with the right people.

Or were they the right people? He'd had reason to doubt that sometimes, especially after the most recent call from Moscow, or rather from the dacha somewhere south of the Russian capital. Oleg parasitized on the city, but he would never live there again. It was too dirty, too poor, with too many cars, he explained. Jeremias Kumlin suspected that it also reminded him too much of history, of the shame and brutality in his childhood and youth.

At Oleg's country place, originally built for one of the leading Party bigwigs, he could live the life of the oligarch he was to its full extent, unconcerned about the city's noise and filth, the alcoholics, the criminality. Oleg's two sons, pale copies of himself, as if they had never encountered sunlight or real life, were already very much at home in the metropolises of Europe. They had also visited Stockholm and Uppsala, with Jeremias as guide. They even stayed at his house for a few days, accommodated in the recreation room.

Their mother had died in the late nineties, of cancer, Oleg maintained, but Jeremias Kumlin suspected suicide. She had been a Party member and with growing fear and sorrow watched the old society being dismantled, the shock therapy when Russia was to be "modernized." To say the least she was horrified by the violence in Chechnya. The few times they met, Kumlin perceived her as the only honorable person in the family, in all of Moscow actually.

Now Oleg was remarried, to a woman who most resembled a parody of a slightly overweight prostitute, with a large, often poorly made up mouth and bad teeth, almost always a little tipsy, a representative of the new Russian economy.

When Oleg wanted to go somewhere he drove the five hundred meters to his own little landing strip, where he had his private plane. He did not trust any other mode of transportation, especially not Aeroflot.

———

I can't blame anyone or anything, thought Jeremias, as the pile of branches got bigger. Right from the start he understood what RHSKL GAS was all about, but chose to ignore his doubts, because he had immediately seen the potential. Just take those damn abbreviations, a leftover from the Soviet period, long combinations which to Jeremias Kumlin stood out as a symbol of nepotism and corruption. So much could be concealed behind a string of letters.

He had made the right choice, but it was still wrong.

And now that infantile policeman Nilsson! The most peculiar thing was that the police only talked about some photo taken decades ago. Nilsson maintained that he was calling around to all the team members to create an image of the murdered man for himself. He immediately sensed that this was only a pretext, but during the course of the conversation became more and more uncertain whether that was a correct interpretation.

Nilsson had also asked whether he had contact with any of the others on the team. Behind that question Jeremias Kumlin sensed ulterior motives. He had become successful in the East, in part because he was good at reading between the lines. Perhaps the police thought someone on the team had something to do with Gränsberg's death?

When he read about the murder in the newspaper he was terrified at first, but as the days passed and nothing happened his worry went away to some degree. But then came that call. About a twenty-year-old photo!

As if that wasn't enough, Oleg called half an hour later. So damn amateurish to phone! KGB, GRU, or whatever their successors were called, were surely listening in like they did in the Soviet period.

Oleg sounded relaxed as usual, but it had been a long time since Kumlin let himself be fooled, a command was concealed behind the velvety words, and a naked threat. He had assured Oleg that there was no danger.

Jeremias Kumlin was a bit player, admittedly somewhat difficult to replace, but in a pinch, if the least friction or uncertainty about his usefulness were to arise, he would be sacrificed. Kumlin did not doubt that for a moment. Oleg was free of loyalty based on nostalgia and human concern.

He should have known better! And Oleg should have too, but when he explained the arrangement it looked reasonably watertight, and would even provide a little street cred that might be exploited in the future. But now in hindsight Jeremias Kumlin realized that it was idiotic to get involved in the environmental business. There were too many wills, too many political considerations, too many idealists. Oil and gas were one thing; you knew going in that it was greed that set the agenda and guided the course of events. The mechanisms were simple and universal, and those involved were definitely not idealists.

And you could simply shoot the heads off of the journalists who started to question and dig. That had been clearly illustrated in the case of Anna Politkovskaya. She paid with her life, as a warning to others.

In Sweden too there were diggers, who loved to poke around in the shit and point out conditions they found offensive, moralistic jaw-flappers. Not least the one on Swedish Radio, one of those Finnish types, stubborn as a dachshund, wanting to go down every single fox burrow. Kumlin had run into him at a reception in Moscow, arranged by one of the "development funds" rigged by the Ural mafia. Then Kumlin didn't know who he was, he took for granted that he was one of the many consultants or aid guys who were looking out for themselves. They talked for a long time, the Finn revealed an exceptional lack of knowledge, asked such naive questions that Kumlin almost felt sorry for him, so he could show off a little to a mutely listening, obviously impressed beginner.

About six months later he heard the same man in a feature on the news program *Ekot* rattle off facts and figures in his characteristic voice, then not the least bit ignorant or shy. That time it concerned an aid project to Russia where Swedish dairy producers and interest organizations were involved. Money had disappeared, unclear where, the established goals were as distant as at the start, everyone blamed everyone else. Everything, in other words, was one big sour milk soup.

He realized too that he was the one who would have to take all the shit, do the payback, an impossible task that would mean the end. Maybe he would even be brought to trial.

Oleg was safely ensconced in Russia. He could always manipulate his way out, there were many judges and politicians on his payroll, so as usual he would get off without a scratch. In the worst case he might shoot some troublesome official to show who had interpretative preference where business methods were concerned.

Without mercy he would sacrifice Jeremias Kumlin, perhaps with a laugh.

Kumlin would soon be forced to travel to Moscow. But first, and as a necessary prerequisite prior to the trip, he had to figure out the problem with Gränsberg, but how? The whole thing was an improbable story that threatened him like a gigantic pile of brush, whose thorns would penetrate deeply. A pile of brush that was growing bigger by the day.

He cursed himself that he let him in at all. Maybe it was a slumbering remnant of team spirit. On the bandy court Gränsberg had been his direct opposite—big, a little clumsy, but with an enormous work capacity. He had compensated for his not terribly advanced skating with a rare eye for the game.

He himself was the elegant one, small and dainty—"a virtuoso on blades," as one journalist had written—who could take advantage of Gränsberg's exquisitely hit, liberating passes, often halfway across the court, rock-hard along the ice or low throws, right on the blade of the club.

They had talked bandy a few minutes, commented on Sirius's wobbly existence. In contrast to Gränsberg he never went to a match at the Students' athletic field. Then, after a brief silence, as Kumlin realized that Gränsberg had a hard time bringing up his business, it slipped out of Gränsberg that he needed money for a "substantial investment."

He had read about his former teammate in the newspaper, how successful he was, and got the idea that Jeremias could make him a loan, at a proper interest rate of course, he was quick to point out.

There was no accounting for Gränsberg, he didn't present his case in a smooth way, not even in an intelligent way. He blabbed too much, got off on side tracks. Jeremias let him carry on for a while before he declined. From experience he knew the danger of engaging in a discussion, asking questions, and giving advice. No, he turned him down right away, not patronizingly, but firmly.

Gränsberg had taken the response unexpectedly calmly, thanked him for the visit, and went his way. A week later he was standing there again. This time Henrietta was home, Jeremias could hear the sewing machine upstairs, and now he was irritated. No meant no. There was nothing to add. His tone became a little sharper, he wanted to get rid of Gränsberg, did not want Henrietta to hear that they had a visitor, come down, perhaps offer coffee, she was like that, always opening her arms, uncritical.

He asked Gränsberg to wait and went up to his study to get a little cash. It took no more than a few seconds. But when he came back the hall was empty. Gränsberg had disappeared and left the outside door open behind him. Jeremias remained standing with two 500 kronor bills in his hand.

It was not until that evening that he realized what had happened. After a couple of days he e-mailed Oleg and told him. Since then his sleep at night had been ruined, every morning he woke with terror as his first visitor.

And now Bosse was dead.

✦

Twenty-four

"The old man's back!" Sammy Nilsson called out as he passed Lindell's office.

"The old man" could be none other than Eskil Ryde, she figured. She sneered. The situation in the tech squad was troublesome to say the least, with half the force on sick leave, Jakobsson on vacation, and three extensive investigations going on: the murder of Gränsberg, Ingegerd Melander's fall on the stairs, and then Klara Lovisa.

So maybe it was necessary to call in Ryde. Lindell could picture him, muttering, but still flattered. Even more so as Jakobsson, the new boss, was away.

Sammy Nilsson sailed past in the corridor again, this time in the opposite direction.

"Hey, Sammy!" Lindell shouted after him.

She heard him stop, sigh, back up a few steps, and plant himself in the doorway. In one hand he was holding a bundle of papers, while the other was drumming on the doorframe.

"Listen, Sammy, you're such a know-it-all, how long does it take to dig out a meter of earth, let's say one hundred eighty by sixty centimeters?"

"That depends on what it's like, if it's hard packed or not."

Sammy Nilsson had a talent for at least appearing knowledgeable about the most widely divergent subjects. Whether he had any experience of excavation work was highly uncertain, but he liked calculating and showing off, and sure enough he left the doorway, pulled up her visitor's chair, and sat down.

"It was, you know, stones, sticks, and dirt."

"Oh, hell," said Sammy Nilsson. "Allan should have heard that precise description."

"Sure, but it didn't look hard as cement anyway."

"Forty-five minutes, an hour," Sammy said. "If you have a decent spade."

"That was the other thing, we haven't found any tools either."

"Either?"

"The grave was clean of everything, besides a silver neck chain. No wallet or cell phone, the pockets were emptied. No fingerprints, which perhaps was not to be expected, but no other traces either. It was neatly done, if I may say so," Lindell said.

It was as if she wanted to churn through everything one more time, now with Sammy as a sounding board.

"In any case he really exerted herself. Most just shovel a little moss on top and hope for the best. If you bury a body one meter down, the chances are very good that it will rest in peace."

Lindell nodded.

"It's the way he went about it that makes me wonder," she said. "Think about it! Fredrik Johansson has just strangled a young girl, a girl he wanted to have sex with or perhaps even raped. Perhaps to shut her up he strikes her, tries to cover her mouth, she struggles, he takes a choke-hold, pushes her down against the floor. She becomes quiet. He discovers that she's dead. He finds a shovel and—"

"Maybe it's in the shed," Sammy interjected.

"Maybe, but otherwise it's almost spic and span in there, a chair and an old wooden box were the only things, so why would a spade be stand-ing there, waiting to be used? But okay, he takes the spade that's there, or, as I think, he brings along a spade, digs a gigantic hole fifty meters away, carries the body there, and covers it over."

"Well, that's probably what happened," said Sammy Nilsson calmly.

"No," said Lindell. "That's not what happened. Fredrik isn't the type. He would wet his pants, curl up in a corner, and fall apart."

"We've seen stranger things happen."

"We have, but this is too professional, if you get what I mean. Not a single mistake. And even if we accept that Fredrik is that cold and does everything right, it collapses on another matter."

Lindell paused.

"And that is?"

"The timing. We will never get him convicted. Klara Lovisa left home at ten thirty. At eleven thirty Yngve Andersson sees them on the road. That seems credible. Fredrik calls her, picks her up somewhere, and they talk a little in the car, drive off toward Skärfälten, have engine trouble, and decide to walk the final stretch. What happens then we can only guess at. An hour and fifteen minutes later, a quarter to one, the tow truck driver Allen Pettersson gets a call. He keeps a log and for that rea-son he's dead certain of the time. Fifteen minutes later he's there. Then Fredrik Johansson is standing by the car, waiting. He seems completely normal, jokes a little with Pettersson, rides along in the tow truck. Half an hour later the car is at the garage."

Lindell's idea of checking with the towing company had been a long shot. To give her thinking some new impetus, she drove out and took a position along Route 72, watched cars, buses, trucks, and other work vehicles pass in a steady stream. How did Fredrik and Klara Lovisa get to Skärfälten? Bus was one possibility; they could have walked up to the bus stop across from Flogsta, which was about ten minutes from Berthåga and Klara Lovisa's home, but was that likely? Fredrik would certainly want to impress her, he wanted to come cruising up in his dad's car, not bump along on an intercity bus.

The conclusion Lindell drew, standing by the side of the road, was that something had gone wrong with the car, but Fredrik hadn't given up. Lust is a peculiar motivating force, and they started walking toward the hut.

She immediately phoned the trainee, Nyman, who willingly took on the task of making calls to the towing companies. She had no idea how many there were.

"An hour or so," said Sammy, "for some pretty words, protests from Klara Lovisa, strangulation, grave digging, and a walk back to the car. But he may have called the towing company from the shed. He knew it would take a while for the truck to get there."

"In principle, I agree," said Lindell. "But during those seventy-five minutes he and Klara Lovisa have to walk the last stretch up to the shed too. I timed it from the place where Yngve Andersson saw them. It took thirteen minutes at a pretty good pace. His attorney is going to pulverize the timetable."

"You think someone else dug her grave?"

Lindell nodded.

"And the court is going to believe that, if the defense plays its cards right."

"How did he come up with the idea of taking her there?"

"He'd been near there picking mushrooms with his mom. The shed looks like it's been there a long time. From what I understand it was not the first time he'd taken a girl there either."

"So you don't think he's guilty of the murder?"

"Guilty of having dragged her there, but perhaps not of homicide."

"Who?"

"Don't you suppose I've racked my brain about that?" said Lindell.

"Three alternatives," said Sammy. "One," he said, holding up his index finger. "Freddy returned later. Two"—another finger in the air—"some local talent runs into Klara Lovisa and strangles her. And three, a third person comes to the shed after Fredrik left, ends her life, and digs the grave in peace and quiet."

"I've been thinking along those lines too," said Lindell, studying Sammy's way of holding up three fingers, thumb, middle finger, and index finger, making it look like an obscene gesture.

"The third man," said Sammy with a smile, and started whistling, but fell silent when he saw Lindell's tormented expression.

Sammy Nilsson raised the bundle of papers in a knowing gesture, making an effort to get up, but sat back down on the chair at once.

"Are there any houses in the vicinity, where Fredrik or someone else could have retrieved a spade?"

"Five houses within three hundred meters, including Yngve Andersson's," Lindell replied. "I've asked Nyman to collect all the shovels and spades from those places. He's a farm boy so that suits him well."

"I heard he was there when you questioned Fredrik," said Sammy Nilsson.

"So someone spilled the beans," Lindell noted with a tired smile. "Well, shock tactics in a broad country dialect can frighten even the toughest guy."

"So now Ryde gets fifty spades to look at?"

Lindell nodded absentmindedly. Sammy Nilsson got up; he realized that in her thoughts she was already on her way somewhere else. She had that thoughtful, clairvoyant expression that had marked her the past week, and he wondered whether there was anything to Morgansson's speculations about an affair between her and Haver. The rumor that Haver was getting a divorce was already going around the building. He had evidently talked with Beatrice, apologized to her, and then asked Ottosson for a few days off to bring some order on the home front.

Haver had not said a word about divorce, but everyone assumed that was the reason for his accelerating dissatisfaction recently. He could "work from home," was Ottosson's extremely generous proposal, and they agreed that Haver would continue to investigate where Anders Brant had gone, whether he was in Spain or had traveled on from there.

Contacts were made with Interpol and the police at the Madrid airport, but producing passenger lists from all the various airlines proved more difficult than Haver could have imagined. But the Spanish machinery was in motion, as Ottosson put it at a meeting.

Sammy Nilsson observed Lindell. Had she lost weight? In any event she looked pale and tired, and Sammy did not believe that Klara Lovisa's death was the sole reason. He considered asking what was up with her, but Lindell anticipated him.

"Sammy, will you stay a moment," she said, gesturing toward the chair he had just got up from.

Something in her voice, but above all the worried expression, her entire posture, made him immediately close the door and sit down again.

She looked inquisitively at him; Sammy Nilsson got the impression that she was assessing him. Was he a suitable audience for what she obviously now had to get off her chest? She lowered her eyes, moving her hands mechanically over the papers in front of her, as if she was trying to put order into the mess, before she braced herself.

"I've not been completely honest," she began, and Sammy Nilsson feared the worst. The last thing he wanted was a soap opera at the unit, with all that would entail. Then she spoke uninterruptedly for ten minutes, gave the background and told how the story between her and Brant had developed, that on Tuesday, the morning after the murder of Gränsberg, he disappeared without saying where he was going and how she then tried in vain to locate him, to get some sign of life, before finally receiving the peculiar—to say the least—message on the cell phone.

"Witness to a murder?" Sammy Nilsson exclaimed. "And he just takes off?"

"Yes, it's completely improbable! And the man I've had with me at my home each and every night, having sex!"

He looked at her with surprise.

"'May be problems,' that flipping idiot wrote. Yes, it's clear there's a problem!"

"Take it easy," said Sammy Nilsson, who had never seen Lindell so off balance. "There must be a reasonable explanation."

"I thought so too," said Lindell. "But why didn't he tell me, instead of taking off as if he were guilty?"

"Maybe he is guilty," said Sammy Nilsson calmly.

Lindell stared at him.

"He knew Gränsberg over twenty years ago, they played bandy together, they have demonstrably had contact—the notebook in the shed, Brant's prints on the window, and Gränsberg's prints in the Toyota."

Lindell closed her eyes.

"What should I do?" she mumbled desperately.

Sammy Nilsson realized that it was not worth saying that she should have put her cards on the table from the start.

"Talk with Otto," he said.

"He'll never trust me again!"

"There's no other way. If you drag it out even longer, it will be ten times worse."

Lindell nodded, as if she already understood the simple fact that a lie creates new lies, until the abscess one day mercilessly bursts.

"I've texted him again," said Lindell, and now there was only resigned fatigue in her voice. "I wrote that he's in a bad way, that he must make contact, preferably come home. I don't get what he's thinking, he knows I'm a police officer. Can you understand?"

"Talk with Otto," Sammy Nilsson repeated, who did not want Lindell to keep speculating about what had happened.

"I'll give him another twenty-four hours," said Lindell.

He looked at her with an expression as if she were an alcoholic who for the fifty-eleventh time pronounced a solemn vow of total abstinence.

"Don't doubt me! Support me instead. There's a lot at stake, don't you get that?"

"Sure," said Sammy Nilsson, "I get it. This is about the murder of Bosse Gränsberg, among other things."

"I know! You don't need to point that out!" said Lindell with an aggressiveness that surprised herself.

"You had a good thing going," Sammy Nilsson observed more than asked, and he was thinking about Brant's apartment and what they found in his bed and the open package of condoms. Lindell's hair color was light, while the strands of hair they found were really dark. He was happy that Lindell was not directly involved in the case and hoped she would never need to read the report from the technicians. But there was an obvious risk that she would find out about it.

Lindell nodded. She was reluctant to say how many hopes she had already associated with this man.

Ann Lindell was not one to talk about her private life at work, which also led to recurring speculations about what was really going on, but Sammy Nilsson was close to her. Behind his roguish image there was seriousness and wisdom, she knew that.

"There are lots of things I'd like to tell you, but we don't have time," she said at last. "It would be too long a story."

"The story of your life?"

Lindell nodded again. She was on the verge of tears.

Sammy Nilsson again made a move to get up and at the same time dropped the bundle of papers, which flew out like a fan across the floor. He swore, got down on his knees to sort the printouts and pick them up in the right order.

Lindell sensed he was doing this out of consideration for her situation; he wanted to give her time to collect herself.

"How's it going for you and Melander on the stairs?"

"It's mostly Bea who's working on that," said Sammy Nilsson from the floor, with his back toward her. "I'm working on the bandy crew. I've talked with all of them except two."

"Is that producing anything?"

"Not much, but it feels good to be dealing with them. The picture of Gränsberg is getting filled out a little more too."

He got up, tidied the bundle, and smiled at Lindell, who smiled back.

She felt relief. Someone knew her secret anyway. Now it was a matter of gathering even more courage and telling Ottosson.

"One thing is peculiar. In the trash bag there was a kitchen towel with Melander's blood on it. One theory is that during the evening she got a smack from Johnny, wiped it off and put the towel in the trash, and later went out to throw away the bag. But how credible does that seem? Get a beating and then clean up?"

"You know how people are," said Lindell. "There's no logic, or there is, it just looks different. She obviously had no intention of throwing the guy out, calling us or the women's crisis center, she just wanted to tidy up. And this is an injury that isn't possible to distinguish from the injuries she got in the fall, you think?"

"The doctor can't see anything that links Johnny to an assault. She evidently tumbled several turns on the stairs, even ruptured her spleen. Johnny admits he threw a chair, but that it didn't hit Melander, just the bedroom wall."

"Question him again," Lindell said.

"We will, but no one really knows where he is. Maybe it was stupid to release him so soon, but we don't really have anything on him. His buddies maintain that he has a lair somewhere but no one knows where it is, or else they don't want to snitch on him. In my opinion Johnny's a bit of a petty thief and maybe a fence."

"What a mess," said Lindell, sighing.

"It reeks," said Sammy Nilsson, leaning over and giving her a pat on the cheek, before he left the office.

✦

Twenty-five

He read the new SMS with growing disbelief. *What were u doing w Bo Gränsberg? Where & when was the murder, who?? Contact me now, return to Sweden! Don't u see how bad this looks for u otherwise? & me! So far I've kept quiet about us. Do u have something to hide? I don't want to believe that. Ann.*

It exuded desperation and confusion. How did she know about his collaboration with Gränsberg? Had he done something crazy and tried to get out of it by putting the blame on someone else? But that was not like him.

Brant had been on good terms with Bosse ever since their bandy days. There were those who found him a bit too reserved, but Brant discovered that when the taciturn Gränsberg finally expressed an opinion, it was often well thought out. He reminded him more than a little of a man Brant had worked with in the Africa Groups of Sweden; besides being a man of few words and a construction worker, like Gränsberg he possessed an unfailing capacity to see through rhetoric. Perhaps this was because they were listeners more than talkers, they didn't fill time and space with unfiltered chatter, didn't drown in their own words, but focused instead on assessing the speechifying of others.

This was a quality in short supply in the various solidarity groups in which Anders Brant had been active, and he envied Gränsberg his sparse but precise comments about the verbal pirouettes of politicians and corporate leaders. There was no dissimulation with Gränsberg. He was a leftist in an unaffected way—that too was in short supply—a perception that Brant understood had its background in Gränsberg's upbringing and experiences from the world of work.

Brant was then living with a woman, Gunilla Tidlund, who worked with Bosse's wife. The two Gunillas were good friends and they socialized a fair amount.

One summer in the early 1990s they rented a house together in the archipelago for a few weeks. This was the time of the banking crisis, wage freezes, the rampages of the Laser Man, and not least the growth of New Democracy, the anti-immigrant party that won seats in Parliament under the leadership of an aristocrat and a pop music impresario.

Bosse figuratively disrobed the party leaders, and, after a couple of drinks on the veranda facing Kanholmsfjärden, could also do a clever imitation of Ian and Bert, both their body language and the racist spewing they so tactlessly provided the world of politics.

When their sports days were over, and Brant's travels really took off with long stays abroad, the contact between them diminished. They might run into each other in town, exchange a few words, but no more than that.

When they came in contact again over the past winter Gränsberg was in poor condition, basically living day to day and usually on the street. The scattered under-the-table jobs he could get were not enough to reestablish his self-esteem or build up his finances and an acceptable life in a lasting way.

For a few months Brant had used Gränsberg as an informant. The former scaffolder was now more talkative, and his analysis was no longer as sharp and penetrating. He communicated his experience of life as a homeless person with barely concealed bitterness.

Brant could not really take his idea of a construction services firm seriously, and even less so after Bosse presented his plan for financing it, a proposal for "mutual benefit." Brant had to smile when he heard him lay out his plan and entice him with a diplomatic phrase that sounded foreign in the context, as if he was talking about an audacious but completely innocent business deal.

Brant had been tempted by the idea, but rejected it almost immediately. But that moment while he considered the proposal, the brief hesitation that arose most likely because it came so unexpectedly, had been enough for Gränsberg. He continued to be in touch, nagging about how foolproof the arrangement was.

At last Brant had to put his foot down. The last time they met was in Gränsberg's temporary home, which he chose to call the job site trailer. Once again he took out the documents and tried to convince him. Brant then made it clear that he had never paid for information and would not do so this time either. Gränsberg evidently realized that this was the last word and gathered up the papers, carelessly pushed them together, and stowed them away again.

Then he started crying, uncontrollable weeping that made his body shake, and the sweat that broke out on his forehead underscored the impression of a fever attack.

Brant thought it was strange to watch the burly construction worker fall apart so completely before his eyes; it was as though he became several sizes smaller.

Brant was embarrassed, a little ashamed on Gränsberg's behalf, but tried to calm him down, even went around the table and placed his arm around his shoulders, but Gränsberg was inconsolable. This unexpected reaction shook Brant; the former teammate had always seemed solid. Now he was crying like an abandoned child.

Finally Brant had to leave. By then Gränsberg had calmed down somewhat, but sat silently with a hollow gaze and his arms stretched across the table.

He felt like a deserter, even though he did not doubt the rightness of his decision for a second. During the drive home he thought about other ways to support the unfortunate man, who clearly had pinned such great hopes on their renewed contact. But he had no solutions, and to be honest, he firmly doubted the project Gränsberg so enthusiastically sketched and attached such hopes to. "This means my life," he repeated several times.

There were also few people who could imagine investing money in a homeless person. Judging by appearances his ex-wife was an exception. Gränsberg mentioned being in contact with several banks, but had been rejected at an early stage.

Now it looked like he was in trouble with the police. And then mentioned his name! And in a context that evidently put him in a bad light, judging by the wording of the message. What was it that looked so bad? And returning to Sweden for that reason seemed terrible, to say the least.

When the initial surprise had abated, his irritation grew, not to mention his anger, at the tone of the message. Wasn't she capable of seeing through an alcoholic homeless person's fantasies and assertions? Did she really believe he was a corrupt journalist who let himself be bought and sold by anyone?

And then the aside that it looked bad for her too! As if, on the basis of loose talk, maybe Gränsberg had even had a relapse and gone on a bender, she would be soiled by the fact that the two of them had a relationship for a few weeks?

She did not want to believe he had anything to hide, but apparently she did. Anders Brant felt humiliated both as a professional and as a person, and that was a feeling he always struggled with. He was touchy, and he knew it, but had transformed that into a virtue, into fuel that could be used to take down an opponent without any scruples. But he never became irritable or sarcastic. In debates and in opinion pieces he displayed a reasonable tone that could be taken for wisdom and reflection. He would polish an article for days to bring out the apparently casual tone that marked his style. Razor sharp but light as a feather, sometimes almost forgiving, as if by charity he tossed off a few lines for the purpose of correcting an antagonist who had gone astray.

Deep inside however he was often furious, seldom forgot an injustice, and could strike back years after a superficially harmless discussion.

In that state of mind he sent an SMS. About the "experience" he did not write a word. Her interest in where, when, and who seemed completely sick in police terms, an occupational injury. She did not say a word about his troubles, not a word of encouragement. For her, murder was probably everyday fare.

Ever since his return from Itaberaba Anders Brant had been feverishly active, but without really getting anything accomplished. He could not find the peace of mind to write, and he cancelled two interviews he had previously scheduled with great difficulty. The most important one was with the provincial governor, a hard prey to catch, which he now voluntarily released.

The agrofuel article, commissioned by *Aftonbladet,* about which they had sent an inquiring e-mail just the day before, was half finished. He poked at it anyway but it would take a few more hours of work to put it into respectable shape, normally an easy match, but now he experienced it as a labor of Sisyphus.

He understood full well the source of his uneasiness. He had witnessed the murder of a homeless person, but had done nothing that might bring justice. He could have contacted the police, he was a credible witness, without personal interest either in the victim or the perpetrator. But he had not lifted a finger.

A homeless man who killed another homeless person, representatives of a group he had written about, collected solid material about in four countries, material that was meant to be compiled into a book.

It felt like a loss. As if the most impoverished killed each other while the injustices remained and increased. He had no illusions, because he had seen far too much irrationality, ignorance, and division among the oppressed and marginalized to be surprised. But that the wrath was so conspicuously directed inward and not against those who created the misery, made him deeply depressed.

On the personal level he had lulled a woman into false hopes, perhaps himself too, and then coarsely betrayed her. Vanessa was a good woman, he sensed that as soon as they met, a perception that only grew. She would have done him good, perhaps he could have been good for her too. They had all the prerequisites, he knew that. Yet he had gone his way. That he now left her in the lurch was a double betrayal besides, against her personally but also against the arrangement that he, colored by political opinions, supported more generally. He thought he betrayed the Brazil he loved when he left Itaberaba. It was an overwrought attitude; sure, love has other conditions than the economic world order, but still the feeling persisted that he seemed to have lost something fundamental, a foundation that crumbled and fell apart.

He felt more uncertain and experienced that he could not assert his opinion with the same precision and force. That was why the articles and interviews were on hold, he realized that. He was talking about the big picture, about the masses, to use an antiquated expression, but betrayed with premeditation a woman from this mass, a woman who without reservation had taken care of him.

His foundations were shaken. Depression, miscalculations, and dissatisfaction were not unusual, but this worry, downright existential anxiety, was new. His self-image had taken a serious blow.

And now, the icing on the cake, Ann's desperate message.

Who was she? A police detective, certainly competent, mother of a bright boy, a woman who clearly had not had it easy on the personal level, who mentioned something about a couple of relationships relatively long ago.

Improbably enough she had connected with him, the journalist with a left-wing past, who saw the police department as a tool not only for maintenance of order on streets and squares and within the home, but also as a guarantor of the continued existence of the economic order, or rather disorder.

In the 1960s and 1970s there was talk about the apparatus of violence, and the police could easily be placed there. Police were brought in against demonstrators, to club them down and then take them to jail because they were "disturbing traffic."

Those who questioned the arrangement had also been monitored during all periods, with their rights taken away by the secret police. Many cases were documented where irreproachable citizens lost positions and career opportunities due to a notation that labeled them as security risks. Perhaps because they participated in a summer camp arranged by a party on the left wing, or for a time subscribed to a certain periodical.

It was not hard for a left-wing sympathizer or even for a rights-conscious liberal to find evidence that the police were just such an apparatus for the maintenance of disorder.

In that machinery Ann Lindell was a cog.

He had fallen in love with that woman and for a few hectic weeks experienced great happiness. For that woman he had betrayed Vanessa.

"A pig," he shouted, sitting in the kitchen, which had become his retreat when the noise from the street and the view from the living room, where he did his writing, constantly reminded him of the murder.

He reached for a sheet of paper, chose with care from the jar of pens, and at last picked a red felt-tip pen. He usually used it to mark galley errors and changes in his articles. The easy, even flow of the pen, the distinct lines formed by the tip—size 0.3—and the sharp color, all contributed to a feeling of security and well-being.

With it he would now right himself. That he chose to write by hand and not on the computer felt appropriate. This was not a feature story or an opinion piece, but something very different, which would be brought forth in red, sharp style. What exactly remained to be seen.

He had, for his generation, unusually beautiful handwriting, and the introduction also turned out, according to what he spontaneously thought, if not beautiful, then promising anyway.

For an hour he sat hunched over the table, writing, virtually uninterrupted, before he took a short break to peel and cut up a mango, mixing the beautiful yellow fruit with the insides of a passion fruit and a couple of strands of flowing honey, his usual snack. This too was a routine.

He ate with good appetite and a newfound sense of well-being, while he skimmed what he had come up with, careful not to soil the blindingly white sheet with the red text in the strangely exquisite handwriting, and continued.

Sometimes he looked up. The sun that shone in through the open window moved gradually and bit by bit mercilessly revealed the untidy kitchen—the soiled counter, with an unwashed cutting board, stains on the floor, piles of dishes that threatened to overflow the sink, the drain covered with grains of rice, fruit peels and coffee grounds—and that created a rising discomfort, this messiness and dirt. He was also less focused, his handwriting deteriorated and likewise his prose.

When the sun reached the refrigerator, a snorting contraption that had been there all these years, and which worked more like a freezer, even though the control was turned down to a minimum, he chose to stop.

He carefully screwed the cap on the pen, childishly satisfied that he had chosen this very one, got up, went out into the living room, and up to the window, now better equipped to meet the sight of the wall where the drama, which had such a disastrous finale, had taken place.

The scene was calm; not a person was to be seen. A few garments on a line were all that indicated that there were people in this ruin.

The main street was also relatively quiet, an occasional bus came careening at full speed, braked abruptly at the stop, and then puffed away again. The fruit seller with his small business, squeezed up against a wall on the sidewalk, stood peering down the street; it looked like he was waiting for a particular customer.

The alley below was deserted. The white flecks of paint on the stone pavement had changed hue, but Brant did not want to believe that it was blood from the murdered man that made the paint darken.

A woman came walking up from the buildings at the top of the alley. He followed her with his eyes. The next woman who goes by, he thought, if the next woman who passes by has a white garment on, I'll go back to Itaberaba and Vanessa. That's how it will be, chance will have to decide, all the wisdom from his writing at the kitchen table fell away, and he was unexpectedly captivated by this idiotic thought experiment.

Now the chance, or risk, was great that the next person would be wearing a white garment. He glanced down toward the main street and could see that white overwhelmingly predominated.

Should I pick a different color, he wondered, but realized that he could not change colors. That was a whim, playing with the irrational, but once the thought had been formulated the whole thing suddenly became serious. Here and now my future will be decided, he thought, captured by the contingencies and excitement of chance.

Suddenly he thought he glimpsed a movement in the alley, but it was only a dog poking its nose in a pile of trash.

He waited; two, then three minutes passed. No one came by. It started more and more to resemble a drawn-out torture, he recalled all the contradictory thoughts that had darted through his brain the past few days. If he did return to Itaberaba, would Vanessa really take him in after having been so humiliated? Did he love Ann? What was it about her really that captivated him so? Could he ever live together with a police detective?

He leaned his forehead against the frame that surrounded the window, closed his eyes, and inhaled deeply.

He started sweating, more and more tormented. Why, why did I get this stupid idea? He hardly dared look down at the alley anymore. With each second his game stood out as a threat.

At last he gathered his courage and looked out at the whole extent of the alley in a single sweeping motion, then yielded, and took a few steps away from the window.

"Now I'll never know," he murmured, filled with a strange mixture of relief and self-contempt.

✦

Twenty-six

Four digging tools of various types, snow shovels included, were the average holdings of the five properties that Fredriksson and Nyman visited.

The first question they asked was whether any of the property owners thought they were missing any tools. Everyone understood the seriousness of the question. The news had quickly spread that the young girl who had been written about so much in the papers during the spring had been found in the area.

Sheds and outbuildings were inspected, all unlocked, the police noted, but no one thought they were missing anything.

While Nyman labeled and packed the tools in garbage bags they had brought along, a task that he performed with great zeal and with an enthusiasm that only a trainee can demonstrate, Fredriksson questioned the residents.

They reminded him of the three monkeys, Fredriksson said later, none of them had seen or heard anything, and none of them was particularly communicative. All of them were obviously sorry about the young girl's tragic fate, but it was as though they thought it was a bad thing that the murder took place within their own domain.

"Did it really have to happen right here?" was an opinion that one of the villa owners expressed.

Another thought that now property prices would surely go down.

"Who wants to live where there's been a murder?"

"The rate isn't all that high," Fredriksson objected, but the woman he was speaking with maintained with emphasis that "one thing leads to another."

Nyman, who overheard the conversation, snorted and got a sharp look from the woman.

"You don't know anything about the real world," she said, turning her back to the two policemen.

The forensic investigation of the tools produced nothing. True, there was organic material on several of the spades, but nothing that could be directly linked to the discovery site. A concrete shovel had dark stains on the blade, but that turned out to be paint.

"If the murderer were so ice cold that he stole a spade and then returned it, he was certainly careful to remove all traces," Nyman said sententiously, when together with Fredriksson he visited the tech squad. Eskil Ryde reported on the lack of anything substantial, and Nyman added something about waste of work time.

Fredriksson recalled a different tune when they were collecting the tools, but chose not to comment, aware that the old technician would surely take care of that.

"You don't know squat, not about police work anyway," said Ryde with such sharpness in his voice that Nyman thought better about making a reply.

Instead, his face turning beet red, he turned and left.

"Which fucking quota did he come in on?" Ryde asked.

Fredriksson shrugged his shoulders.

"We had a Nyman before, and he didn't last long, do you remember?"

Fredriksson remembered. Through his work on the vice squad, Nyman the First had come in contact with an escort service that supplied young women as dinner companions as well as for more physical activities. That Nyman chose to close his eyes, and for his silence was offered services that he eagerly took advantage of. This went on for a few years before the whole thing was uncovered. Nyman was encouraged to resign, but the case was kept quiet, even though a young journalist at *Upsala Nya Tidning* was on the trail of the "prostitution affair."

There was whispering that the whole thing was too sensitive, as several bigwigs within the academic administration also made use of the services, not personally, but by supplying suitable telephone numbers to foreign guest lecturers, among others, in one case to a Nobel Prize winner unusually active for his age.

Whether all this was true neither Ryde nor Fredriksson knew, but they devoted a minute or two to it.

"But we have found something else," said Ryde. "As you recall, there was a chair in the hut. The veneer on the back of the chair was cracked and there was a red thread stuck to it. I don't know if this has anything to do with the case, but it's the only foreign thing we've been able to find. Do you want to see it?"

Ryde took Fredriksson to Johannesson's office, picked up a plastic bag from the desk, and held it out. Fredriksson viewed the thin thread.

"Cotton," said Ryde. "Seven centimeters long. And it doesn't come from the girl's clothing."

Fredriksson sighed. He realized that a thin thread was not much to go on, but did not want to disappoint Ryde. Because even though the technician was an experienced policeman, he often showed unbridled enthusiasm where the possibility of moving forward in an investigation was concerned, primarily if the basis was a detail that the tech squad had fished up.

"Nice," said Fredriksson. "Now it's just a matter of finding the rest of the garment."

Ryde carelessly tossed the bag back on the desk.

"Of course you will," he said and smiled.

"Okay, Eskil, I'll send Nyman up. He gets to escort the spades back." Fredriksson concluded his visit to the tech squad and left a contented Ryde.

Fredriksson returned to his office. Despite the light tone in the gossip with Ryde, when he experienced how much the grumpy old technician really meant to the squad, he was depressed. He felt worn out and confused. He took the resolution of the mystery of Klara Lovisa's disappearance very much to heart.

She had probably been raped. The autopsy could not provide any unambiguous answer but the doctor had expressed it in terms such as "this mostly indicates that" and "one could probably consider." The body had shown injuries that "with great probability" could not be explained other than by assault, but such weak statements could not be used in a possible future trial.

It was bad enough that Klara Lovisa had been found murdered, but the results of the autopsy further darkened the mood.

Fredriksson longed to go home, or rather to the forest. Almost every day he took a long walk along an old logging area, which had good prerequisites for developing into a first-class raspberry patch, followed a ditch toward a marsh, rounded the wet hollows, and then returned home. It usually took half an hour. He noted the daily changes in nature, let himself be intoxicated by the aroma of myrtle. He talked to himself, because his wife was completely uninterested in trudging around in the woods and deep down Fredriksson was happy about that. Here he could be in peace and feel calm.

But the past few weeks it was becoming harder and harder to find that calm. He experienced what all the others also expressed in various ways: It was too much.

He forced himself to focus for a while on the two investigations in which he was involved, Gränsberg and Klara Lovisa. Simply the fact of needing to divide himself was depressing, but with the current personnel situation it was necessary.

It went fine for a few minutes.

Then he chose the forest.

✦

Twenty-seven

"You were looking for me?"

The voice was nasal and light, in contrast to the intense background noise on the phone, like a massive carpet of sound from a busy highway or perhaps a noisy industrial environment.

"And who is this?"

"Håkan Malmberg."

She searched her memory and remembered before the pause was too long. Malmberg was Klara Lovisa's coach. She had tried to find him for a few days, but since then had not given it much thought.

"Exactly. Thanks for returning my call."

"I'm on vacation and don't check my messages very often," said Malmberg, as if to forestall her question of why he had waited to get in touch with her.

"It's okay," said Lindell. "Where are you now?"

"Värmland. What's this about?"

"Klara Lovisa. You were her soccer coach."

"I know that," said Malmberg. "Who have you arrested?"

"What do you mean?"

"I saw on Text-TV that you found the murderer."

"We have arrested someone, yes," Lindell answered evasively.

"So who is it?"

Lindell did not reply; he ought to realize that she couldn't mention any names. She was the one who was asking a few questions instead.

Håkan Malmberg maintained that he had not seen Klara Lovisa

since her departure from the team, only caught sight of her in town on a few occasions. His statements were careful, but below the doctored summary Lindell could detect his irritation, or how he, in September the year before, had become really indignant.

"It was in the middle of tournament play, and Klovisa was a real cog," the coach asserted. "It didn't feel right at all that she just packed up and left."

He could not give any reasonable explanation for her unexpected defection, but was not particularly surprised. At that age many players suddenly gave up sports.

At last Lindell asked the question about what relationship Fredrik Johansson and Klara Lovisa had.

"Is it him? The hell you say! That fucking weasel."

"What do you mean?"

"I couldn't deal with him, he was sick in the head, and not especially good either. And then his godawful staring at the girls on the team. He was . . ."

The continuation drowned in the noise that surrounded Malmberg. Lindell thought it sounded like a whole convoy of trucks passing. She suggested that he should move to a quieter place.

"My battery is low," Malmberg asserted.

"When are you coming to Uppsala?" Lindell shouted.

"In a few days," came the garbled response.

"Call me then!"

"Okay," said Malmberg and ended the call.

Lindell set her phone down on the shelf next to the window. When the call from Malmberg came she had been staring out the window. The heat of the past few days had built up for a proper discharge and now it was pouring down with tropical intensity. The heavy raindrops pattered against the window and the rumbling from the thunderstorm that was first visible as a dark front toward the west was coming closer and closer.

The rain transported her in time and space, to the backyard in the house in Ödeshög, with the rain pouring over her naked body. Her mother stood in the patio door yelling that she would catch pneumonia but Ann could not hear in the thunder, or did not want to hear. She turned her back, shut her eyes and ears, closed everything out, and extended her arms to the sky.

She was seven years old. In the fall she would be starting school. It was a trivial memory, but her earliest one. Many people could recount experiences at an early age in detail, but this storm, the feeling of the rain that whipped her goose-pimply skin and how she felt herself being transformed, was her first real recollection from childhood.

There were other fragments, but the storm of that summer day was her first coherent memory, where she could recall that she had a thought of her own. There was also defiance. Her mother was powerless, she did not want to go out in the pouring rain. Ann was only five meters away, but inaccessible.

She sensed that the talk about pneumonia, which she understood was a disease, was just talk. She did not think she would get sick. On the contrary, the rain would make her healthier.

But if she were to go out naked now and stand in the inner courtyard of the police building and defy both weather and convention, she was not sure the same feeling of purity and liberation would come over her. The innocence of childhood was gone.

It felt like a weight, this experience of being someone else, no longer Ann, the girl in the rain. She was Lindell, a cop; at times very effective, sometimes less so. She was the mother of Erik, age seven, present, needed, and loved by him. She was a woman who loved nakedness and touch, from words, rain, and from another person's warmth and hands.

To what extent and in what order she was all of this, police officer, mother, and woman, shifted of course. Combining it was often the most intricate puzzle of life.

Right then by the window she experienced for a few moments that she was not anything at all. She saw only the girl in the rain before her.

The past few days she had lived as if in a vacuum, her body a walking shell, mechanically performing movements and gestures—speaking, functioning, interacting with others. She functioned in triple roles, but without any meaning or goal.

It ached like mental whiplash. Someone, or something, had hit her hard in the back to make her move forward, and sure enough she took stumbling steps in the direction that was pointed out as the right one. But it ached so much.

She turned around. The rain had eased up somewhat, the storm appeared to be taking a northerly course, would probably pass over Bälinge and Björklinge. On her desk was a plastic bag. It had been there since the morning, but she had not really thought much about the contents, and this lack of involvement, a both unexpected and unwelcome preoccupation, was due to one thing: The sign of life she received from Anders Brant, he who in the past few days had somehow come to incarnate Ann Lindell's three different roles.

What did he have to do with Gränsberg's death? Who was he? Where was he? And on the personal level, did they have a future together at all? Would Erik accept him?

It was as if she couldn't bear to deal with any of the questions and preferred to regress to the first memory of childhood where the girl Ann, in a feeling of bodily freedom, with the rain pounding, in her undeveloped slenderness, took the first careful, unconscious steps toward becoming the woman Ann Lindell. And beyond the purely physical, in the conscious, euphoric defiance of her mother there was a longing for freedom that made her long from that moment to be away, and as soon as it was possible, flee Ödeshög and train to be a police officer, all the time with the goal of becoming a very competent one.

Now she was submerged in melancholy. Extremely absentmindedly she had poked in her investigation of Klara Lovisa and out of pure habit maintained a kind of minimal dialogue with her colleagues, a back-burner Lindell.

She realized that it was Brant's unbelievably brief, almost aggressive message that created this gloom, reinforced by the rain and the recollection of that early childhood memory. It all flowed together—mother, woman, and police officer Ann Lindell. And the result was a melancholy passivity. If anyone were to say anything that might be perceived as the least bit critical of her, she would burst into tears, and if someone were to say that she was a good person, a good police officer, or a good mother, the result would be the same.

She took a deep breath, forced herself away from the window, and over to the desk.

The plastic bag was an ordinary confiscation bag and contained a necklace, consisting of a thin chain and two small silver disks. Each disk had a word engraved on it. Ann read *Carpe Diem,* capture the day. Pathetic and trite to say the least, so that it had lost its significance, she thought, but realized that for a sixteen year old it might be perceived differently.

Klara Lovisa had been wearing the chain. Her parents had not recognized it and maintained that they had never seen it before, which Lindell had no reason to doubt.

So Klara Lovisa received it on the day of the murder, her birthday. From who? Probably not from the murderer, who cleaned out her pockets, took her cell phone, and wallet. Why then leave a necklace behind that perhaps he had given her a few hours earlier?

Lindell's conclusion was that Klara Lovisa received the chain on the morning from someone other than the one who a few hours later would strangle her.

Who was this someone? The one that Lindell immediately thought of was Andreas Davidsson. Wouldn't a silver necklace be a suitable present from an infatuated teenager trying to win his girlfriend back? But he had maintained that he had not seen Klara Lovisa on the morning she disappeared, and why should he lie about that?

Silly question, Lindell muttered immediately, people lie all the time. Sometimes out of habit, many times without realizing that unnecessary lies only hurt their own cause, sometimes instinctively because they believe the truth is dangerous, as if it would be easier to consistently stick to the untruth. Deny everything and you become inaccessible, they seem to think. One untruth leads to another, and then they are sitting helplessly stuck in a tangle of lies. To then get loose, sort out the lies from truth after the fact, becomes a nearly impossible task.

Anders Brant was cheating! The insight came so suddenly that it felt as if she was having a stroke. There was a stabbing pain around her temples as if knives were being driven into her head. She took hold of her head. The pain was indescribable.

He's lying to me, she thought. The pain, which did not last more than a second, was replaced by a massive headache, and for a moment she thought something really had burst, a winding artery that had given up from the pressure.

Lindell took this as a sign, not based on any of the superstitious comments, often ominous, that her mother loved to strew around her, but that this was her subconscious mind's way of sounding an alarm. She concluded that her brain had registered something she was not consciously able to perceive, and was now warning her, trying to get her to understand and formulate.

Duplicity. She pushed the chair back from the desk, and with her elbows on her knees she leaned her head into her hands. She drew on all her strength to read signals that until how had been hidden from her. What had he really said about their relationship? Nothing really. He had a way of expressing himself, in a superficial way clear and lucid, but on closer inspection vague and possible to interpret in various ways. She could now remember several occasions when she experienced just such uncertainty about his words.

On those few occasions they talked about the future, it was as if he either joked it off, or put several layers of information on each other, relativizing what he had just said by adding something new.

She had enjoyed listening to him and took it as a part of his style of reasoning, as if his journalistic activity unconsciously forced him into ambiguities and reservations, like an attorney who talks and talks in long twists and turns, considering all aspects. An occupational injury.

But were the ambiguities perhaps just an expression of duplicity? Had he simply played with her? The idea was completely inconceivable. It couldn't be that way, mustn't be that way.

That man had taken a real hold on her, and if he were now to be torn out of her, the damage would be extensive. Her body, which functioned better than the deficient judgment of passion, signaled betrayal. It ached.

Lindell got up quickly, the desk whirled around before her and she reached for the chair behind her for support.

Ann Lindell went to Ottosson to tell him. She wanted him to listen to her without showing any agitation or even surprise. It struck her that perhaps Ottosson knew about her relationship with Brant and was only waiting for her to tell him what was going on of her own accord.

Ottosson was on the phone, but waved her in. The call was personal, planning a children's party, from what Ann could make out. Ottosson was smiling the whole time and the call dragged on.

Ann made a sign to Ottosson that could be interpreted any number of ways and slipped out the door, relieved that her execution had been postponed, but also with a dawning hatred of the man who had sneaked into her life and crumbled her awkward defenses, brought her down like a hunted animal, and then disappeared with her ridiculous hope as a trophy.

He had also interfered in her professional life in a completely unforeseen and drastic manner. She had become so distorted that through her silence, her duplicity, she had jeopardized her good relationship with Ottosson and her position at the unit.

In the corridor she met Beatrice, who hurried past, clearly on her way in to see Ottosson.

"Everything all right?" said Beatrice in passing, not expecting an answer.

Lindell was prepared to run after her colleague and give her a kick in the rear. She sensed how in the future Beatrice would exploit the Brant affair in veiled comments, peevish stabs that would never be completely understood by the others, and for that reason could not be parried factually. In the unspoken measure of strength between the two women on the squad, the weapons were not fair. And Lindell perceived that she was almost always at a disadvantage. Now it would be even worse.

Back in her office she sank down in the chair, shaken and sweaty. A week ago she was sore and happy.

Hate and love, so close to each other. In her mind Nina Simone was singing "Don't Explain," about a desperate woman's self-degrading appeal to the man to come back: You don't need to explain anything. Just come back!

It was a long time since she played it. She got the CD as a Christmas present from Rolf, long after they separated. He was like that, Rolf, eager to foist his taste in music off on her, and in this case he hit the mark. She liked the record and during long, wine-soaked evenings, while Edvard Risberg was disappearing from her life, she listened to it over and over again, engulfed by Simone's mournful voice, until she learned the lyrics by heart.

Now Simone came back. Don't explain. "You are my joy, you are my pain."

I'm so pathetic, she thought, like a line in a sentimental pop song, like a schoolgirl in love, without any distance, middle-aged but still so immature, easy prey for a man who simply by talking a little, touching a little, cleared away all resistance, to suck on her like candy for a little while, and just as nonchalantly spit her out when the taste got too monotonous, taking away her self-respect and crushing her.

But even so she wanted him to come back! Anything else was too sad, too heavy to bear, in any event at the moment. A respite, that was all. Then, when the worst pains had subsided, perhaps she might take his betrayal and start properly hating him. But now she simply wanted to rest together with him, without explanations, without promises. She wanted to be loved, even if not for real.

That's how bad things were for homicide investigator Ann Lindell.

✦

Twenty-eight

"No, don't call the police!"

"What? He's been standing there an hour, just staring."

"He must be waiting for someone."

Henrietta Kumlin snorted and gave her husband a look that declared him feeble-minded. In principle she had thought that for a long time, but this almost took the cake.

Just when they had finished dinner and started clearing the table, a man came walking by on the street. Henrietta immediately noticed that he did not belong in the area, because she had never seen him before, but above all due to his attitude and dress. Besides, he was obviously drunk or on drugs. She could see that immediately, having grown up with an alcoholic father.

He stopped outside their house, went up to the mailbox, then crossed the street, and leaned against the fence that the neighbor opposite had erected just last week. Now it was seven thirty, and the man was still standing there. For over an hour he had vegetated on the street.

He stood there quite openly, without moving. Sometimes he changed position, resting first on one foot, then on the other. Henrietta noticed that he was whistling. He seemed relaxed and carefree. The few cars that passed he noted with an indifferent expression. When Birgitta Lindén, who lived at the far end of the cul-de-sac, walked by with her collie, he leaned over and petted the dog, exchanged a few words with its owner, and then resumed his position.

It was quite clear that he was watching their house, and the most unpleasant thing was that he was doing it so openly. Henrietta thought her husband's comments that the stranger was waiting for someone were completely sick. She came to the conclusion that Jeremias was afraid; there was no other reasonable explanation for his passive attitude.

At first she tried to get him to go out and ask what this was all about. She did not want to expose herself to the risk of being attacked, well aware of what an unbalanced alcoholic was capable of.

When he refused, she wanted to call the police, but he was against that too.

"There will be so much talk, questioning, and shit. And you know I have to leave early tomorrow morning."

"What does that have to do with it?"

"You never know," said Jeremias, and Henrietta was too upset to comment on his cryptic remark.

"And then maybe he'll want to take revenge," he resumed.

"What do you mean, revenge?"

"Well, if the police arrest him, maybe he'll get beat up in jail, then he'll have a grudge against us."

She stared at him.

"Beat up in jail?" she said with a skeptical expression. "This isn't Russia."

Jeremias shrugged. Henrietta saw that he was trying to look indifferent, but she knew her husband well enough that she could see that the stranger's appearance made him worried.

"Do you know him?"

Jeremias glanced out at the street and shook his head.

"No, but those types are everywhere, people who wander around. You know how it is in Moscow. And remember when we were in California, on the beach in Santa Monica? There was a bum every five meters. He must be sick in some way."

"If he's sick then shouldn't he have medical care? I feel sorry for him."

Henrietta was playing her naive card. That was when Jeremias usually talked about how things "really" fit together, implying that she did not understand a thing. In his blathering he might unconsciously let information slip out that he never would have if she tried to discuss things normally.

But this time it didn't succeed. Jeremias simply let out a deep sigh.

"I'm going to take a peek at the news, maybe there'll be something about the pipeline," he said, leaving the kitchen.

She stared after her husband as he disappeared up the stairs, heard him turn on the TV and tumble down in his creaky armchair.

That damn pipeline, she thought indignantly. Since it became known that the Russians were planning a gas pipeline through the Baltic, an installation that would cut past the coast of Sweden and Bornholm, he had not been himself. He followed the debate with feverish interest, spent hours on the phone, wrote e-mails, and let it be known that Swedish and Danish fishermen were the biggest reactionaries there were.

"Europe has to live, develop, get its energy," he asserted with emphasis.

Henrietta understood that one or more of his companies was involved, but not how and to what extent; she didn't want to know either. He thought it was unnecessary, almost offensive, that "amateurs" got involved. And he no doubt counted her as one.

She had never followed his business dealings too carefully, even though she knew that their affluence, well, their entire existence, was based on Russian contacts and business deals. A few times she had accompanied him on trips but got tired of it. It was too gray, too much alcohol, and above all deadly dull, especially Oleg with his mannerisms, his bragging, and his extravagant dacha.

He tried to get her to shop, but she quickly discovered that Moscow was many times more expensive than either Paris or New York, and a gloomy city besides, with indifferent sales clerks who had developed a rare capacity to look bored.

Jeremias did not like seeing the poverty either. It was enough to turn off the stylish avenue and walk one or two blocks on a side street to discover the enormous difference between the nouveau riche and the poor. She especially recalled an old Russian woman who tried to foist a china set on her, perhaps inherited, beautiful but not complete and with several of the pieces chipped. The old woman, wrapped in an endless number of shawls, held out several cups, pointed down at her feet where the rest of the set was. Her eyes were running, and her hands, partly hidden by cut-off gloves, were chapped. The price was ridiculously low. She repeated it mechanically several times.

Henrietta got the impulse to give her the desired amount and let the babushka keep her porcelain, but could not bring herself to practice charity. She had the idea that begging and street selling should not be encouraged.

A few blocks farther away she changed her mind and returned, but in the archway where the old woman had been standing there was now only a man urinating against the wall. He grinned at her, said something, and turned his body so she could study him more closely. It splashed around her legs.

"If it's like that in central Moscow, what's it like in the outer areas?" she asked the same evening.

They were having dinner at a Swedish-owned restaurant, a few blocks from the hotel. Jeremias was a regular there and was received with almost exaggerated friendliness in the lobby. Already in the bar, where they had a few drinks before dinner, he was tipsy and had that somewhat bloated appearance. It was as if his cheek muscles did not work properly. Henrietta suspected with good reason that he and Oleg had a head start already that afternoon.

"No reasonable people come here," Jeremias had answered. "What do you think, Oleg? You know what it's like. Tell us a little something from the slums, you know!"

He thumped his Russian partner on the shoulder. He pretended not to notice, but Henrietta could see that Oleg did not like either the exhortation or the thumping.

During dinner they talked widely and broadly about business in the *chambre separée* where they were sitting. Henrietta got the impression that her husband wanted to show off, and that made her depressed. She closed herself off and tried to focus on the food.

The only benefit she had from the dinner was when the Swedish executive chef came out in the dining room, made the rounds, and also slipped into their own little section.

"Here's the chef!" Jeremias shouted. "He's the one who prepares all this good food. A damn good guy! He's Swedish! From Uppsala, besides."

He pulled on the chef's sleeve but then completely lost interest.

"That was really good," said Henrietta.

The tall chef had to lean over to hear what she said. He had a nice smile and winked meaningfully at the loud company. Several of the guests had no more than poked at the food, a few had put out their cigarettes on the small plates of mashed potatoes, others had only eaten the meat and pushed the trimmings to the side. The tablecloth was covered with roasted vegetables and turnips. In the middle of the table were two bottles of vodka.

"Ungrateful," said Henrietta, and got a vague movement of his head in reply.

She understood that he could not comment on his guests.

"But you liked the food?"

"Very much," she said, and got another, slightly shy smile. "You shouldn't have to cook for these types," she said.

"I made it for you," said the chef, "and that's more than enough."

"Are you from Uppsala?"

He nodded, smiled again, this time a little broader, placed his hand on her shoulders and squeezed lightly, an unprofessional gesture to be sure, but for her the smile and momentary touch were what she would recall. Everything else about that evening she preferred to forget. Above all the retreat to the hotel, which among other things involved stops at a couple of nightclubs, and then Jeremias's impotent attempt to take her from behind while she removed her makeup. She didn't have the energy to care, she knew he wasn't capable, and just pushed him so that he fell backward and remained sitting on the bathroom floor, stupidly drooling and limply waving one arm.

That was the last time she went along to Moscow. Nowadays she didn't want to hear a word about Oleg, oil, gas, or Russia.

And she did not want to be taken from behind. Or from in front either, for that matter.

She put the last dishes in the dishwasher and started the cycle, then glanced out at the street again. The man had moved a few meters, but still stood just as passively as before.

He was starting to really get on her nerves and it struck her that perhaps that was the point. He was a hired provocation, she realized, his appearance was not such that on his own he would come up with the idea of standing outside a house, just glaring.

His mission was not to injure, no; it was the look of the man, his stubborn staring, that was the message, she suddenly understood.

But why? There could only be one reason. Russia. Business deals. She could think of no other reason. They had no score to settle with anyone, the street where they lived was normally very quiet, nothing unforeseen ever happened, no break-ins and no damage during all the years they had lived there. Everyone knew everyone in the area.

But this man was unknown, an intruder, with intentions that were not good.

She knew, or sensed rather, that Jeremias was moving in a gray area. Probably all Westerners did who were successful in the former Eastern bloc countries. Obviously more or less, but Henrietta had an idea that in Jeremias's case the past few years it had slipped over to more.

Was this one of Oleg's men? He looked like a Russian, dressed in simple, cheap clothing. Oleg was a bandit, she realized that early on. A cruel man, she had seen that in his facial features and eyes. Whenever he smiled it was with calculation or scorn.

She took out a pen and the pad she usually wrote shopping lists on, sat down at the kitchen table and wrote down a thorough description of the man: blue-white gym shoes, stained brown pants, a green summer jacket with breast pockets, under that a dark shirt, maybe blue or green. His hair color was light. The bushy sideburns and beard stubble that was certainly several days old underscored the slightly dismal, worn-out impression. He looked tired and occasionally yawned, as if he was bored, tired of standing there and hanging out, but forced to. Hired in other words.

He had a brown shoulder-strap bag. It did not appear to contain much of anything and did not seem to bother him. She picked a marker on the neighbor's fence, a dark knothole, to use to calculate his height.

When she finished taking notes, she smiled to herself. This felt good. Now she had a description, whatever significance that might have. But she had done something, not just nervously checking every minute or two whether he was still standing there.

If she had not grown up with an alcoholic father, who when he was drunk hit both her and her mother, she might have gone out and asked what his business was, who his employer was.

The news report was over. The remote control rattled against the table and the TV fell silent. It was deathly quiet in the house. After a few moments, which felt like centuries, she heard the rattle of glasses. She knew he was pouring a whiskey.

"Coward," she mumbled furiously, mostly due to the fact that the cowardice applied just as much to her.

The next morning he would travel to Moscow and be gone for three days. That was a relief. Then the idea was that they would sail for a week in the archipelago, for the first time without Malin and Hampus. That was not something she was looking forward to.

Henrietta had to wait another hour before Malin came home. Jessica's dad was driving and let Malin off right outside the gate.

The man by the fence did not move a muscle. It almost seemed to Henrietta that he had fallen asleep standing up.

Her daughter was dragging a bag. Henrietta waved through the bay window and got a tired smile in response.

"How was it?"

Malin immediately took out a glass, filled it with water and a little ice, before she answered.

"The first two days went okay, but then it got too hot."

She drank greedily and filled the glass again.

"Who's the strange guy?"

"I don't know," said Henrietta. "He's been standing there for three hours at least."

"Sick," said Malin, filling the glass again. "Maybe it's the murderer."

"What murderer?"

"The one who killed that homeless guy last week."

Henrietta shut her eyes. The past week the news had been dominated by the homeless murder and the discovery of the young girl in the forest.

"Now I'm calling the police," she said, getting up.

"What do you mean, just because a guy is standing outside? That seems silly. Maybe he's waiting for someone."

"For several hours?"

Malin shrugged.

"Isn't Dad home?"

"He probably fell asleep in his chair."

"Home, sweet home," said Malin, dragging the trunk into the laundry room, which was adjacent to the kitchen.

Henrietta sank down on the chair again, calmed by her daughter's talk. She heard her daughter unpacking her bag and could even make out the odor of her sweaty gym clothes. She smiled quietly to herself. Malin was good, she took care of her own dirty clothes.

"I have to buy a new bikini!" Malin shouted.

"Do it in Bulgaria, it's probably cheaper."

"No way," said Malin, but did not explain why that was so inconceivable. "I'm going into town tomorrow."

"Well, maybe that's better," said Henrietta, because it struck her that perhaps Bulgaria was like Moscow.

She took a look out the window.

"Now he's gone!"

"Who? Dad?"

"No, the guy outside, of course."

"Well, there you go," said Malin, sticking her head out of the laundry room, "you're just a worrywart."

"Malin, sit down a moment."

Her daughter observed her for a fraction of a second, hesitated, then pulled out a chair and sat down across from Henrietta.

How should I talk about it, she thought, smiling at Malin, but noticed her watchfulness and worry, and changed her mind. Soon Malin would be going on her first vacation without her parents, so why tell her now, and add to the tension she probably was feeling prior to the trip?

"You'll be careful, won't you," she said. "I mean, you are four girls."

"We've talked about that," Malin interrupted.

"We have," Henrietta noted, taking her daughter's hand. "I trust you, you know that, it's just that I—"

". . . am a worrywart," Malin filled in with a grin.

✦

Twenty-nine

He recognized him right away. They faced each other silently, for an eternity it seemed to Anders Brant. How did the man get in? The gate by the street and the downstairs door were both locked. Now he was standing, evidently perplexed, outside the door to Brant's apartment.

Brant noticed that he had prepared for the visit carefully, there was an odor of cheap soap and he had put on the best set of clothes he could get hold of, perhaps even borrowed the dazzlingly white shirt and blue shorts. He had flip-flops on.

"Good afternoon," said the man.

"Good afternoon. Can I help you?"

The man nodded. Brant hesitated whether he should invite him in. The landlady was in Ribeiro visiting her sister and would probably not be home before evening. The Dutchman who rented the minimal studio that shared a wall with Brant had been gone for several days, probably on a visit to the woman he spent time with.

If he let him in, what might happen? It was the man's obvious efforts to look proper that decided it.

"Come in," said Brant, stepping to one side.

He went toward the kitchen. Sitting in the combination living room-bedroom felt wrong, too private, and besides the windows faced out toward the alley.

They sat down at the table. The man took a quick look around the kitchen. His eyes settled for a moment on the camera and the little tape recorder on the table, before he cleared his throat.

"Thanks," he said.

Brant suddenly felt thirsty, perhaps it was the man's throat clearing that triggered it, but he refrained from taking a beer out of the refrigerator. He did not want the man to be the least bit affected.

"I know you saw what happened," said the man.

Brant said nothing, but instead waited for what would follow with an expressionless face. This was a technique he used in interviews. Saying too much yourself, filling in, making comments, explaining, giving background and intentions, that could lead astray. The interlocutor, or interview victim, adapted so easily, made a parallel course to try to please or get off easily.

From the inner courtyard was heard the stubborn sound of the bird calling its incessant *nitschevo-nitschevo*, the Russian word for "nothing."

The man sighed, looked down at the table, certainly bothered by his errand, but probably also by the unfamiliar environment, apparently indecisive about how to present his case.

At last Brant felt obliged to break the silence. The bird's stubbornness and the man's timidity were making him nervous.

"What's your name?"

"Ivaldo Assis," he said, extending his hand.

Brant introduced himself and took the man's hand across the table.

"I know that you saw," Ivaldo repeated.

Brant nodded, and that was what was needed for Ivaldo to continue.

"What you see is one thing, but what really happens is another. My son died. I am grieving my son, not the man who died before your eyes. That wasn't my Arlindo. He died a long time ago. Do you understand?"

For the first time their eyes met. The man's left eye was full of blood, red streaks marbled the white of his eye.

"He was not, he did not turn out to be a good man. Not a good son, not a good husband and father. He created a lot of sorrow around him. Arlindo was only twenty-seven years old, but he had three lives on his conscience, and many others I don't know about, because he was not only a murderer, he dealt drugs too. I did all I could to get him to change his ways, but he was so disturbed in his soul. May God forgive him!"

Brant stretched out his arm, opened the refrigerator, and took out a Brahma. There were glasses on a tray on the table. He filled two and set one in front of Ivaldo.

The man waited patiently until the foam had settled and then emptied the glass in one gulp, thanked him with a nod and continued his story.

"Our family comes from the inland, *sertão*, in the vicinity of Jacobina, do you know it?"

Anders Brant nodded. Not because he had visited Jacobina, a city perhaps three hundred kilometers northwest of Salvador, but he guessed that the landscape looked much like around Itaberaba: *caatinga*, bushy vegetation worn by wind and sun, river channels dried out for long periods of time, cactus, merciless heat in the summer, stony, meager soil, which could be made fertile if irrigation could be arranged.

"Then you know. It was poor. We had no land. When my wife died my three sons and I moved here. I thought they might get some education. I had a brother here in Salvador, in Massaranduba, and we moved in with him. It was crowded but we managed. I took odd jobs. My brother was a bus driver. Then he died too, shot during a robbery, and we were evicted. My oldest son had moved to Ilhéus and was doing fine, but two were left, and then my nephew Vincente, who I was taking care of. We were without a roof over our heads, three young men and I. We stole some lumber, put together a few carts, and started collecting rags and boxes. That worked out too. There were four of us and we were strong."

Anders Brant had heard this kind of story many times, in Brazil and in other countries. The details might differ, but the tragedy was the same.

People from near and far made their way to Salvador, hoping that the city would live up to its name, and save them from poverty and misery. The city grew beyond its limits, new *favelas* shot up like mushrooms from the ground, the misery was the same, but also the new arrivals' hope for a better life.

"One day we found this place in the alley, an abandoned building, and we moved in. It was good, we had a roof over our heads. I even planted a tree on the slope outside. Maybe you've seen it, it's five meters tall now. The only sad thing was that Arlindo started living a bad life. He brought a woman here, Luiza. She got pregnant and had a son, but he was born premature and died. He hit his woman. Maybe that was why the child left us. I was a grandfather for thirteen days."

Brant refilled the beer glasses. The same procedure was repeated, when the foam had settled Ivaldo gulped down the beer, nodded, and continued his story.

"He did drugs and for a while he got his little brother and his cousin involved, but at last they got strength from God to say no."

The old man fell silent. Anders Brant studied his facial features, marked by poverty and hard work, a person in this multimillion anthill, dark skinned, the descendant of slaves, born poor, without great demands on life. A man who had lost a son.

Anders Brant had an impulse to put his pale hand over Ivaldo's dark one, but resisted it.

"Now my hope is with you," said Ivaldo.

"How is that?"

"Vincente was reported. We thought you were the one who called the police, but it was a woman in the building on the other side. I recognize her, she always sits in the window and glares, and that's what she was doing that evening too. She saw Vincente push his cousin, my son Arlindo, over the wall."

"What should I do?" asked Anders Brant.

He sensed what the answer would be.

"You have to give false testimony," said Ivaldo.

"And let Vincente go free?"

Ivaldo nodded.

"I won't do it. I can't lie about a thing like that. For a while I thought

I was seeing things, but I saw what I saw. I chose not to tell, but don't ask me to lie."

"Were you afraid?"

Brant nodded.

"You don't need to be. Arlindo cannot take revenge. And God understands."

"This is not about God," said Brant.

"It's not?"

Anders Brant did not know how to get himself out of this dilemma. Discussing a conceivable God's possible understanding was totally foreign to him, and starting to talk about laws and justice was almost tragicomic to a man who had never experienced any justice.

"Don't you believe in God?"

Brant shook his head.

"Not in God, and not in paradise," he said. "I am struggling for paradise here on earth."

"The day after tomorrow you're going to believe in hell anyway."

"What do you mean?"

"We're going to make an *excursão,* you and I," said Ivaldo.

Brant was uncertain what the man meant by that word. He would translate it as "outing," but did not understand the context, and it was so clearly marked on his face that Ivaldo thought it best to immediately tell him what this *excursão* would involve.

✦

Thirty

She remembered how he brushed a strand of hair away from her face and then leaned over to give her a kiss on the forehead. And the aftershave, that he got from the children on his birthday.

That was the last thing, the touch and the smell. She could not remember whether he said anything; sometimes he did, before anyway, a few words to the effect that she could sleep awhile longer, that he would be back soon, or something more affectionate.

That was what she told the police too, that she was barely awake, but realized that he was leaving. It sounded so paltry. She would have preferred saying something else, above all more, a more rounded recollection, that they had made love, had breakfast together, that he was happy his trip would be short, perhaps something about the future, who they really were, what they could have been.

Then she took them out to the street, to the fence, and pointed at the knothole.

"This is how tall he is!"

They did not understand.

"The Russian!" she screamed. "He's Russian! I know he's a Russian. The whole thing is Oleg's fault! The gas, that damn gas!"

Her voice was cutting. She struck the fence with her clenched fists as if to eradicate the figure who had been standing there twelve hours earlier. Beatrice put her hand on her shoulder.

Suddenly Henrietta caught a glimpse of Malin in the kitchen window. A rational thought broke through her confusion for a moment—thank the good Lord I did not tell her yesterday evening—and she freed herself from the female police officer who was trying to calm her, and ran into the house.

"That's the daughter, we'll give them a couple minutes," said Beatrice. "And Fredriksson is in there."

"Who is it that's this tall?"

Sammy Nilsson did not like this. Standing on a street and not understanding a thing. They would soon have an answer to the question of who Henrietta Kumlin meant as she desperately struck her hand against the fence, he was sure of that. But all the other questions?

"It's vacation time, damn it!" he exclaimed.

He would be spending a week kayaking with his crazy sister, who had barricaded herself in a little village in the inland of Västerbotten. No one understood why, but that's where she wanted to live. The only way to see her was to go up there. And sitting in the isolated cabin, with barely enough space for one person, was inconceivable to Sammy; he got cabin fever at the mere thought of it. So they, or rather Sammy, decided they would spend a few days in a canoe, and his sister had unwillingly gone along with the arrangement.

"Do you have any idea how awkward it will be?"

Beatrice Andersson had been listening to his complaints without comment. In principle she was grateful that he was not taking advantage of the fact that his survey of the so-called bandy gang would now perhaps prove meaningful. There was probably a connection between Gränsberg, Brant, and now Jeremias Kumlin, not only as a lineup of team members on a twenty-year-old photo. It would be strange if this were only a coincidence.

"We don't know yet," she said anyway.

Sammy Nilsson stared at her uncomprehendingly, shook his head, and then stomped back to the garage, where Eskil Ryde and Johannesson had just stepped in.

Beatrice Andersson understood that her colleague was tired, worn out; he really needed a week in the wilderness. She also understood what he meant by "awkward." It would be complicated. Vacations would be lost, plans would have to be rearranged. Her own vacation was not planned to start for a month, but yet another case, with a probable connection to a previous homicide, an unfortunate ride down a staircase, and a journalist's mysterious disappearance, all that combined would create chaos in the schedule.

Her own fatigue also made it hard to think, but there was no turning back because she understood that Henrietta Kumlin would be her assignment. This talk about Russians—and gas—was confusing to say the least, and she returned to the house to start unraveling.

Jeremias Kumlin was lying flat on his face, with his arms stretched out over the hood of his BMW, as if during the final seconds of his life he wanted to embrace the symbol of his success.

Sammy was standing in the half-open garage doorway. Two patrol officers had just finished cordoning off the lot and street, and Sammy and the field commander, Simlund, were discussing how they should arrange the door-to-door operation on the normally quiet street.

Ryde and Johannesson were working in silence. Sammy thought it was strange to see the "old man" at work once again, as if nothing would

ever change. That thing about Ryde's retirement was a joke, he had simply fooled them, and would outlive them all.

"How's it look?"

Ryde looked up.

"He's dead," he said.

Sammy Nilsson nodded.

"Head bashed in."

"I know, I saw him. Come on now!"

"You need to calm down."

Sammy Nilsson knew that too.

"Don't stand there stomping your feet!"

Sammy Nilsson left the garage door. A few neighbors farther down
on the street were standing and talking, one of them in a bathrobe, although it was almost nine o'clock. A uniformed officer was on his way
toward them and when they noticed the policeman they pulled back.

"Don't let us disturb you," Sammy Nilsson mumbled.

He walked restlessly down the street, a little fragment of an Uppsala
he seldom or never visited. The well-adjusted, successful types lived here.
So was there a connection between Gränsberg and Kumlin, more than
the fact that both suffered a fatal skull fracture? He tried to recall what
had been said during his and Kumlin's brief phone conversation a few
days ago. Nothing strange or startling he had thought then and could not,
in light of what had now happened, come to any other conclusion. Kumlin had been surprised to be asked about an old photo, perhaps also a
little irritated, but said nothing that aroused Sammy's interest in the
slightest and definitely nothing that would make anyone suspect that
the businessman would meet such a fate.

Did the call trigger some activity on Kumlin's part, perhaps a telephone call to someone else on the bandy team, which in turn led to his
being murdered? Sammy Nilsson realized that he must have another
discussion with the former teammates.

He stopped abruptly and raised one arm as if to keep a train of thought
from disappearing. Had someone decided for some unfathomable reason to eradicate the whole bandy team, player by player? Was that why
Anders Brant took off so hastily, that he realized he was in danger and

fled the country? Or was it the case that Brant had returned from Madrid and was the one who bashed a pipe wrench into the back of Jeremias's head?

Sammy Nilsson looked around as if the answers to his questions were to be found in the well-tended gardens in Sunnersta.

Suddenly a figure emerged from a bush only a few meters away and Sammy Nilsson instinctively reached for his gun which he wore in a shoulder holster—for once he was armed—but calmed himself immediately. A man stepped up to the fence toward the street.

"Birger Luthander," he said.

They shook hands, Sammy Nilsson introduced himself and inspected the man. He was in his sixties, dressed only in a pair of Bermuda shorts; his upper body was bare and he had no shoes on.

"Something has happened, I understand. Is it the Kumlins?"

Sammy Nilsson hummed. He was a little irritated that his train of thought had been interrupted, perhaps a little embarrassed by his reaction.

"You looked so thoughtful, almost sad, if I may say so. Something terrible has happened, I thought right away. And I'm not surprised, I might add."

"I see, what do you mean by that?"

"There's been a little traffic on the street of a somewhat different nature than usual. Nothing good can come of this, I remember thinking."

Do they have to talk like that, wondered Sammy.

"Traffic?"

"Yes, but I'm not referring to motor vehicles. I couldn't help noticing, and I want to emphasize that I haven't made any exertions. I'm not a curious person," he quickly added. "But on several occasions, three to be exact, individuals have appeared on the street, individuals who do not belong to the customary picture of life in the area."

"In brief: You've seen people who don't live on the street."

"Correct. The first occasion was maybe two weeks ago, and he also returned a few days later. And then yesterday, another visitor, this time it was a different man, but with an equally unfavorable appearance; I can't say anything about his inner qualities. The fact was that it was my wife who brought my attention to the man; personally I was watching one of the many sports channels. Completely uninteresting. I definitely think it was some ball sport, you have no idea how quick Asians can be on their feet when it counts. I dismissed him as a peddler, mostly to calm my wife, who sometimes has a tendency to overreact, but the strange thing was that he stayed by Rosén's fence—a not particularly esthetically pleasing construction, in my opinion—for at least two hours, without moving a muscle, in principle completely still, that alone a minor achievement. He was not Asian."

"So what was he?"

"What do you mean?"

"What did he look like?"

"He might very well have been Swedish, but it would not surprise me if he had some foreign background. He was not dark-haired, but not blond either. I guess it's called ash-blond. He was not wearing glasses."

"Clothing?"

"Everyday, but to get details you'll have to ask my wife. That's her specialty."

"Age?"

"Hard to determine, between forty and fifty."

"Yes, that's what we're dealing with," Sammy Nilsson murmured, thinking of the bandy team.

"Excuse me?"

"It was nothing. What makes you think that he might possibly come from abroad?"

"The whole impression," said Birger firmly. "There was something vague about him, something old-fashioned, well, maybe it was the clothes? To the degree he moved it was also with a kind of uncertainty, maybe because he felt he didn't belong here, which was also apparent."

Birger Luthander, who behind all the verbosity proved to be an attentive and clear-sighted witness, except where clothing was concerned, could put words on the unknown man's appearance and to some degree conduct. These were speculations, Sammy Nilsson realized, but it still gave him a good picture of the man who so stubbornly lingered by Rosén's fence.

"If you want to speak with my wife, it's fine to call her cell phone."

Sammy Nilsson took out his phone. Luthander very slowly repeated the number digit by digit.

Mrs. Luthander, who introduced herself as Anita, could quite rightly account for the man's dress: gym shoes, brown pants, and a green jacket that reached to his waist, and under that a dark shirt.

She added something too that Sammy Nilsson found interesting. Right before eight thirty the man disappeared, but Anita Luthander never saw him pass by their house. She thought that was peculiar as it was a dead-end street.

Otherwise she confirmed her husband's understanding. A foreigner, she summarized her impression.

Sammy thanked her for her help and they ended the conversation. In the meantime Birger Luthander had retrieved his business card, which he handed to Sammy.

Publisher Birger Luthander, PhD, he read on the card.

"What do you publish?"

"Mostly bridge books. Do you play bridge? And then a few odds and ends about scientists who have been wrong but right anyway."

"That's an area I'm very familiar with," said Sammy Nilsson, amused at having met this curious character, partly for the testimony, but also because he helped change his own state of mind for the better.

"That was a thought," said Birger Luthander and nodded, obviously content, as if he'd gotten an impulse for new writings.

It was four thirty before an initial summary could be made. A group of noticeably restless, tired police officers had gathered. There was starting to be a shortage of prosecutors too, because even if the prosecutor's office had been spared the stubborn summertime flu that struck the police, several were on vacation and those who were left in the building were all loaded with cases. It was the sanguine Åke Hällström who was assigned the Kumlin murder. And this balanced the gloomy atmosphere somewhat, because even though he too had a heavy workload and was a little confused at the moment, he was endowed with an unusually easygoing temperament for the building.

"Go over that again," said Hällström. "Kumlin's wife maintains that it was a Russian, but has nothing to back that up?"

"No," said Beatrice Andersson. "She explains it by her husband's business deals in Russia, that he might have felt threatened."

"Was there an explicit threat?"

"Not that she knew of."

"Strange," said Hällström.

But Beatrice Andersson did not think so at all. She had listened to Henrietta Kumlin's story, about the constant trips to Moscow and some place farther east, the name of which she could not remember, and about Jeremias's worry, which had increased recently. And then this Oleg Fedotov, who to Henrietta was clearly the image of evil incarnate.

"His business seems to have moved in the well-known gray zone," Beatrice continued. "There are, as we know, less conventional methods for getting your way."

"Even murder?"

"Yes, that had occurred to Henrietta."

Hällström nodded.

"But she knows this Fedotov?"

"They've met, but he was not the one watching their house. According to her, Fedotov prefers not to travel abroad. On the other hand his sons have visited Sweden and Uppsala, even stayed with the Kumlins."

"But we don't know if it was the fence man who murdered Kumlin," Sammy interjected. "He evidently went up in smoke at eight thirty. Either he left the area or else he went into the garage, waited there all night, and went to work in the morning when Kumlin was going to take his car and drive to Arlanda. That could mean he knew that Kumlin would be leaving the house in the morning."

"He didn't leave a trace," Beatrice Andersson observed in the antiphony that arose between her and Sammy Nilsson.

"A pro," said Hällström, and Beatrice gave him a tired look that showed what she thought about that comment.

"Then we have Luthander's information that there have been several unexpected visitors on the street recently," Sammy resumed. "On two occasions he saw what he characterized as a stranger on the street. If that person was on his way to Kumlin we don't know, no one else on the street noticed the man, and no one has expected or received a visit either. If we rely on Luthander's information that this wasn't the 'Russian,' if we're calling him that, then who was he?"

"It may be someone who tried to visit someone on the street two times, but this someone was not at home," said Beatrice Andersson.

"Someone doing reconnaissance," Fredriksson tossed out.

"What bothers me, seriously," Beatrice resumed, "is that the 'Russian' hangs around so long, completely visible. We have three witnesses, besides your buddy Luthander, who saw him standing there by the fence. Why? If the idea was to kill Kumlin that was unusually stupid."

"It went wrong," said Sammy. "The mission was to frighten, then it went overboard."

"Did he stay in the garage the whole night?" Hällström asked. "I have a hard time believing that."

For an hour they argued back and forth, until they started repeating themselves. It was the prosecutor who proposed a break, and it was as if that suggestion let the air out of the gathering.

The group broke up, but Sammy Nilsson stayed behind. He could not settle down. He was thinking about the Gränsberg-Brant-Kumlin connection. It had barely been discussed but it was arguably the most interesting.

If they could establish and understand such a connection, everything would be resolved, that was his firm conviction.

He left the meeting room and went to his own office, where he sank down in his chair and put his feet up on the desk. He ought to go home, but was unable to relax. He took out the photo that he had taken from Brant's apartment and studied the team members.

Brant, the joker in the deck, Lindell's lover, the Spanish traveler Brant, whom Ola Haver had all the trouble in the world locating. Sammy Nilsson guessed that Haver was not making any great efforts, he probably had his hands full working things out on the home front. Probably he had just dutifully sent a few e-mails to the Spanish police with questions that were now floating around in the virtual world of cyberspace.

Why did Brant take off? Why do people leave the country anyway? To get away, to work, or simply to go on vacation. At the start of the investigation Sammy had been convinced that Brant was hiding; now he was no longer so sure, perhaps due to what Lindell had told him. Would she have dated a murderer?

Suddenly it occurred to him that among all the piles of papers on the journalist's desk there was a folder marked *Putin*.

He looked at the clock—six thirty—reached for the phone and called Lindell at home, who answered after the first ring.

"Hello!"

There was suppressed tension in her voice.

"How's it going?"

"Huh? Is that you, Sammy? With what?"

Lindell's voice seemed to be coming on scratchy connections from the other side of the globe.

"Life. Have you talked with Ottosson?"

She had not. An e-mail from Brant had changed the picture, as she said, but did not want to tell what it was about. This irritated Sammy Nilsson, and he let her know it too.

"But he's clean," said Lindell. "In any event where Gränsberg is concerned, I mean."

"Where is he?"

"Brazil, in a city. In the atlas . . . I looked it up. It's called Bahia. Or Salvador actually."

"The atlas," said Sammy Nilsson, as if he found it unbelievable that people looked things up in something as old-fashioned as an atlas.

"He knew Gränsberg but has nothing to do with the murder. It was a different murder."

"What do you mean, different?"

"In Salvador, of a homeless person," said Lindell tiredly. "He witnessed it."

"Unbelievable," said Sammy Nilsson. "That sort of thing doesn't happen. Would—"

"One moment!"

Sammy heard Lindell set down the receiver. In the background bizarrely loud sounds from a TV were heard and he understood that she was yelling at Erik. The volume was lowered somewhat and Lindell returned.

"What did you say?"

"Have you been drinking?"

"Well, I, no, no," Lindell protested. "Erik is just a little—"

"Are you depressed?"

Lindell did not answer. He could picture her, even if he hadn't seen her new apartment, which she claimed to feel so at home in, but it was not comfort and coziness that Sammy Nilsson associated with Ann Lindell at just that moment. He knew she'd been drinking, he recognized the signs, the slightly elevated pitch in her voice and the bad syntax.

"Ann, listen to me! I'm coming over, so we can talk."

The only thing he heard was Erik singing along with a song that boomed from the TV.

"Ann, are you there?"

Was she crying?

"Sure, a while longer anyway, but it's a little heavy right now," she said at last.

"Is 4B your apartment number?"

She hummed in reply.

"No entry code?"

"Three-eight-three-eight," said Ann Lindell. "My shoe size times two. I do have two feet."

But not particularly steady ones, thought Sammy Nilsson.

"Don't drink any more! I'll be there in half an hour, maybe an hour, just have to swing by home. Put on some coffee. Sit down with Erik on the couch, talk with him."

"Okay," said Lindell. "I'll . . ."

She fell silent, Sammy Nilsson waited for a continuation, and when it came it was suddenly a sober Lindell who was talking.

"I think I know who murdered Klara Lovisa."

Sammy Nilsson parked on Österplan, a short distance from Lindell's residence, and remained standing a moment. It was a lovely evening, the air was warm and trailing from a grill on one of the courtyards was the aroma of meat cooking.

A freight train lumbering north made the ground vibrate. The heavy train creaked and lurched. He counted the cars, forty-eight of them, and it occurred to him that he had wanted to be an engineer when he grew up. Imagine sticking to a track and never leaving it.

Höganäs was an area he seldom if ever visited, either personally or on the job. In statistical terms it was a peaceful part of Uppsala. He had had one assault there, and as he walked past the building where the wife of a glazier had been severely beaten, he peeked into the yard, and stopped in amazement. The glazier's wife was sitting in a lawn chair, reading. Sammy Nilsson could see that it was the same novel, by the most recent Nobel Prize winner, that he himself was trying to read in the evenings. The glazier himself was in front of a grill with a spray can in one hand and a beer bottle in the other. He said something, the woman looked up and smiled, but immediately went back to her reading.

Sammy Nilsson hurried on before they caught sight of him. He would surely be recognized and he felt embarrassed, as if he was guilty of something indecent.

Ann had freshened up both the apartment and herself in the hour that had passed since they talked. There was a scent of cleanser, mixed with coffee, and she had showered.

"Erik just fell asleep," she said.

Sammy carefully closed the door. The evening sun was shining in through the windows in the living room, capturing the swirling dust and giving the apartment a strangely suggestive, opaque character, a romantic but at the same time ominous introduction to a French noir film from the fifties, with a woman placed like a fragile, dreamlike detail at the outer edge of the picture who would slowly back into the room and disappear.

"I made coffee," she said barely audibly, as if she was testing whether her voice would hold, while Sammy kicked off his shoes and curiously looked around in the dark hallway.

He still had the feeling from his encounter with the glazier and his wife that he was intruding, peeking into something extremely private. He did not socialize with his colleagues; the barbecue every summer at Haver's was actually the only occasion they got together in an organized way. He might have a beer sometimes with Morgansson in tech, in any case before Morgansson met the woman he had now moved in with, but he was the only one.

The impression of intruding was unexpectedly mixed with a feeling of tenderness for Ann Lindell. She was sitting on the couch, her hair wet, straight-backed, ready to pour coffee. A plate of cookies was set out, as well as a jug of milk.

"You have a really nice place," he said. He was seized by an impulse to take hold of her, pat her on the cheek, or something physically tangible, but realized that would be idiotic. She was on tenterhooks and was doing everything not to show her emotions. A pat might make her fall apart, he knew her that well.

Once before, a few years ago, he had picked up the pieces after her. That time she was sitting alone at a bar, drinking. A patrol officer, who was there to have a bite to eat and dance, phoned Sammy and told him that his colleague probably needed to go home and go to bed, otherwise things might go very wrong.

Sammy had gone there immediately, found her blind drunk, and carted her home. That time he stayed with her the whole night, slept on the couch they were now sitting on, and the next morning had a long chat with a hungover, regretful Lindell. A chat that sank in, he realized afterward, even though they never brought up the incident later and what had been discussed that morning at her kitchen table.

He had asked her where Erik was and she said he was staying with his "relief family," and explained that occasionally it felt so heavy that she did not know whether she could manage bringing up her son, and that he was really the one who needed to be relieved from her, not the other way around.

He called the patrol officer and asked him to keep quiet about what happened, and as far as Sammy could tell he had done that, he had never heard any comments or gibes at work anyway.

After that she pulled herself together and from what Sammy had heard Erik stood out as a well-adjusted boy. It seemed as if that morning Ann definitively decided to put her love and longing for Edvard Risberg on the shelf, even if she later admitted to Sammy that for long periods it still hurt a lot. As recently as last year, in connection with her investigating a murder in the archipelago, and in doing so came geographically very close to Edvard, the misspent love story put her out of balance for several weeks.

He sat down alongside her. The living room was, if not boring, conventionally furnished. He understood that Ann had not spent any time looking through home decor magazines. It was dutiful and functional. The only thing that deviated was a large oil painting on the opposite wall.

She noticed his interest and told about an artist, now a very old man, who had painted a single motif his entire life, Lake Vättern, on whose shore he was born and had always lived.

"I bought it twenty years ago, I actually borrowed money from my parents to get it, and I don't regret it. It goes with me. It's the only advantage with Ödeshög, being close to Vättern, or 'the sea,' as Dad called it."

"He's succeeded," said Sammy.

"Lovely but cold," said Lindell, lost in thought.

"Klara Lovisa," said Sammy, who wanted to break the slightly ominous mood, at the same time pouring milk in his coffee mug.

"The last Mohican," she said, and dismissed Sammy's perplexed expression with a hand gesture. She then told about the necklace they had found on Klara Lovisa and that no one, not even her parents, recognized. She had drawn the conclusion that it was the murderer who had given her the jewelry.

"Nice," said Sammy. "First a chain around the neck and then a chokehold."

"I asked a teenage girl here in the building, she takes care of Erik sometimes, where she bought her jewelry and whether this particular type was popular. She listed a number of stores and today I've been making the rounds. Got a bite at the first one, Silver and Such, on Drottninggatan. The clerk recognized the necklace immediately and said they had sold a lot in the past six months, with the exact inscription *Carpe Diem*."

"That doesn't sound like much," said Sammy. "I mean, that's a lot of customers. It would be better if it were something unusual."

"I was prepared," Ann resumed, and now she smiled for the first time. "The clerk pointed out my candidate right away."

"What the hell?"

"I'd gone around to three schools and picked up yearbooks, you know, with photos of everyone in class. I let her browse and speak up if she recognized a customer. In the third yearbook I showed her she put her finger on a face without hesitating: It was the last Mohican. She was dead certain of it."

"He had a Mohawk haircut, in other words."

Lindell nodded.

"I thought like this: If and when Fredrik Johansson left Klara Lovisa alone in the forest hut, what did she do then?"

"Tried to get away from there," said Sammy, happy at the change in Lindell, from slurring to lucid, but he was also listening to her with a feeling of unease. He had seen something similar before, when she stubbornly shifted into higher gear on the last drops of fuel like a gasoline engine before it finally coughs and falls silent.

"It was her birthday, she wanted to go to town, she was angry besides and maybe shocked at Freddy's attempt, but she could not readily call her parents and ask them to come and get her."

"She called the last Mohican," Sammy interjected.

Lindell nodded again.

"Andreas Davidsson. He has such an unusual hairstyle that you remember him, and that was what I was hoping for. Like I said, the clerk was quite certain about it. My theory is that Andreas got on his moped right away and took off. In the morning he had sent her an SMS, Klara Lovisa knew he would show up, and that he would certainly not tattle, the boy was deathly in love with her. This would put her in his debt, so of course he showed up. Then it goes wrong. She gets her present and hangs it around her neck, but when Andreas wants to screw her, it goes wrong. Perhaps she lets something slip, tired of all the horny boys, and Andreas suddenly understands that he is never going to have a chance."

"A lot of assumptions," Sammy Nilsson objected. "Does he have a moped, for example?"

Lindell nodded and continued.

"She leaves home without jewelry, afterward murdered with jewelry. Anders bought just such a necklace a few days before. Signed, sealed, and delivered."

Sammy sighed. He realized that Klara Lovisa and Andreas might just as well have met earlier in the day, and that she then received the chain as a present. On the other hand, why would the boy lie about such a thing?

"And one more thing," Lindell resumed. "But this is just a feeling. I think his mother knows something. She seemed more than allowably confused and nervous. If I bring in mother and son and put pressure on them separately, then someone will break down, sooner or later. I actually think sooner."

Sammy Nilsson had great respect for Lindell's "feeling." It didn't always lead right, but often enough that you could take it seriously. She seemed to have recourse to a kind of inner direction finder, an instrument that made her the capable police officer she was.

"Have you talked with Ottosson?"

Lindell looked at Sammy Nilsson in confusion.

"About what?"

"This?"

"Yes, we're bringing in Andreas and his mom early tomorrow, early as hell."

Sammy Nilsson nodded, drank the last of his coffee, which had gotten cold.

"Then you're not allowed to drink anymore this evening," he said, fixing his eyes on hers. She returned the look a few seconds before she lowered her head like a penitent.

"Do you know what I did after we talked?"

"Showered."

"Yes, but first I stuck my fingers down my throat and vomited. Erik didn't hear anything, he has his own karaoke club right now. He's been at it constantly for a couple weeks now, he sings along with every single TV program and video, sweet but tiresome after a while. I had just had two glasses of wine and you know I don't need much, even more so when I haven't been eating right. Then I drank a liter of milk and showered. I didn't want to be drunk when you came."

"Anders Brant," said Sammy.

She nodded.

"What's happened?" he continued.

"Do you really want to hear? It's a depressing fucking mess, filled with stupid love, a lot of hope, but just as much disappointment and anguish, dreary to listen to if you're not involved."

"Tell me," Sammy encouraged her, knowing that it would sound just as drearily predictable as Ann foretold.

"I think he has a woman in Brazil," she said. "He didn't say that flat out in his e-mail, but between the lines it was clear enough. Maybe she's the one who was here and visited. And now he's there."

The tears welled up and made their way down her cheeks.

"And when you read his e-mail, you opened a bottle of vino," Sammy observed.

"It's so petty," said Lindell. "I feel so deceived, as if someone holds out a bag of candy and then pulls it back right when you're about to feast on it. The senseless thing is that I think he was in love too. We had a good thing!"

Sammy Nilsson wondered whether he should tell what he had found in Brant's bedroom, but not everything needed to be told. She had drawn the right conclusion on her own, so why sprinkle more salt in her wounds by giving her the details?

She seemed to have shrunk on the couch, her voice had also gotten smaller. How long could she bear to be alone? How long would she manage to control her emotions? When would the wine drinking take over? In silence he cursed Brant, who had unleashed this.

"He's coming back," he said instead.

"Can you love two at the same time?" she asked no one in particular.

"I don't know, I have my hands full with one," said Sammy Nilsson.

"I can't take it," she said, her voice cracking. "The loneliness. I have Erik and he's everything, everything! I like my job, I don't have many friends, but I have you and a few others. But I want someone close. Is that so strange?"

"No, not at all," said Sammy, taking her hand.

"It's as if this life is not for me. That sounds like a bad soap opera, but that's really how it is. I had Edvard, and say what you will about him, he was a man with substance, maybe not always fun, but solid. I lost him by getting knocked up. Should I have kept my mouth shut and had an abortion? Do you think I've wondered about that, wondered what my life would have been like then. But then I look at Erik and I don't understand how I could even think that."

"He's a great kid," said Sammy.

"I'm really lousy at living," said Lindell. "I get jealous of all the others, who are living as couples or single and happy with that. How the hell do they do it?"

"It's not a given that they're happy," Sammy Nilsson objected. "Look at Ola."

"I know, but they have the tools, the recipes for it. I'm completely lost, confused when it counts, like a social caricature. If there's a pill that makes you numb I should take it, go ahead like a mechanical apparatus."

"I don't believe that at all," said Sammy, who was starting to get tired of the self-pity.

"No, me neither," said Lindell downheartedly. "But the thoughts are there, that's bad enough."

"He's coming back," Sammy repeated. "If it's as you said, that he was in love too, it may turn out that way. He's just indecisive."

"Do you believe that?"

"I don't believe anything," said Sammy Nilsson. "But it may be that way, you know that too. Don't kick out like a terrified horse, just wait until he comes home. Sit down here on the couch together and talk about everything. You're not very good at talking about what you're thinking and feeling. Isn't that right? You don't believe anyone can like you."

"It's not like that," Lindell protested.

"Yes, it is like that, Ann. It's the same at work. You're one of the best we have, but you diss yourself all the time."

Lindell burst into tears. Sammy Nilsson pulled the sobbing body next to him. It occurred to him that he had never hugged her before. It was possible that she had awkwardly tried to imitate the lives she observed around her, but she had never adopted the weakness for hugging at all times.

She freed herself, straightened up, drew her hand over her face, sniffed, and tried to arrange her facial features.

"My life is filled with lies and a whole lot of blood," she said. "That's what I get."

She got up and went over to the window next to the balcony. On the table was a chipped saucer. One of his cigarette butts was still there. The sun had gone down and the yard was slowly settling down into darkness. One of the neighbors was sitting by the mock orange, smoking a pipe. His wife, a woman Lindell had seen in line at Torgkassen, was gathering up the remains of a meal. They were talking.

"A little love wouldn't be bad," she said, with her back to him.

"You have Erik, he's an exceptional boy," said Sammy Nilsson, realizing how paltry that sounded.

Ann tossed her head as if to show what she thought about that comment.

✦

Thirty-one

Avenida Oceânica extends all the way from the lighthouse in Barra, the district located on the southwest tip of Salvador, to the Rio Vermelho district. Both areas are relatively prosperous, dominated by the middle class, but with small favelas here and there too.

On the avenue one of three parades takes place in February during Carnival, the world's biggest outdoor party, which goes on for a week.

The parade in Barra, starting just south of the harbor, is dominated by whites, a number of them coming from São Paulo and Rio, who pay to be part of a *bloco,* one of the sections that make up the parade. Each *bloco* is led by a gigantic trailer with musicians and singers, followed by those who have the money to buy a T-shirt or costume to participate. Those holding the ropes that keep out those who don't have the money are overwhelmingly black, as are the observers crowded on the sidewalks.

Preparations for Carnival starts weeks in advance. Along the entire parade route bleachers are set up where for 100 or 200 dollars you can buy a seat. An inconceivable expense for most.

Carnival had become business. Brant preferred the one in Pelourinho, the historic part of the city, which is more like a folk festival, where people drink beer, splurge on trinkets, dance, listen to music at a couple of permanent stages or by groups of musicians that wander through the narrow, cobbled alleys.

At eight o'clock in the morning Anders Brant and Ivaldo Assis got into a taxi on Avenida Oceânica. Before that they had coffee, which they bought from a woman who had set up a portable stand, some thermoses, and a pile of plastic mugs, on the sidewalk.

The coffee was too sweet, but Anders Brant suspected he would need energy to survive the day.

Right across the street, on the shore promenade, the white, or half-white, Salvadoran middle class was running in brand-name shoes and fluttering linen. They silently observed the joggers; nothing needed to be said. Pointing out that a pair of Nikes cost as much as a minimum monthly wage was unnecessary. Brant knew that, and Assis had experienced it.

The taxi ride was short, the jail was only a few blocks from Campo Grande, and when Brant paid he said something to the effect that they might as well have walked. It struck him that Assis probably seldom took a taxi, and perhaps he liked getting out of a taxi in front of the entry to the jail where his nephew Vincente was imprisoned. It looked good; maybe he hoped that someone on the staff would notice the arrival.

Besides, his comment might be taken to mean that he thought he was wasting money on an unnecessary taxi ride, and he was ashamed.

"But a little air conditioning was nice," he said. It was hot and sticky outside and the taxi's air conditioning had cooled them for a few minutes.

The jail, one of forty-two in Salvador, was a circular structure whose exterior did not reveal anything surprising. It was also surprisingly calm, both outside the entrance and in the small reception room into which they stepped. Anders Brant had expected groups of relatives, police cars arriving to drop off persons under arrest, agitated voices, and heart-wrenching scenes.

In the room a wall-mounted TV was blasting out a cooking show. The program host was white, of course. The picture rolled, but no one bothered to adjust it. It was on simply because that was Brazil; something has to make noise.

There were three small open booths, like in a Swedish pharmacy, where the arrested person was admitted and where the general public could also report crimes. Only one booth was manned, which reinforced the quiet impression.

Everyone's eyes were turned toward Brant and Assis. Everyone took it for granted that the *gringo* had been robbed or the victim of some other crime, and that the older man would help him, possibly submit information important to the case.

Ivaldo Assis stood passively, perhaps expecting that Anders Brant would act, which he had no intention of doing. It was Ivaldo who had taken the initiative, and it was his relative they were going to visit.

After a period of mutual indecision, the official in the booth waved them up.

"Good morning," Assis began. "Is everything okay?"

The policeman nodded, somewhat nonchalant but still curious.

"This gentleman has an important errand," Assis continued.

His white shirt was already stained dark with sweat.

The police turned his eyes toward Brant.

"If it's a report, then it's better if you talk with the federal police," he said, in an attempt to avoid paperwork and other inconvenience.

"It's not about a report, but a visit," Brant explained.

"Wednesday is visiting day," the policeman interrupted. "You can come back next week."

"By then I will have left the country," said Brant quietly.

"Then that takes care of it automatically."

Brant knew from experience that it was pointless to get worked up. It was crucial to preserve dignity and remain polite.

"It's about a murder," he said.

Consciously he had raised his voice to capture the other policemen's attention; one of them had retrieved a chair and was fiddling with the TV.

The policeman got down from the chair and came up to the odd duo.

"What's this about?" he asked.

"Vincente Assis," said Brant.

The policeman nodded, as if to confirm that he recognized the name and was interested in continuing.

He was solidly built, more dark than light, with the sleeves of his T-shirt rolled up, perhaps to show the swelling biceps, and his gaze was alert. I must gain the man's confidence, thought Brant, choosing his words with the greatest care.

"I witnessed an incident that was shocking, a man died before my eyes. I would like to visit Vincente and with my own eyes see if he is the one I believe."

"And who are you?" the policeman asked, turning toward Ivaldo.

"Ivaldo Assis."

"Father of Vincente?"

"Uncle. It was my son Arlindo who died."

The policeman's expression did not reveal what he was thinking, but with a head movement indicated that they should follow him.

They passed a door, following a passageway that looped in an arc between the windows on the one side and small rooms on the opposite. Anders Brant was reminded of a roundhouse. A number of doors were open, Brant looked in and was met by indifferent eyes.

The policeman stopped suddenly and opened a door.

"Here we won't be disturbed," he said. "This is actually our lunch-room."

They sat down at a small, wobbly table.

"You want to see Vincente?"

Brant nodded.

"To identify him."

"You witnessed the incident, you say. Why didn't you come forward earlier?"

"I was in shock," said Brant, but realized at once that this was not a good answer. "And then, I didn't want to get involved. The incident was tragic but didn't concern me directly. But since then things have changed so that—"

"You speak excellent Portuguese," the policeman interrupted. "Do you live here permanently?"

"No."

"Do you have problems with your visa? Was that why you didn't want to talk with the police?"

"All my papers are in order," Brant answered, making a motion to take his passport out of his money belt, but the policeman waved dismissively.

"We'll deal with that later," he said, getting up quickly. "I'm going to take you down to the cells. You will get to see Vincente, but you may not speak with him. I want you to point at him. After that we can sort this out. Senhor Assis, you can wait here."

"But he's my nephew."

"It will be fine," said the policeman. "Visiting day is Wednesday, and then you are welcome. We can't make any exceptions."

Anders Brant was astonished. He had encountered the Brazilian bureaucracy on many different levels and contexts, and was surprised by the policeman's directness and efficiency.

They left the lunchroom and continued a dozen meters to a staircase with some fifteen steps leading down below ground. The smell of human excretions was tangible.

The policeman stopped and looked at Brant with a serious expression.

"This won't be a pleasant sight," he said. "The jail is meant for thirty-five prisoners but right now we have ninety-six."

"I understand," said Brant. "But I'm not here to describe your jail."

"I didn't think so for a moment either," said the policeman, offering for the first time what Brant with a little good will might characterize as a smile.

They went down the stairs. The smell got stronger. The voices of the prisoners, echoing between the concrete walls, made it hard for Brant to hear what the man was saying, but he understood that there were three sections: one for murderers, one for drug dealers, and one mixed, with everything from petty thieves to assailants. This was where Vincente Assis was being held.

At the bottom of the steps there was a small room. That was where visits normally took place, the policeman explained. Five prisoners at a time were taken there and they had fifteen minutes to talk with their relatives. Brant wondered whether the visitors could bring things to the prisoners.

"Clothes, sanitary articles, and cookies," said the policeman.

"No food?"

The man shook his head, but did not explain why cookies were allowed.

He unlocked a barred iron grate, gestured for Brant to wait and went to the left in a narrow circular passageway. In the middle of the building was an exercise area, from which shouts and yelling were heard. Cells ran along the passages in both directions. Brant saw hands squeezing the bars.

The policeman stopped at a cell five or six meters away, silenced the prisoners by holding up both hands and saying something that Brant did not understand.

"We have a visitor," said the policeman. "He's only going to look. I want you all to line up. No one says anything. Anyone who says a single word will have me to deal with."

He waved to Brant, who kept as close to the wall as possible to avoid the hands reaching out through the bars. All of them were young and black, dressed only in dirty shorts and barefoot.

"I'm innocent," whispered a man in the first cell. "My family doesn't know I'm here."

When Brant came up to the third cell everyone's eyes were turned toward him. Their gazes were mournful and soulless, young boys and men without hope.

Brant counted ten persons. Vincente Assis was the third man from the left, in a cell that was perhaps meant for four.

He raised his hand and pointed without meeting Vincente's eyes, and then quickly went back to the gate and slipped out to the visitor's room.

Immediately the taunts came thick and fast after him.

———

They returned to the lunchroom where Ivaldo Assis was waiting, standing by the window. He immediately turned around. Anders Brant lowered his eyes.

"Well, was that the man who shoved his cousin over the wall?"

The policeman's immediate, direct question caught Brant by surprise. He took a deep breath, felt the sweat running down his back, his nostrils still filled with the stench from ninety-six people crowded together, and he realized that the hopelessness he had seen in the young men's eyes would stay with him a long time.

He gave Ivaldo a quick glance and then answered with as firm a voice as he could.

"No, the man I saw down there was standing at least five meters from the wall when Arlindo Assis fell."

The policeman's eyebrows arched a few millimeters, but he was otherwise able to maintain his poker face. Ivaldo Assis on the other hand gasped. Brant did not dare look in his direction.

"You're certain?"

"Completely. I was standing by my window, maybe five or six meters from the wall, I saw what happened plainly and clearly. No one, neither Vincente nor anyone else, shoved Arlindo."

"Do you understand what this means?"

Brant nodded.

"You also know that we have a witness who maintains the opposite?"

Brant nodded again.

"And you're still certain?"

"Yes."

"Why? Are you being paid? Do you know the Assis family from before?"

"Payment? That's an insult," said Brant. "You're just saying that to provoke me. And I have never seen the Assis family before."

That was yet another lie. He had seen them the year before when he lived at the pension, but that time he had not taken specific notice of them, they were one family among others. Then their whole building also had a roof and was not the half-open stage it later became.

"Are you prepared to testify?"

"Yes. No innocent person should be convicted."

The policeman let out a snort. Ivaldo Assis was crying by the window.

"Who shoved him?"

"No one," said Brant.

"You mean he jumped head first over the wall himself?"

"He fell. Maybe he was drunk. I saw how he was leaning over the edge and then lost his footing. Maybe he wanted to see what was on the ground down in the alley. The day before they had thrown out a lot of things. Maybe they quarreled."

"Lots of 'maybes,'" said the policeman.

Brant nodded.

"How did you find out that Vincente Assis was in jail?"

"I saw Ivaldo on the street yesterday and expressed my sympathy."

"You said you didn't know the family."

"I saw everything from my window, including how Ivaldo embraced Arlindo and closed his eyes. I realized they were related. Ivaldo told me that the police accused Vincente of the murder of his cousin."

"Arlindo was a criminal, a murderer who dealt drugs besides. Maybe you think it's good that he died?"

He looked at Ivaldo, as if he expected a protest from him, but he said nothing about the description of his son.

That man is dangerous, thought Brant, but was able to adopt an expression of surprise, and shake his head, as if he thought the policeman's question was unreasonable.

"What do you think about his death?" Brant asked instead.

The policeman observed him silently. Brant realized that the decision would be made at that moment. He opened the bag and took out mineral water, unscrewed the lid, and greedily took a few gulps.

"You'll have to meet with one of our investigators, the one who's taking care of the case. You'll have to sign a statement."

"And then?"

The policeman made a movement with his head as if to say: Who knows, or maybe, who cares?

✦

Thirty-two

"Magdalena Davidsson," said Lindell, after recording the mandatory interview information, and then waited in silence for ten seconds—a pause that she used to read from her notes what she already knew—before continuing.

In the meantime the attorney, Petter Oswaldsson, a forty-something well-coifed sort, as Fredriksson characterized him, and a friend of the Davidsson family, was staring at her, which she noted in the corner of her eye.

She then raised her eyes and gave the attorney a blank look. She sensed that the struggle would be between the two of them, in any event if he had his way.

"I have a son, Erik, who's going to start school this fall. A spirited kid"—she used an expression she had not heard since her father used it a very long time ago—"who, like your son, is just starting out in life."

Magdalena Davidsson took a deep breath.

"We have a great responsibility, as mothers," Lindell continued.

"Really!" the attorney exclaimed.

Lindell turned her head very slowly, as if her neck were hydraulically controlled and the oil very cold and turgid, fixing her eyes on Oswaldsson, before she again turned to Andreas's mother, and continued.

"And through your lies you are letting him down. It's that simple. He's made himself guilty of a crime, you are protecting him, or you think you're supporting him, but in reality it's the exact opposite: You are shoving him away."

She waved her hand and realized to her surprise that her strategy was holding up. Oswaldsson was grimacing, but remained silent.

"He has no one but you. Your lies are transmitted through him. Give up while there is still time."

"What constitutes the crime?" the attorney asked.

"Obstruction of a murder investigation and in the worst case manslaughter, perhaps homicide," said Lindell calmly, as if she were discussing something very ordinary, without taking her eyes off the woman.

Magdalena Davidsson flinched as if she had been hit when she heard the word "homicide."

"Yes, it's that bad," said Lindell. "And you are the only one who can fix that. Andreas will not manage this on his own."

"What do you mean 'fix'?" Andreas's mother said hoarsely.

Lindell took a photo of Klara Lovisa from the folder before her, and set it on the table. The attorney stared at the picture of the young, smiling girl.

"If it is the case, and there is a lot that suggests it, that your son is involved in Klara Lovisa's death, he must have support to manage. He's only fifteen. His whole life is waiting. Right now he is suffering terribly, and he will be for a long time, if you don't help out. He will never really be free from anxiety, because he is not a hardened criminal who lacks empathy, but he must be able to go on."

"What should I do?" Magdalena Davidsson whispered.

"Talk with him! Now, right here, the rescue of your son's mental health and life begins. Let him understand that he has your support, no matter what happened, and that for his own sake, and for Klara Lovisa's and her parents' sake, he must be honest."

Lindell let the words sink in. It was not surprising that she was broken down; what was surprising on the other hand was Oswaldsson's passivity. She gave him a quick look and did not know what to believe. Either he was unusually dense or he agreed with her, whatever he thought about her emotional overacting.

"You lied about his alibi the day Klara Lovisa disappeared," Lindell resumed. "I think he's lying when he says he didn't see her that day. It was her birthday, and he gave her a present, a necklace."

Lindell recounted her theory of how Klara Lovisa phoned Andreas and how he went to Skärfälten on his moped, and how they quarreled, a dispute that ended in violence.

The woman listened with bowed head, and when Lindell stopped talking she had nothing to say. Nor did attorney Oswaldsson, who put his notes in his briefcase and thanked her for an interesting lecture.

Lindell felt a twinge of desperation. She had hoped that Magdalena

Davidsson would break down and that a story would gush out of her that would be the beginning of the end of the drawn-out investigation.

None of this happened. The woman's silence and Oswaldsson's only slightly camouflaged scorn made her depressed, and she concluded by saying that Magdalena Davidsson could either stay there, sit in, and listen during the questioning of Andreas, or go home.

Both of them knew that Andreas would not want his mother to be there, he had made that clear, but Lindell could not refrain from mentioning that alternative, with the dim thought that in some way she wanted to get back for the woman's compact silence, by pointing out how Andreas distanced himself in this way from his own mother. Cheap revenge, and it bothered Lindell that she treated the poor woman so basely.

"I think Magdalena can wait here in the building," said the attorney. "Then I'll drive her home later."

Lindell wondered whether it was Oswaldsson who had encouraged the mother to keep quiet, which obviously was her right, and whether he had advised the boy to do the same. That would soon be seen.

It was a given that Oswaldsson would sit in and assist Andreas. If the outcome of that interview was the same, they would be forced to release Andreas, which the attorney very nicely pointed out.

✦

Thirty-three

The afternoon meeting, called by Ottosson and the prosecutors Fritzén and Hällström to summarize the investigation of the murder of Bo Gränsberg and subsequent events, Ingegerd Melander's death, and the murder of Jeremias Kumlin, was a long, trying sitting. It was Friday and everyone had been working intensively the whole week, the majority with hours of overtime. The force was decimated by illness and vacation, and the investigation had swelled out to almost unsurveyable proportions. So despite the widespread fatigue, a summary was needed.

Ottosson had Sammy Nilsson make a chart on the whiteboard, with photos of those involved and brief information below each. Arrows ran across the board in an intricate system, not entirely clear to everyone, pointing to connections between those involved, established links indicated with solid lines, and others with dotted lines. Question marks, written in red, were abundant.

The given question was: Were they dealing with the same murderer where Gränsberg and Kumlin were concerned?

It was not obvious. The only known link that existed between them was a twenty-year-old photo. Henrietta Kumlin had never heard the name Bo Gränsberg. When she and Jeremias met, he had just finished his bandy career. She said that later they went to a few Sirius parties, including an anniversary dinner, but could not recall more than a handful of names, and Gränsberg was not one of them.

She could not identify him on a photo either, either in the group photo or pictures taken later.

"So did she recognize the journalist, that Brant?" Riis asked.

Sammy Nilsson shook his head.

"Where the hell is he?"

Sammy Nilsson looked at Riis, who had a talent for letting every question sound like an insult or an accusation.

"In Brazil," he said, smiling.

"A fucking Nazi," Riis exclaimed, whose line of thought was not always easy to follow, but Sammy Nilsson and most of the others understood that he was thinking of the many Nazis who fled to South America in the final stages of or after the Second World War. "What the hell is he doing there?"

"That's less interesting," said Sammy. "I think we can remove him from the investigation. He met Bo Gränsberg in his work. Brant is writing a book about homeless people in different countries, and it was in that connection he visited Gränsberg. They knew each other from before. The notebook we found in Gränsberg's shed that he got from Brant was to write down some of his experiences."

"How the hell do you know that? Have you talked with Brant?"

"No," said Sammy Nilsson.

"You, Haver?" Riis continued, turning around.

Ola Haver, whose task had been to trace Anders Brant and who to the surprise of everyone except Ottosson had returned to work that morning, shook his head.

He looked so miserable that even Riis thought it a good idea to leave him alone.

Sammy Nilsson seized the opportunity, giving Ottosson a quick glance before continuing, hoping that Riis would let go of Brant.

"Then we have the question of Henrietta's absolutely certain assertion that the 'fence man' was Russian."

"Do we know what her husband was working on right now?" asked the prosecutor, Fritzén.

"Not entirely, and perhaps we'll never know," Fredriksson interjected.

He was the one, along with Olof Myhre at the financial crimes unit, who had taken on Kumlin's business activities.

"Jeremias Kumlin owned several companies, some on his own, some with Russian partners, among them this Oleg Fedotov, and almost all of them concerned gas and oil. There are a few exceptions and those involve surveillance systems and alarms. It's impossible to speculate about what was worrying Kumlin. It's a tangle of companies, and for that reason there are any number of conceivable explanations," Fredriksson summarized his and Myhre's impressions.

"Are there any relevant documents?"

"Yes," said Fredriksson. "A whole room full. He used a room on the top floor as an office. Myhre thought it would take at least a month to go through all the papers, and what might be considered relevant is impossible to say."

"A hitman from the East," the trainee Nyman said for no reason, seeming to find the thought of the Russian mafia appealing.

"But Kumlin was just about to go to Moscow," the prosecutor resumed. "He must have prepared for the trip, wouldn't there be documents packed in his bag?"

"No, his packing consisted solely of a computer, clothes, and a toiletries case," said Fredriksson. "We found a locked bag on the garage floor. It's clear that Kumlin was on his way out and was surprised by the murderer in the garage."

"The murderer may have brought the bag with him," the prosecutor objected.

"Maybe," said Fredriksson calmly. "But Henrietta doesn't think so. Her husband had the habit of getting his bag ready the night before and putting everything by the door to their garage, or by the outside door if he was going to take a taxi. That particular evening, according to his wife, there was only the suitcase with clothing, nothing else, by the door. Kumlin fell asleep early in the evening in front of the TV, was awakened by Henrietta at eleven thirty and then went straight to bed."

"But going to see a business partner in Moscow without any documents seems improbable to say the least. He may have had them in his office and brought the papers down in the morning," Fritzén countered.

Fredriksson shrugged.

"It's possible," he said. "My theory is that when Kumlin came into the garage the 'fence man' was there, ready with the pipe wrench. Then if there were papers or not—"

"But maybe it was those very papers that were the target of the attack," the prosecutor persisted.

"We may never know that," said Fredriksson.

"How did he get in?" Fritzén asked.

"The garage door to the street was unlocked."

Fritzén pushed his glasses up onto his head and rubbed his face.

"What a mess," he said, and that probably expressed what they were all feeling that Friday afternoon. "An unknown man who disappears. The only thing we have is a pretty good facial description, which fits a few million Russians, and Swedes too for that matter. And Henrietta Kumlin maintains that her husband did not recognize him."

Fredriksson had slid far down in his chair—the others were convinced he was dreaming about walks in the forest—so it was Sammy Nilsson who continued the brainstorming.

"It was probably Jeremias who said that, and we can imagine he did not want to admit it to his wife. He was also against calling the police. He did not even want to go out and ask what the man was doing. Completely passive, in other words, and that's a little peculiar."

"It doesn't indicate great fear exactly," said Fritzén. "I don't think he recognized him or felt any real threat. Then surely he would have acted differently."

Submerged in his own musings, Sammy Nilsson thought, where does

Brant fit in? Was it too hasty to remove him from the list of interesting persons? He remembered again the material he had found on the journalist's desk that prompted him to call Ann, but that had been forgotten in her agitated state.

Russia. Putin. Was there something in that? Anders Brant was an investigative journalist, perhaps he had dug up something that had to do with Kumlin's business deals, even something about Oleg?

Sammy Nilsson kept this to himself, and decided to plod ahead on his own on that line of inquiry. This would mean having to get into Brant's apartment one more time. Nilsson, the building manager, would surely no longer be as accommodating.

After two hours of discussion and arguing, the gathering broke up. Their collective fatigue was monumental, and nothing new had actually emerged, but it had been a necessary session, everyone realized that. Seemingly meaningless talk might waken slumbering insights to life, perhaps not during the meeting, but over the weekend or next week or in a month. That was how police work functioned. It was only Riis who complained loudly of wasted time.

Sammy Nilsson went past Ann Lindell's office, but it was empty. He had heard about the disappointing result of the questioning of Magdalena and Andreas Davidsson. Both had been able to leave the building, without Lindell having become any wiser.

Fredrik Johansson had also been released, after Prosecutor Molin and Lindell had conferred. It could not be proven that Fredrik was the perpetrator. The timing was the reason, and as long as they could not present evidence that Fredrik had returned to the shed in Skärfälten, or that his father's car had been driven to the garage, they had no case.

Sammy could imagine Lindell's disappointment. Twice convinced that the murder was about to be solved, twice forced to see it would not hold. Would there be a third time?

He sauntered back to his office. It was already three thirty and he should go home. The weekend was earmarked for a visit to Tärnsjö in northwest Uppland, the promised land of mosquitoes, where the livestock went crazy and the camping sites were going out of business due to bloodsucking insects, who propagated at a magnificent rate in all the windings of the nearby Dala River, and then visited the area in dense clouds to attack every living thing.

It was not an enticing visit, but Angelika's coworker and close friend was turning forty and having a party. There was no avoiding it. Sammy Nilsson had a feeling he would get drunk, and perhaps that was the only way to put up with the mosquitoes. The Tärnsjö mosquitoes ate insect repellent for breakfast, and mosquito candles and other types of incense only got them excited. But on the other hand, in that part of the landscape they were surely accustomed to alcohol too.

Just when he had decided to leave the building, the phone rang. He hesitated before answering, but picked up the receiver after the fifth ring. It was Morgansson.

Sammy Nilsson immediately noticed in the northerner's serious voice that he had something unusual to tell. The technician said that Lindell had just stopped by and asked to look at the protocol from the investigation of Anders Brant's apartment. When she left the tech squad she looked completely destroyed, did not say a word to Morgansson or anyone else, simply closed the folder, sat awhile staring blankly, and then more or less staggered away like a sleepwalker.

Sammy Nilsson realized immediately what had turned her into a zombie, but had no time for a follow-up question before Morgansson barreled ahead with an intensity that Sammy had never experienced before.

"I've also secured a print in Ingegerd Melander's apartment." Sammy Nilsson could not avoid noticing how the excitement was mixed with pride. "You know how Bea is, she's extremely nitpicky. I've been trying to get hold of her but haven't been able to."

Sammy Nilsson was not surprised. Beatrice had an unfailing capacity to disappear and cover her tracks when the weekend was approaching.

"And?"

"Hold on now," said Morgansson. "It's Anders Brant's fingerprints, a clear index finger on the toilet paper holder."

"What the hell are you saying?"

"Yes," said Morgansson contentedly. "Crystal clear. He used the john at Ingegerd's."

Sammy encouraged the technician to immediately call Ottosson so that he could inform the prosecutors.

"What are you going to do?" Morgansson asked.

"Go to Tärnsjö and fight mosquitoes," Sammy replied. "Well done, Charles! But call now, so you don't miss Ottosson!"

Sammy Nilsson hung up and immediately called Lindell's cell phone. No answer. He went back to her office. Empty. Irresolute, he stood awhile going back and forth before he took the elevator down to the garage.

✦

Thirty-four

The mild summer rain dampened her cheeks. She knew she had to pull herself together, there was no other alternative. She slammed the car door behind her. I don't even have an umbrella, she thought.

Most of all she wanted to disappear in a fog, just go, leave everything, give up. But Erik was waiting. She had fled the police building, but she could not flee from her son.

Emma's mom, Carolina, came walking up. She lived nearby and could walk to the preschool. Ann Lindell opened the car door again, turned her back, and pretended to be looking for something in the front seat.

"Hi, Ann, did you lose something?"

I'm looking for a life, thought Ann, wanting to fall head-first into the car and just lie there, but straightened up and turned around.

"Yes, a piece of paper," she said.

"Papers always disappear," said Carolina. "It's nice to get a little rain."

Ann thought so too, because it hid her tears.

"Please excuse me," she said. "I have to make a call."

"Sure, about dreadful murders, I understand," Carolina said cheerfully, and left. When she came up to the day-care entrance, she turned around and called out something like "Have a nice weekend." Ann waved back.

Feeling ashamed, she picked up her cell phone. Who should I call? Who would want to listen to what I have to say? She did not even want to listen to herself, so why did she think anyone else would be interested? And what did she have to say? One word said it all: degradation. Maybe shame, even hate.

She realized that Sammy knew, maybe even Morgansson. No, Sammy was not mean enough to tell the technician about her and Brant. But the very thought that Morgansson had gathered pubic and head hair with a tweezer from Brant's bed, hair from a dark-haired woman, made her crazy with jealousy and bitterness. Hair that was now in a plastic bag as evidence of his duplicity.

I'll kill him, she thought, and she felt a new anxiety attack making her body cramp up.

Over and over again she played the scene in her mind. How he had gone from her bed to the other woman, whispered words of love, pushed a pillow under the woman's belly, caressed, licked, and penetrated her. Her too.

What was her name? Ann wanted to know her name, what she looked like, and how old she was. Probably a young beauty, with a firm body and a smiling mouth. Maybe she was twining her legs around his back at just that moment, panting in his ear?

Now of course he was sleeping with her in Brazil. Did they talk with each other about the policewoman in Uppsala? An escapade that didn't mean anything, that would be forgotten and forgiven. She could hear him making his assurances.

He declared his love to the dark-haired woman, whispered indecencies in her ear, made her laugh and willingly part her legs.

She was riding him, sucking his cock, massaging his balls. Right at this moment.

Lindell struck the roof of the car, stroked the finish with her hand and pushed away the raindrops in a wild dance, drawing air into her lungs. Hated. She wanted to throw up in his mouth, kick him, make him suffer.

"I can't take this," she mumbled, but knew that there was no going back. Erik had to be picked up, fed, put to bed, woken up, and taken to daycare and school. Not just today, but every day—ten, fifteen years ahead. He would grow, become a teenager and a man, step out into life on his own two feet. She was the one who would guide that journey. It was her duty. Who else would do it? Who would ask about how she was doing? Who would take her hand and listen to her needs and wants? Who the hell would love her?

"Are you still there?"

Carolina's voice, Emma's talk, but Anna did not turn around, did not have the energy to be polite, remained leaning against the car. They could think what they wanted to. The rain picked up. Everything was damp. Drops pattered and divided into small cascades on the roof of the car. The asphalt shone black. The crowns of the trees in the little park outside the preschool were moved by a sudden breeze.

She was submerged in grinding bitter thoughts, unaware of the rain and the world. Her inner drive belts were slackened, gears and wheels turned more and more slowly, there was no drive, the machinery was being turned off.

Suddenly she felt a hand on her shoulder and she jumped.

"Ann, what's going on, don't you feel well?"

"I'm fine," she blurted out.

She closed her eyes, wanted to close everything out. Let me be, don't talk to me, don't touch me.

"Are you coming in? It's raining. We are getting worried."

Suddenly Ann turned around and fell into the woman's arms, sniffling and sobbing. Just then a car pulled up. It stopped right behind Ann's and Sammy Nilsson got out.

"Hi, what's going on?"

He was noticeably moved by the scene. Ann, his colleague and friend, helpless in an embrace outside the preschool.

"I'm a colleague of Ann's," he continued.

The woman nodded.

"She's not feeling well," she said.

"We're having a tough time at work," said Sammy. "I can take care of her. I'll park her car here, then I'll drive Ann and Erik home. She needs to rest."

"Will you do that? Do you know Erik?"

He saw the relief in the preschool teacher's face.

"We've met," Sammy answered, putting his hand in Ann's jacket pocket and fishing out the car keys.

Together they made sure that Ann got into Sammy's car. The pre-school teacher went to get Erik. After a few minutes he came running.

"Hi, there," said Sammy. "Your mom is a little sick. She has a tummy ache, so I'm going to drive you home."

Erik observed him big-eyed, then peeked carefully in the backseat where Ann was sitting. She tried to smile. The boy got into the car without a word. Maybe he thought it was exciting to ride in a newer, sportier car than his mom's.

"Drive fast," he said, as he put on the seatbelt. "Mom never does."

Sammy nodded and turned out of the parking lot.

He took command immediately and bedded Ann down on the couch in the living room, draped a blanket over her, let Erik feed her strawberry ice cream. It was good for her stomach, Sammy said. Ann looked at them with sad eyes. Erik held out a spoonful of ice cream and she swallowed dutifully.

Her silence made Sammy Nilsson nervous. If only she had protested, but she let herself be fussed over. Wordlessly she lay there watching her son as if he were a person she had seen before but had not paid close attention to until now. Sometimes she let out a barely audible whimper or smiled faintly, as if she found herself seeing the comedy in the situation, being fed by a seven year old. But she continued opening her mouth and taking in spoonful after spoonful. At last she held up her hand.

"Now I think her tummy feels better," said Sammy.

"Thanks," Ann whispered, reaching for the boy with an awkward motion, but too late, he had already slipped away with the container of ice cream.

Sammy heard him open the freezer and put the ice cream back.

"I'll stick around awhile," said Sammy.

"I'm a piece of shit," Ann hissed.

Sammy understood that she was trying to whisper, but that something went wrong. He shook his head.

"Yes, letting myself be deceived like that."

They heard Erik turn on the computer in his room and then the clamorous sound of a computer game.

She was stretched out on the couch. The blanket moved very slightly when she breathed. Her bare feet were sticking out at one end, and it occurred to Sammy that all that was missing was a thread around one toe, a thread with a tag and a number written on it.

"Hold me," she said quietly, this time with better control over her voice.

He reached out his hand and stroked her wet hair.

"We'll manage this," he said.

"You knew," she murmured.

Sammy nodded.

"Morgansson and I were there, you know."

He could not deny that he had seen the package of condoms, the dark hairs, and the semen stains in Brant's bed, even though it increased her torment that he had known, while she only sensed that something was very wrong.

"But you didn't say anything! What a fool I am!"

"Lie down," said Sammy, with a touch of irritation in his voice, because while he knew that treachery was the worst blow a person in love could be subjected to, he could not help feeling that her self-pity was tiresome.

"I know," she said. "It's pitiful, but I was really in love. For the first time since Edvard, and that feels like a hundred years ago."

There was desperation in her voice, but Sammy was glad that she was talking at all. For a time he feared she would sink into a trance-like state, which would require different measures than he could contribute.

"Do you want to call anyone? Your friend, what's her name? Görel?"

"No, not her," said Ann.

She closed her eyes; he continued stroking her hair. It was as if the two of them were calming each other. From Erik's room plinging and clamor was heard from the computer.

"Take a few days off. I know it sounds silly, but you need to rest. You'll have more energy, and things will look different."

"I can't," said Ann.

"You can't go on like this, with this tension, and you know it too. You'll break down."

"Work is the only thing I have outside these walls," Ann replied, opening her eyes.

"That's what's wrong."

"I've tried," Ann sobbed.

"I know," said Sammy. "I know you've struggled. But have you done it in the right way, on the right grounds, and with the right means?"

Instead of answering she raised herself up on her forearms and started telling about the experience of finding Klara Lovisa, about how at the edge of the pit she promised Klara Lovisa to find her murderer.

"We shouldn't make those kinds of promises," said Sammy. "That's the sort of thing that hollows us out."

Ann shook her head and sank back on the couch, closed her eyes, and grimaced in pain.

"Should I go get some pizza?" Sammy asked after a while.

Ann opened her eyes in confusion. She looked dazed and was barely able to keep her eyes on him. Sammy realized that for a few seconds she had been somewhere else.

"I'll take Erik and get some pizzas, okay? We have to get a little food in our stomachs. I'll call home and say—"

"Not a word about me!"

"I'm working late," he said, smiling. "Angelika will understand."

She observed him thoughtfully a moment before her gaze fluttered away, and he realized that she was trying to imagine a man *she* could call, a man who would understand.

Erik did not go with Sammy to the pizza parlor, but instead stayed in front of his computer. He did not seem to understand how far down his mother had fallen into the black hole at whose edge she had tottered for so long.

Or else he did understand, thought Sammy, in that instinctive way children have. Maybe he had seen the tottering, seen her torment, and now he was silently rallying by her side, and by not showing any visible worry he was safeguarding their day-to-day life, the fixed points that Ann could connect to. If she lost her footing, he would stand steady.

They were eating at the kitchen table. Sammy asked questions about what Erik thought about starting school in August. Erik explained that he already knew all the letters and could read, and that he was not a bit nervous.

Sammy observed Ann. She cut up her pizza with slow movements and ate slowly. But at least she's eating, he thought, and wondered what he would do. He had called home and explained the situation, and that he did not want to leave Ann alone. He understood that she did not want to contact anyone who might come and keep her company. Ann had always been careful to show a controlled exterior. She was the one who could manage everything—work, Erik, and being single—without cracks. It was bad enough that at the preschool they had seen her fall apart.

That she was extremely bad at talking about herself, her needs and desires, Sammy believed was one reason for her problems. He had never heard her talk about dreams and plans for the future, never about desire and men, at least not more than in brief, self-ironic comments that she nonchalantly threw out in passing. But he had seen through her for years. Behind the self-sufficient, cocky surface, tumult reigned. Alarm bells were ringing inside Ann Lindell.

She never invited anyone over, never flirted, seldom took any initiative to break her isolation. Instead she sat at home, swilled wine, and gnawed on the bones of loneliness. He knew that Olofsson had discussed her drinking habits with her, most likely very cautiously in his low-key way, careful not to criticize her. He had also discussed the issue with Sammy in confidence, and had been worried and irresolute. That was two or three years ago, when Ann's life appeared to be falling apart, when she showed up hollow-eyed and uninspired almost every morning.

Ann put down her knife and fork after forcing down half a pizza and now sat and observed Erik putting away the last pieces of his. It was slow going, but he seemed to be making an effort not to leave a single crumb on his plate.

"Well done," said Sammy.

Erik gave him a smile. Sammy realized how like his mother he was, that slightly wry smile and momentary expression of mockery in his eyes, a moment that in Ann's case could light up the darkest corners, and that made people smile back. Sammy could not remember when he had last seen that in her face.

But Erik's smile made him remember what it was like when Ann came to the unit. Then she shone; she was eager and curious, she loved life, and could not get enough. The contrast to the Ann of the last few years was suddenly so clear. Life had truly treated her roughly. Sammy took a deep breath to conceal his emotion, got up, and started clearing the table. He turned his back to them, moved by how things were for all of them, how fragile life was, how those few seconds of the deepest warmth and love in life so easily and so often were crossed by pain and desperate fumbling.

He scraped off the plates and rinsed them, to break the silence with rattling and the rushing of water, painfully aware that after all it was these moments of connection and perceived love that were the only things that could save a person, that made you a person. All the rest was struggle. All talk about work satisfaction was bullshit, if the other person wasn't there. At arm's length or on the other side of the ocean made no difference, if only the other person was there. But even as he was thinking that, it felt like a simplification, almost a lie.

"Maybe love is all" he had heard a choir sing once, at Culture Night many years ago. He and Angelika were on the square listening in a downpour. Then, even though Angelika took his hand and squeezed it, the words felt false, but the phrase had taken hold in his mind. Now he didn't know what to think. Every person was the designer of his own life. There was no solution that suited everyone. But was love really all?

Ann's transformation was a deconstruction. She was slowly but surely collapsing; she struggled against it but the collapse continued. The moments of joy, eagerness, and curiosity had been replaced by duty; only if she solved the murder of Klara Lovisa would her existence be justified, but Sammy knew from his own experience that the satisfaction was shallow; only if she was able to give Erik love and care, bring him up to be a well-adjusted person, then her life would be meaningful, but Sammy sensed that the task in itself was no guarantee that she herself would feel like a whole person. There were many things troubling her.

He was roused from his thoughts by Erik, who thanked him for dinner and left the kitchen to resume his computer game.

Ann was still at the table. Sammy felt her gaze and guessed what she was thinking.

"I have a dishwasher," she said suddenly.

Sammy turned his head and smiled.

"I like doing dishes."

He folded up the pizza cartons and scrunched them into the trash bag, wiped off the table and counter, and closed the door to the hall, before sitting down across from her.

"Tell me about Brant's work with Russia," he said.

"I don't know anything about it," Ann answered after a moment's hesitation, "other than that he's been there. He doesn't like the country, that much I understood. What about it?"

Sammy did not know whether this was the right tactic, but he hoped that by disrupting her line of thought he could get her to talk about Brant from a police perspective, and then perhaps bring up their brief but intense relationship. He was convinced that it was in conversation, in talking about what she had experienced and felt, that she might find relief.

He told about Jeremias Kumlin's business deals, the little he knew, and Henrietta Kumlin's conviction that it was a Russian who had murdered her husband.

"What does this have to do with Brant?"

"He's been in Russia, he's an investigative journalist. In his apartment we found material about Russia—books, lots of computer printouts, newspaper clippings, and such."

"You think that Brant ran into Kumlin there?"

"Or his deals, shady or not. He did know Kumlin."

"You want to link him to the murder of Gränsberg and Kumlin?"

Sammy shook his head.

"At first I thought he had something to do with the murder of Gränsberg, but not now. I guess he's in Brazil, right? He hasn't come back, has he?"

"No, not as far as I know."

They sat quietly for a moment and Sammy assumed that Lindell too was thinking about the possibility that Brant had quietly returned.

"We've found his fingerprints in Ingegerd Melander's apartment, so he's certainly still relevant in the investigation. He has connections to both Gränsberg and Melander, and through bandy to Kumlin. He e-mailed you that he had interviewed Gränsberg for an article about the homeless, and it is conceivable that he was at Melander's to meet him on the job, so to speak."

"You think he's physically been there, at Melander's?"

Sammy Nilsson nodded, but did not say where they found Brant's fingerprints.

"He has a lot to explain. How tall is he, this Brant?"

Ann looked at him with surprise.

"Like me?"

"Shorter, maybe a couple, three centimeters taller than me."

"That's good," said Sammy. "The Russian outside Kumlin's was about one hundred eighty centimeters."

Normally Lindell would have asked how he knew that, but now she simply nodded, absent, already on her way elsewhere.

"Brant said that the Russians lacked sympathy, that was something he read in a book. Do you know that he read out loud to me sometimes? I don't read much, but he consumed everything. It was a little tiresome sometimes. He might be reading a paragraph, and when he stopped he looked at me as if I should comment on what he'd read. What could I say? I felt so stupid."

Sammy smiled.

"You should have told him about the pain," he said.

Lindell looked at him, perplexed.

"Your pain, what they try to write about in books. Do you remember Enrico and Ricardo from Peru? The one murdered and the other pressured into suicide. I was there, I saw your pain when you were told about it. Do you remember the mother and daughter by the roadside out in Uppsala-Näs, massacred, the girl had been picking flowers and Josefin, dying, who tried to crawl to her Emily, but didn't make it? We stood there beside each other. Do you remember Jansson's tears? That monster of a patrol officer was crying like a child."

"Stop!" said Ann, but Sammy would not let himself be stopped.

"Those are the true stories. People don't believe that we see, smell, and feel pain. No, we should be cops, some kind of caricature from a video, or . . . fiction, to put it simply. That beats all Brant's reading out loud. The best thing would be if all of us were like Riis, then we wouldn't have to think about what's happening around us. Then we could be like Persbrandt in a TV series, with a little fake angst for the sake of effect, but in reality machines to create smutty headlines about our cleaning job."

"We can't—"

"No, we never can!" Sammy interrupted her. "People don't want to hear that sort of thing. They want to know everything else about our job, but not what it's really like. For us, for the ones who shovel up from roadsides and concrete floors, pick up along the railroad tracks, for those we met, for those we are compelled to visit with horrible news."

Lindell nodded and looked very tired.

"And it will only get worse, no one understands anything anymore. Think if we were to write down—"

"We can't!"

"We shouldn't. We mustn't. The true story would tear everything apart, the politicians' talk and all the empty words. Behind every crime is greed and the imperfection of our society, people's anxiety. And not only our stories. On the way to us, the final station, there are lots of truths that should be told. Away with the fine words, the lies in the newspapers!"

"You sound like Brant," said Ann.

"We would avoid eighty percent of all crimes if . . ."

Sammy fell silent, as if the air had gone out of him, and suddenly looked very helpless.

"If what?"

"I don't know," he retreated.

"That other twenty percent, what's that about?"

"Craziness," Sammy replied, after thinking a moment. "Craziness and love."

"It's the same thing," said Lindell.

He started to say something, but changed his mind. They heard a car drive into the lot, car doors opening and closing, voices and laughter.

Sammy thought about getting up, going to the open window, and looking out, curious about the life outside, but he remained seated.

"We needed that pizza," he quietly said at last.

"Do you want to go home?"

Sammy shook his head.

"You wanted to get me to talk," said Ann. "But what comes bubbling out is your own terror."

Sammy made an effort to protest but knew she was right.

"I know all about the lies, but I hoped that here at home I could bring a few truths to life," she resumed. "Instead I got lies here too."

"What got into you outside the preschool?"

Ann closed her eyes, took a deep breath, and exhaled, as if it required an enormous effort of will to remember what had happened.

"I got tired," she said at last. "I just wanted to lay down and sleep, go away. I couldn't cope, couldn't take another step. All my reserve energy was gone. The mask fell, you know. The preschool, chat a little, answer all of Erik's questions, fix dinner, put Erik to bed, and then . . . keeping your inner self closed, picking up around here, and then—"

"Have some vino to fall asleep," Sammy observed.

"But you wake up again. When he was here, then . . . well, you know. I got a taste of intimacy for a few weeks. I was starved. In the beginning I was just happy and satisfied, then came the thoughts, hopes, plans. It got serious. Besides, he's different than anyone I've ever met, even if he did remind me of you, Sammy. A kind of restlessness, close to sweetness, but also to fury, an inconceivable fury. He could get hopping mad over a trifle."

"Did you ever suspect anything?"

Ann shook her head.

"Never. But I guess that's how it is. You don't see the cracks, or pretend not to. I feel hate, but perhaps mostly self-contempt. That's how much of an investigator I am. And now Klara Lovisa. I thought I'd solved the whole thing. First Fredrik and then Andreas, and I had to let both of them go. Andreas said finally, when I pressed him about the necklace, that he put it in Klara Lovisa's mail slot the morning she disappeared. And I can't disprove that."

"That may be so. But you think it's Andreas?"

"I don't really know. I can't separate lies from truth there either."

"Only hate and self-contempt?" Sammy asked.

"If it were only hate, I would manage better."

"Hate burns," said Sammy. "It may feel good in the short term, but you get deformed."

"As if I didn't know," Ann hissed.

She got up, stole a glance at the sideboard—he guessed that was where she stored the wine—before she went up to the kitchen counter, filled a glass with water from the tap, and drank it.

"You still want him," Sammy observed.

Ann slammed the glass on the kitchen counter.

"Are you going to take sick leave?"

She turned around.

"You know the answer to that question," she said. "It would be fatal to stay home and brood."

"Maybe you can go somewhere for a few days."

"My job is the only thing I have left."

"One thing," said Sammy Nilsson. "What would you say if I e-mailed Brant a few questions, maybe asked him to call? I mean, it's more awkward for you to get hold of . . ."

The question hung in the air between them. Then she shook her head, but tore off a piece of the pizza carton anyway and wrote down his e-mail address.

It was eleven before Sammy went home. He was tired, but happy about the long conversation with Ann. She needed it, and maybe he did too. They seldom sat down and talked things out.

The air was still warm, people were walking on the streets or sitting on balconies and patios, enjoying the night. Sammy was struck with a bad conscience, he ought to have been at home. But Angelika would understand.

During the short walk from the parking space to the town house he thought about Henrietta Kumlin. That besides the terror and grief at her husband's violent death, she seemed relieved.

✦

Thirty-five

Twenty-three murders in the course of forty-eight hours. Anders Brant read the headline in *A Tarde,* let his eyes run over the photographs of the murder victims—among them a local politician, two shopkeepers, a coconut vendor, three teenage boys, a young mother and her two-year-old son. A gallery of young men and women, famous for a day.

All of them looked serious in the photos, as if they were aware that they would meet a violent death. Who would I vote for, thought Brant.

No picture of any perpetrators. He skimmed through the text. No, no one had been arrested.

With those figures it was not particularly surprising that the jails were overcrowded, even though many of the crimes of the past few days would remain unsolved. He was also convinced that more murders had been committed, deeds that would never be reported, either in the statistics or in the mass media. People simply disappeared, were buried, thrown into the bay, or incinerated.

Perhaps a few of those pictured had been victims of police bullets, not policemen in service, but moonlighters, earning an extra buck by taking the lives of criminals and homeless youth. Contract jobs, where the payment was settled when the victim had his picture printed in the newspaper. A newspaper the victims seldom if ever read themselves.

He pushed the paper aside. He was not surprised at the sensational headlines. He was aware of the Brazilian reality, but could never get used to the ever-present violence. Once he had a taste of it himself, but got away with only a scare, and a scar. It was during an outdoor concert at Farol da Barra. He had walked around the lighthouse to find a place to relieve himself. On the slope down toward the sea a couple was necking, a few others were sleeping off a bender. The sea, which had gathered momentum all the way from Senegal, was whipping its white cascades against the rocks.

Out of nowhere a gang of boys and young men suddenly appeared. They came toward him on the narrow cast-iron passageway. He sensed the danger and stepped aside, looking around. It was dark, there was no one nearby, the loud music would drown out all calls for help. The group surrounded him. There was no hesitation in their movements, this was not the first time. No pardon would be given.

Immediately, without a word having been spoken, he took a blow to the back of his head and fell forward, was caught up by a swipe that hit above the eyebrow. He felt the pain and the blood, and now felt really afraid. Someone laughed, it sounded like glass cracking.

He had a rather slender build and knew that he would never escape by muscular strength, but he was agile and limber and that was his only chance. Blinking away the blood in his eyes he saw a gap between two of the attackers, feinted to the right but threw himself to the left.

His experience from bandy helped him. He knew, as he slipped between two bodies, vainly grasping arms that reached out a tenth of a second too late, that he would escape. A feeling of triumph made him let out a howl. With blood running down his face he ran crouching like a rugby player around the lighthouse, and was soon surrounded by people.

A group of policemen took care of him, and at the Portugal Hospital he got seven stitches. The scar, a white line right above his left eyebrow, was the only evidence of what he had experienced.

He had never told anyone about his experience. Even if it was a true picture of Brazilian reality, it felt like a betrayal of the country to brag about the incident behind the lighthouse. He could tell about anything else—the landless, the poverty, the homeless, the struggle for justice, the corruption, but what people would remember was that he had been assaulted.

He had not seen Ivaldo Assis since they visited Vincente in the jail. The neighboring building, or what was left of it, was silent. Brant peered through the window several times a day. The scene was deserted, as was the alley. The dark stain on the cobblestones was the only evidence of what had happened. The trash along the wall had been removed and nothing new had been collected. The carts with which the Assis family gathered rags and boxes were quietly parked with their shafts in the air. Perhaps the Assis family had gone away?

There was no peace and quiet, and he accepted that in the time until his departure not much would be accomplished. He could only wait. The problem was that things were not going very well. It was not just the murder and his false testimony that worried him, but above all, thoughts of Vanessa and his own life.

The day before he had decided to go back to Itaberaba, took a taxi to the bus terminal, bought a ticket, but then never got on the bus. Instead he remained sitting on the bench and watched it disappear in a cloud of exhaust fumes.

The 10,000 reais he should have given her were now rolled up in a sock hidden under the sink. What should he do with the money? In a few days he would be going home. He could exchange them again, at a significant loss, or save them for the next trip, but he sensed it would be a while before he returned to Brazil, if he ever did.

The material he had collected was more than enough—statistics, a hundred interviews with homeless people, politicians, public officials and others, and thousands of photos. He was perhaps the Swedish journalist who best knew the conditions of the most marginalized in Brazil, the smiling country, the country with the samba and Carnival, but also the devastation of nature, especially to produce agrofuel.

And a Brazil with a woman he had betrayed in a degrading manner.

He dreamed about Vanessa, devoting nights as well as days to the settling of accounts. He was out of the running, waiting for a flight that could take him out of the country; for a policeman at his door, who would give him a summons; for Ivaldo Assis.

The cowardice, the lies, and betrayal haunted him. The boundaries of his personal life were becoming blurry, everything was being mixed into a bitter concoction that he was forced to swallow over and over again.

He put on his shorts and a linen shirt, left the apartment and went out, strolling aimlessly, headed up toward the lighthouse, took September Seven Avenue north, stood for a long time by the wall above the little beach by the harbor and studied the bathers, thought he saw

Vanessa several times, strolled over to the small square, sat at the out-door café, and ordered a beer. He had always liked the little square by Barra's harbor, even though it was a haunt for a number of shady char-acters. Various drug deals were settled around the pay phone; the fences, pimps, and whores wandered around. Others picked up cans or begged.

He took several sips of beer, rejected a few offers of getting a massage, and studied the people. Some faces he recognized from previous years. The waiter was the same, always equally furious at Lula and the other politicians, "bandits" he called them. It struck him that this was where he felt at home, in this swarm of contrasts.

It was as if he was seeing himself for the first time, as the person he really was. He was bursting with knowledge of Salvador and Brazil, but also almost completely isolated. He had experienced that before, the dilemma of the temporary visitor and passive observer of a reality that he would never be a part of. Until now he had managed to keep that feeling in check, handled it; he was a journalist, and could temporarily dampen the discomfort and alienation with alcohol. After that he had again plucked up courage, dutifully continued to record and industri-ously gathered material. Then he went home, simply to depart once again, apparently tirelessly curious.

It was his duty to tell the truth, how things really were. That's how he had viewed his work.

The new insight that slipped up on him was that he was also isolated in Sweden. He only existed as the eternal activist, but without roots.

He had been given a chance with Vanessa to become part of the Bra-zilian reality. He could have bought a house, married her, had children, and settled down, but he had chickened out.

I'm too much of a European to feel at home here, he thought. Perhaps that was the ultimate reason for his flight from Itaberaba. Or was it? Yes, that's how it is, he continued his monologue—now on his second beer—I love her, or in any case what I think is love, she loved me, but I put my tail between my legs and ran.

I miss Europe . . . Sweden. It's that simple. But what is in Sweden? A little Spartan two-room apartment in Uppsala, a number of contacts with newspaper and magazine offices, where I have a fair reputation, a few friends I've neglected over the years, a mother I haven't seen in two years. That's it.

And then Ann Lindell. Is she what's different from before? Do I love her? Can I imagine a life with a policewoman? What would that be like?

What exactly it was about Ann that made him so deeply attached he did not really understand. Maybe it was an unspoken wish for a kind of normalcy, just to be part of a context, build something lasting with a completely normal woman.

She was bright, pleasant to be around, her son seemed to be a good kid and would certainly not create any problems, they'd had an amazing time in bed. Ann seemed to be starved for love and affection, and she had made up for that with a vengeance. He had probably never experienced such intensity.

They had widely disparate backgrounds and experiences. He was a politically oriented journalist and, from what he understood, she was a politically indifferent police detective, but that no longer worried him.

He was facing a choice, perhaps the most significant in his life, and he had no answer. Soon he would go home to Sweden. The distance to Vanessa would become, if not insurmountable, then considerable. And perhaps she never wanted to see him again, or even hear from him. He had burned his ships and there was no point in going ashore and searching. But if . . . if he changed his mind, would she want him back, despite his treachery? The question tormented him. He hated making the wrong choice.

He thought about Vanessa's amazing body, got excited there at the outdoor café. She was a true Brazilian mix—a little white, a little red, and a lot of black. Her mother came from south Bahia and had half-Indian blood in her veins. Her grandfather was an Italian engineer from the southern part of the country, while the other relatives were descendants of African slaves from Benin and Senegal.

There was nothing to match Vanessa's beauty. She attracted attention wherever she went, especially during her visit in Sweden, and he had often been proud to walk by her side.

During her stay in Sweden they did not spend many days in Uppsala. For a week and a half they stayed in a borrowed cabin outside Ludvika. The cabin was completely isolated by a small lake. Vanessa had watched in amazement as he threw himself into the water from the wobbly pier. She never got in more than up to her thighs. For a week they did Stockholm, acting like real tourists, stayed at a hotel and ate at nice restaurants every night. He wanted to spoil her, but sensed that she had been most at home in the simple cabin in Dalarna, taking care of themselves and with nature at their doorstep.

He lost himself in memories, ordered a third beer, and built on the painful feeling of loss, longing, and guilt.

When they separated at Arlanda, she was sure he would soon follow her to Brazil, where the mutual promises would be fulfilled and plans for the future take more substantial form. Doubt had started to gnaw in him, but he kept up appearances. After his return home he started brooding, sat in his apartment, and got nothing done.

Her visit had clearly shown that she would have a hard time adapting to Sweden, which she had also expressed in her careful way. But could he imagine living in Brazil?

Only a few days after her departure, he called Ann. He was ashamed afterward of his faithless initiative and how their first encounter immediately developed into a violent, uninhibited sex orgy.

He had a hard time admitting to himself that he called and asked Ann out because he had been attracted to her at Görel's dinner, which took place only a few days before Vanessa showed up. Yet until he was standing in front of her, with her wrapped in a bathrobe, he convinced himself that it was only about dinner, some nice conversation, and nothing else. Deep down he knew differently.

Now he was torn between two women. And he didn't know what love was.

The third beer was finished. The proposals for massage came more often, quickly whispered invitations, and he decided it was time to get up and make his way homeward.

On the other side of the square, right where September Seven Avenue begins its climb up toward Vitória, a young woman was standing, with one hand against a railing, one leg raised and crossed over the other. With the other hand she was adjusting the heel strap of her shoe. Their eyes met.

"Everything okay?" she asked.

Instead of answering dutifully with the same phrase, he shook his head.

"No, an inferno," he said, and stopped.

As if by silent agreement they left the square and without exchanging a word along the way they went to a small hotel on the beach promenade.

The desk clerk looked bored as they stepped into the cramped, dirty lobby. An unbelievably large grandfather clock stood ticking in one corner, a Portuguese product, Brant saw on the face of the clock. The clock was wrong, almost exactly five hours slow. It showed Swedish time.

For 25 reais they got a room to use for an hour, and a condom. The woman took the key and he the condom. She led the way up the stairs; he plodded behind, stumbled, laughed.

The air was stifling and still. The woman, who introduced herself as Monica, seemed to be familiar with the room, because she went up to the window at once and opened it. The breeze of the trade wind immediately came in with an odor of sea and rotting garbage. A threadbare curtain billowed listlessly. She fastened the curtain to a nail, turned her head, and smiled.

Anders Brant had the feeling that she was buying a little time, that she wanted a moment with the view over the Atlantic. He went up and stood beside her.

On the other side of the bay was Itaparica, the island where he had stayed so many times. For a few moments they stood together as if they were a couple who had just arrived on vacation to a charming beach hotel and were taking in their first impressions, not wanting to say anything before they each formed an impression of the place and tried to judge whether they would like it.

His eyes spanned the coastline south of Mar Grande and tried to work out on which beach he had stayed.

Monica slipped out of her dress with minimal movement. She had a white lace bra and matching tanga, which shone against her dark skin. Afterward he wished they had frozen the scene there. She could have leaned her head against his shoulder, he could have put his arm around her waist, told about Itaparica, about the fishermen who pulled their nets and about the carnival where the men dressed up like women.

She would tell him something about her family, about where she came from, what she dreamed about, perhaps lie a little, but he would be treated to a story, something personal, testimony that he could store along with all the others.

Without having said more than perhaps ten words to each other she kneeled before him and loosened his belt, pulled down his fly, and then his shorts and underwear. She did it slowly, carefully, and patiently, careful not to scratch him with her long, red-painted nails, as if he were a little boy being lovingly undressed by his mother at bedtime.

He observed her pale belly and her blackness, which in the folds around her armpits took on a bluish-black hue. He was leaning against the windowsill, she was on her knees.

She sucked him off while he tried to remember the names of the villages on Itaparica, from Mar Grande all the way down to Cacha Pregos. It went fine, he could remember almost all of them.

Monica disappeared into the bathroom; he heard the gushing of the shower. When she came back a minute or two later she was naked. On her belly a few water drops glistened like pearls.

She lay down on the dirty-brown, stained bedcover, and looked at him with what seemed to him a peculiar smile, perhaps critical, taunting in an elusive way, perhaps conditioned by boredom or fatigue, probably both. She turned indolently onto her belly, thrust up her ass, but changed her mind almost immediately and rolled over on her back again. Her eyes were warmer now, he wanted her to say something that reconciled them, something forgiving, but he was not able to meet them in earnest to see. Instead he inspected her body, she was very beautiful, the light ruptures across her breasts and crotch revealed that she had a child. A child who could be his grandchild.

"What does it cost?" he asked, regretting it at once, but it was too late.

The illusion that they had come together because life was an inferno could no longer be maintained.

A drop of sperm fell from his shriveled sex to the floor. He happened to think of the desk clerk who would have to mop up after him. Or certainly there was some woman who had to clean, the man in the lobby appeared to be stuck behind his counter, and he too was probably always five hours too late.

He lay down beside her and pushed his head into her dark hair.

When Anders Brant came home to the pension, Ivaldo Assis and his nephew Vincente were sitting outside the gate. Between them on the sidewalk was a bottle of Primus beer.

On Ivaldo's face Brant saw for the first time a hint of a smile, relief, that made him years younger, while the darkness from the jail still rested heavily over Vincente's facial features.

Brant opened the gate, signaled with his hand that they should wait, went up to the apartment and returned after half a minute. The two men had gotten up, there was something guardedly compliant about them. In his hand Brant was holding a sock, stuffed like a sausage. Without a word he handed it over to Ivaldo.

"*Obrigado*," said Vincente.

"*De nada*," Brant replied, who did not want to be thanked, actually did not want to hear anything from anyone.

A group of schoolchildren came running on the sidewalk, their uniform T-shirts, white with a blue line across the chest, made them look like a soccer team. Brant backed up a step out into the street to give the noisy youngsters free passage, happened to see Ivaldo's gesture, the outstretched arm, before the right side of his face was hit by the side mirror on a bus. He fell headlong to the ground and struck the sidewalk face first.

✦

Thirty-six

Becalmed. A feeble wind from the south that was making a halfhearted attempt on Saturday morning to create a little movement in the air quickly gave up, settled down over the Uppsala plain, and created a trembling haze of heat over city and countryside.

Allan Fredriksson was sweating. He was upset besides. For the *nth* time in a row he was on duty over a weekend with brilliant weather, and he felt a major injustice.

The building was quiet. Everyone who could had fled of course. He was sitting in his office, tapping away on a report of a disturbance at the Central Station. The whole story was simple and predictable. Two loosely composed gangs had collided. Five personal injuries, one of which somewhat more serious, a knife in the buttock of a twenty-year-old youth from Märsta, eight police reports including damage, unlawful threat, unlawful possession of weapons, everyone blamed everyone else, what a life, five of them in jail, a real mess that only created paperwork, because he knew it would all run out in the sand. In six months, maybe a year, a few fines levied, possibly a suspended sentence for one of those involved, if that. The issue of guilt was not crystal clear.

No one was particularly worried, besides a Lebanese whose sausage stand was destroyed and an elderly woman who fell down the steps in the disturbance outside the railway station and broke her wrist.

Fredriksson wiped his brow with a napkin. This was really not his job. Why should he, an experienced detective, have to deal with such trifles when they had three murders on their agenda?

The whole procedure took two hours. Then he left the building and tried to think about considerably more pleasant things, horses that were running at Solvalla and hopefully crossed the finish line in the right order and made the cash register jingle.

Allan Fredriksson was a successful gambler who in just the past six months had pulled in over 150,000 kronor. The free time he did not spend in the forest he devoted to gambling programs and speculations and tips in the newspapers. The fact was that he also spent more and more of his work time thinking about horses.

Sometimes he thought about resigning to become a full-time gambler. He was casually acquainted with a few people who devoted their lives to harness and quarter horse racing, and they seemed to be thriving and living well. Why not? It seemed worry-free, no cocky, loud-mouthed youths creating piles of paper, no weekend shifts, no nagging sensation that the job occasionally, and more and more often, was meaningless.

In an hour he would be meeting the on-duty prosecutor, Gunnel Forss, and decided to take a walk before that. He walked through Svart-bäcken, followed Timmermansgatan, and made his way in among the villas north of Gamla Uppsalagatan. A climbing rose against a wall made him stop.

I'll take Nelson Express, he decided, while he admired the luxuriant buds, and then moved on. His decision created a certain relief but also a tingling excitement, because the fourth run was a real hornet's nest, and if that nail went in, the round could be very interesting and lucrative.

When he reached Sköldungagatan, a woman came walking toward him. He immediately recognized her and she obviously remembered him, because she slowed down and smiled carefully in recognition.

Allan Fredriksson, together with Beatrice Andersson, had gone with Gunilla Lange to the morgue to identify Bo Gränsberg, her ex-husband. He wondered what he should say; he could hardly thank her for their last encounter. But Gunilla Lange solved the problem by stopping and saying something about how amazing the weather in Sweden could be. Fredriksson agreed, even if he would probably spend the rest of the day indoors.

Gunilla Lange talked on about the weather. Fredriksson cursed his decision to take a walk on these particular blocks.

"I've been thinking about something," she said after a brief pause.

"I see, and what might that be?" he said, trying to look interested.

"The last time I saw Bosse, it was only a couple of weeks before he died."

Fredriksson nodded encouragingly.

"Well, he was happy somehow, or maybe excited. I thought it was strange, because otherwise it was mostly problems, the company he wanted to start, and that he didn't have an apartment. He was always saying he was blacklisted by all the landlords. But this time he was optimistic, like he could be in the past. He said that he and Bergman, who he was going to start the company with"—another nod from Fredriksson—"now had everything as good as arranged. When I asked whether they had scraped enough money together, it costs a hundred thousand just to register a corporation, did you know that?"—nod—"he said that it would work out."

"How is that?"

"I asked that too. There was talk that I was going to loan him a little.

He started talking about an old buddy who was well-off, as he put it, someone who had more money than he needed."

"And who could make a loan?"

"Yes, as far as I understood. Or even go in as part owner, but without working in the company. Bosse and Bergman really believed in it, that the company would make money and then someone else might come in—"

"Did he mention any names?"

"Well, he didn't want to say who it was, but that I had met him. He was like that, Bosse, he liked to be a little secretive and then surprise you."

She suddenly smiled, as if she were remembering the Bo Gränsberg she had once known.

"He gave no clues?"

Gunilla Lange shook her head.

"He said something about old times, but that can mean anything. Someone on the work team from before, was what I understood."

"He said team?"

"That's what I understood," said Gunilla.

"How well do you, or did you, know his coworkers from construction?"

Gunilla Lange thought a moment before she answered.

"Not that well. I met some over the years, but not so that we socialized. Bosse probably had enough at work."

"Maybe he meant the bandy team?"

She shook her head skeptically.

"Could it have been Anders Brant?"

"You mean the journalist? Would he be interested? That's hard to believe. True, they played bandy together, and we saw each other quite a bit at that time. He had a girlfriend named Gunilla too, she and I worked together for a while besides. But he doesn't have money, does he?"

"We know that Brant saw Bosse right before he died. Did he say anything about that?"

"No, not a word that he had seen Anders. It was strange. I mean, he should have mentioned it, he liked talking about the past, when he played bandy and that."

The good times, thought Fredriksson. The unexpected meeting had, against expectations, improved his mood.

Fredriksson thought about the photo that Sammy Nilsson had taken from Brant's apartment, and how he called around to everyone on the team.

"Did he mention anything about a Jeremias Kumlin?"

"I know who that is too," Gunilla Lange replied.

"Sadly he was murdered yesterday," said Fredriksson.

The news of the murder had appeared in *Upsala Nya Tidning*, but no name had been mentioned, as they had not yet been able to get hold of Kumlin's mother. She was in northern Sweden. Henrietta Kumlin had a vague recollection that her mother-in-law had talked about Padjelanta, where she would be hiking with a friend. Ottosson had contacted the police in Jokkmokk and asked them to locate her in the wilderness.

Gunilla Lange was staring at him.

"It's not true," she exclaimed. "I saw that in the newspaper this morning, but that it was him . . . Poor Henrietta."

"You know her?"

"We've met at a few parties, then, when everything . . . and they have two small children, a boy and a girl."

"They're almost grown up now," said Fredriksson. "Can Kumlin be the one Bosse was talking about?"

Gunilla Lange had turned pale. There was nothing left of her initial light mood. Fredriksson understood that it no longer mattered that Sweden, on a day like this, was amazing.

They went their separate ways after a few minutes of additional small talk. Fredriksson had done his best to try to give Gunilla Lange back some of the carefree feeling she had shown only a few minutes earlier, but failed completely. Her day was ruined, he realized that, and he was not without a touch of bad conscience.

His day on the other hand looked brighter. Now nothing was left of his slow strolling gait, and he paid no attention to the gardens, but instead walked at a rapid pace toward the police building, with his eyes fixed a few meters ahead of him. His thoughts were circling around Gunilla's scanty, but perhaps significant information.

He formulated various theories to himself, but wanted to talk this over with someone. There was no point in trying to get hold of Beatrice, she always made herself inaccessible, Sammy was in Tärnsjö, you couldn't talk with Riis, Lindell seemed completely engulfed by the murder of Klara Lovisa, and Ottosson was presumably sitting in his summer house in Jumkil playing with the grandchildren.

He phoned Sammy Nilsson on his cell. Sammy answered immediately, as if he was expecting a call. He had not left yet, but would be leaving in a matter of minutes. He was packing the last few things in the car.

Sammy listened, hummed, and asked a few follow-up questions. Fredriksson thought he detected a satisfied tone in his comments and sensed why: the bandy lead, to which Sammy had devoted so much time, might perhaps prove to be a navigable road.

They both realized that Gunilla Lange's meager information that someone from Bosse's previous life had perhaps been prepared to put money into the company, could be a possibility, a thread to spin further on.

"It might be anyone," said Fredriksson, to restrain Sammy's growing enthusiasm. "Some old friend from work won at the track, or—"

"Or Jeremias Kumlin," said Sammy.

"Or Anders Brant," Fredriksson countered.

"Or Lasse Svensson, the restaurant owner," Sammy continued. "I'm sure he has a few hundred bills over."

"Then he would have said something about it when we talked."

"Maybe he was hiding it," said Sammy, not sounding completely convinced.

However much they talked back and forth they got no further. They were stuck in speculations. Fredriksson heard Sammy's family talking in the background, an angry teenage voice and a car door slamming.

"Go ahead and head off for the sticks," said Fredriksson generously.

They ended the call. Fredriksson had arrived at the police building, went in the main entrance, and took the elevator up to the waiting Forss.

But instead of the prosecutor, he encountered Beatrice Andersson and Berglund standing in the corridor outside Ottosson's open door. Unlikely, he thought. Beatrice has a free Saturday, and Ottosson there besides. And Berglund! But then he understood the connection, Ottosson had called them in.

Beatrice turned around.

"Good that you came," she said. "A few things have emerged. Kurt Johansson has started to talk a little."

Who the hell is Kurt Johansson, wondered Fredriksson.

✦

Thirty-seven

Ann Lindell did her level best not to burst into tears. Beside her at the kitchen table, Erik was having breakfast, yogurt with cornflakes and a caviar-paste sandwich on rye. He smiled a little uncertainly.

"I couldn't wait," he said, "I got so hungry."

"That's fine, honey, you're very clever."

She tousled his hair, bent over, and kissed his neck.

"Are you still sick?"

"No, I feel a lot better," she reassured him.

After preschool on Fridays they always shopped at Torgkassen, buying a little something special before the weekend. Breakfast, especially on Saturdays, was usually substantial, with warm sandwiches, boiled eggs, smoked ham, fruit, sometimes pancakes with strawberry jam, and other things they didn't have during the week.

But yesterday had not been a typical Friday, no shopping and no cozy evening. Erik fell asleep in front of his video and when Sammy Nilsson left, Ann carried Eric to the bedroom, undressed him and tucked him in, and then sat for a long time by his bed looking at her son.

She did not go to bed until two. She limited herself to one glass of wine. Sleep would not come until it was starting to get light. It was now ten o'clock in the morning. She was awakened by the phone, sat up half asleep and answered, sure that it was about work. But it was Sammy Nilsson wondering how she was feeling. He also told her that in the morning he had e-mailed Anders Brant and that Tärnsjö was waiting. He ended the call by encouraging her to phone if anything came up.

"We'll have a big breakfast tomorrow instead, okay?" said Ann.

Erik nodded, but did not look convinced.

"I want to do something fun."

"And what would that be?"

"Go swimming," he said.

"We'll do that," she said. "It looks like it's going to be a nice day."

"It's super hot out."

"Have you been on the balcony?"

He nodded.

"You're not allowed out on the balcony alone, you know that."

"I was afraid the food had run out," he said morosely.

In a big box on the balcony Erik was cultivating tortoiseshell butter-flies, small caterpillars that he fed with nettles he gathered in the bushes at preschool where he had also found the caterpillars and come up with the idea of raising his own. A few had already pupated and he was now waiting eagerly for the arrival of the butterflies. Ann thought the cater-pillars were disgusting but let him have his way.

"We'll go to Fjällnora," she decided. "But first I have a few things to take care of."

She was not clear what it was she had to take care of, but she felt she needed to think things over properly. Yesterday's feeling of total dejection at a life that lacked meaning had rocked her foundations. She had had real lows before, but Brant's duplicity triggered some-thing she had never experienced, a wish to just lay down and let go of everything.

She was drained of all energy, there were no reserves left. Sammy's intervention had rescued her from total collapse. She felt anxious when she thought about what might have happened if he hadn't shown up; maybe the preschool staff would have called for an ambulance or taken her to the nuthouse. In the state she was in she would have been unable to protest or even care. She would have let herself be taken anywhere, and that was what frightened her the most. She had jeopardized Erik's well-being.

Now she had escaped with no more than a scare, and admittedly Erik was hesitant, she noticed that in his actions, but he did not have to experience a total shipwreck.

She sat down on the couch with a new notepad, a white, blank sheet before her, and her pen at the ready. It did not worry her that no words came immediately to jot down. She was accustomed to that. Many times she sat that way, sometimes for an hour or more, before she started writing.

But now she did not have the time, and Erik would soon start pattering around her like a lost soul.

"Car" was the first thing she wrote, then "moped." Then five minutes passed before the next notation, "spade."

In between a murder happened, she thought, trying to imagine the scene at the old shed. So common, a shed. Did Fredrik believe, and later perhaps Andreas, that Klara Lovisa would want to lose her virginity that way, on a dirty floor, in that setting? The girl who wanted to wait. Ann Lindell could understand her decision, imagine her tension, her expectation, but not that she would ever accept such a scenario. Never. Lindell had read her diary, the girl was a romantic, but in a touching, mature way, perhaps even more aware of the conditions of love than Lindell was, almost thirty years older. That was what she thought when she read the diary.

"Rape," she wrote. The word screamed violence. The one who supplied the violence was capable of pushing Klara Lovisa down on the floor, pressing his hands around her neck, watching her gasp for air and finally stop struggling and go limp. He must possess not only physical strength but also anger beyond what Lindell could imagine.

Perhaps the scene of the murder and the discovery site were one and the same. Perhaps she had tried to run away, in her confusion dashed into the forest and been caught, pulled down into the moss, and murdered.

Fredrik and Andreas, were they capable of this? It could not be ruled out, but something told Lindell that they lacked just that anger. They were excited, they were eager to have sex with her, they were in a hurry, they wanted to take her virginity as a trophy, to win. But were they capable of violence?

Fredrik had reacted with childish rage, left her to manage as best she could. How did Andreas behave? Pleading, a little pathetic, perhaps. He was also a romantic. The necklace, that was certainly just the right thing for Klara Lovisa, but she could do without his teenage, panting eagerness; his begging puppy-dog eyes. He would have been angry too, but mainly sad. Tears came easily to him, Lindell had seen that.

He had slouched away, crushed, with a shock that turned into anxiety when she never came back again, either to him or to life. If he was innocent of murder, he probably felt guilty of her death. He must be constantly asking himself whether he could have saved her life by acting a different way.

That was the reason for his lies! He could not bear to tell what had really taken place. He could not admit to anyone that he could have driven Klara Lovisa home, but didn't; he, the only person on earth who could have saved her life. He betrayed her.

The insight came to Ann Lindell just as Erik came into the living room. He had a pair of swimming trunks in his hand.

"They're worn out," he said.

"I bought you a new pair," said Ann.

"What color?"

"Blue."

Erik looked at her a moment, their eyes met. She smiled.

"Is that okay?"

Erik shrugged and disappeared.

Ann looked at the words she had written. If she could get Andreas to admit that he had gone to the shed, because she was convinced he had, then the timetable could be improved. Every minute that she could chart the last part of Klara Lovisa's life also brought Ann Lindell closer to the murderer. Maybe Klara Lovisa said something to Andreas before he went back to town? Something that might cast light on what she intended to do. Perhaps Andreas had seen something, encountered someone on the way home, met the third man? A little shard would be enough. It might lead her closer.

What am I doing, she wondered suddenly. It's Saturday, a beautiful summer day, and Erik wants to do something fun.

She closed the pad and got up.

"Let's go now," she called, and Erik showed up immediately, as if he had been waiting in the hall.

Ann wanted to embrace him, promise him that everything would be fine, but she refrained from hugs and promises. It would just make him even more nervous, and could she really say that everything would be fine?

✦

Thirty-eight

"We've sewed on your ear," someone said.

He assumed it was a doctor, a man in his fifties, with tired, greenish brown eyes, a thin mustache, and puffy cheeks, who was leaning over him. His eyes were fixed on him the way doctors' eyes do.

Anders Brant had a feeling that the doctor had been talking to him for some time, he could faintly recall someone repeating his name, a hand on his shoulder, a vague odor, antiseptic, but also onion.

"My ear?"

The doctor nodded, smiled a little, probably pleased at having made contact.

Brant closed his eyes. His head was aching, pounding. He remembered Monica, sank bank into the darkness, his body felt heavy as lead, formless, as if it didn't belong to him. He exerted himself to the utmost to remember anything other than the whore he had bought.

Someone was moistening his lips.

"Señhor Andrés?"

A hand on his chest. Worry, thought Brant, they're worried. He was not able to open his eyes.

"Ivaldo?"

"Yes."

"What happened?"

"A bus. You stepped out into the street, the Pituba bus came."

Geography came first. A map of Salvador slowly appeared in his mind.

"Ondina, Barra, Sete Portas," he mumbled.

"No, Pituba."

The map became clearer and clearer. Memories flowed up and merged like dream sequences: Largo Santana. A boy came up and asked for a chicken bone. When he was refused, he spit on the food and ran, rounding the church in the middle of the square and disappearing down toward the sea; a demonstration on a square, a man separated from the group, he spoke without amplification but his voice sounded surprisingly strong; the mussel gatherers, their sinewy backs against the light, the shouts and laughter across the banks and how he loved life then.

"You gave us money. Why?"

Money. It costs money. What does it cost to sew on an ear? I have to ask. The darkness came back, the map disappeared, the memories were eradicated.

"Vanessa," Anders Brant mumbled.

✦

Thirty-nine

"We're old sports buddies, after all," Berglund explained.

He was smiling quietly to himself, as if remembering something. The others—Bea, Ottosson, and Fredriksson—waited.

"Sometimes we run into each other in town. Kurt works downtown, you might say, collects cans and panhandles a little change from people. He's shrewd in some ways, inventive, but a little out of his mind sometimes. It's hard to know what he's thinking. He often starts crying, but then he was a painter."

"Why do painters in particular cry?" Bea wondered, but Berglund continued as if he hadn't heard the question.

"This morning when I was out with the pooch, I ran into Kurt outside the old prison. He had been sleeping on a boat down at Flottsund and was on his way to town."

"Walked from Flottsund? That must be ten kilometers at least."

Berglund smiled at Fredriksson.

"Kurt has always been in good shape. And he can't take the bus because then he throws up. Balance, you know. And a bus ride is a lot of cans."

Beatrice could not keep from smiling at her colleague.

"Today was a good day for Kurt, he remembered things. He was at the party at Ingegerd Melander's and remembered the quarrel between her and Johnny Andersson. It was about Bo Gränsberg. She accused Johnny of having caused Bosse's death."

"Caused, but not murdered?"

"That's how Kurt understood it," said Berglund. "What the exact words were he doesn't know, but it was a big conflict."

"Was it about something as common as jealousy?" Beatrice threw out.

"I don't think so," said Berglund. "Bosse had been out of the picture for a month."

"Why haven't the others at the party said anything?" said Beatrice. "They should have heard what the quarrel was about too."

"They were gone," said Berglund. "Kurt was the last one still hanging around."

"So where the hell is Johnny?"

Ottosson's interjection put the finger on a sore point. Because even though there had been a search warrant out for Johnny for several days and they plowed through his circle of acquaintances for tips, it was as though he had been swallowed up by the earth.

"Dead, maybe?" said Fredriksson.

The discussion went on, they considered various angles, looking for connections between the various investigations. Fredriksson felt like he'd heard it all before and felt more and more tired, excused himself that he had to go see Forss, and lumbered off.

The last he heard was Ottosson, as he asked what business Anders Brant had at Ingegerd Melander's, and then Beatrice's reply.

"Urgent needs."

The meeting with Forss was not a long one. The prosecutor decided not to do anything for the moment about the trouble at the train station. There was no reason to arrest any of those involved. The alleged crimes were too minor.

Fredriksson was both pleased and displeased with the decision. Pleased because he could immediately put this behind him, and displeased because he wanted at least one of the creeps he had encountered in the questioning, the one who probably wrecked the hot dog stand, to have to rattle bars for a while, preferably a long while, and preferably soon.

Instead of returning to the conversation outside of Ottosson's office, he looked up Myhre. Fredriksson guessed that he was sitting hunched over all the binders and other material they had taken from Jeremias Kumlin's office.

"Nice of you to visit," said Myhre without any ceremony, looking sincerely happy that Fredriksson in particular came by.

Myhre was a workhorse. There were those who thought that the success of the financial unit depended on his efforts. He had been recruited from Malmö in connection with the former police commissioner's decision to make financial crimes a higher priority, and this proved to be one of the few successful personnel efforts on the part of leadership.

In front of him on the desk were papers in such an enormous quantity that even an experienced man like Fredriksson was amazed.

"Is this all Kumlin's?"

Myhre nodded and threw out his arm toward another table where at least as many papers were piled.

"Oil, gas, and Russia equals money," he said. "And money equals papers."

"Money also equals crime," Fredriksson quipped.

Myhre looked surprised for a moment, as if it struck him for the first time that he was dealing with crime. Most of his colleagues were convinced that Myhre was not driven by any fervent devotion to law or desire to put financial criminals in jail, but that the motivating force for him was numbers, columns, and balance sheets.

"Have you found anything interesting?"

He regretted the question at once, as Myhre would almost certainly go off on a detailed account of Kumlin's various undertakings, but the financial policeman surprised him by taking out a single sheet from the drift on the table.

"This," he said.

"And this is?"

"A purchase," Myhre answered contentedly.

"Of what?"

"Of a certain Sture Millgren," said Myhre. "Millgren is an expert on energy issues and somehow associated with the Swedish embassy in Moscow."

"Trade attaché?"

"No, some kind of special service from what I understand. I've snooped around a little and Millgren got the position over a year ago, for the sole purpose of issues about oil and gas. He came most recently from Brussels where he worked as an expert on energy issues."

"And you think Kumlin bought him?"

"Yes and no. Kumlin's partner, Oleg Fedotov, was probably the one who took care of the actual transaction, but Kumlin was aware of it. And our Mr. Millgren was not cheap."

"A case of Russian caviar, perhaps?"

Myhre shook his head.

"Considerably more, about a million to be more exact."

Fredriksson stared at the contentedly grinning Myhre.

"Dollars," he added.

"That's over six million kronor!"

Fredriksson sat down.

"Then you can imagine what kind of money this is about in the end," said Myhre.

"And what would Fedotov and Kumlin get in return?"

"That's just what I was thinking about, but obviously it has to do with oil and gas."

"Jesus H. Christ," said Fredriksson. "This is getting too big."

"And why does Kumlin die? Did he get cold feet, was he careless with the money, or what?" Myhre speculated.

"We had a similar case many years ago, before you came to town," said Fredriksson. "Then it was the CEO of a pharmaceutical company, Cederén was his name. A pure contract job."

"So Fedotov sends one of his torpedoes to silence his partner?"

"It may have happened that way," Fredriksson mumbled, who was taken back in his thoughts to the Cederén family's horrible fate. "Maybe we can set up protection for Henrietta Kumlin," he said. "It is conceivable—"

"Then we would have found her in the garage too," said Myhre. "No, I think it was Jeremias who was the target and no one else."

"We'll have to present this to Ottosson and Hällström," said Fredriksson. "You can compile what you've come up with so far. It's a little delicate of course with a Swedish diplomat involved."

"He's not really a diplomat, more a consultant associated with the embassy."

"Bad enough," said Fredriksson, getting up.

"There's more," Myhre resumed. "Millgren also has his own company, Neoinvest, but it is registered with his wife, Carolina, and his brother Arnold. Although I am quite convinced that it is Sture Millgren who stands for the substance in Neoinvest."

"Is that allowed?"

"They work with environmental impact analyses, as it's so nicely called on their website, primarily where exploitation of oil assets is concerned. It may concern the effect on the marine environment of extraction of oil offshore or, like now, the pipeline that the Russians and Germans want to lay through the Baltic Sea. So he and the little woman also have a more commercial connection to the industry."

"Is that allowed?" Fredriksson repeated. "On the one hand working as a semi-diplomat, and on the other hand making money through your own company?"

Myhre shrugged.

"That's how it is, a fucking mess. Money talks. They're the same type of people, the whole lot of them."

"One more thing," said Fredriksson. "How are you able to even find this information? So unbelievably stupid to leave a trail behind you."

"Fedotov seems to be a self-confident type," said Myhre. "He writes about it in a regular e-mail. On the surface it appears to be an ordinary business transaction, but considering how it works we can assume that this million dollars should be seen as a bribe. Millgren probably doesn't need to do too much analysis, instead it's about paving the way. He writes a report, perhaps for the sake of appearances including a few critical viewpoints and side comments, but basically positive to RHSKL GAS, as Fedotov's and Kumlin's biggest and oldest company is called. And just like that they can bring home a pile of cash, and now we're talking lots of zeros. So a million dollars to Millgren is a good investment."

"But this pipeline is a Russian project, isn't it?" Fredriksson objected. "How can a Swedish consultant's statement play any role?"

"I don't know," said Myhre. "But there is a connection of some kind, I'm convinced of that. Maybe Millgren's report is intended to look good internationally. The project has gotten a lot of criticism, and if Putin and the boys in the oil mafia can show an honorable document from an honorable Swedish expert, that looks extremely confidence inspiring. A Russian statement doesn't impress anyone at the EU, but Millgren is known in Brussels as an irreproachable Swede. Perhaps the Fedotov-Kumlin duo have also hired others? They have contacts with several other European consulting companies, including one in France. Possibly the idea was that they could present a whole bundle of independent reports. A mess, like I said, and somewhere in that pudding is an almond that's worth millions."

"But Kumlin seems to be a small-timer," said Fredriksson, who was thinking about his little office with all the binders. "If this was about billions, he ought to be sitting in a nice office."

"Appearances deceive," said Myhre. "He was certainly good for a couple hundred million."

Fredriksson was amazed.

"So why does Kumlin die?" he asked.

"That's your thing," Myhre grinned. "I pull out the numbers, you capture the Russian mafia."

Fredriksson made a face that showed what he thought about that mission.

"But I don't believe in chance," he said.

"What do you mean?"

"First Gränsberg, then Kumlin. Those two knew each other from before. Add to that Ingegerd Melander's fall in the stairway. And then this journalist on top of it, an old buddy too."

"Maybe Gränsberg was Kumlin's man," Myhre threw out. "Kumlin brought in his old bandy teammate for some dirty jobs. Gränsberg needed the money."

"Where does Brant fit in?"

"Maybe he was on the trail of something and was threatened by Gränsberg, who was sent out by Kumlin. Maybe this talk about Brant writing about the homeless is just bullshit. His real work was about Russian oil."

"Gränsberg didn't seem to be that type," Fredriksson objected.

"Money," said Myhre.

"Inheritance," said Fredriksson.

Myhre grinned.

"The merry widow who invents a Russian," he said.

Fredriksson sighed heavily.

"Jesus H. Christ, such a beautiful day!" he exclaimed.

"I'm comfortable here," said Myhre with another grin.

Fredriksson shook his head and left his colleague who had the nerve to be happy at work on a beautiful summer Saturday.

He went slowly back to his office while he considered whether he should slip out, but realized that was a little too much. First he had to write down what Gunilla Lange had told him and make sure that Sammy Nilsson and Beatrice Andersson got a copy. It was not sensational information, but along with everything else they had collected perhaps a pattern would emerge.

Could it be Jeremias Kumlin who had been the cause of Gränsberg's optimism, that the former teammate, now a multimillionaire, would contribute capital to the planned construction company? But who then would have an interest in killing Gränsberg? And why did Kumlin have to die? Had a Russian been dispatched? Was it just mere coincidence that the two murders involved mutual, old connections? Improbable, but still a conceivable possibility. Over the years chance had played numerous tricks on Fredriksson, but he was an experienced investigator and gambler, chronically suspicious of coincidences.

Those were the kinds of questions that Fredriksson devoted his time to as he suffered through the afternoon. He was not noticeably wiser when he left the police building at five o'clock.

✦

Forty

Anyone who saw Ann Lindell return to the police building on Monday morning would not have guessed that the Friday before she had been close to a definitive breakdown. She walked briskly into the elevator, inspected her face in the mirror, and adjusted her hair.

As the elevator door slid open, she walked right into Sammy Nilsson. Lindell took a quick look in both directions before giving her colleague a hug that was as quick as it was unexpected.

"That was a pretty nice welcome," he said.

"Anything new?"

Sammy Nilsson told about Fredriksson's conversation with Gunilla Lange and that Myhre has been hunched over Kumlin's accounts all weekend. Lindell realized at once that this opened several possible pathways that might raise the investigation from the question mark level, but she could not keep from thinking about Brant's possible involvement.

"Although we must have a chat with Brant," said Sammy Nilsson, as if reading her thoughts. "And now a chat is actually approaching. By some miracle Haver managed to find out that Brant is booked on a flight from Brazil to Madrid tomorrow, and from there to Stockholm by Spanair."

Sammy Nilsson leaned forward and pressed the elevator button.

"Who should—"

"Me," said Sammy Nilsson. "I'm going to Arlanda to meet him so he doesn't disappear again. You don't want to come along?"

Lindell shook her head.

"You could do a separate interrogation," said Sammy Nilsson, trying to strike a light tone.

"Doubtful," said Lindell.

"Take the chance," said Sammy, getting into the elevator and blowing her a kiss.

Lindell headed for the coffeemaker but changed her mind when she saw that Riis was standing there. Talking with him would be a real step down after the encounter with Sammy and probably ruin her good mood.

Instead she went into Ottosson's office, mostly to make an appearance. She considered telling him that she hadn't had a drop of wine, either on Saturday or Sunday, but such information would surely make Ottosson nervous. He was a specialist in finding reasons to worry in anything that deviated from the usual. "Are you sick?" he would probably ask.

"You look frisky," he said enthusiastically.

"Blame it on the booze," she blurted out.

Ottosson looked surprised at her before his face cracked open in a smile. The message was received.

She went up to the desk, leaned over, and patted him on the cheek.

"What now?"

"It's WHO International Pat-on-the-Cheek Day, didn't you know that?"

Ottosson, sometimes painfully lacking in imagination, looked even more confused.

"I didn't know that," he said. "But that was a good idea from the UN."

"I thought about skipping morning chapel this morning," said Lindell. "I have a few ideas."

Ottosson started to protest, but stopped himself and nodded. Like no one else on the unit, Lindell was allowed to run her own race, and she knew how to exploit this to the breaking point.

"A few ideas," she had said to Ottosson, but the fact was that she had turned onto two dead ends, Fredrik and Andreas, and now did not have a single reasonable idea of a passable way to proceed.

"Horny little bastards," she mumbled.

She devoted an hour to making a clean copy of her notes from the interviews with both of them. Sometimes it helped to go over everything again with fresh eyes and a rested brain. But the results were the same this time as well.

The question of the grave in the forest constantly returned. That was the key. Deep and carefully dug, by someone who was cold and calculating, not a rush job. The only weak point was that it was so close to the shed. For the only thing that might lead to a discovery of Klara Lovisa's body was that someone could say she had been there. There were two to choose from, Fredrik and Andreas, but both had kept quiet. They could have gone to the police but didn't, afraid and ashamed.

The murderer must have realized that but took the risk anyway. That argued for Andreas, but against Fredrik. Did he come back, unaware that Andreas had also made a visit and then disappeared? Perhaps there was no third man? Andreas, one visit, but Fredrik two. The latter with Klara Lovisa's death as a result.

Her musing was interrupted by the phone. She answered immediately, happy to break the vicious circle.

"I'm back now," he said in his light voice.

It was Håkan Malmberg, Klara Lovisa's soccer coach.

"I see, that's nice," said Lindell absentmindedly.

"You wanted me to call."

"Exactly. I have a few questions about Klara Lovisa, perhaps you can fill in a few things."

"I doubt it," said Malmberg. "What's it about?"

Lindell glanced at the clock.

"Is it possible for you to drop by this morning?"

"Drop by," Malmberg laughed. "That sounds like a social visit, but sure, I'm going into town, so I guess I can drop by."

Håkan Malmberg was a tall man—Lindell estimated his height at 190 centimeters—and when he took off his motorcycle jacket it was clear that he spent many hours at the gym. He radiated energy in an unexpectedly attractive way to her. Otherwise she had a hard time with tattooed, leather-clad men with bandannas around their necks and ponytails, maybe because she associated them with biker gangs. There was also something pathetic in their attempts to radiate masculine energy, which in Malmberg's case was dampened somewhat by his shrill voice.

He also lacked a ponytail and was constantly rubbing his hand over his shaved head. Lindell guessed that he had very recently shaved his head and was not used to it, perhaps unsure whether it had been a good idea.

He was noticeably nervous. She could only speculate why. His body language gave her the impression that he had something to hide, or else he was just uncomfortable about being at the police station.

"How well did you know Klara Lovisa?"

"Pretty well, she was on the team for several years."

"Have you played soccer yourself?"

He simply nodded, and Lindell noted that he did not take the opportunity to tell when and with which club, an area that was reasonably not a minefield.

"Do you know Klara Lovisa's parents?"

"Well, not really, I guess I've seen her mom at a match sometimes."

"Did you have a relationship with Klara Lovisa?"

Malmberg looked up at her, then his eyes wandered toward the reception counter and around the reception area, where people were coming and going in a steady stream, the majority on their way to the passport department, before he answered.

"No, damn it, she was jailbait."

Those were Fredrik's words.

"She definitely did not look like a fourteen year old. Was she flirtatious?"

"No, I don't think so," said Malmberg. "More or less like the others, a little giggly sometimes. You know how girls are, like hens, cackling."

"And you were the rooster?"

"Sure," said Malmberg. "No, damn it! You have to keep your distance. I'm a coach and I like it. The girls are good for the most part. We have a good time together."

"But the club wasn't doing so well," Lindell observed.

"Not good? It wasn't working at all."

"Do you know why Klara Lovisa stopped playing soccer so suddenly?"

Malmberg shook his head.

"Were you upset?"

"Of course I was," he muttered.

"What did you have against Fredrik? He was forced to quit."

"He was too on all the time."

"What do you mean? Where soccer or the girls were concerned?"

"Both," said Malmberg.

"Was that why she left the club? Did he hit on her?"

"I don't know, but I guess it's not inconceivable."

"Do you think he murdered Klara Lovisa? You said something about that when we talked on the phone."

Malmberg hesitated. He was obviously unpleasantly affected.

"Do you know or do you suspect anything that you ought to cough up?"

"Well, no . . ."

"But you think—"

"No! In a way I was completely floored when I heard you'd arrested Fredrik, but at the same time not particularly surprised, because he's a really smarmy type. But to be honest I had a hard time believing that kid would have the nerve to kill someone and then bury the body. I didn't believe that about Fredrik. He's a bastard, but—"

"Have you talked with him lately?"

"No, not since he left the club. I thought I saw him in town last winter."

"Alone?"

"I don't know," said Malmberg.

"Don't know?"

"It was so quick. He went past in his dad's car and maybe there was someone in the car."

"Klara Lovisa?"

"It was a light-haired girl anyway."

Lindell tried to ferret out more detail about where and when Malmberg thought he had seen Fredrik and a possible passenger, but he could not remember more than that it was on Kungsgatan, near Stadsteatern and that it was some time in March, because it was before he had taken his motorcycle out for the season.

"When do you do that?" Lindell asked.

"It depends on the weather, but usually in the middle of April."

"Have you talked with anyone else about this, I mean since Klara Lovisa was found? Anyone in the club?"

"I've been out with the bike and got home yesterday. My sister called right away. I'm going to help her move."

"Can you imagine anyone else in Klara Lovisa's surroundings who may have anything to do with the case?"

Malmberg shook his head.

"So to summarize: You haven't heard or seen anything, and you think Fredrik in principle is an oily bastard but not capable of murder?"

"He's probably capable, but I was a little surprised."

"Okay," said Lindell, extending her hand. "Thanks for taking the time for this social hour."

Håkan Malmberg smiled at her. She guessed that smile had put ideas in the heads of many soccer players.

Ann Lindell accompanied him to the entrance, watched him leave the building and straddle the motorcycle, which he had parked right outside. He waved to her, pulled on his helmet, kick-started the motorcycle, and disappeared onto Svartbäcksgatan.

A feeling of calm came over her: She looked down at the notebook. There was a single word noted: March.

✦

Forty-one

"Shadows," said Allen Fredriksson. "They're there, but we don't see them, other than as shadows."

He said this quietly, as if he had thought of something but did not have the whole context clear.

"What do you mean?"

Sammy Nilsson sensed what his colleague wanted to say but wanted to hear more, how Fredriksson developed a theme that he had never put into words before.

"Kumlin, that Fedotov guy, and now consultant Millgren in Moscow, and then everything behind that. There must be a lot. Gränsberg and the others, we understand them well enough. They assault and kill each other, get drunk, throw up and act out, stink, yell and scream, lie and make flat denials. But this gang is just formless figures. We know they exist, we see them on TV, and read about them in the newspapers—successful, promising, but that's just bullshit. Just the surface. Kumlin, for example, who the hell would believe he was good for over two hundred million? Where does the money come from?"

Fredriksson threw out his arms and stared encouragingly at Myhre, as if he could explain.

"You're just jealous," said Beatrice. "You play the horses and want to win the big pot every week. You wouldn't turn down a few million."

"No, of course not!" Fredriksson hissed.

He was unrecognizable. Obviously he had spent Sunday thinking and concluded that life was unfair. Seldom had they seen or heard him so upset.

"Where Russia is concerned it's a little different," said Myhre thoughtfully.

It was noticeable that he was slightly ill at ease being the center of everyone's attention, perhaps also due to Fredriksson's unexpected aggressiveness.

"In what way?" Sammy Nilsson asked.

"It's a sick bandit economy," Myhre resumed. "The ones who enter the Russian game, like Kumlin, have to be prepared to apply somewhat unorthodox business methods. For one thing this concerns enormous sums of money, for another the mafia runs the economy, and third, the forces that could serve as a corrective are completely out of commission or even mixed up in it. I'm thinking about the politicians, the police, and the courts. But the price is high. I think Russia is the only industrialized country where the average life span is going down, and drastically, it's not a matter of six months or so. The country is heading for a demographic catastrophe, and mostly for the Russian population, which is declining the most, while other peoples in the Federation are increasing. The result will be black as night, with ethnic cleansing and civil war. I can picture to myself how Putin starts a crusade, more Chechnyas in other words. The ones who are drinking themselves to death today may be the most fortunate."

Myhre paused and turned toward Fredriksson.

"There's the answer, Allan, to where all Kumlin's millions come from: liquor, oil, corruption, and misappropriation of everything that can be sold."

"So we can't count on any help from the authorities?" Sammy Nilsson asked.

"Hardly," replied Myhre.

"And Millgren will probably not cooperate?"

"Not in the slightest now," said Myhre.

Sammy Nilsson smiled at the expression and how the modest Myhre was so sure of himself.

"The process goes on," Myhre resumed. "Russia's economy is like a giant organism that floats around. If a tentacle is cut off, the body twitches, but the cut surface heals quickly and new tentacles grow out."

"Kumlin was only a tentacle, good for two hundred million," Beatrice observed.

Myhre nodded and continued his lecture.

"Millgren continues his activity, his agreement with Fedotov and Kumlin probably rests on relatively solid legal grounds, he's probably not that dense. Maybe he has to take a little shit, there will be some talk about divided loyalties, but who will really be surprised?"

"There is a catch," said Sammy Nilsson. "The neighbor lady with the dog, the one who walked past Kumlin's house, maintains that the man by the fence did not sound foreign, that he said something about the dog. She maintained that he said the word "pooch," "nice pooch," or something like that. How probable is it that a Russian—"

"But she wasn't sure, and besides her hearing is very bad," Beatrice objected. "When I talked with her I had to more or less shout."

"The lady with the dog," said Fredriksson. "It's always some bastard with a dog."

"You're in top form," Sammy Nilsson grinned. "Did the system break down over the weekend? Was there a free-for-all in the fourth race?"

Fredriksson only glared. The fact was that Nilsson's dig was right, his system had broken. If Nelson Express had behaved himself Fredriksson would have taken home almost four hundred thousand. Now he had to be content with a miserable eighteen grand.

"I won," he muttered.

"It shows," said Sammy Nilsson ironically. "And how does it feel when you lose?"

"But why does Kumlin have to die?" Beatrice said suddenly.

Her question expressed what they were all thinking, that the motive was decisive for whether they would have a reasonable chance to solve the murder. If there was a connection to the Russian mafia, the probability was great that the murderer was already out of the country and forever inaccessible to justice.

"Maybe he was playing both sides," Sammy Nilsson threw out at last.

"With who?" asked Myhre, well aware that they would probably never get a clear picture of the whole thing.

✦

Forty-two

Moments of happiness, when fate smiles gently and generously, came seldom to Ann Lindell, but now she was experiencing such a moment of grace.

She had called Klara Lovisa's parents to confirm what she already believed.

Now she was sitting in her office, completely motionless, with her hands clasped on the desk, smiling broadly, even grinning occasionally.

She sensed that what she was experiencing at that moment was like the feeling a craftsman or artist has before a completed work.

The only sorrowful thing in the context, which somewhat soiled it all, was the sad finding against which she experienced happiness at this time. It was after all about the death of a young girl. But that did not take much away from the feeling of quiet triumph. Detective Inspector Ann Lindell had succeeded.

She thought about looking for Ottosson to tell him, but more than anything else she wanted to sweep into his office and submit a finished package to him and Prosecutor Molin, where everything was signed, sealed, and delivered, so she decided to savor the sweetness a little longer.

Then came the worry. Basically it had been lurking there the whole time, but suddenly the fear of failure struck with full force. She could not be 100 percent certain; did her eagerness to solve the murder make her draw hasty conclusions? Her intended submission of evidence was fragile, to say the least.

She got up indecisively and gave the notes on her pad a final look before she hurried out of the office, shut the door, jogged over to the elevator, and pressed the button. But she then changed her mind, and took the stairs to Forensics.

✦

Forty-three

"I saw Bosse the day he died."

Gunilla Lange looked up. The information came unannounced, spoken in a casual tone of voice, as if he were telling something very ordinary.

"What are you saying? You were at work, weren't you?"

"That day I was in town," said Bernt Friberg. "I was helping Gurra with a leak."

"And you're just telling me now?"

He nodded in response.

"Where?"

She feared the worst and did not want to hear. She was afraid that the relative calm of the past few days, when she fought her way back to some kind of normalcy, would now be over. Was this the start of a confession? Was her husband a murderer?

"I saw him walking along the road, so I stopped and picked him up. He was going to the trailer."

"Why was that?"

Gunilla's voice was shrill and challenging.

Talking was not easy for Bernt, the words often sat deep inside, but this time it seemed as if he wanted to get rid of a burden. That was how Gunilla understood his unusual talkativeness.

He told her that right before the nine o'clock break he was on his way to Spikgatan, where the company had its storeroom and office, to have a bite to eat and pick up a few spare couplings and bends for the job he and Gunnar Melin were working on. He went on in great detail about the difficulties they had with the leak outside an apartment building in Gunsta. It was an emergency call. The foreman called in the morning and told him to skip Stockholm and instead join up with Melin who was already on the scene with a backhoe. Unfortunately first thing in the morning they had severed an electrical cable, which admittedly was completely outside the cable plan, but that obviously created even more problems.

Gunilla let him go on with his exhaustive account, afraid of what was to come. As long as he was talking pits and backhoes everything was calm.

According to Bernt, Bosse Gränsberg had been radiantly happy that morning. There was no sign of the usual slightly bitter, careworn air that was his trademark, an attitude Bernt always had a hard time with. During the short car ride Bosse had chatted. He was sober and reasonably well-dressed. He explained that he had been forced to look for a phone booth as his cell phone had disappeared.

Bernt drove him all the way up to the trailer. An impulse made him get out of the car. They chatted awhile about old times.

"I really had nothing against Bosse," Bernt explained. "You may not know it, but we worked together many years ago. We got along fine then."

Gunilla Lange became more and more surprised. Never before had Bernt spoken so calmly about her former husband. Neither of the two had mentioned that they had worked together before either. But was the reason for the admission was that Bosse no longer constituted a threat?

"Who did he call from the phone booth?"

"He didn't say, other than that it was important as hell. But before I left he said something strange. He said something like 'Now Ivan would get a good thrashing.'"

"Who's Ivan?"

"No idea," said Bernt. "And then he added that he was 'going to make big money.'"

"He said nothing else about Ivan?"

"No, nothing except that he would get a beating. Actually there is an Ivan, a pipefitter from Gamlis, who I worked with a long time ago, and who Bosse knew too, but he must be retired now. I have a hard time believing that's the Ivan Bosse meant. And then there's a paver named Ivan, who worked at BPA a long time ago, but—"

"And then you left?"

"Then I left."

He looked at her with a steady gaze. I have to believe him, she thought. He can't lie, he mustn't lie.

"I felt a little uneasy," Bernt continued. "I mean, Bosse was happy and all, but that talk didn't sound pleasant. And it wasn't either. He died a few hours later."

"Why haven't you told this to the police?"

Bernt looked at her a few moments before he answered.

"What would they think? And what would you think?"

"But now you're telling me."

He nodded.

"I wanted you to know. If it should come out, I mean. If anyone saw us."

Bernt suddenly got up from the table. After every meal he usually cleared the table and loaded the dishwasher, but now he left the kitchen and disappeared into the living room. Gunilla heard the lid of the old secretary desk being lowered. Bernt returned with an envelope in his hand.

"Here," he said, handing over the envelope. "We're going to take a trip."

"Trip?"

"In August."

"We're taking a trip? Where to?"

For several years she had nagged that they should travel abroad and suggested different destinations, but Bernt had always resisted.

"Cape Verde," he said.

She stared at him incredulously.

"Not that many people go there. I thought it would be nice to avoid the crowds."

"Where is it?"

"In the middle of the Atlantic," said Bernt. "It's an island."

She could not keep from laughing.

"Of course it's an island," she exclaimed, "if it's in the middle of the Atlantic. You're completely out of your mind!"

He nodded and smiled for the first time since he came home from work.

Gunilla took the travel documents out of the envelope. Two weeks on Cape Verde with departure on the fourth of August. That was when her vacation began.

"But you—"

"I've moved up my vacation," he said.

She browsed through the travel documents, but did not really understand anything other than that the hotel was called something with Vista.

"I think it will be fine," he said.

She pushed the papers to the side.

"You have to tell the police that you met Bosse," she said.

"They're going to think it was me."

For a moment it struck Gunilla that perhaps it was Bernt who had killed her ex-husband. She looked at the colorful brochure about the Atlantic island group, read a line about a music festival on one of the islands, raised her eyes and looked at Bernt, who had started clearing away dinner. He could have done it. He was overcome by anger sometimes. Then he was changed beyond recognition. Once he hit her. Then she was prepared to leave, but he asked for forgiveness, and she stayed.

Was the talk that he and Bosse had a friendly chat about old times a lie? Had they quarreled? About her, about the money that she might conceivably loan out?

She dared not ask, afraid to trigger his anger.

"You have to talk with them," she said.

He turned and looked at her, but she dared not meet his eyes. In one hand he was holding a plate, the other was holding hard onto the edge of the counter.

It was here in the kitchen that he hit her. That time his anger was triggered by what she considered a trifle. One of her coworkers had unexpectedly called and asked whether they could go out. Bernt was working late and Gunilla thought she could take advantage of that, she seldom went out, and left a note on the kitchen table.

They went to Hijazz, had something to eat, and listened to a blues band. When Gunilla came home she found Bernt drunk at the kitchen table. She had had wine and stumbled a little when she went up to give him a kiss on the cheek. She was met by accusations of infidelity and a hit across the mouth.

"Cape Verde is beautiful," he said.

Gunilla Lange did not want to go to an island in the Atlantic. She wanted to get rid of the growing sense that something was wrong, shake off the feeling of worry and fear. She wanted to grieve alone, it occurred to her.

After the murder of Bosse at first she only felt a great sorrow and loss. Bosse had been the love of her life, and now he was gone forever.

Then when she found Bernt at the kitchen table early that morning, the fear had come. There was something in his behavior that she did not understand. And now this, that Bernt had encountered Bosse perhaps only an hour or two before the murder. Was he concealing anything else? What had they really talked about? The feeling of not being able to trust the man she lived with made her uneasy.

And Cape Verde of all places! Was the trip only a way to confuse the issue, get her to think about something else?

✦

Forty-four

It was as if Friday's collapse rinsed a lot of waste products out of Ann Lindell. Was it the chat with Sammy Nilsson that created this peculiar sense of inner purity, or was it as simple as the fact that she had not had a drink in four days?

"I don't care about you," she mumbled, but knew that this was partly just play-acting. Her thoughts this morning revolved around Anders Brant, and she could not decide what to think. One moment she felt a thrill of happiness at his arrival, and the next moment remembered the events of the past two weeks.

"Mom!"

Erik was tugging on her sleeve. She could hear from his tone of voice that he had asked her something, but she had not registered what it was about. She crouched down and put her arms around his shoulders and neck.

"Kiss," she said.

Erik shook his head with an expression beyond his years, as if he wanted to say: *Give it up now!* But he gave her a quick peck on the check before he freed himself and set off.

Ann Lindell left the preschool behind her with a feeling of energy.

For the police, Tuesday was an in-between day, with few reports and alarms. Even the number of visitors in reception went down significantly on the second day of the workweek. It was as if even criminals were low on energy.

But for her it would be a different kind of day, Lindell realized. Sammy Nilsson would be meeting Brant at Arlanda and in the meantime she would break a murderer.

The day before she had summoned him for questioning at ten o'clock. He expressed no surprise, only a poorly concealed fury that "a whole day would be ruined."

"There are just a few additional questions we need to have on tape," she said to calm him, smiling to herself and thinking that she would be very pleased to help ruin ten or fifteen years of his life.

It was Allan Fredriksson who went to meet Håkan Malmberg at the reception counter.

"Where's Lindell?"

Allan was making small talk with a colleague at the counter while he pointed with one finger vaguely upward.

"Excuse me," he said at last. "Lindell is up there, she asked me to get you."

"What do you want?"

Fredriksson observed him with surprise.

"Solve a murder," he said. "That's all."

Fredriksson took the lead and led Håkan Malmberg to the interview room where Lindell was waiting. She got up and welcomed him.

"Would you please take off your bandanna and jacket," she said. "It can get very warm in here."

He shook his head, but obeyed and hung the leather jacket on the back of the chair.

"I'll take care of the bandanna," said Fredriksson, snapping it up.

"Why's that?"

"Listen now, Malmberg!"

Lindell's voice cut through the room.

"We think you've been doing a little too much talking. Yesterday when we spoke you stated that you had not talked with Fredrik Johansson since last fall. Is that still true?"

"Yes, damn it! Why would I talk with him?"

"What do I know? Have you spoken with Klara Lovisa's parents since she was found?"

"No, I don't know them."

"You haven't spoken with anyone at all about Klara Lovisa since she was found, is that correct?"

"Yes! Like I told you, I've been on vacation."

Ann Lindell observed Malmberg.

"Think now, you have a chance to change your mind. We're record-ing our conversation, do you realize that?"

"What is this?"

"You haven't spoken with anyone, okay," said Lindell. "When we dis-cussed Fredrik Johansson, you said something to the effect that you thought he was a bastard but that you didn't think him capable of kill-ing Klara Lovisa and burying her. Do you still think that?"

"Sure," said Malmberg. "Do you have to do everything twice at this place? And why aren't you arresting him, instead of taking up my time?"

"Tell me how you knew that Klara Lovisa's body was buried in the forest," Lindell challenged.

"Huh?"

"You heard me," said Lindell calmly.

"Everyone knew . . . What do you mean? Huh? How . . . ?"

Håkan Malmberg's confusion was immediate and total.

Ann Lindell observed Håkan Malmberg's sweaty forehead and lis-tened patiently to his flat denial. When he realized he was in a bad way, Malmberg demanded that a lawyer be present. One joined them after an hour-long break in the questioning, looking almost indifferent. Ann Lindell got the feeling he didn't like his client, but concealed his antipa-thy behind a bored expression.

The third man, thought Lindell. Is this going to work? Håkan Malm-berg stood firmly by his story that perhaps he had heard something about Klara Lovisa being buried, but that he could not remember when or from whom. That would hold in a courtroom, she realized, even if Malmberg first stubbornly maintained that he had not talked with any-one about the murder after the body was found. That could be explained by his feeling pressured.

"You have a Kawasaki?"

"Yes, what about it?"

"I don't know that much about motorcycles, but it looks unusual."

"There are only a few in Sweden."

"Easy to recognize," Lindell continued.

Håkan Malmberg stared at her without commenting.

"I think we'll take a break here," said Lindell.

"Then I'm going home!"

Lindell shook her head.

"You'll be staying here awhile," she said.

"What was that with the motorcycle?"

Lindell grinned.

"Just trying to make him a little nervous."

"It hasn't been seen in Skärfälten?"

Lindell shook her head.

Allan Fredriksson had been generally passive during the questioning. He had seldom felt so strongly that this was Lindell's case and that it was her business to break down Malmberg's resistance.

Malmberg was taken to the jail, and his bandanna to Forensics. Everything was hanging on a red thread. If it could be established that the thread they found in the forest hut came from Malmberg's bandanna, they had an indictment, otherwise not.

"Were we too quick?" Lindell asked self-critically.

Fredriksson did not think so.

"There was no alternative, everything else has been threshed over," he said.

"The harvest of chance," said Lindell.

Fredriksson nodded. He felt out of sorts and tired and mostly wanted to put his feet up on Lindell's desk, lean back, and close his eyes.

"Today Sammy is meeting the journalist coming back from Brazil," he said, mostly to have something to say, perhaps to break Lindell's tense expression, but the comment had the opposite effect. She looked like she'd been slapped.

"I know," she hissed.

"Relax," said Fredriksson. "You can't do anything before Forensics has had their say. If the thread holds, that would be marvelous, otherwise we'll have to try something else."

"Something else," Lindell muttered.

✦

Forty-five

There was no doubt that Anders Brant was clearly the most interesting passenger on the flight from Madrid to Stockholm. His head was bandaged. He was also walking with a cane. The pain in his legs and hips, which had not bothered him much to start with, had gotten worse. The whole right side from the hip on down was basically one big bruise. Despite the doctor's assurances that he would recover completely, he was worried about his future ability to move.

Even so, it gradually occurred to him what incredible luck he'd had. He ached all over and one ear was sewn on, but he was alive.

The Salvador–Madrid leg passed in a daze. Before departure he took two of the pain pills he got when he was discharged from the hospital and then had a cognac on the plane. The effect was quick and tangible. The flight attendant had to wake him when the plane landed. He had dreamed about Vanessa: turbulent confrontations, filled with shouting and tears, hatred and ill will.

Anders Brant staggered around the airport in Madrid, so captured by his dreamed experiences that he felt sick. He had presence of mind enough however to make his way to the right gate and sink down in an uncomfortable plastic chair. He was sweating profusely. His head ached and the pain in his hip was getting worse and worse as the pain reliever wore off.

This is my punishment, he repeated his mantra from his sickbed. That he would be punished was a given. He had not only betrayed Vanessa but also his own convictions. The experience with Monica in the shabby hotel room was a death blow to his whole outlook on life. He had deprived her of a piece of her human dignity, he was a whoremonger, a john.

The nausea made him lean back and swallow. He breathed in deeply, tried to focus on details in the terminal—a little crack in the dirty panorama windows, a vending machine with soft drinks, and scattered passengers walking past.

"Forgive me," he mumbled, and hated himself even more for being such a sorry sight. How could she forgive him? Idiot, he thought.

He stood up but immediately sank back in the chair, dizzy and terrified that perhaps he would not be able to take care of himself. Would he even be able to write the articles on Brazil he had promised? Would he ever be able to write about . . . ?

"Lay off," he mumbled.

Would he be able to look Ann in the eyes and explain what had happened? Or would it be best if he gave her up too, without pathetic attempts at explanations?

I have to start over, he thought, and tried to logically construct a prelude to normalcy and everyday life, to the person he had been before. But soon he began to worry that he was in the wrong place, at the wrong gate, maybe even in the wrong terminal.

He stared at the information board above the gate, but Stockholm had not come up yet. There was less than two hours until departure. Maybe the gate had been changed? Helplessly he sat and stared stupidly ahead of him, remembering the man who had lived in an airport for years. That felt like an attractive alternative, floating, vegetating without purpose or goal, in a departure hall.

He closed his eyes, rocked his upper body a little back and forth in a hypnotic swaying, a trick he had used before to reset himself and try to regain control over his thoughts.

When he opened his eyes a short, skinny man was standing in front of him. His furrowed face expressed unveiled curiosity.

"I hardly recognized you," said the man. "But isn't it Anders?"

Anders Brant did not recognize him, but something in his voice sounded familiar, a harsh tone that made Brant think of the endless Sunday dinners of childhood.

"And who are you?"

The man grinned.

"You don't recognize me?"

Brant took a deep breath.

"Did you get beat up?"

Anders Brant felt his anger growing.

"Maybe you've lost your memory?"

The man let out a dry laugh, looking around as if searching for an audience.

"Go to hell, you fucking nobody," said Brant.

The man was startled.

"You curious little piece of shit," Brant continued, and immediately started laughing.

It was not so much the man's astonished face that made him burst out in uncontrolled laughter, but rather the liberating feeling of being able to say something in Swedish, and above all to tell someone off.

He got up from the chair, took his cane and shoulder bag with his computer, and limped away.

"You think you're so fucking remarkable, huh?" the man shouted after him.

Without looking around Brant raised his cane.

"But all you write are lies!"

Brant stopped and looked over his shoulder. The man was gesturing and his mouth was moving, but Brant didn't care about the words. It was as if he had left something behind on the spot he had left.

"Lies!" the man shouted again.

Brant nodded and went on. He needed a restroom.

"A pretty solid hit," Sammy noted when Anders Brant told him about the accident. "Do you still have a headache?"

He had met the journalist in the arrival hall, introduced himself, and explained that the Uppsala police had a number of questions. If I get coffee right away, Anders Brant had said, and they sat down at a coffee bar.

Brant did not answer but instead stared without seeing at the people streaming past. He was actually not surprised to be met by the police, but felt too tired to answer questions, much less argue.

"A number of things have happened—"

"I know," said Brant. "But I don't get what this has to do with me."

"Bosse Gränsberg," said Sammy Nilsson. "You saw him the day before he was murdered, and I think you know why he was murdered."

"What does Ann say?"

"About what?"

Brant shook his head.

"I met Bosse to interview him, that's all," said Brant.

He told how he and Bo Gränsberg ran into each other by chance and exchanged a few words about old times, bandy and so on, but pretty soon got on to the homeless situation in Uppsala.

"I'm writing a book about the homeless in several countries, and Bosse was simply an informant."

"Do you see any motive for the murder? Did Gränsberg say anything about feeling threatened?"

"No, the only thing I can imagine is the 'Russian papers,' as Bosse called them."

"The Russian papers?"

"He claimed he had come across valuable documents about Russia."

"Tell me more!"

"I don't know that much, he was very secretive. He tried to sell the papers to me."

"Sell? What would you do with them?"

"I'm a journalist."

"And you said?"

"No, thanks."

Sammy Nilsson looked at him pensively. Brant wanted to get home as soon as possible, the headache had come back with full force, but he understood there were more questions.

It was Sammy Nilsson who unexpectedly got up from the table.

"I'll drive you home," he said. "You don't have any other baggage?"

"I'm guessing you know where I live."

"I know *how* you live," said Sammy Nilsson, taking off.

It took a few moments before Anders Brant understood what he meant, and he quickly caught up with the policeman, who had now made it to the exit.

"What do you mean? Have you been in my apartment?"

Sammy Nilsson nodded, but without slowing down.

"I'll explain," he said, pointing to the black BMW parked in a space reserved for taxis.

"That's a break-in, damn it!"

Sammy Nilsson stopped short.

"Listen up now," he said. "If you had talked with Ann, been a little more upfront with her, then that wouldn't have been necessary. So stop the shouting. Do you want a ride or not?"

They stared at each other for a few seconds.

"No, thanks," said Anders Brant at last. "I'll take a taxi."

He saw the vacillation in the policeman's face.

"Then I'm compelled to take you with me anyway," said Sammy Nilsson.

"You're a senseless character," said Brant. "First a little small talk and coffee, then you bring out the coercive measures."

"You were actually suspected of complicity to homicide."

"And now?"

"Stop talking nonsense, damn it!"

Anders Brant smiled for the first time in several days. Most recently was when the Assis family visited him for the last time in the hospital. He opened the back door, threw in his bag, and made himself comfortable in the back seat.

It was not until they passed the exit to Knivsta that Sammy Nilsson broke the silence.

"You played bandy with Gränsberg, is that right?"

"Why do you ask about things you already know?"

"And Jeremias Kumlin. He's dead too, struck down in his garage. Did you know about that?"

"What the hell are you saying?"

Anders Brant leaned forward. Sammy Nilsson turned his head and their eyes met for a moment.

Sammy Nilsson briefly told how they had found Kumlin's body in the garage.

"What the hell is this?" Anders Brant exclaimed.

"We're wondering that too. What were you doing at Ingegerd Melander's place?"

"Who's that?"

"We found your fingerprints in her bathroom."

"Is that Bosse's lady friend?"

Sammy Nilsson nodded and gave him a quick look in the rearview mirror.

"I was there, but I didn't remember her name. Bosse took me there. We were going to talk, I was going to record a little, Bosse and a few others in his gang. You can listen to it if you want."

"Okay," said Sammy Nilsson. "Tell me about the documents Bosse wanted to sell to you."

"Like I said, I don't know what they were about. Bosse was really desperate and thought he was sitting on a gold mine, but I had a hard time believing that. It would never occur to me to throw away fifty thousand on something without knowing what it was. Besides, I don't have that kind of money. And I don't buy information, which I explained to him."

"Did he show you any samples?"

"No, he waved a few papers, that was all. I took it as a little confused talk. He was going to start a company and needed money."

"We know about that," said Sammy Nilsson. "Where did the papers come from?"

"I don't know."

"He never mentioned Jeremias Kumlin?"

"No."

Sammy Nilsson stopped his questions. They came out on the plain south of Uppsala and the city's thorny profile emerged, with the cathedral, the castle, and the chimneys of the heating plant as the most prominent landmarks.

When Anders Brant saw the industrial area on the south edge of the city, he was reminded of Bosse Gränsberg, his desperation, how he had burst into tears in the trailer. I betrayed him, he thought, but dismissed the self-reproach. He could not have acted any other way. Or could he have?

"What kind of condition are you in?" the policeman interrupted Brant's thoughts.

"Pretty good now," he answered.

He told about the accident in a little more detail and could not keep from mentioning that he had visited a jail in Salvador and about his impressions.

"What were you doing there?"

"Giving false testimony," Anders Brant answered.

He saw the policeman's wry smile in the rearview mirror, and found himself liking him more and more.

"I'll drive you home, okay? I'll wait while you get rid of your baggage, then we'll go to the police building, so we can get everything on tape. Maybe you want to towel yourself off too?"

"Preferably not in the police building," said Anders Brant.

"You don't want to run into Ann?"

Anders Brant did not reply. He did not think the other man had anything to do with it. Ann and his story was their business, but at the same time he was curious about what Ann had said.

"She's a good woman," he said at last.

"So treat her like one," said Sammy Nilsson.

"What do you mean?"

"You know what I mean."

Anders Brant perceived it as a verbal wrestling match, an exchange of words he did not want to have, that he was not prepared for. What did he know about Sammy Nilsson? Nothing. And regardless of that, he only wanted to go home, lie down in bed, and sleep.

"I'm just about done," he said. "Can we have this chat tomorrow?"

"We've got to do it today," Sammy Nilsson decided.

✦

Forty-six

Johnny Andersson poured another glass, the last one. He was crying. Alcohol always made him teary eyed, but some of it was the real thing. Maybe it was the old knick-knacks, dusty but otherwise untouched by the passage of time, that made him boozily sentimental. Hadn't the vase with the inscription *Souvenir from Leksand* been there for ages? Johnny seemed to recall that sometime in the fifties his parents cycled around Lake Siljan. How did they come up with the idea of cycling all that way? And why drag a vase home with them? But that's how it was then, he thought with a mixture of envy and contempt.

The whole cottage was like a nostalgia museum, and he willingly let himself be carried back to his childhood. He sobbed over vanished smells, memories, and possibilities.

This is what I have, he thought, and I'm not responsible for any of it. He turned, stroked his hand tenderly across the flowery wallpaper, and then tipped over in bed.

"If only I could sleep," he mumbled, but knew he was too sober to fall asleep. The alcohol was really gone now, and along with it the possibility of fooling his body.

For three days he had stayed at the allotment garden cottage. Sleeping over was not allowed, but he did not think anyone even noticed he had been there. He stayed inside and did not make himself conspicuous, did not even turn on the radio. He had been given notice; the annual fee to the association had not been paid for several years. The only reason the association had not taken action was that his parents were among the original gardeners; his father had been chairman for many years. He knew that as soon as his mother was gone, he would be thrown out.

The old Nordlander woman, who had the cabin right across the narrow street, had been digging in her plot for a couple of days, and then biked home in the evening. But if she had seen him she wouldn't dare say a word. She was afraid of him, always had been.

He was living on rye bread, sausage, and powdered mashed potatoes. But now supplies were running low and what was worse, all the beer was consumed and the bottle of aquavit he brought with him was empty.

There was a time when there was always a bottle of wine or a few beers in reserve in the cottage, a time when he could sit under the apple tree and look out over his mother's flower beds, often with a beer in his hand. Sometimes he had to go out and give her a hand, prune a branch or dig up a flower bed. No major exertions, but the old lady had always been grateful, especially for the company.

The cabin at the allotment garden had been a retreat. He never brought any of his drinking buddies there, did not even talk about the cabin. It was his and his mother's territory where they could maintain the illusion of the industrious allotment gardeners. He had to fill in for his father, who died in the early eighties. She must have thought that a few beers for his assistance and company was a low price, because the pantry under the hatch in the kitchen floor was always filled.

Now he had to leave. He stared out the window; the poorly tended beds made him sad. During the spring he tried to weed out the worst of it, but it was as if a little resistance only stimulated the couch grass and thistles, because now the perennials were barely visible. Only the angry red poppy was able to show off.

He didn't know what time it was, his wristwatch had stopped and the phone was turned off, but he guessed it was fairly early.

He looked around the cabin. It struck him that this might be the last time he would be there. Otherwise I could live here, he thought, I don't need anything bigger.

He shut the door with a slam, did not bother to lock it, stood quietly on the stoop, and drew the fresh morning air into his lungs.

"I could live here," he repeated out loud.

He felt no regret, only a great fatigue. They could have done it together, but Bosse had always been a stubborn bastard.

He heard the sound of the bicycle before he saw Nordlander come pedaling, but did not bother to hide.

She opened the gate to her patch, pushed in the bicycle, and then turned around, as if she unconsciously registered his presence.

To his surprise she smiled. She parked the bicycle, came back, and stood by the gate.

"Up early," she observed, and Johnny could only nod.

"Have you had coffee?"

He shook his head.

"I'm putting some on. Why don't you come over in ten minutes. I can make a few sandwiches too."

Has she had a stroke? Sure, he'd had coffee many times at the Nordlanders, but always with his mother, and the last time was at least five years ago.

He could not bring himself to answer, but of course coffee and a sandwich would be nice.

"So you'll come by later?"

He nodded. The neighbor lady gave him another smile, turned on her heels, and disappeared into her house. He sat down on the bench under the apple tree. Coffee and a sandwich; he remembered her egg-and-anchovy sandwiches, but that was probably too much to hope for.

He glimpsed Anna Nordlander behind the curtains, rummaging around in the kitchen. She was a retired teacher and it showed, she almost always had that gentle, forgiving expression on her face, which he associated with his own time at the Tunaberg school. The teachers had given up before he even tried.

Johnny leaned against the apple tree, enjoying the warmth. After the frosty nights earlier in the month it had been getting steadily warmer every day. It sucks that I can't live here, he thought, then I could sit here every morning, feel the rough bark against my back and the sun against my face, enjoy life.

Having access to a cabin but at the same time not having an apartment was frustrating. He got the idea of talking with the Nordlander bitch, she was the only one in the vicinity who would have an opinion on whether he could stay in the cabin over the summer. Maybe she could be convinced. He could even help her with a few chores.

Johnny got up from the bench, certain that at least ten minutes must have passed. He left the lot, crossed the road, and went up on Nordlanders' stoop. Through the thin door he heard her voice. Was she talking to herself? He carefully opened the door.

"You have to hurry," Johnny heard her say, and he realized that Nordlander was talking on the phone.

"Ralf, do you hear what I'm saying? He might get away," she said in her teacher's voice.

Suddenly he understood. She was talking with her son, that fucking busybody policeman. Ralf must have tattled to her that the police wanted to get hold of Johnny.

He and Ralf, who had played together in the garden area, were in the same class the first six years of school. Now he would march out and become a hero.

The old lady was calling the cops on him! The invitation for a cup of coffee was only a way to keep him in the area.

Johnny Andersson was consumed by fury. This happened to him more and more often.

He opened the door wide and threw himself into the cabin.

"You damn witch! 'Have you had coffee?' You lying sack of shit!"

Anna Nordlander picked up a knife from the counter and held it in front of her with both hands. On the counter was a loaf of bread.

He stared at the shaky hands that held the serrated knife.

"I see, you're going to cut me?"

Johnny Andersson took hold of a chair and raised it. For a moment in his mind he saw his mother and Nordlander as they were sitting in the kitchen, shelling peas, a childhood memory. Thirty-five years ago maybe. Then he and Ralf had stormed into the kitchen, out of breath and thirsty and Nordlander poured rhubarb juice from a pitcher.

He lowered the chair.

"Leave my house!"

He raised the chair again and swung it toward the woman. A chair leg hit the left side of her head and Anna Nordlander was thrown toward the window, pulling down a couple of flowerpots with her arm as she vainly tried to hold herself upright and then collapsed on the floor.

Johnny Andersson knew now that flight was everything. From Nordlander's kitchen, from all the memories, from the Ralf of childhood, from the garden cabin—his only property and fixed point.

He grabbed the loaf and took a bite. The woman at his feet whimpered. Hatred welled up inside him, hatred for which he had no target. He leaned down and picked up the knife from the floor.

"You wanted to stick this in me," he said.

Anna Nordlander slid up in a half-sitting position. Her eyes were cloudy and blood was dripping from her temple. She shook her head. She opened her mouth but was not able to say anything. Johnny wanted to hear her voice, listen to her lies and excuses, simply to have a reason to release his rage. He wanted to hear her say her obvious lies in her teacher voice. He wanted her to crawl in front of him, beg him, she who had always given the orders. Then he could scream at her, spit and kick her, but he could not attack a mute elderly woman lying at his feet with a foggy gaze and shaking hands.

He threw the bread at her and left the cabin with the knife in his hand.

✦

Forty-seven

It turned out to be a long talk, more and more taking the form of a monologue. Sammy Nilsson did not need to ask many questions. After a few minutes Anders Brant already felt a growing satisfaction, being able to talk about Bosse Gränsberg and what had happened the past few months.

He began to feel a kind of optimism. He was talking with a person, admittedly a policeman, who seemed to be able to put two and two together without everything having to be explained. Brant talked about the time on the Sirius bandy team with a sense of joy, even pride. He had been a pretty good player, a team player.

Brazil and Salvador faded away. Lately his brain had been working in high gear: the ignominious flight from Vanessa, the e-mail from Ann, witnessing the killing on his street, the visit to the cell, and finally the accident—all this had built up a tension that was now relieved as he talked about something as trivial as bandy. There were no lies, no betrayal, no personal or political complications. He experienced it like the joy of a reunion, as if he and Sammy Nilsson were two old teammates who unexpectedly ran into each other and were now exchanging recollections.

Brant sensed that the relief perhaps had to do with Ann Lindell, even though he had no basis for optimism in that area. Sammy Nilsson had hinted that she was extremely sad. It would surely be a painful showdown. He realized that she had somehow found out about Vanessa's existence and his duplicity. Of course she was angry too. He was sure to be raked over the coals, and there was something in Sammy Nilsson's attitude that made Anders Brant uncertain, as if it no longer mattered what he said or did. Had Ann grown tired of him and given up the thought of a relationship for good?

But let it come, let the waves rage over him! He was not worth anything else. Maybe he didn't even want to see her anymore. Was it the case that it was neither Vanessa or Ann? A cop, he thought, how would that work?

"Is she in the building?" he asked suddenly.

Sammy Nilsson nodded.

"She's questioning someone we believe to be a murderer and rapist."

"Nice," said Anders Brant.

During their intense weeks together he had not really thought much about her job. He tried to picture her sitting in front of a violent perpetrator, but the image of the Ann he knew did not tally with murder and rape.

"She's a police officer," he said, as if that had only just occurred to him, and Sammy Nilsson laughed.

"A good police officer," he noted. "With all due respect to bandy, let's return to Gränsberg. What do you think he had to do with Jeremias Kumlin?"

"Nothing," Brant answered immediately.

"Could those Russian papers have come from Kumlin? Did you know he worked with oil and gas?"

"Not a clue," said Brant, although he had a vague memory of an article about his old teammate who had become so successful in the former East bloc.

He started to feel the headache more and more. The doctor at the hospital in Salvador had encouraged him to take it easy. The blow to the head had caused a serious concussion and minor internal bleeding. He should be at home in bed, licking his wounds.

"I realize you're feeling a little shaky, but just a few more questions," said Sammy Nilsson. "Do you know Johnny Andersson, a buddy of Gränsberg?"

"I interviewed him the week before I left for Brazil. He was funny somehow, tried to stand out as a little superior, but in a moving way. He actually came to my place a couple days later."

"What did he want?"

"No idea. I was just leaving and in a bit of a hurry. I told him to come back another day. But to be honest I did not particularly want him running around my apartment."

"How did he get your address?"

"It's in the phone book."

Sammy Nilsson grinned.

"You know that Johnny succeeded Gränsberg as Melander's boy-friend?"

Brant shook his head.

Sammy Nilsson told how Ingegerd Melander was found dead in her stairwell and that they were now looking for Johnny Andersson.

"Have you been to the Tuna allotment garden? He has a cabin there."

Just then Sammy Nilsson's cell phone rang and he answered immediately. Brant heard an agitated voice. Sammy held the phone away from his ear.

"At the Tuna allotment garden perhaps?" he said with a derisive smile, giving Brant a bemused look.

✦

Forty-eight

"Was it better before?"

Ann Lindell's question got no answer. She did not expect one either, since she was alone in her office.

For fifteen years she had been employed with the Uppsala police, or was it longer than that? She couldn't bear to even count. It was not an especially long time, one of her colleagues had forty years in the building, but long enough that she should be able to answer the question.

She decided that it was better before. In any event at Violent Crimes, in any event for her, in any event according to her own hasty, subjective analysis.

Had she been better before, that is, was she worse now? She grinned. Okay, she was older, a little heavier, more wrinkled, perhaps more cynical, not as curious, but no worse as a police investigator. She did not want to believe that, not even consider it. Had her associates gotten worse? Where some of them were concerned, she answered yes without hesitation. Riis definitely, maybe Allan too, mostly because he showed such a depressing resignation, more clearly than the others. Ottosson?

Haver mostly went around seething. Beatrice? Well, she had definitely gotten heavier anyway, thought Ann with a hint of a smile. Sammy?

The majority had no doubt undergone a development similar to hers—more wrinkled, heavier, more experienced, individually perhaps more skilled, but on the whole worse.

There was something at Violent Crimes that didn't add up. Ann had a hard time putting her finger on it. The percentage of cases solved was roughly the same over the years, despite an increased workload, not compensated for by more personnel. Productivity had increased, in other words, but something else was missing.

The joy was gone, she decided. Less and less often was there a gleam in her associates' eyes. It was as if they all had a virus that produced out-of-sorts, downhearted police officers. There was grumbling, she decided. She was no exception, on the contrary, her own grumbling had increased dramatically in recent years, as if she was never really satisfied, either with her own efforts or her colleagues'. Or rather, there was grousing about an uncomprehending environment—the politicians, the National Police Board, the county police commissioner, the union, the media, the general public, young people, immigrants, social workers, the correctional system, prosecutors, the healthcare system, they all got their share. Seldom expressed and factually formulated, instead it usually went no farther than muttering from the corner of your mouth.

The whole morning she had thought about Sammy Nilsson's words that the true story would destroy all the empty words, tear away the politicians' veils of meaningless talk and promises. In a previous discussion, one of the now rare outbursts of meaningful debate at coffee break, he maintained that they all knew what was wrong, that there were simple, reasonable solutions to the majority of problems. Eskil Ryde protested and maintained that Sammy only wanted to spend the taxpayers' money for no purpose. The technician thought that people's most fundamental motivation was egoism, a characteristic that was genetically determined besides. In other words, not much could be done other than try to correct, mend, and repair, and lock up the worst idiots. Humans were incomplete, so why dream about a paradise? It only made you tired.

"Klara Lovisa," she mumbled.

The name had become like an incantation. Why, she did not understand, but knew that the true story about the girl who was raped and then strangled could never be told. Or rather, there were several stories, tangent to each other, layered over each other.

Ann was convinced of Håkan Malmberg's guilt. There was something very helpless about his massive form. During the latest interview she had seen something in his eyes. Perhaps he wanted to tell what had happened?

The information of whether the thread from the shed matched Malmberg's bandanna would take time. It was a complicated analysis, and Prosecutor Molin explained that to file an indictment there could be no doubt whatsoever about the thread.

To break her passivity, Ann Lindell decided to visit the jail and say hello to Malmberg. Perhaps that environment, which he was now forced to see as "his," would make it easier to get to know him better.

As she passed Ottosson's office he called her in. He was sitting behind the desk, leaning back with his hands behind his neck. A button in his shirt had come loose, and in the gap that formed white skin was visible. He looked strikingly content.

"The national forensics lab is prioritizing the thread," he reported. "You still think this is the right guy?"

Lindell nodded.

"Fredriksson found a spade," said Ottosson. "Malmberg has one of those collapsible kinds, camping type, that can be stored in a packing case on his motorcycle. Ryde will take a closer look at it."

"Yes, I heard that."

Ottosson let his arms fall down on the desk and observed her.

"Sammy picked up that journalist today."

Maybe he's in the building, Ann thought.

"I've got to go," she said.

"How are you doing?"

"Fine," said Lindell curtly. "I'm going to see Malmberg now."

In the elevator she took a deep breath and exhaled. Brant, yes! May he rot in hell!

✦

Forty-nine

Surprisingly enough the hole in the fence was still there, perhaps thanks to the fact that it was hidden by some tangled bushes. That was the opening he and Ralf used when they wanted to go down to the Fyris River, forbidden excursions. On hot days they undressed and splashed around in the water, swam upstream and then let themselves be brought back by the current.

Johnny Andersson stood by the river's edge. It must have been thirty years since he'd last been there, but everything seemed so familiar and near. For a minute or two he was carried back to the games and memories of childhood. The episode that usually showed up when he thought about playing at the allotment gardens was the memory of his father, who only came down to the cabin if there was digging or carpentry work to be done, and who once joined him in the forbidden crawl through the fence. Johnny did not remember what they did, only the memory of his father wriggling through and then standing on the river bank, peering, as if he was thinking about fleeing from everything.

An angry dog's barking was heard from the other side of the river. Johnny looked around. He had no plan, but he realized that soon Ralf and his cohort would be swarming around the allotment area. He took a few steps in the thick vegetation, turned on his heels, and started walking south, toward the city.

After some ten meters he came upon a boat, a leaky old rowboat, partially hidden in the dense meadowsweet. It was secured with a frayed piece of rope to the trunk of an alder. No lock, only a knot. He untied the knot and pulled the rowboat into the water. It floated, but for how long? There were no oars, but he tossed in a crooked branch that was on the bank and then carefully stepped into the wobbly vessel, pushed off with the branch, was caught by the weak current and carried away.

When he determined that the boat would not immediately capsize or sink, he felt a sense of calm. This was what Ralf and he had dreamed of, being able to take off like Tom Sawyer and Huckleberry Finn. Admittedly the Fyris River was a very pale copy of the Mississippi, but that was the waterway he had.

Johnny Andersson sat very still on the bench and watched the shore glide past, as if he were a well-adjusted, curious participant on a sightseeing cruise, where everything was arranged and predetermined.

Soon he passed the badminton hall. At the camping site a teenage couple was sitting on a bench. Johnny waved, the couple waved back. At a level with Fyrishov he heard sirens from a patrol car, but he had difficulty making the connection to himself. It was as if the recent events, even the showdown with the old Nordlander woman, had faded away and were replaced by a strange equanimity. Slowly the rowboat carried him closer to the city center.

After the Fyrisvall bridge, the half-finished buildings rose on the right and to the left was the old retirement home where his grandfather had died. A few construction workers had made their way down to the river. Johnny guessed they were on a break. One of them shouted something that Johnny did not catch, but he answered anyway with a wave and a smile.

The vegetation was thick, big trees lowered their crowns toward the water. There was a scent of sediment and summer. Johnny took a deep breath and laid down in the boat. He watched the light clouds sail along, and it was as if everything faded away, now there was only him and the light veils against the blue sky. After a while he got dizzy from staring at the sky and sat up in the boat.

Without thinking of anything in particular, Johnny Andersson was traveling at a moderate pace through his city. The Fyris River passed like a dividing line through Uppsala. In the past the inhabitants were sorted according to which side of the river they lived on. As an illustration of the ancient division, he passed the old shoe factory on the east side, his grandfather's workplace once upon a time, and to the west the Fyris school, where in his youth he committed a totally meaningless burglary and to top it off was arrested.

It was as if he was floating along in no man's land, and that feeling made him forget his sorry situation. He caught himself sitting in the rowboat, grinning, suddenly and unexpectedly reconciled with the events of the past few weeks.

It was not until he glided under the bridge by Skolgatan that he remembered the milldam at the Uppland Museum. At the annual shooting of the rapids at the end of April, most of the boats would capsize there, either at the crown of the ramp or as they tumbled along. The homemade boats broke apart and the students ended up in the water. Johnny had never seen the spectacle, but read about it in the newspaper.

Then there were divers ready to fish out the ones who suffered shipwreck, but he suspected that no one would jump in to rescue him today.

He first tried to paddle with the crooked branch, then use it as a steering oar, but with equally meager results. The current placed him in the middle of the river and was steadily carrying him toward the falls.

Now he also had an audience. At the Åkanten Restaurant people were flocking by the iron railing and shouting encouraging words. On the other side a gang of youths was yelling, and outside the museum Japanese tourists were filming as the rowboat approached the edge, tipped over, and disappeared from their field of vision. Those who were standing on the Cathedral Bridge had an even better view, and Johnny happened to see a woman pointing and screaming in terror. Johnny Andersson had become an attraction.

He crouched, preparing for the worst. The rowboat turned over, he was thrown out of the boat and dragged down into the murky water under the Cathedral Bridge.

He had not been swimming since he was a teenager, but instinctively he started vigorously moving his arms and legs, to avoid being thrown against the side stones. He gasped for breath, getting a mouthful of cold water, reached the surface for a moment, flickeringly saw a man up on the bridge. His mouth was wide open. Maybe he was screaming. He reached out his arms as if he wanted to take hold of Johnny, who was however five meters below, inexorably being flushed down toward the New Bridge.

He was sure he would die. The possibility of getting a hold and hanging on to the perpendicular walls was nonexistent, and it was several meters up to the edge. There had been a chance upstream of the milldam where he could have crawled up on land, but now it was too late. He kept taking in mouthfuls of cold water. He was caught and sentenced to drown.

At the New Bridge someone threw down a life buoy but it missed him by several meters and Johnny watched it float away. He was pulled by the current toward the west side, scraping against the rough stones. I don't care anymore, he thought, but at that moment he glimpsed a figure and felt a hand take hold of his arm.

On all fours he threw up, emptied himself completely. He looked around. He had completely forgotten the stairs down from West Ågatan. He had sat there many times before, drinking beer. Now it was his salvation.

"How are you feeling?"

A young man was leaning over him.

"Fine," said Johnny, getting up.

"Do you need to go to the hospital?"

Johnny shook his head and went up the stairs on shaky legs. Several curiosity seekers had gathered. The sound of sirens was coming closer and closer. Someone must have called an ambulance, maybe the police too.

He stepped out into the street, stopped a car, opened the door on the driver's side. A young woman was sitting at the wheel.

"Beat it," said Johnny. "And keep your mouth shut."

✦

Fifty

"Give up, damn it!"

Håkan Malmberg sat straddle-legged on his cot, with his back toward the wall and his arms crossed on his chest. He smiled, showing a perfect row of teeth.

Ann Lindell looked at him, trying to find the slightest hint of a crack in the scornful attitude, but, on the contrary, Malmberg showed nothing to make her optimistic.

She looked down at the floor, closed her eyes for a moment, and made another attempt. She coaxed, shifted perspective somewhat, but once again found herself stuck in the same meaningless repetition. He obviously had no empathy she could appeal to, and if he did he was hiding it very well. Maybe he was innocent? Lindell had gone back and forth on that question. No, he had murdered Klara Lovisa. No one had leaked the information that the girl had been buried, Lindell was sure of that.

Now he was smiling again, this time not scornfully, but more sympathetically, as if he was sorry that she was on the wrong track.

She happened to think of Anders Brant. Why, she did not understand, because there was no connection between them, other than that they were both men.

"You're wasting your time," said Håkan Malmberg, interrupting her train of thought.

"I guess I am," said Lindell. "But that's nothing compared to what you'll be doing the next few decades."

He laughed.

"Decades may be pushing it."

"You'll get life," said Lindell. "Raping and strangling a young girl does not give you any credits in court. The only thing that can help the situation at all is if you cooperate."

Malmberg shook his head dejectedly.

"Lay off," he said.

Ann Lindell was overwhelmed with disgust, and not only about Malmberg. It was the whole atmosphere, the institutional shabbiness of the jail and the musty odor that clung to her skin.

Håkan Malmberg smiled again, which made Lindell stand up quickly. She really wanted to spit on him, strike him, see him tortured. Never before had the feeling of hatred and revenge overcome her so.

"Take a vacation," he said in a derisive tone.

"That's none of your damn business!"

Lindell turned toward the door and waited for the guard to open and let her out. She felt Malmberg's eyes on her back. For a fleeting moment she had the idea that he was going to knock her down from behind.

"You need a dick," Håkan Malmberg whispered just as the door opened.

Ann Lindell left the jail without a word, her body bathed in sweat and her face bright red.

✦

Fifty-one

He was forewarned, but it still came as a shock. They had been snooping around in his apartment, the traces were obvious. A folder that was not where it should be, piles of papers that had been moved a few centimeters, and a closet door that was wide open were some of the signs.

Anders Brant walked slowly around his apartment. It suddenly felt soiled, and foreign in a peculiar way. I don't want to live here! The little apartment in Salvador, two rooms and a kitchen with minimal furnishings, suddenly seemed like his true home.

He recognized this, a sense upon returning of being at home in two places, and yet nowhere. He knew the feeling would go away, usually within a few days, but this time the rootlessness and alienation were underscored by the visit by the police.

"Vanessa, what should I do?" he mumbled, leaning his forehead against the refrigerator door.

He was tired, had a pounding headache, and did not know what his next step should be. At his feet was the small travel bag.

He laughed at his own pettiness. What should I do? A non-question. He knew what he had to do—transcribe and edit all the interviews, compile texts, get to work in other words, but for the first time he saw no way out of his state of doubt and suspicion of himself.

"Ann."

He tried her name. He had tried to pump Sammy Nilsson for a little information about what Ann had said, but only got a wry smile and a few cryptic words about patience. What did he mean? Who was the one who should show patience?

Ann Lindell, a very everyday name, police detective, all the more sensational, at least for him. What was it about Ann that he was drawn to? In superficial terms they did not have much in common. She showed no great interest in the issues that had occupied him for almost twenty years.

He could not remember a single occasion when she had brought up a social issue, recommended a book, or commented on a story on the TV news. She had been remarkably passive and evasive. On the other hand he had not been particularly talkative or open either, or for that matter not overly interested in her job. They had made love and cuddled, and enjoyed it.

He opened the refrigerator door and took out a bottle of beer. When he finished it he would lie down on the sofa, pull a blanket over himself, and sleep, hopefully until the next morning. With his head more or less clear and his body rested he would start dealing with all the work that was waiting.

How he would handle Ann he did not know. With an unusually fatalistic attitude for him, he decided that it would work out. Perhaps Ann would resolve it all by making a decision. Based on Sammy Nilsson's evasive insinuations he could absolutely not predict what such a decision would look like.

He was wakened by the doorbell ringing. In his dream he had been in Salvador, at the hotel room in Barra. The view had been the same, the harbor, the bay, and in the background Itaparica, but the interior of the room was different—paintings on the walls, thick carpets on the floor, a gigantic bed where someone, perhaps the cleaning lady, had decorated the bedspread with flowers in the form of a heart. Monica was there. From the bathroom singing was heard. A good dream, a dream without guilt.

He got up, but his legs barely held him. Confused and a little shaky he rocked back and forth. The ringing from the door cut into his head and the ache returned like a blow across his skull.

As his dizziness abated he shuffled out into the hall. Just then the door was thrown wide open.

"What the hell, at least you can open the door!"

Anders Brant stared in surprise at the intrusion. It took a moment or two before he recognized Johnny Andersson—homeless, informant, and sought by the police.

"Is it raining?"

Johnny did not answer but instead took off his shoes and threw the soaked jacket on the floor.

"I have to borrow some threads from you."

"What's happened? Have you been injured?"

Johnny shook his head, despite the trickle of blood on top.

"What do you want?"

"Clothes," said Johnny. "Don't you get it? I have to change."

"Why come to me of all people?"

He realized that Johnny was in trouble and that he had appointed Brant to solve his problems. He had no time to feel afraid before Johnny's right fist reached out and grabbed the front of Brant's shirt.

"Clothes," he hissed. "I'm cold, do you get it?"

"Okay," said Anders Brant, putting up his hands.

The grip on his shirt slackened a little.

"Do you have any food too?"

Anders Brant decided to play along.

"I'll get out some clothes, though they may be too small, so you can change. There's not much food but I can probably arrange a beer and a few sandwiches. Okay?"

Johnny Andersson released his hold. He looked almost surprised.

"I've been out of town," said Anders Brant as an explanation for the meager fare.

They were sitting at the kitchen table. He thought it was strange to see the other man in his clothes. He had bought the shirt and pants prior to Vanessa's visit.

Johnny quickly consumed three pieces of toast and a beer.

"But I heard what happened, that Bosse is dead."

"He had himself to blame."

"What do you mean?"

"He talked too much," Johnny hissed.

Brant chose not to prolong that discussion. He did not want any agitated emotions. Johnny Andersson was not the smartest guy in the world, Brant had figured that out during the interviews he conducted. So why get him riled up? The best thing would be if he left the apartment as quickly as possible, and Brant suspected that gentle persuasion would be most effective.

"Was that good?"

Johnny nodded.

"Unfortunately I don't have any more beer."

"That's okay," said Johnny generously, placing the empty can on the table. "Did you see the papers Bosse had? The Russian ones? Were they worth anything?"

"I saw them only in passing," said Anders Brant.

" 'In passing'?"

"I saw them, but I didn't read them," Brant clarified. "So I don't know if they were valuable."

"Bosse was going to sell them for a lot, he said so anyway, but he talked a lot of shit. I didn't get a dime for them."

Anders Brant nodded and made a move to stand up.

"Listen up, sit down! You're going to help me. Think up something. They're chasing me, even an old childhood friend who's a cop. Not a bastard I can trust."

"What do you want to do?"

"Do you have a car?"

Anders Brant shook his head and got up. He wanted to indicate that he wouldn't let himself be controlled so easily, even more so not in his own kitchen. While he cleared away the empty can and margarine container, he wondered how he could get rid of the intruder.

"So get a car!"

He's a caricature, thought Brant, and observed Johnny. It struck him how improbable the events of the past few weeks were. Four deaths—Bosse, Ingegerd Melander, Jeremias Kumlin, and Arlindo Assis. Two separations—one of which definitive—and on top of that he had been mangled by a bus. And now Johnny Andersson.

"I have a buddy who owes me a favor," he said. "Maybe you can borrow his car. I can call and ask. It's a piece of junk but it works. He was going to trade it in, but he got so little for it that he kept it. Where are you going?"

Johnny grinned.

"I'm not saying, but it will be on the way to hell."

"Then my buddy will probably want to get paid, but we can arrange that later."

"You can forget about that. Call now!"

"I have to pee first," said Brant, leaving the kitchen, snapping up the wallet that was sitting on the hall table, and went into the bathroom. There he took out a business card and as he flushed he memorized the number, left the bathroom, picked up the portable phone, and returned to the kitchen.

Johnny Andersson was still sitting at the table.

"What kind of buddy is this?"

"A guy I usually—"

"Go ahead and call!"

He punched in the number and had to wait five rings before he got an answer. He made a thumbs up to Johnny.

"Hey, it's Brant. I'm in a bit of a fix, or rather Johnny is, he's a buddy of an old bandy teammate, and he needs a car. He has to go away quickly and his car just broke down. I was thinking we could borrow your old Golf."

He nodded at Johnny and gave him a conspiratorial smile.

"Sure! He's sitting here waiting in my kitchen. You can come by with the car. You have a few things that . . . Bring your girlfriend along too, it's been a while, although maybe she isn't too pleased with me anymore."

He fell silent and made another thumbs up to Johnny.

"Great," he said, ending the call.

"Is he bringing the car?"

"It will take ten minutes max," said Brant soothingly.

"I need money too."

"I'm not a bank, but I may have five hundred you can borrow."

"Are you trying to fool me?"

Anders Brant looked up in surprise.

"Why would I do that?"

"You're sweating so much."

"I've got a headache," said Brant. "I was run over by a bus."

Johnny Andersson observed him without a word.

"Do you have to sweat like a pig because of that? And why should you loan me five hundred?"

"I have to take my medicine," said Brant, leaving the kitchen.

His headache was pounding. He looked at his face in the bathroom mirror. He was truly sweating copiously and for the first time he felt scared for real. Maybe there was something wrong. Did he have injuries they hadn't noticed in the hospital in Salvador?

How long would it take before Sammy arrived? And did he understand what this was about? He didn't know how he could get rid of Johnny.

"Brant!" Johnny shouted from the kitchen.

Anders Brant took one of the pain tablets he got in Brazil.

"Come here!"

Johnny's howl from the kitchen made Anders Brant consider whether he should try to get out of the apartment. If he carefully opened the outside door and threw himself down the stairs and out onto the yard, maybe he had a chance. But how far would he get, considering his miserable condition? True, Johnny did not look like he was in very good shape, but he would surely catch up with him anyway.

Johnny stood by the window and looked out toward the yard, but turned around when Brant came into the kitchen.

"You thought you could fool me," said Johnny, smiling, and perhaps it was Johnny's calm that frightened Anders Brant the most.

"The cops are coming," said Johnny. "I recognized them right away. The bitch that questioned me forgot to hide her fat ass."

Anders Brant looked around, Johnny rushed forward, took hold of one arm, and threw him down on the floor in a single motion. The pain from his head and the recently repaired ear was indescribable. The scream surprised himself. He perceived the astonished look on Johnny, a surprise that changed to an expression of triumph.

"No bastard can fool me!"

Johnny aimed a kick at his crotch, but Brant had instinctively drawn up his legs and turned to the side so that the kick hit one kneecap.

The next one hit near his kidneys. I'll die in my own kitchen, thought Anders Brant. He tried to crawl under the kitchen table. The pain and the shock made him belch up something sour. He had the harsh taste of airplane coffee in his mouth.

Another kick drove him closer to the wall. Johnny turned the table over. A knife that had been on the table rattled on the floor alongside Brant. Johnny immediately reached for it, held it up in front of Brant's face and sneered at him.

"I can pay!" Brant shouted.

Johnny Andersson looked surprised for a moment.

"What should you pay for? Pay to keep on writing shit about us?"

Johnny's face was disfigured by hatred. He spit out the words.

"I'm writing—"

"Parasite," Johnny screamed. "What do you know about me, about us? Not shit! Lies!"

He raised the knife. Now comes the punishment, thought Brant. He saw Vanessa's closed face before him.

Johnny Andersson smiled, aimed the knife, and made a couple of stabs in the air as if he were playing with him. Then he cut Brant on the face. A rapid movement, no pain, just blood that ran down over his face.

✦

Fifty-two

"Damn, it stinks," Riis muttered.

"Honeysuckle," said Beatrice Andersson. "Are you allergic?"

Riis did not reply and she did not expect him to either.

They were standing behind a screen of climbing plants that enclosed a play area. They were keeping an eye on Anders Brant's backyard. Second entry from the left, one flight up, according to Sammy Nilsson.

Two patrol officers were placed at the end and prepared to intervene if needed. Beatrice felt confident. The one, Conny Holmlund, was Swedish police champion on the low hurdles. True, that was a few years ago, but she was sure he could still catch up with anyone trying to get away.

The idea was that two colleagues from the uniformed police, but in civilian clothes, would go up to the apartment and get an impression of what Brant's call was about. Sammy Nilsson, whom Johnny had met and would surely recognize, would wait a half-flight down. If no one opened, they would go in with the key Sammy had appropriated after a brief, heated discussion with the building manager.

"That journalist," said Riis.

"Yes, what about him?" said Beatrice.

There was a crackle on the radio. Sammy Nilsson's voice: "Screams from the apartment, a fucking commotion. We're going in."

The radio was silent.

"I think he's screwing Lindell," said Riis. "I saw them when I donated blood at the hospital."

"Are you a blood donor?"

Beatrice's surprise was unfeigned. That Riis would donate blood was completely improbable; it was the first time she had heard of Riis performing a philanthropic act.

"Are we going to hang around?"

Riis left their hiding place and set off toward the outside door. Beatrice followed after a few moments of hesitation.

When Sammy Nilsson called her, Ann Lindell had just sat down at the Café Savoy with a cup of coffee and a filled doughnut. She had gone there to try to dampen her fury over Håkan Malmberg's arrogance, his scornful sneer, and his parting words.

That he would slink out of the net was an appalling thought. She had expended a lot of energy and much thought to Klara Lovisa's fate. Twice she thought she had solved the case, but saw her hopes dashed.

Besides, she hated herself for having felt attracted to the tall motorcycle rider the first time they met. She realized that he had read her thoughts and now could mock her that way too.

She pushed aside the cup of coffee. Johnny Andersson at Anders Brant's apartment, Sammy's message said. She had heard about Johnny's escapades at the Tuna allotment gardens and how he came climbing up the stairs from the river just south of the New Bridge, jumped right into traffic, a stopped a car on West Ågatan, forced the driver out, and without further ado took possession of the car. The car was found twenty minutes later on Svartbäcksgatan, crashed into a tree. According to the witness the driver had left the scene running east on Sköldunga-gatan.

From Savoy it was not far to Svartbäcken and when Ann Lindell arrived she saw Beatrice Andersson and Riis rushing out of their hiding place and running toward the back entrance. Lindell drove up onto the grass to quickly park, leap out of the car, and follow her colleagues.

In the stairwell clamor and yelling was heard. Between the thin railing she glimpsed Bea's legs disappearing through a door. At the same moment a shot rang out, immediately followed by a howl. It was Sammy Nilsson's voice. Lindell ran up the half-stair and into the apartment.

The odor of gunpowder. Once before she and Sammy Nilsson had been involved in gunfire. That time a man had died, shot in the head by her.

In the report that Sammy Nilsson wrote that evening he described, in the best police prose, how the kitchen floor was "bathed in blood." Ottosson asked him to change the formulation. He thought it was more likely Anders Brant and Johnny Andersson who were bathing in blood on the floor.

Johnny Andersson was lying with his head at a strange angle toward the radiator under the window. The strange thing was that he had Brant's checkered shirt on, the one he'd had on the first time he came to see her. Johnny's eyes were unfocused. Shock, thought Lindell.

The other body was only visible from the waist down, but Lindell knew who it was. She recognized Anders Brant's worn sandals.

Sammy said something she did not catch. Johnny Andersson turned his head a little and spit blood out of his mouth.

Riis was on his knees, leaning over Anders Brant.

"That looks really bad," he shouted. "See about getting a couple of ambulances here. As soon as possible!"

"Ambulance en route," said Beatrice.

The odor of gunpowder was mixed with the raw smell of blood.

For a few moments a kind of stillness rested over the kitchen, before Beatrice rushed in, pulled on her plastic gloves, crouched next to Johnny Andersson, put her hand under his neck, and moved his body somewhat so that the head was at a more comfortable angle. Then she started unbuttoning the shirt that was already stained dark with blood.

"I need bandages!" shouted Riis. "He's bleeding like a pig. He has abdominal injuries too. I think he's dying."

The ambulance sirens came closer and closer. Sammy Nilsson had lowered his gun but remained standing in the doorway. One of the patrol officers took the pistol from his hand.

Ann Lindell registered all of this before she turned on her heels, went into the bedroom, and sank down on the bed.

✦

Fifty-three

"Often all it takes is a single stab for a person to stay lying down for good," said the surgeon.

The surgeon Bertil Friis told that Anders Brant had been stabbed nineteen times—four on his arms, one in the throat, six on his legs, and eight on his upper body, not counting the cut on his face. He had lost more blood than anyone Friis had heard of. The injuries in his abdomen were the most serious.

Several times during the operation the doctor thought about the foreign minister Anna Lindh, who with similar injuries had been lost on the operating table. Brant's injuries were even more extensive.

For eight hours the surgical team was at it, a total of four doctors and just as many nurses.

"Is he going to make it?"

"We don't dare say anything."

Although the doctor was beyond tired, he did everything to appear fresh, but hinted that it wasn't going that well. The woman before him also looked hollow-eyed, to say the least.

"Are you related to Anders Brant?"

"I'm a police officer."

She stared at him as if it were his fault the prognosis was uncertain.

"Police," said Friis.

Ann Lindell nodded.

"I want you to save that man," she said, and then turned on her heels and went her way.

Sammy Nilsson caught her just as she came out in the fresh air. It was an unusually lovely day. Right outside the entry stood a group of smokers.

"I wish I smoked," he said, mostly to have something to say.

Lindell tried to smile. She appreciated his concern. Ever since the bloody showdown in Brant's apartment, he had followed her closely. It struck her that perhaps this was also for his own sake. He was the one who fired the shot that dropped Johnny Andersson. Johnny's life was not in danger, and he would not have lasting injuries, but a policeman is normally put on leave after a shooting.

That was also Ottosson's obvious decision, but nothing could keep Sammy Nilsson from keeping Lindell company. They could say that the visit to the hospital was personal.

"Will he make it?"

"They don't know."

"Will you make it?"

"I have to pick up Erik," said Lindell.

Görel had picked him up at preschool and Lindell knew that Erik was not lacking for anything, but she had a bad conscience anyway.

They stood quietly a moment. Sammy Nilsson let out a big yawn. The group of smokers broke up. A great emptiness came over Ann Lindell, as if she were only a walking shell.

She slipped her arm behind Sammy's back and leaned her head against his arm.

"He'll make it," said Sammy.

Autumn

Anders Brant crept next to her. His thin body was shaking. Ann Lindell realized that he had been dreaming. Perhaps he was still dreaming. He whimpered.

Like so often they were lying front to back, usually him behind her, coiled together, naked.

It was still dark outside. Ann did not want to lean over to check the time. She guessed four o'clock.

The nights had been unsettled ever since he left the hospital. He had incorporated his anxiety, sleep betrayed him. Sometimes he woke up screaming, sweaty and filled with a pounding anxiety.

Even his body failed him. He caressed her. He himself was often limp.

Anders Brant spent the days in Ann's apartment. He seldom went out.

The texts flickered on his computer screen. He talked about what he was writing, and what he wanted to write, but Ann suspected that not much was getting accomplished.

They had not talked about Vanessa. He mentioned her name, but nothing about their relationship, other than that he had left her for good.

She wanted to believe him, chose to do so. His obvious helplessness made such hope easier. Earlier in the year, when they met and started their relationship, he was the stronger one. Now, after his return from Brazil, the knife attack, and the hospital stay, he was like a disheartened child.

Many times she was irritated at his passivity, even at his anxiety, but also saw how he suffered, so she could never get really angry.

One day when Ann came home, he was sitting on the balcony, smoking a cigarillo. That was the first time since he left the hospital. He had obviously not heard her, because he continued talking to himself, with himself, it looked like he was arguing with himself. He argued and gesticulated. She took that as a good sign.

And gradually he had come back. At the end of September he had an article accepted in *Aftonbladet,* which made him, in Ann's eyes, ridiculously exhilarated.

She needed to sleep, but realized there would not be much more of that. Carefully she slipped out of his grasp and left the bed, closing the door behind her and hoping that he would not wake up.

The kitchen clock showed 5:14, much better than she had feared. The vigil before Erik would get up would not be very long. He was like a clock and always woke up around six thirty.

She retrieved *Upsala Nya Tidning* and sat down at the kitchen table, but did not open the newspaper. Instead she sat with a cup of tea before her.

In the morning the trial of Johnny Andersson would begin. He was indicted, in part, for two homicides and attempted homicide. During the first round of questioning he had already confessed that he clubbed down Bo Gränsberg. He had hidden the murder weapon, an iron pipe, in a pit, where it was later also recovered. The reason for their fight was the so-called Russian papers, which Gränsberg had stolen from Jeremias Kumlin's house. Johnny, like Gränsberg, believed they were very valuable.

When Johnny later looked up Jeremias Kumlin to blackmail him for not revealing the contents of the documents—he had threatened to go on TV—Kumlin laughed in his face. That laugh became his death.

Henrietta Kumlin also identified Johnny Andersson as the "Russian," the man who stood outside their villa in Sunnersta. Johnny had entered the garage and slept there. In the morning, when Kumlin came to get his car and go to Arlanda, Johnny was waiting in the semidarkness.

Beatrice Andersson had expended great effort to bring clarity into what happened the night Ingegerd Melander died. Her theory that Johnny Andersson pushed her down the stairs could never be proven. If on the remaining points of the indictment he was, if not cooperative, at least grudgingly compliant, he loudly denied that he was responsible in any way for Ingegerd's death. Johnny asserted that "you don't kill an old lady," which Beatrice was quick to point out was just what many do.

Ann Lindell had nothing to do with the case. Anders Brant on the other hand would be called as a witness, but that would not happen for another day or two.

She opened the newspaper and read the headlines. The only thing that caught her interest was an assault in Årsta. A seventy-year-old home-owner had quarreled with his neighbor, about a tree branch that was hanging over the property line and which had caused discord for several years. The exchange of words ended with the retired bank official striking his antagonist on the head with a rake.

Ann could not help but smile. There was something almost laughable in the fury of the middle class. In Johnny Andersson's hatred and flashes of violence there was no comedy, his actions, his whole being, were only frightening. Now he had clearly resigned himself and was strangely silent. It seemed as if he wanted nothing more than to crawl into an institution for life.

Suddenly the phone rang. She threw herself forward to stop a second signal from sounding.

"Good morning, Forsberg here. Excuse me for bothering you so early, but something has come in that I think will interest you."

"I see."

"Håkan Malmberg is dead."

"What?"

"It seems as if a kind of justice has been rendered. The girl's father has confessed. He called half an hour ago. We sent a patrol car and it's true. Malmberg is done."

"Klara Lovisa's dad?"

Could that little mouse-gray man have murdered the powerful Håkan Malmberg?

"Yes."

"How?"

"He went to see Malmberg yesterday evening and shot him in the head. Then he sat with the dead man the whole night. Maybe he intended to shoot himself too but changed his mind. Allan Fredriksson is at the scene. He asked me to call you. True, it's early, but I thought you'd want to know right away."

After the call, Ann Lindell went out on the balcony.

Håkan Malmberg was dead. In the end Klara Lovisa's father, a taciturn man her own age, had snapped. How did he get hold of a gun?

It suddenly struck her that perhaps he had murdered an innocent man. It had never been established that the thread in the shed really did come from Håkan Malmberg's bandanna. The only thing that argued against Malmberg were his own words that Klara Lovisa had been buried. He had stubbornly maintained that he heard that from someone, but could not remember from whom, not when or where either.

According to the prosecutor it could not be ruled out that he spoke the truth, and Håkan Malmberg went free. Now he was dead.

Ann Lindell realized that she would never be certain who had murdered Klara Lovisa on her birthday.

On the balcony was the ashtray with three butts neatly lined up on the edge. There was also *Aftonbladet* open to Anders's article. He had made notes in the margin, underlined and crossed out. She read the introduction. It was clearly a polemic aimed at Green Motorists, an organization she had never heard of. But there were many things she did not know about in Brant's world, what sugar cane looked like or a plundered rainforest, for example.

Lindell understood that he was on his way back. What if he could write about Klara Lovisa, Gränsberg, Sammy Nilsson, me, and all the others? What Sammy Nilsson had talked about, what couldn't be written.

Leaning over the balcony railing she started to cry. Uppsala was bedded in a cold, gray October fog. The whole city was weeping.

"Stay with me," she whispered.

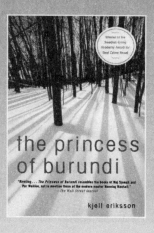
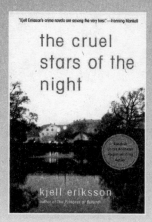
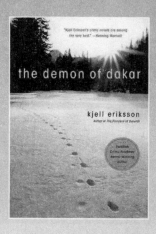
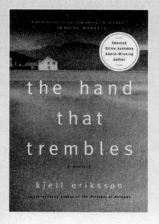
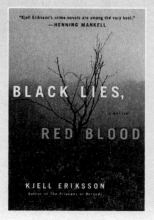